Read

or

Alive

Also available by Nora Page

Bookmobile Mysteries

Read on Arrival
Better Off Read

Read
or
Alive

A BOOKMOBILE MYSTERY

Nora Page

NEW YORK

PUBLISHER'S NOTE: The recipes contained in this book are to be followed exactly as written. The publisher is not responsible for your specific health or allergy needs that may require medical supervision. The publisher is not responsible for any adverse reaction to the recipes contained in this book.

Published in the United States by Crooked Lane Books, an imprint of The Quick Brown Fox & Company LLC.

Crooked Lane Books and its logo are trademarks of The Quick Brown Fox & Company LLC.

Library of Congress Catalog-in-Publication data available upon request.

ISBN (hardcover): 978-1-64385-301-7
ISBN (ePub): 978-1-64385-322-2

Cover illustration by Jesse Reisch
Book design by Jennifer Canzone

Printed in the United States.

www.crookedlanebooks.com

Crooked Lane Books
34 West 27th St., 10th Floor
New York, NY 10001

First Edition: May 2020

10 9 8 7 6 5 4 3 2 1

To Eric, with love

Chapter One

L ibrarian Cleo Watkins prided herself on living a modest life. In all her seventy-six years, Cleo had never craved designer shoes, flashy jewels, or a new-model car. She was judicious in her use of air conditioning, although a tad flagrant with the furnace. Cleo canned peaches and put up her own pickles. She still darned socks.

However, everyone has a weakness, some little luxury they can't resist. An obsession?

Obsession sounded extreme.

But then, so was Cleo's love for books.

"Hold tight to your wallet, Cleo Jane." Mary-Rose Garland, Cleo's best friend since infancy, clapped a protective hand over her purse, so slender Cleo doubted it could hold sunglasses, let alone important purchases.

Like books! Armloads and bags of books!

They paused at a crosswalk, allowing Cleo to take in a sight that made her heart go pitter-patter. Sunlight glittered off the emerald-tile cap of the historic Catalpa Springs Railway Depot. The last train had departed decades ago, but the long brick build-ing lived on, now hosting special events. There were weddings and expos and a recent gathering of pedigree-rabbit enthusiasts. Then there was the present event, which was very special to Cleo.

"The Georgia Antiquarian Book Society Fair," Cleo said, blissfully reading the banner stretched over the entry. She mentally replayed the fair's promise: *a one-week extravaganza of rare books, old books, used books, maps, manuscripts, and bookish ephemera beyond imagination.*

Cleo felt as giddy as a kid on Christmas morning, Halloween, and her birthday combined. It was opening day, and Cleo had taken the morning off from her bookmobile duties to attend. Taking time off wasn't something Cleo did lightly. She adored captaining Words on Wheels, her retrofitted school-bus bookmobile. She knew how much her patrons depended on the mobile library too.

Cleo again rationalized that it was her professional duty. Cleo was a librarian, and thus books were her business. She and her young protégé, Leanna, had made up special displays of collectible library books and ephemera in honor of the fair. Cleo would be driving hers around in Words on Wheels, while Leanna had hers on prominent display in the main library.

Cleo was also supporting her "gentleman friend," antiquarian bookdealer Henry Lafayette. Henry had the honor and anxiety of hosting the fair. Each year, the society selected a location with an esteemed book business. Henry's shop, the Gilded Page Antiquarian and Rare Books, was certainly that. In the handful of years Henry had lived in Catalpa Springs, he'd established a sterling reputation as a book restorer and dealer. His shop brimmed with literary treasures, and Cleo considered it as dignified, handsome, and filled with wisdom and wit as its owner.

"Henry's been running every which way," Cleo said, as she and Mary-Rose waited for a slow-moving sedan to pass. "Antiquarian bookdealers seem to be a high-maintenance bunch."

Their demands could fill a card catalog, from frigid air conditioning for their books to stall positions optimized for visibility, fêng shui, and flow. One bookdealer had even lobbied to ban all ink pens and children under eighteen from the Depot.

Cleo could understand the pens. Page-marring implements had no place around precious books. She'd go further, adding gum and neon highlighters and anyone who'd ever dog-eared a page.

"Henry feels his reputation rides on everything going smoothly," Cleo continued. "I keep reminding him to have fun too. Did I tell you, we've been taking dance lessons for the final soiree?"

Cleo stepped into the crosswalk, eager to get inside.

An arm whipped across her chest, halting her. "Proceed with caution, Cleo," said Mary-Rose, more firmly than the sparse Monday-morning traffic on Main and Elberta streets warranted. "Let's agree right here and now. We'll do a full scoping lap around the booths first, remembering that we're sensible, mature women on budgets."

Cleo shelved the words under *recommendation*. Subcategory: well-intentioned but unrealistic, like the proper serving size of french fries being six pieces. Who could possibly hold to such a tiny number? Who would *want* to? Not Cleo, but she wouldn't argue with a friend on such a fine, sparkly day.

"Of course," Cleo said, twining fibbing fingers behind a purse the size of carry-on luggage. The purse was empty except for her wallet and several expandable shopping bags.

Mary-Rose snorted and allowed them to proceed. "The look in your eye, Cleo Jane Watkins. You're like a kid about to dive into a chocolate swimming pool. All I ask is that you don't go drowning in temptation. No falling in love with a book you can't afford and getting your heart broken."

It was Cleo's turn to scoff. "How could I *ever* get my heart broken among books and booklovers?"

Cleo picked up her pace. "It's the atmosphere I'm after. Can you feel it? It's like the very air is quivering."

"That's heat waves," Mary-Rose said, determined to be unromantically realistic. She tugged her floppy hat lower. Her patterned sundress flapped gently over red sandals. "It feels more like August than the first week of May. I'm just saying, Cleo. We're both susceptible to book temptation, but did you see the price list for the showcase items? Good gracious, you could buy a yacht for the cost of the same stories you and I have gathering dust on our shelves."

"I have no desire for a yacht," Cleo said primly. She politely refrained from mentioning that dust wasn't gathering on *her* bookshelves. "Pricy collectibles won't tempt me. If I buy a book, I want to read it on my porch with a cold drink and my cat."

"Good to hear," Mary-Rose said. "These are *sales*people. They smell weakness and desire. Remember the time you and I went shopping for that oven? Those salesmen were like piranhas fighting for prey. These book*sellers* are no different."

Cleo remembered. Mary-Rose had needed an industrial-sized oven for the Pancake Mill, her family restaurant, famous for serving up pies and flip-it-yourself pancakes.

A mosquito floated by. Cleo waved it off, along with her friend's concerns. "That was different. Those were *appliance* salesman. In *Florida!*"

Cleo held a certain leeriness of the state a mere few miles to their south. Florida was lovely, no doubt. However, it had an unsavory association with something Cleo feared more than piranhas. *Retirement.*

"These are *book* people," Cleo said, head held high. "Book people are *nice and honest.*" Cleo spotted just such a nice, honest person now. Henry stood at his demonstration table under the broad eaves of the Depot. A small crowd watched as he aimed a sharp tool at a hunk of leather. Cleo didn't want to interrupt. She'd stop by on her way out, she decided. Then she could show him her purchases—all her new, old books!

Hurrying on, Cleo pushed through arched doors wide enough for a carriage. Inside, the long, open space brimmed with bookstalls and browsers. Iron trusses crisscrossed the ceiling and stained-glass rainbows spilled across the space. *A cathedral of books*, Cleo thought, savoring her favorite incense: the vanilla aroma of ink and paper.

Mary-Rose caught up and continued her warnings. "Not *all* book people are trustworthy, Cleo. Not from what I've been hearing."

But Cleo didn't want to hear anything to dull the shine of her day. She barely heard anyway. Her eye had alighted on a cover, and her mind soared to another place and time.

* * *

"*Gone With the Wind*," Cleo said dreamily. "Remember that summer at the coast, when we about drove my father mad, noses stuck in our copies? He said we were 'wasting' our vacation. I loved this book as a teenager."

"Then, now, and forever," Mary-Rose said, her tone softening. "What a lovely edition. I've never seen it before."

She and Cleo stood with heads lobbed left as if they could make the page tip and turn too. The book remained unmoved in its glass case, open to a whimsical watercolor of Scarlett O'Hara in a red ruffled dress. Watery purple flowers and a horse-drawn carriage formed the backdrop.

Cleo recalled her earlier statement about craving only books she could hold and enjoy. That surely wouldn't be this book, locked in a case. Still . . . she wouldn't mind looking through it. Her cousin Dot would love a look too. If possible, Dot was an even bigger *Gone With the Wind* fan than Cleo and Mary-Rose, although it was close to a three-way tie.

Dot wouldn't need a warning about pricey books. Cleo's cousin was firmly frugal and a wise businesswoman. She had to be. Dot ran one of the few remaining general stores in the area— or anywhere, for that matter. The Drop By made her rich in happiness, Dot always said, suggesting that the monetary profits weren't as generous.

"It's in French," said Mary-Rose, tapping a small card bearing a typed description. "No wonder we've never seen it. Just as well too. Look at that price! This is not a book for librarians or pancake makers, Cleo."

A platinum blonde had been tidying up boxes and books at the back of the stall. She turned and thrust a manicured hand at them. "Kitty Peavey, proprietress of Southern Delights." Her breathy voice matched her Marilyn Monroe appearance, from the round fifties-style curls in her stiff-set hair to the red wrap dress highlighting her curves. "You ladies have fine taste." She waved an open palm over the glass case.

"Just looking," Mary-Rose said firmly. She elbowed Cleo for emphasis.

Looking to look inside this lovely book. Cleo kept the thought to herself. Some folks suffered from a devil on their shoulder, urging wicked deeds. Cleo lugged about the burden of good manners, instilled by her mother and grandmothers and generations of proper southern ladies before her. It wouldn't be right to get Kitty's hopes up or paw through a book she had no intention of buying. Cleo grudgingly echoed Mary-Rose's sentiment. She introduced them both and praised Kitty's shop.

"You *do* have delights here," Cleo said. "We're huge fans of southern settings and authors. So is my cousin. She absolutely adores *Gone With the Wind*. I'll send her over to your shop."

Kitty beamed, her lips as red as her dress. "Your cousin is a GWTW fan? Then I'm her woman. GWTW delights are my specialty!"

Cleo decoded the acronym and smiled, picturing Dot amid a pack of Margaret Mitchell lovers, all dropping the insider lingo. MM. GWTW. Was there one for *Frankly, my dear, I don't give a . . .*? FMDIDGAD?

Kitty leaned over the glass case, her voice dropping to husky. "Let your cousin know, I just picked myself up some gems. Some are such treasures, they're for special eyes only. My *personal* book scout came to town early and made some amazing discoveries that I—*exclusively*—will be offering for sale here at the fair. I was skeptical about meeting here, I'll admit. But this little town is a treasure!"

Cleo glowed, pleased with the praise and eager to pass it on to Henry. She'd assured him that his fellow antiquarians would be charmed by Catalpa Springs.

"So, *imagine* . . ." Kitty was saying, or rather, exhaling. "Imagine a first edition of GWTW, signed by Margaret Mitchell herself. Her hands opening the cover, caressing the pages. Her pen, pressing down . . . Woman to woman, I'll tell you, I get a tingle in my fingers when I touch books like that. Can you imagine the thrill?"

Cleo didn't have to imagine. She knew. So did Dot, who owned just such a rare copy. She'd discovered it in a box of "throwaway" books from an estate sale. Cleo would always remember the moment she and Dot opened that cover for the first time. They hadn't swooned, but they'd come close.

7

"So how much are you selling *that* for?" Mary-Rose asked, with businesswoman brusqueness.

Kitty straightened and fluttered ruby-red fingernails over her heart. "I'm not sure I could bear to part with such a gem. But . . . then . . . I *am* sharing the proceeds with my book scout. Since y'all are my first customers, I could do a special deal. Say, twenty-five."

"Twenty-five dollars?" Cleo said, as Mary-Rose simultaneously said, "Twenty-five hundred?"

Kitty's giggles had sharp edges. "So precious! This town is ripe for the picking, isn't it? Twenty-five *thousand*. That's cutting you ladies a sweet deal."

Cleo gasped.

Mary-Rose grabbed Cleo's elbow and tugged. "How nice," she said stiffly. To Cleo, she whispered, "Moving on. We're moving along."

Cleo remained rooted, boggling at the price. *Good gracious!* Could Dot's copy be worth that much? She almost didn't want to tell her cousin. Dot would worry. She'd need to buy expensive insurance and keep it somewhere safe. Cleo pictured them visiting the book behind bars, locked away in a cold safe-deposit vault deep inside the bank.

Kitty's smile twitched. "Now, if y'all are looking for more affordable fun, I have other delights too. First-customer discount applies. Come this way."

Cleo obediently followed Kitty to the end of the table, making sure to praise books that were just as lovely without trios of zeros in their price tags.

"Then there are these beauties," Kitty said, sailing her hand over photographs in individual cellophane sleeves. "Photos from the 1939 film of *GWTW*, ready for framing. Picture Clark Gable on your wall, say, in your powder room." She fanned them out. "Here he is with stuff burning in the background. Look at those *smoldering* eyes. I'd recommend getting five for a nice gallery-wall arrangement. I'll give you a package deal."

Cleo's head had lobbed again, this time in confusion. "But these are all single pages . . ." Pages that belonged to a book she knew well, the 1940 motion-picture edition of *Gone With the Wind*. Dot kept a copy in her sitting room, with pride of place on her coffee table.

"I don't think you want to know, Cleo," Mary-Rose muttered.

Kitty beamed. "I extracted the pretty pages from a book that was in *fair* condition, at best. It'd suffered too much use. Some crayon damage too."

Cleo and Kitty shuddered as one, in shared crayon revulsion. Cleo forgave children for their artistic urges. However, she couldn't forgive crayons, the waxy ruiners of far too many library books.

Kitty said brightly, "That's the problem with people loving their books too much! The pictures are more useful this way."

More useful and profitable for her, Cleo translated. Each photo bore a price that was probably more than the whole book. Cleo reminded herself that not all books could be saved. Even at the library, they had to periodically thin the collection to make room for new items. Someone would enjoy these photos, and that was a good thing, wasn't it? That *someone* wouldn't be Dot Moore or Cleo Watkins, though. They preferred their books intact!

Cleo inched away, glad now for her promise to Mary-Rose. "We're just starting out," Cleo said, a little shakily. "We're doing a full lap of the fair before making any decisions."

"Send your cousin round," Kitty trilled. She thrust a business card at Cleo. The paper was thick and scarlet with embossed gold script.

Cleo slid the card in her bag out of politeness. She turned to go, taking one last look at Clark Gable. As she did, her heart flipped again. Not in a pleasant pitter-patter but a thud.

Chapter Two

Cleo tugged Mary-Rose down the narrow aisle between Kitty's stand and a cheery table with a picnic-worthy red-and-white-checkered tablecloth. Kitty was busy charming new customers.

A brimming trash basket stood inside the rectangular table corral of Kitty's stall. Cleo pointed to it. "Look! Look at the bookplate!"

Atop the trash, a cover lay open, bare but for a fringe of ripped pages and a bookplate. The plate featured two live oaks arching over the words *Ex libris. From the library of.* The signature beneath was in pencil too pale to read.

Mary-Rose inhaled sharply. "Is that *Dot's* bookplate?"

Years ago, Mary-Rose had hosted a foreign-exchange student with a mastery of wood-block printing and a love of books. The student had made personalized bookplates for Cleo, Mary-Rose, Dot, and the Catalpa Springs Public Library too.

The library's design featured the Victorian cottage that was the library's home, with the name forming a blocky border. On Cleo's bookplate, a cat sat atop a stack of books in a moonlit window. A lady in a sundress read beside a sparkling spring on Mary-Rose's plate.

Then there was Dot's plate, framed in lovely arching oaks. Just like the plate on the dismembered cover, Cleo thought with a sinking dread. A cover matching the size and color of the motion-picture edition of *Gone With the Wind* that should be sitting on Dot's coffee table.

Cleo immediately talked herself down. *Dot would never sell that book. Certainly not to someone who'd hack it apart!*

"No, this has to be some kind of mistake," Cleo said to Mary-Rose.

But Mary-Rose had turned away. She nodded toward the entry. "We can ask her. Look."

Dot stood in the entry. A slice of red light flared on her silver hair, cut in the short bangs and bob she'd sported since childhood. Tall and stretched to slender, Dot wore a ruffled apron, her preferred uniform for work, dining, gardening, and even driving.

Cleo frowned through her bifocals. The view was perfectly clear but all wrong. Dot looked . . . *angry. Enraged.* Neither the words nor the look fit Dot. Her usually serene face was pinched. Her hands balled in fists at her apron-covered hips. Before Cleo and Mary-Rose could react, Dot stormed off into the crowd.

* * *

"Where are my books? I *want* my books back!" Dot's voice cut across the milling din.

Cleo wedged through bodies and knee-bumping totes to find Dot pointing at a dark-haired man. Cleo didn't recognize him. He looked like a cover model for a cruise ship, tall and tanned and a touch too good-looking for Cleo's taste. Dark hair waved rakishly at the collar of his light linen jacket. Expensively weathered jeans skimmed canvas boat shoes and bare ankles.

Cleo guessed he was in his fifties and denying it with the help of hair dye.

"Do I know you, ma'am?" he was saying in deep tones stretched in a haughty drawl.

"Do you *know* me?" Dot gripped her apron ties. "You came to my home. We had tea and cake. You *took* my books! I changed my mind. I want them back. You *must* have gotten my many messages. I've been trying to contact you."

Bookdealers and browsers glanced their way. Gawkers inched closer.

Cleo reached Dot's side. Her cousin jumped at her touch.

Dot spun around wide-eyed, taking in Cleo and the gathering crowd. Red splotches blossomed on Dot's cheeks, and she withered toward Cleo.

The man smiled. "Yes," he said, drawing out the word. "I remember now. You served a lovely cake, but I'm afraid I wasn't able to purchase any of your *used* books. Remember, ma'am? You must be confused."

"Dot? What's happening?" Cleo put her arm around Dot's thin shoulders, feeling a burst of big-cousin protectiveness. Dot might have just turned sixty-nine, but she'd always be Cleo's little cousin.

Dot opened her mouth but then slapped her hand over it.

A crowd was coalescing, inching toward the spectacle of conflict. Sideward glances turned to outright staring and titillated murmurs.

"Hunter Fox," Mary-Rose declared. She stepped up, arms akimbo, her fighting stance. "*I* know you. Remember *me*? I kicked you out of my pancake shop the other day for buttering up my customers with your sweet-talking schemes. Did you try that with this good woman?"

Dot's head whipped side to side in denial.

Sweet-talking? Cleo worried. Could that account for something as incomprehensible as this man getting his hands on Dot's books? It would explain Dot's mortification.

Mary-Rose raised her voice. "*This* is what I was trying to warn you about, Cleo. This man is a snake-oil salesman with a sugary tongue. From what I hear, he's been going around town, targeting ladies, talking them out of valuable items." She lowered her tone to ominous. "Talking them out of *books.*"

Cleo gasped. How had she not heard of this? She'd been busy with the bookmobile and library, with Henry and dance lessons and the loveliness of springtime. Busy was no excuse if books and booklovers were in danger.

"Ah, yes, Mrs. Garland," said the now-named Hunter Fox. "I do recall you and your equally beautiful pancake establishment. I was merely offering my assistance and expertise, helping folks find profit in the old books cluttering up their homes." He flashed dimples at the audience. "I offer exclusive, personal, in-home consultations and special incentives for the ladies."

Titters and giggles erupted. Hands reached out for his card.

Mary-Rose scoffed. "Right. That's what you were doing. *Helping.* Is that what happened to you, Dot?"

"No . . ." Dot stammered. "No!"

"See?" Hunter said. "This woman is awfully confused. Can someone bring her some water?"

"Dot?" Cleo said carefully. "Did you sell this man books? We saw—" She didn't want to upset Dot further by mentioning the maimed volume. "We noticed your bookplate at another stall."

Dot grabbed Cleo's hand. "Where? I just want my books back, that's all. This man misled me. I thought we had a deal, but he tricked me. I see that now. I've been trying to contact him. I was at the Drop By and I saw him, coming this way, and followed him and . . ."

Hunter shook his head in exaggerated pity. "Following me? You must be under a misimpression. I have no records of any deal. Do you, ma'am? No?"

Dot held her forehead as if in pain. Her silver hair fell forward, covering her face. From underneath, she whispered, "I'm an old fool . . ."

Cleo squared her shoulders. "My cousin might not have a contract, but we can identify one of her books right now. The dealer who has it can surely help us trace it back to you, Mr. Fox. Follow me!" With Dot, Mary-Rose, and the crowd at her heels, Cleo led the way to Southern Delights.

Kitty stood behind her table, flouncing a puffy pink feather duster at nothing in particular. When she saw them coming, she trilled, "Hey, ladies. Y'all are back soon. Oh, and you've brought friends! Is this your cousin the GWTW fan?"

Cleo kept going, scooting around Kitty's booth to the view of the wastebasket, the wounded book, and evidence of misdeeds.

She stopped short. The basket was empty.

"What did you do with the discarded cover that was here?" Cleo asked.

Kitty's laugh twinkled to the high rafters. "I deal in *delights*, darling, not discards. I don't know what you mean." She looked beyond Cleo, her face brightening, her manicured fingers waggling in a wave. "Hey, Hunter."

His eyelids dipped seductively. His voice did too. "Kitty, what a lovely display."

Kitty's cheeks turned as rosy red as her lipstick.

Cleo's stomach sunk. Was Kitty among the women under Hunter Fox's spell? "Miss Peavey," Cleo said sharply, aiming to cut through any romantic trance. "Did this man sell you a movie edition of *Gone With the Wind* with a bookplate depicting live oaks?"

Dot gasped. She stared down at the photos, sliced and sealed in their clear cases.

Kitty grinned and bopped Hunter teasingly with the fluffy duster. "You *hound*, you. What are you up to?"

"That book was mine," Dot stammered. "He had no right to sell it. You had no right to . . ." She turned away from the photos.

"Oh, honey," Kitty cooed with syrupy sympathy. "Did you fall for that old show-me-your-books line? Can't you see this man is slippery? I mean, just look at him! The tip-off's right in his name too. *Hunter*: always on the hunt. *Fox*: wily like a fox. Or is it *sly*?"

Hunter flashed sharp white canines. "I *do* like to *hunt*," he said suggestively. "I trust you have no complaints about our business arrangements, Miss Peavey?"

She giggled but stifled her laugh as a tall man with salt-and-pepper hair stepped up beside her. He wore a stiff dark suit and an even stiffer expression.

Kitty trotted out from behind her stall and latched on to his arm. Cleo noticed a hefty diamond ring glittering on her finger.

He patted her hand and introduced himself. "Dr. Dean Weber, president of the society."

"And my pre-fiancé honey," Kitty tittered, gazing up at his rigid jawline.

He continued on, his stony gaze landing on Hunter Fox. "What's the problem over here?"

Book theft and butchery, Cleo thought.

Hunter Fox issued a smooth smile and an oily answer. "I'm afraid there's been some confusion, Professor. These ladies are getting overly emotional. Books can have that effect on the fairer types."

Mary-Rose huffed.

Cleo concurred, but she partially agreed with Hunter Fox too. Books could arouse passionate emotions like righteous indignation.

"I'm afraid," Cleo said, rephrasing his insincere words, "That this man stole from my cousin."

Dear Dot murmured apologies. She was sorry for bothering his fair, she said, and for causing a fuss and—

Mary-Rose drew in air until she looked ready to burst.

Cleo knew what was happening. Challenged to shush up, Mary-Rose would do just the opposite. Dot, on the other hand, dreaded causing trouble or putting anyone out, even when the situation called for it.

Cleo put a placating hand on Mary-Rose's elbow and a soothing one on Dot's. If she explained the situation, surely the society's president would act on Dot's behalf. Cleo laid out the facts as she understood them, checking for jerky head bobs of affirmation from Dot. Through it all, Professor Weber exhibited the emotional range of granite.

"Mr. Fox?" the professor said after Cleo finished with a rousing demand for the return of Dot's books. "Did you buy books from this woman?"

"I can honestly say I did not *buy* her books," Hunter said with a devilish twitch of a grin.

"You fox." Kitty whapped him with her duster.

"He, he . . ." Dot stuttered. "He said he'd take the books and give me eighty percent of the profits when they sold. When I couldn't reach him, I got worried. It didn't seem right, and I changed my mind and . . ." Her words withered. "I just want my books back."

The professor remained unmoved. "What kind of books? Valuable or sentimental?"

"Both," Dot said. "There was my book of Georgia birds and a boxed set of Mark Twain, various classics by southern authors, and a diary, and . . . oh, I can't say the others, not here." She avoided Cleo's eye.

Cleo thought of Kitty's newest "delight," the signed copy of *Gone With the Wind*. No, surely not, she told herself. Dot would never, ever let go of that book.

Professor Weber, in the tone of a disappointed principal, said, "A private transaction—without documentation—is not the purview of the Georgia Antiquarian Book Society. Mr. Hunter is an affiliate member and thus not subject to our rules of ethics, although I will remind every one of you to set a good example. Provenance. Authenticity. Integrity. Those are our cornerstones."

He turned to Kitty. "If *he* sold you this French translation of *Gone With the Wind*, he's taking advantage of you too, my dear. You'll never get that price."

A flush returned to Kitty's cheeks, whether embarrassment or anger, Cleo couldn't tell. Professor Weber didn't notice. He was already striding off through the stalls.

Hunter gave a scoffing snort. "No offense, Kitty, my dear, but I wouldn't trust your *pre*-fiancé to understand the value of such a gorgeous treasure." His hand rested on the glass case, but his eyes lingered on Kitty.

"Thanks for the cake," he said, flashing an alligator smile, flashy and treacherous, at Dot. "Let me know if you find that book you're looking for. Sounds like something I'd be interested in selling."

Dot's knuckles were white on her apron ties. "You are a wicked and deceitful man!" she cried. "You'll be sorry. Awfully sorry!"

A chill swept over Cleo, and not from the air conditioning puffing from industrial vents far above.

"Let's get some fresh air," she said, but her cousin was already rushing for the door.

Chapter Three

In heart and mind, Cleo Watkins felt forever young. However, certain things could prompt Cleo to acknowledge her true age. Wisdom was one. Young folks' bafflement around such items as card catalogs and rotary telephones was another. Then there was running.

As a child, Cleo had galloped whenever her mother, with her polite-little-girl rules, wasn't looking. Cleo bounded up staircases and dashed across fields, arms outstretched, flying to wherever she was going, even if that was nowhere in particular.

Nowadays, Cleo valued the slow life. She kept her speeding to vehicles, although she'd curtailed that as well, having a few too many traffic tickets to her name. When she did run, her knees protested in creaks and a nagging arthritic ache.

Cleo feared she'd lose Dot. Her cousin had a tricky hip, but Dot was still younger and speedier on her long legs. What Cleo hadn't factored in was cuteness.

Cleo and Mary-Rose burst out into muggy brightness to find Dot diverted. She'd stopped at Henry's table, not for the bookbinding demo, which appeared to have ended, but for his dog. Mr. Chaucer, an elderly fawn pug, lay on his back, an upside-down grin stretched across his wrinkly muzzle. Dot rubbed his belly. A front paw twitched, and his googly eyes closed in bliss.

Henry was tidying his table. Leather, canvas, and parchment stood in neat stacks. He wedged tools into a wooden carrying box that reminded Cleo of a picnic basket. The tools themselves looked too lethal for a picnic, and definitely too dangerous to keep around books. There were hammers with sharklike heads and fins, metal piercers and sharp incisors, and implements resembling miniaturized hybrids of pizza cutters and medieval weapons.

Cleo hesitated. She wanted to comfort Dot, but Mr. Chaucer had that job covered, and Mary-Rose was joining in the therapeutic pug pampering too. Catching Henry's eye, Cleo sent a silent message, bobbing her head for emphasis. He understood and followed her a few yards down the shaded portico. She wished she had happy news to share. Her earlier joy at Kitty's praise of Catalpa Springs had soured. What had Kitty really been cheering? Small-town gullibility? The ease of pilfering residents' books?

"Dot seems upset," Henry said in a low voice. "Is everyone okay? I asked when she came running out, but she said she and the family were fine."

His concern put the situation into perspective. Books were hurt. So were Dot's feelings, but there hadn't been a death or accident or dire disease, at least not that Cleo knew of, thank goodness. As briefly as possible, she explained.

Henry rubbed his temples. "Hunter Fox has been around for several of our recent fairs. There have been rumors that his scouting methods aren't entirely ethical, but some dealers do business with him anyway. He has a knack for discovering amazing books. He's like a magician, a true treasure finder."

Cleo put it bluntly. "I think his knack comes from conning folks. Mary-Rose heard he was targeting ladies around town. Like Dot."

Poor Henry looked devastated. Cleo hurried to say, "It's not *your* fault. He's one bad apple."

"That could give the whole society a rotten reputation," Henry said. "We can't have any more of that. Last year's host got wrapped up in a forgery scandal. There was a rare-book theft the year before and rumors about a problematic antiquarian map the year before that." He gave her a pained smile. "The 'fair curse,' we call it, but please don't let that get around. We old bookdealers have nothing if it's not our reputation."

Henry rubbed his beard, which was neatly trimmed for spring. His white hair tufted over prominent ears and his wire-rim glasses tilted slightly askew, as did the lavender pocket square in his light-gray linen blazer. He always looked adorable, Cleo thought, although she hated to see him so worried. She reached out and patted his elbow. "No one can blame you or the other bookdealers for that man's actions."

"I know," he said, not sounding fully convinced. "I am sorry about this, especially for Dot's sake. I'll do whatever I can. I'll talk to Hunter Fox and Professor Weber too. If neither will rectify the situation, then maybe the police can."

Police. Cleo liked that idea. She imagined her favorite neighbor, Deputy Gabby Honeywell, snapping cuffs on Hunter Fox. He might be sly and slippery, but he couldn't slither out of those.

Dot was coming their way. Cleo intercepted her.

"We can have that awful man charged with theft," Cleo declared, stepping into Dot's path. "Fraud. Breach of verbal contract." *Book-slaughter?*

Dot nimbly sidestepped Cleo and kept going, speaking rapidly over her shoulder. "Please don't worry, Cleo. I'm sorry I bothered everyone. Go back inside, both of you, and enjoy the fair." She moved at a scurrying speed-walking pace, with Henry and Cleo trailing behind.

"Wait, Dot, please," Cleo pleaded. They neared the crosswalk. Just up a gentle rise lay downtown, the quaint brick buildings, Dot's store, leafy Fontaine Park, and the library, with Cleo's bookmobile resting out front, a bright spot of school-bus yellow.

Cleo assumed that Dot would stop to look for traffic. Dot, however, stepped into the crosswalk with barely a glance. Cleo was about to follow when a man's voice halted them both.

"Hey, hello? Ma'ams?"

They turned to see a bald-topped man approaching at a lumbering jog. He was around Dot's age, Cleo guessed. Young to middle sixties. Faded denim overalls rose over a round belly. A red paisley bandana fluttered from his front pocket, and an official book-fair tote bag bounced at his side.

He was panting, and as he caught his breath, he drew a manila folder from the bag. "I couldn't help but overhear. I was at my stall—the table beside Miss Peavey's . . . you probably didn't notice."

"The checkered tablecloth," Cleo said. She assured him that his display was eye-catching and tantalizing.

"Yeah, that's me," he said. "The shop, I mean. I'm not tantalizing. I'm Buddy Boone." He shifted the folder to his left hand and offered vigorous if sweaty-palmed handshakes. "Mr. Lafayette, we've met online and in your shop. I don't know if you remember."

Henry issued pleasantries: of course he remembered; how nice to see Buddy again. Bookish small talk ensued, and Cleo's nerves settled. She hoped Dot's would too. At least Dot had stepped out of the crosswalk and was making polite murmurs in mostly the right conversational places.

Buddy said he'd come to town a day early to do some sightseeing, but most of all to visit the Gilded Page, the bookshop of honor.

"First thing, first day in town, I stopped by this man's store," he said to Cleo and Dot. "I'm still debating on whether to buy that photo history of the Okefenokee you have, Mr. Lafayette. It called to me again last night. Sure would look fine on my side table." He chuckled. "I'm supposed to be here to *sell* books, not buy more! I can't seem to stop, if you know that problem."

Cleo assumed she could safely speak for all of them. "We certainly do!"

Henry blushed when Buddy gushed about the social Henry had hosted for society members at the Gilded Page the previous evening. "Sure was awesome to see those old manuscripts and whatnots you work on," Buddy said. "Those folks who collect medieval stuff were drooling over your pages. Not literally, I hope."

Cleo shot Henry a happy told-you-so smile. She'd stopped by the social briefly and assured him later that everyone had been having a lovely time. He'd worried that he hadn't spoken with everyone individually. The dear, silly man had even thought he'd bored his guests by showing off some medieval illustrated texts he was restoring for a museum.

Henry flushed. "I'm afraid I got carried away when you asked me about gilding. I can go on forever on questions of rebinding too."

Buddy laughed. "Just shows what a bunch of book nerds we are that folks get riled up about glue and stitching." He turned to Cleo and Dot. "We all have a little book . . . ah, problem."

"I empathize with that," Cleo said.

"Cleo's a librarian," Dot piped up. "She's fortunate. She gets to work around books all day."

"That'd only make the problem worse for me, I expect," Buddy said. "I'd probably wanna take 'em all home at night."

"I do just that," Cleo said. "I drive a bookmobile and often park it in my driveway. If I get an urge in the middle of the night, I go out and browse."

Dot politely asked what Buddy collected.

Cleo thought one of her cousin's superpowers—along with kindness and making the best chocolate-chip cookies in Georgia—was her gift of listening. Folks stopped by the Drop By not only for groceries and Dot's delicious deli items but also for talk therapy. Dot's sound advice often came with a free cookie.

Dot was listening intently to Buddy.

"I collect simple stuff," he was saying modestly. "Georgia-themed and southern books are my big thing. I go for things I like, like book jackets and even bookmarks and bookplates. Of course, I do the actual books too, which makes me eligible for the society. That and I'm a natural gabber! Get it? Georgia Antiquarian Book Society, GABS?"

Cleo guessed the gag was as well-worn as his boots. As a librarian, she heard more than her share of repeated, corny jokes. Some of her patrons had been uttering the same puns for decades. Cleo never tired of them. They were a comforting constant like the sun rising and setting.

Dot said seriously, "That sounds wonderful. You offer items that bring people joy. That's as important—no, more important—than money."

"It is!" Buddy said, as if Dot had hit on the key to life. "Collect and read what you love!" He quickly turned hesitant, scratching behind an ear. "That's why, well, I hate to be a bearer of bad news. Like I said, I overheard your troubles about your books. You love 'em, right, and want 'em back? Well, it occurred to me that I might be part of the problem."

Dot's smile sank.

Buddy hurried on. "I bought this here bird picture last night from that Hunter Fox dude." He opened the folder to reveal a painting of cardinals on a branch of flowering dogwood. "He's staying at the same bed-and-breakfast as most of us bookdealers. After the social, he offered up deals. I liked this picture and it seemed like an okay price, so I snapped it up."

Dot's mouth opened, but no sound escaped.

"It's a watercolor," Buddy said, gabbing on faster. "George M. Sutton's the artist, but y'all probably know that."

Cleo's heart sank. Oh no . . . had another one of Dot's books been butchered? Cleo knew the book and artist. She knew Dot owned a copy too. She glanced at her cousin. Dot yanked at her apron ties, loosening them only to cinch them tighter.

"Is it yours, Dot?" Cleo asked.

"Maybe you can tell by this little spot." Buddy pointed to minor discoloration at a corner. "That's what made it affordable for the likes of me."

"My book was intact," Dot said in a small voice. "Cleo, you know the book. It was perfect except for some age spots. My movie book is—was—fine too."

"I just have this one page here," Buddy said, flipping the folder shut and biting his lip. "I'm happy to get it back to you. May I call you Dot? Miss Dot?"

Irritation bubbled up in Cleo. Another fine book, chopped up for pieces? It wasn't right. It was book murder! Deliberate and malicious book butchery! And now this man wanted to rip Dot off again by selling it back to her?

"For what price?" Cleo said, unable to keep a snap from her voice.

Buddy looked wounded. "No price, ma'am." He extended the folder toward Dot. "Here. Please. Take it. I wish I had the complete book, but a page is better than nothing. Better than a kick in the behind with a frozen boot, as my granddaddy used to say."

Dot clutched her middle as if she'd been kicked. She swung around and took off at a shuffling run, heading toward downtown. In the middle of the intersection, Dot turned to Cleo and the two worried men following after her.

"Please, let me handle this," Dot said. "I got myself in this mess. I'll fix it."

Chapter Four

"I'm sure Dot will call today," said Henry, ever the optimist. He and Cleo sat at her kitchen table. A fine, sunny Tuesday and the second day of the antiquarian book fair stretched out before them. Henry was finishing off the final crumbs of a morning-glory muffin, a treat Cleo considered exempt from her doctor's joy-stifling prescription of a low-sugar diet. Morning glories contained pineapple, coconut, raisins, whole wheat, and even carrots. Anything involving carrots and whole wheat had to be healthy. They'd each enjoyed two.

Henry collected their plates and carried them to the sink. He offered Cleo a refill on coffee and a concerned smile.

"Thanks," she said, glad for his company and that she'd convinced him to keep pajamas, toiletries, and a few changes of clothes at her house. For too many nights, the dear man had slept curled up on her sofa or trudged home alone in the dark.

Cleo cupped her warm mug and a warm feeling. Until meeting Henry, she'd assumed her senior years would be spent solo. Her husband had passed away some ten years ago. She'd always miss Richard, but she'd gradually discovered some new joys too.

On her own, Cleo could read in bed at all hours and cook whatever she wanted, whenever she wanted. She slept in on

Sundays and let visiting grandkids sail down the banister and make outrageous noise, messy art, and pancakes in deliriously abstract shapes. Then there was a joy that Cleo hadn't even known she was missing: driving. In her version of a swinging single, Cleo had dusted off her father's classic convertible, kept cooped up in the garage far too long. Best of all, she'd learned how to captain a school bus full of books.

However, it was awfully nice to have company for breakfast, Cleo thought, watching Henry rinse the dishes. Drifting off to a dimming e-reader was surprisingly pleasant too, especially if it included a fellow booklover at her side. Even if his pug did snore and her gossipy neighbor to the north, Wanda Boxer, delighted in disapproving.

Outside, the sunrise lit up the powdery peach blossoms in the old orchard behind Cleo's back fence. Soon the warm rays would burn off the dew and morning mist. Not soon enough for Rhett Butler, Cleo's cat. Cleo watched out the window as her fluffy orange Persian attempted to extricate himself from trouble of his own making.

After gobbling his breakfast, Rhett had meowed demands to go outside. He'd then barreled straight into a patch of damp grass. Rhett detested water in any form except in his bowl and clearly considered himself stranded. He held up a front paw and flicked it, before putting it down and flicking the other. In between, he shot accusatory glares toward the house.

They could both take this as a lesson, Cleo thought. Yesterday, she'd barreled into Dot's business. She'd bullied her cousin with loving concern, leaving phone messages and dropping by Dot's home and store. Dot hadn't answered the phone or the doors.

Cleo would have been beyond worried if she hadn't heard from Dot's niece, April, who'd reached Dot by phone. April reported what Cleo had suspected: Dot was mortified and didn't want to talk about it.

"Something about making a scene?" April had said, incredulous. "She said she got caught up in the excitement of some big book festival and made a silly, spontaneous mistake?" Dot and April were as close as mother and daughter. Dot had raised April since she was seven, after April's mother passed away and Dot's older brother—April's father—failed to cope.

"Auntie Dotty will be fine," April had said, adding with less confidence, "Won't she?"

April lived on the West Coast, with a busy job and busier family life. Cleo knew she'd fly home in an instant if she thought Dot was in trouble.

"Of course! Everything will be fine!" Cleo hoped the false enthusiasm covered her concerns. She'd promised April that she'd keep in touch. She'd promised herself that she'd give Dot some space.

Cleo spoke the vow aloud as a reminder. "I will not push. I will not rush in . . ."

"Wise," Henry said, setting dishes in the drainer. "Meanwhile, I'll ask around about Hunter Fox's transactions."

Cleo smiled at him. "I will too." She was taking Words on Wheels out this morning. She hoped she wouldn't find swindling victims among her patrons, although she feared she might. Cleo sipped more coffee, fueling up on caffeine and indignation.

Henry checked his watch. "I should get going. The fair opens at ten. I'm giving some of the antiquarians a tour of my workshop beforehand. I need to tidy it up."

"I'll give you a ride," Cleo offered. "I need to stop by the library and pick up some holds for Words on Wheels. Let me get Rhett inside and dry his paws." Cleo forbade food, drink, gum, and dewy cat feet in her bookmobile.

"Chauffeured in a bookmobile? I accept," Henry said, gazing out the window. "It's a sunny, fresh day. I predict problems will fizzle away like the fog."

Cleo hoped he was right, but she didn't quite feel as sunny. She believed April's report of Dot suffering a painful case of chagrin. What she didn't buy was that Dot had gotten caught up in a spurt of book-fair excitement.

As a child, Dot hadn't taken off running like Cleo. Dot wasn't spontaneous. She didn't pretend to fly or even wish she could. Dot was solid, rooted, and cautious.

Something had to be wrong. Something deeper and possibly even more important than books.

* * *

Stepping off her porch, Cleo's ears picked up faint sounds of butchery. She cringed inwardly. Outwardly, she waved brightly to Wanda Boxer, looming at their shared side fence, clippers aimed at a wounded gardenia. Cleo's neighbor to the north was on spring break this week and using her free time to garden, an unfortunate situation for the plants. In gardening—and life in general—Wanda derived her greatest joy from hacking at the happy and exuberant.

Rhett, already grumpy from damp grass, toweled toes, and being clipped into his cat harness, shot Wanda the frown she deserved. Wanda had once chased Rhett with a broom for sunning on her porch. He'd never forgiven her.

Henry and Mr. Chaucer wisely kept moving toward Words on Wheels, parked in Cleo's driveway.

Wanda smirked at their departing backs. "Shacking up with your boyfriend again? No wonder you're getting lax at work, Cleo," she said. "I needed a book yesterday. I walked all the way to the park to find your bookmobile closed."

"I took the morning off to attend the book fair," Cleo said, letting Rhett tug her down the path.

Wanda's laugh demonstrated the distinction between a happy chuckle and a malicious cackle. Reinforcing the latter, Wanda beheaded a gardenia bloom. It fell, like so many others, at her rubber-booted feet.

"I heard all about that book fair," Wanda declared. "Sounds overpriced and boring, except for your cousin making a silly fool of herself. Did she really fall for some hot man and give away her books? Let that be a lesson, Cleo. Fawning is unseemly at her age and even more so at yours, if you ask me."

Cleo hadn't asked. Besides, Wanda was only a few years younger than Dot and had been unseemly in her rudeness for decades.

Wanda took aim at another bloom and gave it a snip. Then she eyed Cleo, waiting for a rise, a rightful reproach of her unnecessarily cruel words and pruning practices.

Cleo bit her tongue. She wouldn't give Wanda the pleasure. Instead, she employed her mother's go-to polite brush-off. "I shouldn't keep you," Cleo trilled, adding a cheery wave. "I'm off to work. 'Bye!"

"You're actually *working*? I'll come over right now, so I don't waste my time later if you decide to close without notice."

Manners wrestled in Cleo's mind. Good manners for both neighbors and librarians dictated that she welcome Wanda and wait patiently while the woman griped and grumbled and likely rejected all of the many fine books on offer.

On the other hand, manners required that Cleo get Henry to his shop as she'd promised. She needed to prepare for her appointment at a nursing home this morning too. It would be rude to keep the residents waiting for their books and audiobooks. She planned to show off her special display of library collectibles too. Cleo was sure the residents would be appreciative and happy, unlike Wanda.

Wanda smeared muddy handprints down her beige windbreaker. Clippers swinging, she started toward her gate. Cleo pictured mud on her floor and her pages.

Wanda *could* have said please, Cleo reasoned. She *could* wait until regular opening hours. Most of all, she could refrain from insulting Cleo's kind and virtuous cousin!

Cleo made a show of checking her watch. "Oh, so sorry, Wanda. Look at the time! I really do have to run. Words on Wheels will be parked down at the Depot all afternoon. As you know, the main library opens at nine." Cleo pitched her words as bright and sunny as her buttercup-yellow cardigan.

"You want me to walk all the way to the main library when you have a busload of books parked right here?"

"It's lovely weather for a stroll," Cleo trilled. To avoid Wanda's glare, she bent to scoop up Rhett. His claws dug into her shoulder as she hurried for the bus, assuring herself she had nothing to feel guilty about. It was a gorgeous morning, and visiting the main library was always a treat, even more so since its extensive renovations.

Last year, a toppled tree and town turmoil had nearly felled Cleo's beloved library, where she'd worked for over five decades. Thanks to an unexpected benefactor and Cleo's efforts to uncover criminal activities, the building was back. Cleo was still the head librarian, but she no longer spent her days at the circulation desk. She'd entrusted main-library operations to her young protégé, Leanna. That didn't mean Cleo was retiring or resting on her library laurels, though. *Heavens, no!* Cleo was as busy as ever, crisscrossing the county in Words on Wheels.

When the main building was out of commission, Cleo had enlisted the bookmobile as the full-time library. The experience had been eye-opening in many ways. Personally, Cleo had come to realize how much she loved the open road, the wind in her hair, and visiting patrons where they lived and worked. Professionally, Cleo had seen how much joy and benefit the mobile library delivered. Folks lit up when they saw the bookmobile coming. Some even flagged her down at red lights, hoping to hop on board. Everyone loved a bookmobile.

Well, almost everyone, Cleo qualified, as Wanda's complaints chased her down the walkway.

Henry stepped aside. "It's locked," he said with an urgent glance back toward Wanda.

Cleo unlocked the bookmobile and hustled Henry and Mr. Chaucer up the steps. She followed with Rhett's tail swishing at her chest. Once inside, she lowered her cat into his traveling box, a padded peach crate bolted to the floor by her captain's seat. Henry buckled up on the front bench seat, clutching Mr. Chaucer on his lap. The big bus roared to life.

When they were clear, Cleo glanced in her rearview mirror, happy to be free of Wanda and always delighted to be in Words on Wheels, the prettiest bookmobile in Georgia, if not far beyond.

Cleo's clever grandson Sam had retrofitted the retired school bus as his Eagle Scout project. Sam and his friends had crafted handmade bookshelves to replace most of the bench seats. The back bench remained to provide a kids' nook, along with soft seating. Squishy rainbow floor tiles ran the length of the aisle.

The exterior was just as fun. *Words on Wheels* looped across each side in opalescent green cursive. Airbrushed flames fanned the grille, and cartoon text spelled out READ above the front and back windshields.

Cleo adored the newest feature too. For a Christmas present, Sam had surprised her with a Plexiglas display case with handy clips for securing it to a bookmobile shelf and a leather handle for easy carrying. Cleo had given the case pride of place on the *New Reads* shelf directly behind her captain's seat.

"Whew," Henry said, exhaling as they drove on. "Good job escaping Wanda. She scares Mr. Chaucer. And me . . ."

The pug affirmed with a whimper.

"Wanda's worse in springtime," Cleo said. "I think it's all the new life, the baby birds and fresh flowers and oak pollen. It turns her meaner. I never can understand why she takes a spring break. Maybe her coworkers insist." Wanda worked in human resources, an ill-fitted position given her dislike of most humans.

Henry asked, "Was she gossiping about Dot? How'd she know? I didn't see Wanda at the fair, although there was quite a big crowd."

"Tentacles," Cleo said darkly. "She has a long reach for gossip." If there was something bad to hear, Wanda knew of it, faster than the dark webs of the Internet. For a second Cleo almost regretted rushing off. Wanda knew about Hunter Fox. Maybe she'd heard of other victims. If so, she'd be happy to mock them, as she had Dot, and Cleo could collect some names.

The bus lumped over a speed bump, and Cleo affirmed her Wanda-avoidance instincts. There were nicer and more trustworthy ways to get information.

"Maybe it's good that Dot is lying low," Cleo said. "At least until Wanda moves on to other gossip."

"She has us to talk about," Henry said.

In the rearview mirror, they grinned at each other like two teenagers.

Cleo turned on a route that would take them around Fontaine Park. She planned to let Henry off at his shop and then loop around again to stop by the library. Even though she'd be going inside soon, Cleo couldn't resist admiring the building as they passed. The Victorian cottage that was the library's home sported palm-frond-green paint and a shiny metal roof, fresh with last year's renovations. The lawn was neatly trimmed, and a young redbud bloomed against a lacy backdrop of dogwoods.

A little farther on, Cleo's head swiveled to the park, where the azaleas were downright gaudy. In fact, all the colors seemed especially bright this spring, even the chartreuse glitter of oak pollen. They rounded the corner, and the ebony panels and gold trim of Henry's shop came into view.

The Gilded Page Antiquarian and Rare Books occupied a former pharmacy. Henry had restored the building from its plank floors to the tin ceiling. Best of all, he'd packed it with shelves and cozy reading spaces.

The shop was his "working retirement," as he called it. In the back, he operated a book surgery, a workshop where he mended cracked spines and brought new life to ancient illuminated manuscripts, often donating his services. He and Mr. Chaucer lived on the second floor in an apartment with views over the park.

Cleo's mind shifted to their plans to meet for dinner, if not sooner. They could go to Dot's Drop By for a picnic lunch and check-in. It wouldn't be pushy if Cleo was there to buy lunch . . .

"Let me know if you hear from Dot," Henry said, reading her mind. "Perhaps we could stop by for a bite. It's the biscuit-sandwich special at the Drop By today."

Cleo murmured agreement. Her attention was divided between the street ahead and the sidewalk to her left. A toddler raced up the walkway, giddy and wobbly and waving at the bookmobile. Cleo waved back. The little boy's father jogged to catch him, swooping him up in his arms.

Cleo smiled and loosened her grip on the wheel. But when she turned back to the street, she gasped and stomped on the brakes.

"Hold on!" she cried. Her heart thumped, the brakes moaned and wheels skidded, and the big bus jolted to a stop.

Dot had run into the middle of the street. She stood, feet planted, arms waving frantically. Apron ruffles poked out from under a spring jacket the color of mint ice cream. Her bangs were askew, and the hem of her jacket looked dirty.

Cleo flung open the door and wrestled to release her seat belt. In her urgency, the school-bus stop signs flung open. Cleo let them be. Dot was already at the bottom of the steps.

"Oh, Cleo! It's that awful man, Hunter Fox!" Dot's voice wavered. She gasped and staggered back. "No, no, *I'm* the awful one. *He's dead!*"

Chapter Five

"Dead?" Cleo stepped back, bumping against the supportive padding of Henry. He rested a steadying hand on her shoulder.

A terrible prayer passed through Cleo's mind and heart. *Oh, please, let it be an accident or natural causes.* Cleo knew from unfortunate experience that her pretty little town was not immune to crime, including murder. Last year, Cleo had discovered several victims of unnatural demise . . . and their killers. Henry had been at her side then too. It was a wonder the dear man dared spend time with her, she thought wildly. But she hadn't stumbled on death this time. Dot had, and that was worse.

Her cousin's face was gray and slack with shock.

"Dot, come up into the bus," Cleo urged. She imagined swinging the door shut behind Dot and speeding away. Cleo sighed heavily. They couldn't do that, of course, and Dot wasn't getting on board anyway.

Dot edged back, pointing with zombie-armed stiffness toward Wisteria Street, which ran along the side of Henry's store. "Hunter's all alone. In the alley."

Cleo grabbed her purse and rooted around for her cell phone. Her kids and grandkids had given her the phone for emergencies.

They'd likely imagined crises no worse than a flat tire or a forgotten grandmotherly birthday call, not reporting corpses.

Cleo brought up her contacts screen, which included her deputy neighbor. Gabby's face smiled out from a little round photo. Cleo's finger hovered and then moved on. She didn't want to get Gabby in trouble by breaking emergency protocols. She should call 911, but what would she say? Who would she ask for? Only an ambulance, or the police too?

Cleo dropped the phone back in her purse. To be most helpful, she needed to see the scene. Dot was backing that way, mouthing something that Cleo interpreted as "I'm sorry," right before she disappeared around the corner.

Sorry . . . Yesterday, Dot had said the word in a much different context to Hunter Fox. *You'll be sorry! Awfully sorry!*

*   *   *

The pets were safe in Words on Wheels. Henry was at Cleo's side, and Hunter Fox was as Dot had reported: alone in the alley.

And dead. Cleo could see that from a few yards out. The book scout sat in a low slump against a telephone pole, surrounded by an exuberant patch of thistles. His face was dipped but unmistakable, despite the grim pallor behind his tan.

"I checked," Dot said in a small voice. "I went to touch his neck for a pulse, but then . . ."

Then she would have seen his neck.

Henry inhaled sharply.

A red stain blossomed under Hunter Fox's collar.

Cleo looked away, to anywhere but at the man. To her right was Henry's back patio, mostly hidden behind a lattice fence woven thick with honeysuckle vine. They'd sat out on many an evening, snug at a café table tucked in a mesh-netted gazebo.

Henry Lafayette was as attractive to mosquitoes as he was to Cleo.

To the left stood the tippy carriage garage and wild garden of Madame Romanov, the self-proclaimed "premier psychic seer" of Catalpa Springs. Cleo granted the "premier" label. As far as she knew, Madame Romanov was the *only* psychic in town. However, Cleo didn't quite believe in Madame's seeing abilities. She had even more doubts now. A light glowed behind lace curtains in Madame's home/psychic center. If the psychic was in, how had she failed to sense a death inches from her own backyard?

Dot hovered at Cleo's shoulder. "When I first noticed him, I was irritated. How awful of me! I thought he was sitting out here drunk or sleeping."

"How did you notice him?" Cleo asked. From the street, she hadn't, even knowing he was there. A row of trash bins blocked the view, one tipped and spewing out shredded paper.

"The psychic's little dog," Dot said swiveling around. "He's always getting out of that fence. I was walking by and saw him in the alley. He shouldn't be out alone on the streets . . . we should look for him."

Cleo knew the dog, a chubby dachshund named Slim. Despite his double-wide size, Slim managed to slip out of his fence and often pranced around town, getting treats, which explained his escape urges and his girth.

"I wanted to catch him and get him back home, but he ran off back down the alley. I followed a little way, and then I saw . . ." Dot bit her lip.

Cleo fished for her phone, which always managed to wiggle back to the depths of her purse. She pressed 911 and half listened as Dot fretted about a tipped trash can, litter, and Slim.

Suddenly the dispatcher spoke in Cleo's ear, asking what her emergency was.

"A body!" Cleo blurted. "A man has been murdered." None of them had said that word yet, but it was clear that neither a medical condition nor an accident had taken Hunter Fox's life. With her free hand, Cleo tugged her sunny cardigan tight.

Dot was reaching for the tipped trash can.

"Dot, no," Cleo called over. "Don't touch anything!"

Dot yanked her hand back as if shocked.

"Sorry!" Cleo said. "It could be evidence."

"Hello?" the dispatcher said, more stridently. *"Miss Cleo,* is that you?"

Cleo blinked. She recognized the voice of her favorite neighbor and deputy. "Gabby? I'm sorry, I thought I called 911."

"You did. I'm covering dispatch for a spell. Did you say *body*? You didn't find another, did you?"

"My cousin Dot did," Cleo said, explaining briefly and assuring Gabby they were all safe.

"The chief is already out on another call," Gabby said. "I'll send him right over. I'll be there too, as soon as I can get someone to take over the phones. You're right—don't touch anything. Do you want me to stay on the line with you?"

Cleo politely declined. She wanted to talk to Dot before the chief came blustering in. He wouldn't be happy to see Cleo at another crime scene. He'd be even less happy with another murder.

* * *

"I was walking to work," Dot said. She and Cleo stood at the corner of Henry's shop, waiting to flag down the chief. Henry had nobly volunteered to keep watch at the end of the alley so that no one else stumbled into a shock.

"I have a lot to do at the Drop By," Dot continued, hands nervously twisting her jacket tie. "I wanted to go early, to get inside before a lot of folks were around downtown."

Gossiping folks like Wanda, Cleo interpreted. "And you spotted Slim," Cleo prompted when Dot fell silent.

"Yes," Dot said, managing a weak smile. "He's a little teaser. He let me touch his head and then ran off. I went down the alley after him. I hope he's okay."

Cleo assumed she meant Slim. Hunter Fox certainly wasn't okay.

"And there that man was," Dot said, her tone suddenly calm and chilly cool. "That awful man who stole my books."

This time Dot didn't chide herself or say she was sorry. She firmed her jaw and folded her arms across her chest. Cleo chalked it up to shock.

Chapter Six

A silver pickup the size of a small yacht pulled up in front of Words on Wheels, one tire bumping up over the curb. Cleo would need a stepladder to get to the wheel. Chief Silas Culpepper had many inches on Cleo's five foot three, but even his boots dangled in empty air before he slid down to the pavement.

Back on solid ground, he puffed his chest and stretched out his suspenders with both thumbs. Suspenders were the chief's indulgence, Cleo thought, like books were for her. The man likely had enough for a new print every day of the year and then some. Today's featured crawfish dancing beside their boiling pot. They were joined by fellow culinary victims, grinning ears of corn and wide-eyed potatoes.

Cleo felt her eyes widen in surprise as she approached the truck. The passenger door had opened, and slender legs in gold strappy heels emerged. The chief let his suspenders snap back and hustled to assist as the Marilyn figure of Kitty Peavey flowed out.

The "purveyor of southern delights" wore another formfitting red dress. The hem rode up as she slid down. Kitty steadied herself on the chief's shoulder. "Such a *big, tall* truck," she said breathily.

Red spots blossomed on Chief Culpepper's cheeks as sunlight flashed on his wedding ring. *Bless her heart*, Cleo thought for the long-enduring Mrs. Culpepper. The chief's wife was a stout and stolid woman who preferred her books in audio form. Better for filtering out her husband, Cleo assumed, whose utterances ranged from blustery orders to exhausting explanations.

Cleo sensed one such bluster coming her way. She shifted protectively in front of Dot and got in the first question. "Why is Miss Peavey with you?"

The chief huffed. "I'll ask the questions here. Who'd you find dead this time, Mrs. Watkins?"

"It's not Cleo's fault," Dot said. "It was me!"

Cleo clarified. "Dot was walking by, noticed someone in trouble, and as a good Samaritan, tried to help. Seeing he was . . . deceased . . . she ran to summon assistance. I happened to be driving by, and together we called you."

"Of course you drove right into another death," the chief muttered. He glanced back at his truck, where Kitty practically reclined on the fender. She appeared engrossed in her cell phone.

The chief grumbled on. "Finding bodies is all in the family for you, isn't it, Mrs. Watkins? Let's hope you're wrong and this one's a simple accident. Let's hope it's nothing to do with books too. This fair's already taking up too much police time with crime, and it's barely started."

Crime? Another crime? Cleo opened her mouth but quickly decided against asking. She wouldn't give him the pleasure of denying her information. She'd find out from Gabby. "I'm afraid this is a murder," she said.

"If that's true, then what's the public doing messing around my scene?" The chief pointed a thick finger at Henry, who still stood staring glumly down the alley. "You there," the chief bellowed. "Clear the scene."

"You too, Miss Cleo," the chief added. "Go wait on that book bus of yours. We only need the witness who found him." He jerked his head at Dot. "Ma'am, come with me."

"Me?" Dot said, sounding less certain of her role.

"Yes, ma'am. *You* said you found him, correct?"

Dot liked to be helpful. Sometimes she was too helpful for her own good. Cleo moved to hold Dot back, but her cousin slipped away and hurried toward the alley. The chief held up a mitt of a palm.

"Nope. Not this time, Miss Cleo," he said. "I don't need your help."

Worry gripped Cleo. It was Dot who might need her help. Dear, kind Dot had threatened a man in anger and in public. Now that man was dead, and Dot had discovered his body.

The chief would surely hear about the argument and swindled books. When he did, he was apt to overreact. In past cases, he'd suspected Cleo of murder, and Mary-Rose and Cleo's grandson Ollie and other innocent members of the public too. Cleo had helped in those cases. She would step in again if she needed to protect Dot.

Henry trudged toward her, hands deep in his pockets, head dipped. "I'll go check on the pets," he said, his voice a dull monotone.

Cleo pitched her response to perky. "Great idea! I'll be right there to join you all. I just want to talk to someone first."

A throaty Dodge Charger was pulling up, sporting the logo of the Catalpa Springs Police Department. As Cleo had hoped, Gabby Honeywell hopped out. Her glossy curls swung in a ponytail, and she managed to make the beige polyester uniform look stylish. The style was no surprise. Gabby, a former beauty queen, was a yoga enthusiast, brimming with poise and polish. In her midtwenties, Gabby was also the youngest member of the Catalpa Springs Police Department, the only female, the sole African-American officer, and Cleo's favorite neighbor, not counting Cleo's grandson Ollie, a recent college graduate who was currently residing in Cleo's backyard cottage.

Gabby gave Cleo a quick hug. "Are you all okay?"

"Honeywell!" the chief boomed. "This isn't a social call. Get this scene secured. Close off the street and both entrances to the alley. Move it! You're already late."

Chief Culpepper puffed his chest importantly and glanced toward Kitty. If he'd hoped to impress Kitty, she hadn't noticed. Her focus remained on her phone. After heaving a sigh of disappointment, the chief stomped off down Wisteria Street.

"I think Dot's pretty shaken up," Cleo said, following Gabby to her vehicle and explaining what she knew as Gabby rummaged in the trunk. Gabby emerged with a large roll of crime-scene tape and sympathy for Dot.

"Dot was just walking by," Cleo stressed. "It's bad luck, that's all. If she hadn't found him, someone else would have. She's in shock. She's not thinking—or talking—straight. I should get her home."

Gabby gave her an assessing look and seemed to read Cleo's concerns. "Don't worry," she said. "I'll get Dot back to you as soon as possible. You should all stick around, though. We'll need to get statements from everyone. Are you sure it's murder? Not that I doubt you, Miss Cleo, but I don't want another springtime crime spree."

Neither did Cleo, but she saw no way of sugarcoating it. "I'm certain," she said, wrapping her arms tight to her middle. "He was stabbed, I'd guess. Look for something sharp."

Gabby hoisted out a duffel and looped the roll of crime-scene tape around her wrist. "Did you recognize the vic?"

All too well, Cleo thought. "Yes, his name is Hunter Fox."

"Should I know him?"

Yesterday, Cleo had definitely thought Gabby should get to know Mr. Fox, by way of arresting him for bad book behavior. She didn't want to bring that up yet. "You wouldn't know him, probably. He's in town for the book fair."

Gabby groaned. "The chief isn't going to like that. A visitor, killed? It's not even a half year into his safety campaign."

After last year's murders, the chief and the tourism board had gotten together and designed a new campaign to boost the town's image. Mostly it consisted of glossy photos and a logo of questionable factualness: *Catalpa Springs, Safest Little Town in the South.* The statement was prominently endorsed by the chief, who'd look bad if it wasn't true.

"Mr. Fox was a book scout," Cleo said. "I think he came to town about a week ago, in preparation for the fair."

"A book scout? Like a Boy Scout?"

"Not quite," Cleo said diplomatically. She briefly explained Hunter's job, how he hunted down books and sold them on to collectors. "Like a middleman, a finder."

"So kinda like that reality show about garage-sale pickers?" Gabby said. "But with books? That sounds fun! I can't see him making enemies by discovering and selling books."

Cleo could. She was still deciding how to politely explain Hunter's slippery practices when Culpepper bellowed again.

"Honeywell, stop your yapping and secure this scene!"

Young Gabby had an admirable ability to turn serene under the chief's outbursts. Cleo watched, taking it as a lesson, as Gabby centered her already perfect posture. Gabby inhaled, exhaled, smiled calmly, and said, "We'll talk later."

"We will," Cleo said, already dreading it.

Chapter Seven

Cleo glanced at Words on Wheels. Henry stood inside the bright, happy bus, staring glumly out toward his shop. Rhett Butler sat atop the next shelf down, grooming a rear leg for all to see. If anyone had been looking at the bookmobile. To Cleo's dismay, the crime scene was drawing keen attention. Cars drove by at rubbernecking pace. Pedestrians stared. Some turned away and hurried on. More clumped in little groups at the caution tape strung across Wisteria.

"What is going on?" Kitty Peavey had finally detached from her cell phone. She breezed over to Cleo with a wave of perfume and a scowl. Her lips matched her cherry-red dress, and her golden hair was set in stiff curls, slightly flattened on one side.

Before Cleo could come up with an answer teetering between truth and outright fib, Kitty struck a pouty pose. "The chief wouldn't tell me. He said he didn't want to upset me since I'm a lady and already shaken up."

Kitty inspected ruby-red nails and a chip on her right index finger. She fussed at the imperfection, giving Cleo time to assess her state, which hardly seemed shaken at all. Then Cleo remembered what Gabby had said when she'd called 911. *The chief was already out, responding to another call. Did that call involve Kitty?*

"Did something happen to you earlier?" Cleo asked. "Are you okay?"

Kitty gave up on the nail. Her hand fluttered at her heart. "My room was ransacked! While I slept!"

Cleo's hand slapped at her own heart. Female solidarity overcame any previous suspicions of Kitty. She pictured a prowler, creeping into Kitty's room in the dark. How terrifying! "How awful!" she exclaimed.

"I know!" Kitty said. "My room was a mess and a half this morning. Some of my inventory is missing too. Thank goodness I had my best treasures and cash in the safe. Of course, the safe was too tiny for all my southern delights."

Ransacking *and* book theft? Cleo's hand remained firmly at her breast.

"That bed-and-breakfast looks pretty enough, doesn't it?" Kitty said. "But the security is atrocious. What if I had been in my bed in my negligee? The thought gives me the chills. I'm thinking of suing for emotional distress. Chief Culpepper says I'll have a better chance if I make out a police report. That's where we're going, to the station. He's offered to hold my hand through it. He's such a gentleman."

Cleo's sympathy slipped. A robbery was a violation, and how upsetting to lose books. But then Kitty hadn't shown any concern for Dot's missing books, and suing the Myrtles Bed and Breakfast seemed extreme. Cleo knew the hardworking owners. The Flores family took care with every amenity, and Henry had told her about their above-and-beyond efforts to accommodate the demanding antiquarians.

"It's upsetting, most certainly," Cleo soothed. "But criminals strike. Sometimes there's nothing that good, honest folks can do to stop them." She knew all about that. "Unless you think it's someone who works there? But then it would be that person's fault, and the police would charge them."

"Like the maid? I can't see a *housekeeper* caring about *books*, can you?"

Yes, I can, Cleo thought, but she occupied herself with cleaning her glasses.

Kitty rattled on. "Those innkeeper people say it's my fault for forgetting my room key at a bar. Well, *I* say it's still *their* establishment and *their* key! When I discovered the mess this morning, all they did was offer me a free stay and condolences and a fruit basket! Fruit hardly makes up for theft, does it? I won't be letting housekeeping in after this, just in case."

Cleo had been having a pretty wrought morning herself. Thus it took her a moment to work out the situation.

"You weren't in your room when it happened?" Cleo asked, guessing the answer as soon as she spoke. "Oh, of course, you were probably with your fiancé. Thank goodness!"

Kitty twisted the glittery diamond on her ring finger. "Oh, right . . . I guess I shouldn't kick up too much of a fuss. I wasn't exactly with my Dr. Dean. I think I mentioned, he's my *pre*-fiancé, if you know what I mean?"

Cleo didn't, but she firmly believed in letting others love as they liked. She nodded and smiled, but a new worry was growing.

"Deany's a good man," Kitty continued with a touch of defensiveness to her tone. "He knows his books and takes care of me and supports my collecting interests, but he's no fun on trips. Can you believe, he brings his own food? He goes to bed by nine o'clock sharp too, lights out and quiet hours. That's why I have to get a separate room, so I can conduct my own business." She giggled. "And a single gal at a book fair should have some fun too, don't you agree?"

Cleo continued her polite nodding. She was all for fun around books, and how Kitty spent her evening was none of Cleo's concern. Unless it included a certain book scout.

"Did your fun or business happen to involve Mr. Fox?" Cleo asked, careful to keep her tone neutral.

"Now, that's my business," Kitty said in mock chastisement. However, her sly smile and the rosy glow blossoming on her cheeks suggested the answer.

Kitty tapped a foot impatiently. "Speaking of business, what is taking that policeman so long? I suppose it's a sign I should forget the whole thing. You're probably right."

She made it sound like Cleo had twisted her arm. "Now I'll have to walk *all that way* back to the bed-and-breakfast. I don't suppose y'all have Uber here?"

Cleo had no idea. She did know that the Myrtles was just a few blocks away and a pretty walk through the park and downtown.

"They better have some carb-free breakfast items by the time I get there," Kitty was saying, in the same ominous tone she'd used to threaten the Flores family with financial ruin. She turned on her gold heels to go.

"Wait," Cleo said.

Kitty spun back too quickly, catching Cleo in indecision. It wasn't Cleo's place to inform Kitty of Hunter's death. Such awful news should be handled by professionals. On the other hand, Kitty might have helpful information, for the police and for Cleo too. If Kitty cared about Hunter Fox—which Cleo was certain she did— then she'd surely want to help bring his killer to justice.

"When did you last see Mr. Fox?" Cleo asked.

"Why?" Kitty's eyes narrowed under mascara-heavy lashes. "Oh . . . I get it. This is still about your cousin and her old books, isn't it? Well, you tell her to stop bugging him. Honestly, did you know, she was pounding on his door in the middle of the night? Rude!"

Cleo felt her mouth open. No words came out, being stuck in the worries whirling in her head. Dot had gone to the Myrtles and banged on Hunter's door? And Kitty knew. At the very least, Kitty had spoken with Hunter Fox last night.

"That's right, your cousin was making another fuss," Kitty said, clicking her tongue in disapproval. "Since you're so determined to pry, I'll tell you. Yes, I was over at Hunt's room, talking books. He didn't open the door to your cousin. He said there'd be no way to reason with her. I mean, you saw what happened at the fair yesterday. She made a *scene.*"

Kitty's cheeks remained rosy as she talked on about Hunter Fox, how sweet-talking was in his nature. How it got him the *best* deals.

Cleo felt a pang of sadness, for Kitty and for Hunter too. He'd been devious and underhanded—possibly criminal—but he hadn't deserved death.

A huffing sound from Kitty cut into Cleo's thoughts. "This is taking forever," Kitty said. "I'm leaving. Maybe Hunt'll turn up for breakfast. That man, I swear; you can't trust him any farther than you can throw him, but that's part of his charm, isn't it?"

Cleo's head spun in a should-she, shouldn't-she dither.

Another police car pulled up, lights flashing and sirens blaring.

Kitty pressed her palms to her ears. "What a racket! What did you say is happening? It looks kind of serious."

"There's been an . . . incident," Cleo said obliquely.

"Must be some *incident* if it tops my room-invasion robbery. This town isn't as sweet as it seems, is it? *Safest Little Town in the*

South, ha! Hunt keeps telling me, this is the most innocent place around. Wait till I tell him. A robbery and an *incident*. He better watch his backside too!"

She poked at her phone. "Why won't that man respond? What's he up to so early?"

"Oh, Kitty," Cleo said, deciding she had to say something. She took a breath, but someone else let the words out first.

"Murder . . . a murderer is among us . . ." Madame Romanov, premier psychic, spiraled toward them, moaning in watery tones. Palms outstretched, she spun in a slow circle. She wore a shimmery purple robe that brought out the lavender streaks in her long, black hair. Bells jingled from bangles as thick as barnacles. A dusky scent of incense hovered around her.

"The chimes of the beyond call. A man calls to me. His spirit cries out. He cries to be heard." Madame waved her hands and bangles clanked.

"Murder? A man?" Kitty wrinkled her nose and jerked back as Madame Romanov jangled a hand close to her ear. Then she gasped. "Oh. My. Gosh! Was it another room invasion? Thank goodness I was with Hunt. I could have been killed! I *should* sue."

"Hunter," Madame Romanov intoned. "The huntsman. The *fox* in the henhouse. His body lies on the earth, but his spirit waits overhead. Waiting for justice . . ." Her eyes rolled back, flashing wild whites. She muttered on about angel bells.

Kitty stepped back, mouth agape, eyes aimed at Cleo. "Hunter? What is this weird woman talking about?"

"Kitty, dear, I'm so sorry," Cleo said, reaching for Kitty's hands. Kitty yanked away. This wasn't how Cleo would have broken the news, but now it was out. "It's true. Mr. Hunter has been . . ."

"Slain! Knocked down . . . down, down, down, dead," Madame Romanov supplied, her eyes popping open.

Cleo quickly said, "I am so very sorry, Kitty. The police will tell us more soon, and they'll want to talk to you."

Kitty backed away, pointing at Cleo. "You! They need to talk to *you*, that's who. You and that cousin of yours! That's why you were asking all those nosy questions. You're looking for someone else to blame! Well, he was alive and happy with me. Oh, Hunter!"

"The hunter in the great beyond," Madame Romanov intoned, eyes slithering upward.

"Shush!" Kitty spat.

"Kitty, please," Cleo said. "You can help bring him justice. When did he go out? Was he meeting someone?"

"Leave me alone, both of you!" Kitty shoved by Cleo and the chanting psychic, running toward Wisteria. Cleo followed, rounding the corner in time to see Kitty smack into Chief Silas Culpepper.

Wailing, Kitty gripped the chief's suspenders, releasing a hand only to point toward Dot, exiting the alley. Gabby was at her side. A chubby dachshund panted at their heels.

"She did it!" Kitty wailed. "She threatened Hunter— everyone heard her!"

Slim barked sharply and ran off. The clumps of onlookers had coalesced to a blob rumbling with sounds of scandal. Cleo recognized locals—friends and patrons. She saw strangers too, visitors with tote bags, antiquarians with name tags, and the toddler and dad who'd waved to the bookmobile.

"A killer is among us." Madame Romanov approached in a slow, jangly waltz. "The killer walks *with* us."

"Is that so?" Chief Culpepper said, his gaze following Kitty's pointing finger and narrowing in on Dot.

Chapter Eight

An hour later, Cleo sat with Dot, Henry, and the pets in the Gilded Page. In other circumstances, the bookshop would have been a lovely place to while away a morning. Mr. Chaucer snored on his window-seat bed. Rhett was curled up beside him, methodically kneading his pug friend's back. Beyond were pretty views of Words on Wheels and the park, a fluttering postcard of new greens and rowdy floral magentas.

Cleo reached for her coffee cup and sipped the tepid brew, mainly for something to do. She wanted action, information, and assurances. They were waiting to give statements. Waiting wasn't action.

Beside her on the green velvet love seat, Henry flipped through a photographic history of the great Okefenokee Swamp. Black-and-white blurs of nubby cypress knees passed by. Men in coveralls and brimmed hats forever fished from flat-bottomed boats.

Buddy Boone had been drawn to the book, and Cleo could see why. It was the kind to enjoy again and again, picking out details and imagining the scents and sounds at the moment the photographer clicked the shutter.

Henry wasn't savoring the words or the images. He flipped pages in rapid succession. In rigid contrast, Dot sat as upright as her armchair. A book lay open on her lap, but she hadn't turned a page.

A rap at the door gave them all a jolt. Faces appeared in the picture window, fingers cupped to the glass. Mr. Chaucer woke with a confused woof. Rhett threw back his ears and swished his tail. The rapping intensified.

Henry groaned. "Oh no, the workshop tour. I called the bed-and-breakfast and left a message with Mrs. Flores to cancel it. She said Professor Weber was in the breakfast lounge and she'd tell him right away. Maybe he left or she forgot."

"Or maybe no one listened," Cleo said, getting up and peering out the far side of the window. Bookdealers in name tags were descending on the door. They looked a tad too buzzed, even for a bunch of antiquarians about to talk about bookbinding. Red flashed across Cleo's view, and she saw Kitty hurtle toward her colleagues. Kitty threw herself, sobbing, into their collective arms.

The rap came again, sharp and loud.

Henry stood and smoothed his light tweed jacket. "Professor Weber," he said, unlocking and opening the door. "I'm sorry, I tried to send a message canceling the tour, and—"

"We got your message." Dr. Dean Weber stepped inside, with the other bookdealers and Chief Culpepper streaming in behind him. The chief stepped aside to a dim corner and leaned against a shelf, watching.

The professor wore his undertaker attire again, dark and gloomy and now entirely appropriate. "We're not here for your tour," he said. "Obviously, we came to show support for Kitty." He added, belatedly, "And Mr. Fox too. Most unfortunate."

"Of course," Henry murmured. "It's terrible. I can bring out tea or coffee, cold or hot, or—"

"There she is!" Kitty burst in. She rushed to the professor and grasped at his sleeve. "I told you she'd be here, guiltily hiding. Mr. Lafayette is aiding and abetting her. I hear he's in cahoots with her cousin the librarian."

Dot staggered up from her armchair. "Henry's not abetting. We're all just waiting to give our statements. We're awfully sorry for what's happened and want to help."

"Do you deny you threatened Mr. Fox?" Kitty demanded.

"No, I didn't intend to threaten," Dot stammered. "Oh, it might have sounded like that. If it did, I'm sorry! I didn't mean for him to get *hurt*."

Cleo murmured shushing sounds to her cousin, but dear Dot barreled on.

"I meant that he'd be sorry for hurting others. Later, at the end of his life, if he looked back and took stock of how he'd treated folks and books, he'd be sorry. That's all I meant."

"At the *end of his life*?" Kitty said, her voice rising with each word. "You hurried that on, didn't you?" She threw her hands over her face. Her shoulders heaved, and she sobbed in loud, dramatic gulps. "Poor Hunter. Our beloved colleague."

A few bookdealers moved in to comfort her with awkward pats. The professor put an arm stiffly but protectively over her shoulders.

Only Buddy Boone backed up Dot. "I heard you yesterday, Miss Dot. I get what you're saying. You meant, like, he'd be sorry if he had to account for his actions, facing the afterlife and repentance and whatnot. That's what I'd think about."

"Oh, what do you know, Buddy?" Kitty spluttered, hands parting so she could cast a look of utter disdain. Her mascara had held firm, but her lipstick smeared up on one side, giving her a half-clown grin. "You collect trinkets and garage-sale paperbacks. You wouldn't know the allure of a true delight, the tingle of holding a rare treasure in your hands. I bet you don't even understand the power of *Gone With the Wind* and the passions it arouses. Like driving this woman mad to murder." She seemed to remember that she'd been passionately weeping. She hid her face again and wailed through her hands, "Rest in peace, Foxy!"

Dot had backed up into a wall. Fortunately, it was the front wall by the picture window and pets. Mr. Chaucer toddled over to pant up at her. Dot patted his wrinkles. Rhett held down the satin bed. From his newly claimed throne, he scowled at the gathered bookdealers. Cleo silently cheered on his guard-cat instincts.

"I know *Gone With the Wind*," Buddy said, shuffling his boots. "It's one of my own personal favorites, and I sell a bunch of copies too. 'Course I do. It's real popular." He shot Dot a twist of a smile. "I understand . . ."

Cleo saw a grim opportunity. She'd intended to ask Dot gently and privately about her rare, signed book. But Kitty had alluded to it, and Kitty was bullying as much as grieving. "Did Mr. Fox give you my cousin's signed copy of *Gone With the Wind*, Ms. Peavey? If so, it was not intended for sale, and you'll have to return it."

Cleo glanced over at Dot. From Dot's crumpled expression, Cleo knew she'd guessed right. It also meant that Dot had a twenty-five-thousand-dollar motive for murder.

Kitty hesitated, her lip quirking until it rose in a smug smile. "Y'all weren't listening. I told you to *imagine* such a treasure. If you're imagining something, it's not real, is it? I will say, I bought your cousin's movie edition of GWTW fair and square. I did it a favor too, chopping it up and making it relevant again. Now loads of folks can enjoy it, hanging on their powder-room walls. Right, hon?" She patted the professor's stiff arm.

A hint of a sneer cracked his stoic expression. "*Gone With the Wind*? Popular pulp. Much too dated for modern sensibilities. If *that's* the book at the heart of this trouble, it's even tawdrier business."

Kitty covered a flash of irritation with a syrupy giggle. "Darling, have you even read *Gone*? You should. It's a romance and a thriller. A *saga*!"

Professor Weber ignored her and turned to Henry. "We can't have this sordid event or wild rumors sullying our fair. The Georgia Antiquarian Book Society selected this out-of-the-way town based on your proposal, Mr. Lafayette. You assured us that it was a quality location worthy and befitting of our reputation. Now I hear that it's not as safe as you made it out to be. I hear there have been serious crimes. Murders. Recently too."

Cleo patted her hair, half expecting it to be bristling with her irritation. The pompous man had no right to chide Henry or Catalpa Springs.

"Every place has crime, unfortunately," she said briskly. She realized the tourism bureau wouldn't appreciate that argument. She pictured a new glossy brochure, Mary-Rose's scenic Pancake Mill embellished with the slogan *Catalpa Springs: Flip your own pancakes, solve your own crime!* A burst of inappropriate giddiness struck, along with an alternate motto. *Catalpa Springs: Not many more murders than most!*

Cleo pushed back her bifocals, thinking Dot wasn't the only one in the aftereffects of shock.

"This is horrifying to us all," Henry said. He reached for Cleo's hand. "We all need to cooperate with the police and help them identify the culprit quickly."

The other bookdealers seemed to be losing interest. Several were browsing the shelves. Buddy drifted to the Okefenokee book. Others checked their watches and slipped out the door. A few grumbled pointedly about how *their* choice of venue would have been better.

Atlanta, a woman declared in a carrying whisper. *Atlanta would have been much preferable. More Ubers, better Thai food, fewer murdered members.*

Henry rubbed his temples.

"There are murders in Atlanta too," Cleo said indignantly. "Catalpa Springs may have no connection to this crime other than being the unlucky setting. You all know each other. You're associates and business rivals. The killer might be one of you. *You* might have brought crime to *our* town."

The response was momentarily gratifying. The book browsers glanced up, startled. The Atlanta proponent clamped her mouth shut.

Cleo raised her voice so the chief would be sure to hear too. "The police will want to know about Mr. Fox's activities last night, when he was last seen, who he was with." She looked pointedly at Kitty. "They'll need to know who he was close to and any enemies and—"

Kitty interrupted. "I *told* you who his enemies were. Your cousin and any other desperate old ladies who *misinterpreted* his attention. As for us antiquarians, we're all good friends, isn't that right, y'all? Friendly competitors?"

Mild murmurs of agreement and noncommittal grunts filled the air.

"Right," said Henry, clasping his hands as if they'd settled something. "So I'll reschedule the workshop tour for later this week when hopefully this is all wrapped up."

His intent was as clear as large-print font. Henry was trying to hustle them out. No one made a move for the door, except the chief, and he returned too soon. When he did, he had Gabby at his side. The young deputy held up a clear evidence bag in her hand.

"I need your attention," Gabby said. "Does anyone recognize this item?"

"That must be the murder weapon," Cleo whispered. She glanced over at Henry, expecting he'd be interested. She didn't expect his ashen-faced shock.

* * *

"Obviously, that's an awl," Professor Weber said. "As anyone in the book world would know, this particular tool is used in bindings, especially Japanese stab bindings."

Cleo cringed at the word. *Stab*. Had he used the word on purpose?

The professor droned on about other bindings: stitches and skewers, secret Belgian, Coptic, and slingbacks. As he pontificated, Gabby slipped behind him. She stepped over to Henry and Cleo.

"Do *you* know this tool?" she asked softly, holding the bag up for Henry to see.

Henry's hand trembled as he took it.

"I think it's mine," he said, and Cleo's heart jolted. "That mark, there, on the handle, it's a forger's mark. It's unique. Yes, it's mine." His voice was soft. Cleo was sure only she and Gabby, standing inches away, could hear. But the professor had stopped talking. All eyes were turned their way.

The antiquarian bookdealers stared. For a moment no one said a word. Then voices erupted, filling the room with outrage and accusations.

"See! I told you! He did it!" Kitty cried, seeming to forget that she'd been just as sure about Dot.

The chief roused himself and started toward Cleo and Henry. Cleo read *arrest* on his mind.

"No," Dot said, finally speaking up. "He didn't do it!"

"No," Cleo repeated, louder. "Please, listen, all of you. Mr. Lafayette had no motive to hurt Mr. Fox, and besides—"

"He did too have a motive!" Kitty crowed. "He confronted Hunter yesterday too, later in the afternoon, outside the fair. He threatened to get Hunt banned from Georgia antiquarian events if he didn't stop wooing ladies. Jealousy, that's a motive. Mr. Lafayette here was jealous of Hunt scooping up all the book treasures in his town and wooing all the ladies too."

Henry reddened. "That's not what I said—"

Cleo was sure he hadn't. She finished her sentence in a booming voice. "Mr. Lafayette *couldn't* have done it. He has an alibi. He was with me."

The chattering hushed. The chief raised a quizzical eyebrow.

Cleo put a protective hand on her gentleman friend's elbow. "Henry Lafayette was with me all night long and this morning until we arrived here," she said firmly, eyeing the crowd, daring anyone to question her.

"Well, I . . . ah . . ." Henry stammered. "I didn't stay at my apartment upstairs last night . . ."

"I can vouch for that!" exclaimed a gruff voice from the doorway. "I live next door to Cleo Watkins, heaven help me. That man's over there all the time. *All night long!*" Wanda Boxer stood in the doorway, cackling happily.

For once, Cleo could have hugged her.

Chapter Nine

G abby Honeywell was a wonder of swift efficiency. Cleo watched her young neighbor usher the bookdealers and onlookers from Henry's shop. As each person filed by, Gabby collected their name and contact information and arranged for interviews.

"You know full well where *I* live," Wanda griped, running a hand through pink-gold hair as choppy as her gardenia. "You wake me all the time, driving that police cruiser up and down our street on your odd shifts. It's not right to park a police car on a nice, residential street. It makes it look like a crime scene." She jabbed a finger in the air. "*That* encourages crime!"

Gabby politely nodded. Wanda had long held the mind-boggling theory that police cars attracted criminals.

Wanda shot Cleo a wickedly triumphant grin. "Of course, with Cleo as our neighbor, it's likely to be a crime scene any day of the week. You're a magnet for trouble, Cleo Watkins, you and your bus. Now your bad habits have rubbed off on your cousin." She surveyed the bookshop. "Where is Dot? Did she run off and hide?"

Dot had wisely retreated to the peace of Henry's workshop. Mr. Chaucer and Rhett had followed her. Pets, Cleo thought, could always tell when someone needed furry, four-legged therapy.

Wanda departed in a trail of muddy boot prints, off to muck up the town with gossip, Cleo was sure.

The chief puffed his chest and pushed out his suspenders. "*I'll* escort Miss Peavey someplace *nicer* to give her statement. She's had a most distressing morning."

Kitty sniffled and dabbed at her eyes. She'd fled to the restroom earlier, claiming to feel faint and needing to "recover her composure." Her pre-fiancé hadn't waited for her or her composure. Professor Weber was among the first to leave. Someone, he'd said pompously, had to be in charge and keep the fair on schedule.

"Why, thank you, Chief," Kitty crooned now. She leaned against Culpepper's arm. "I'd be so scared without *you* here."

"I'm here to serve and protect," the chief said, glowing.

She's a suspect, Cleo yearned to yell. She saved the thought for practical Gabby.

After everyone else had left, Gabby took statements from Cleo, Dot, and Henry. Cleo had hoped they'd all talk together, sitting around the coffee table, maybe with the extra comfort of treats from Spoonbread Bakery down the street. Most of all, Cleo wanted to be present when Gabby asked the key question: why had Dot ever thought of selling her books to begin with?

But Gabby interviewed them separately, using Henry's workshop for privacy.

"Procedure," Gabby said, explaining the one-by-one statements. Dot went first and fled right after, saying she was going home to rest. Cleo couldn't argue with that. She couldn't follow Dot either.

"You're up," Henry said, after his interview. He tried for an upbeat look, but the smile lines fanning his eyes drooped and he looked as worried as his pug.

Still, Cleo had to smile when she entered the workshop. Rhett Butler lay on the workbench, stretched from paws and claws to the tip of his plumed tail. Gabby had claimed a few feet of the soft soapstone tabletop. Rhett faced her, front paws flexing in what Cleo thought of as his "air biscuits."

Cleo took a seat across from Gabby, on a stool that felt both too high for her legs and too short for the tabletop. As Cleo got settled, she breathed in a perfume of leather and paper, glue, paint, and ink.

On a pegboard panel, white-paint outlines marked where each tool should go. About a dozen outlines were empty. Tools lay scattered at the end of the workbench and crowded in the wooden carrying case. Shelves and boxes bulged with items of the book-repair trade. There were inks, paints, glues, and tissue-thin tape, parchment, vellum, and paper. Here was Henry's indulgence on full display, Cleo thought. His joyful obsession.

Gabby smiled at her. "Deputy Honeywell and Deputy Rhett Butler, commencing the interview of Miss Cleo," she joked, flipping to a fresh sheet on the legal pad in front of her.

"Who's the good cop?" Cleo asked.

"Me," Gabby said. "Most definitely. Deputy Rhett here tried to lure me into touching his belly. I know that trick." She addressed Rhett, who stared back with wild round eyes. "I'd be in for an all-paw attack if I touched that belly, wouldn't I?"

Rhett purred and rolled, flexing his claws.

Cleo reached out and rubbed her cat's fluffy shoulders, a safe zone in his playful mood. She told herself to be careful with Gabby too. Gabby was a friend and neighbor, but she was also a deputy investigating a murder.

"I don't suppose you can tell me what Dot said?" Cleo asked, getting in the first question.

Gabby apologized, citing procedure. "I would like to show you this, though."

She turned back in her notepad and pushed it over to Cleo, avoiding Rhett's reach.

Cleo stared at a list of favorite books. For a second, she was lost in their stories. Then her mind registered the handwriting. Dot's careful cursive. This was a list of some of Dot's favorites too.

"Oh no," Cleo said, tugging the list closer. "Are these all books that man stole from Dot?" A lurch of her stomach reminded Cleo where "that man" was. A few yards beyond the back wall, where voices filtered in from the alley.

"Allegedly stole," Gabby said, before confirming Cleo's guess. "Dot said some are very precious to her," she added, watching Cleo intently.

Cleo's gaze fixed on one title in particular. *Gone With the Wind*, after which Dot had noted in parentheses, *signed*, *first first*, and *purple crayon mark on back inner cover*. The crayon was from Dot's niece. The double *first* wasn't a typo—not on Dot's part, at least. Unlike the crayon marking, this typo made the book more valuable.

The very first printed copies of *Gone With the Wind* gave the publishing date as May 1936 instead of the actual month of June. At the time, some unfortunate typesetter likely got a berating or a pink slip. But now—inconceivably to Cleo—collectors paid top dollar for the slipup. Collecting was a different world, Cleo realized, suddenly wondering how well she understood the antiquarians. They loved books, surely, but not necessarily for their reading value.

She slid the list back to Gabby. "May I have a copy of this? Henry and I can keep our eyes out at the fair."

Gabby said she'd be typing up the list. "I'm going to give it to Professor Weber too. Dot may be able to take legal action to get the books back if we locate them."

If . . . Cleo mentally corrected the word to *when*. Aloud she said, "We suggested legal measures to Dot yesterday. But you know Dot. She doesn't like to bother anyone. She'd certainly never *kill* someone. I hope you're not taking Kitty's outburst seriously. She's upset. Understandably."

Gabby tapped her pen, bouncing the end on the notepad. After a few beats, she said, "I know Miss Dot, but not as well as you do. Let me ask you. Your cousin said something I don't believe."

Cleo tensed until Gabby said, "Would *you* believe that Dot let some stranger take her books because she got caught up in fair excitement? No other reason? Not for love or money or . . . ?"

Cleo could only shake her head. "Dot told her niece that too. I'll admit, I didn't believe it either. I'll talk to her. I think she's embarrassed."

"About that public outburst?" Gabby turned to a fresh page of her notebook, pen poised. "Kitty Peavey made sure we all heard about that."

Cleo swiveled in her stool, considering her words carefully. She didn't want to be on the record spreading conjecture. On the other hand, Cleo believed compiling and organizing facts was always helpful. "I wouldn't want to gossip about Miss Peavey," Cleo said, as a polite prelude to doing just that.

"It's not gossip if it's the truth," Gabby replied. "None of us know these booksellers except Henry, and he only knows them from conferences and online interactions."

"Well, then," Cleo said. "You should ask Kitty about last night. From what I gather, Kitty was in Hunter Fox's room.

That's why she wasn't in her room when it was robbed. Obviously, Mr. Hunter left at some point."

A metallic squeak crept in from the alley. *Wheels*, Cleo thought. *A cart or trolley. Or a stretcher . . .*

"Obviously," Gabby said darkly.

Cleo spoke louder to block out the backdrop. She told Gabby about Madame Romanov revealing the murder. "Kitty did seem truly shocked. Of course, it could have been an act."

Cleo replayed Kitty's behavior, but couldn't decide. Kitty seemed to wear her outward image like a costume. Was she someone else on the inside?

Gabby bounced her pen again, attracting Rhett's wild-eyed attention. "Madame Romanov . . . she offered us her psychic services," Gabby said, rolling her eyes. She consulted her notes. "She said she could facilitate 'talking to the recently deceased,' 'spirit translation,' and 'bridging the bardo.' *Bardo* . . . do you know what that means?"

"The bardo is a state between life and death," Cleo said, happy to be helpful as a librarian and a reader. "It's Buddhist. I recently read about it in a novel about President Lincoln." Cleo wondered if Madame Romanov had checked out the same book. Cleo had featured it on Words on Wheels' *Recommended Reads* shelf for a while.

Gabby took a note. "Good. I can cross that off my lookup list, at least. We already have enough to do. Murder. Burglary . . ."

Rhett purred loudly.

Sometimes Cleo thought her cat liked a bit of chaos. "Speaking of burglary," Cleo said. "What do you think of Kitty's robbery? Doesn't it seem unlikely to have two separate, serious incidents on the same morning?"

"I can't say," Gabby said, "and not just because of procedure." She allowed a wry smile to slip across the workbench to Cleo. "The chief's handling that. He seems to be taking a personal interest."

"Oh, I noticed his *interest*," Cleo said.

Gabby bravely risked a rub of Rhett's belly. He got in a double-paw kick before Gabby whisked her hand away to ruffle his head. Gabby said, "Off the record, the chief has a thing for Marilyn Monroe. I've seen his garage. She's his calendar girl."

"Well, this Marilyn could be a suspect," Cleo said.

"Because she saw Hunter last night?" Gabby mused. She made more notes in her palm-sized notebook. Cleo waited as Gabby wrote, appreciating Gabby's neat handwriting and knack for cataloging information. Gabby was a good reader too, especially of people. She'd have made a fine librarian if she hadn't found her calling in crime. Cleo had told Gabby this once.

Gabby had countered that the reverse was true for Cleo: Cleo Watkins might have been chief of police or a CIA operative if she hadn't been so attached to the world of books.

Gabby turned over a fresh page and said abruptly, "What else should I know, Miss Cleo? I suspect you're ahead of us already on whatever book stuff's going on."

Cleo swiveled uncomfortably in her stool. She didn't want to get Dot in trouble, but she didn't want to withhold valuable information either. "Kitty may have been in possession of a rare, signed first edition of *Gone With the Wind*. I gather she was selling it in collaboration with Hunter."

Gabby raised an eyebrow and flipped back to Dot's list.

"Yes," Cleo said with a sigh. "I think it's Dot's book. It has more than sentimental value." Cleo named the price Kitty had suggested.

"Whoa!" Gabby gripped the table. "Over twenty grand? Wish I had one of those lying around. But you didn't see this gold nugget in Kitty's possession? You can't confirm it's Dot's?"

Cleo couldn't. "I asked Kitty before you came into the shop earlier. The chief was here, but I'm not sure he understood the importance. Kitty said she'd been describing a hypothetical book. *Imagine a page touched by Margaret Mitchell.*"

"Interesting . . ." Gabby jotted more. "I can *imagine* cashing a twenty-thousand-dollar check. Imagining's the closest I'll be getting."

Dot must have been imagining the payoff too. But what did she need so much money for? Guilt stabbed at Cleo. What had she failed to see or ask? What was wrong?

"Dot's probably not the only local who lost books," Cleo said. "Hunter Fox was going around conning booklovers, particularly women, out of books. I heard so from Mary-Rose and planned to make inquiries on my bookmobile route today."

"So they'd all have motives too." Before Cleo could protest, Gabby raised a palm. "I know. You don't want local booklovers involved. I don't either. I'm only saying who *could* be connected so we can narrow down on means and motives. I'd like to know who else Hunter visited."

Cleo would too. She wondered something else as well. "Hunter wasn't from here. How did he know where to go?"

Gabby ran her pen just beyond Rhett's claws as she mused. "So we have conned local booklovers. Any other suspects, Miss Cleo?"

"Professor Weber," Cleo said, glad to move on to someone who wasn't a friend, family member, or patron. "He's Kitty's 'pre-fiancé.' Did you notice that diamond on her finger?"

"I noticed. Pre-fiancés and overpriced rocks aren't my things, but that ring is hard to miss. So she's been dating—or seeing or whatever—both Hunter *and* Dr. Weber? Do you think the professor knew?"

It was Cleo's turn to use the phrase "I can't say." She added, "But I suspect he did. He seemed chilly—chillier—yesterday when he suggested that Hunter had sold Kitty an overpriced book."

"I can't quite see him as the fiery passionate type," Gabby said, "but I do see him as my next interviewee. I hope he doesn't lecture me more about tools." She slid off her stool and patted Rhett, who rumbled back a purr. "You've been a great help," she said. "You too, Miss Cleo. Will you listen if I ask you to let us handle it from here?"

Cleo smiled at her neighbor. "I'll listen," she said agreeably.

Gabby shook her head. "I know what that means. You'll listen and then do what you want. Just promise me you'll be careful around these book people, okay?"

Cleo remembered Mary-Rose's similar warning. To think, all Mary-Rose had worried about was Cleo's wallet if she became overly enamored with a book. "I'm already on guard," Cleo said. *And on the case.*

Chapter Ten

L ater that afternoon, Cleo's mind spun as fast as her wheels, rolling with facts, theories, and unanswered questions. She and Rhett were back in Words on Wheels, cruising out of town through lush forests painted in every shade of green. An egret soared across a cloudless sky. Warm air ruffled Cleo's hair, and she thought again that among the most shocking aftereffects of murder—or any death—was how the world carried on. Birds sang, rivers flowed, and folks went about their mundane business. Appointments remained too, even if she was hours late.

After giving their statements, Henry had gone to the fair. He needed to surround himself with books, he said. Cleo understood that. She'd driven straight to the library. Her colleague Leanna had been reshelving and happily oblivious to the awful events just across the park. Leanna, at twenty-three, was Cleo's protégé in all ways but one. Thankfully, Leanna showed no propensity for getting wrapped up in crimes.

Leanna, however, had known of the slippery book scout. To Cleo's surprise, Leanna thought she'd met him.

"Dyed hair? Too tanned? Shiny teeth?" Leanna said. "Good-looking in a slick kind of way, like he'd try to sell you low land in a swamp?"

"That sounds like him," Cleo said.

Such a man had dropped by the library about a week ago, Leanna reported. He'd just gotten to town and was inquiring whether she—clearly a beautiful and astute young woman—knew of anyone "looking to get rid of some old, useless books cluttering up their attics."

"That was the tipoff," Leanna said, scowling through retro cat-eye glasses. "Not the cheap flattery. That's too common. But 'useless books'? That's no way to butter up a librarian! I do know of folks interested in book assessments with the fair in town, but no way was I going to let that guy near them."

Leanna was wise beyond her years, and Cleo had thanked her for fending him off. The problem was that Cleo had no idea who Hunter Fox had visited other than Dot.

"We'll put the word out," Cleo said to Rhett, who snoozed in his padded peach crate. Cleo inched her window open wider and let the warm wind bat her cheeks.

At a crossroads, Cleo turned toward Golden Acres, a nursing home built on a former farm with pretty views of meadows and a feathery backdrop of cypress. The home itself resembled a squished-down, stretched-out White House. There were ornate columns and two symmetrical wings, with a rose garden to one side, and a curving drive with a space designated for *Buses and Bookmobile Parking Only.*

"Remember, Rhett, no talk of murder," Cleo said, rattling Rhett's canister of tuna treats. He hopped from his crate. While he was happily munching, Cleo slipped on his harness. Rhett stopped crunching and fell to the floor.

"Oh, stop," Cleo chided. "You're acting. You don't do this when Henry puts on your harness." Rhett's tail slapped at the floor tiles. "I can't carry you and the display," Cleo informed him.

She unlatched the Plexiglas case, which was light and had a handy leather handle, but was still the size of carry-on luggage and filled with books and other library ephemera.

While Rhett played stricken, Cleo thought of the case's designer, her grandson Sam. He was studying architecture at college, and she couldn't have been prouder, as she felt about all her grandkids and her two sons too.

"You're going to miss out on the fun," Cleo told Rhett as she hefted the case and started down the steps. Rhett moped, sending her a sulky, wounded stare.

"You're going to miss out on the fun," Cleo said in a singsong voice. Halfway down the steps, a blur of orange fur passed her, and Cleo was glad his leash extended more than a bus length so she could keep up.

* * *

"The bibliophile group is in the sunroom already. Here, let me take that." Franklin, Cleo's favorite nurse, reached for the display case. Rhett adored Franklin too and trotted with doglike devotion at his heels.

"I hope they haven't been waiting in there for hours," Cleo said, chagrined at her extreme tardiness.

Franklin's chuckle rumbled in baritone. He towered over Cleo by a good foot, with his cloudlike hair adding a few inches.

"No worries, Miss Cleo. We occupied ourselves with audiobooks."

He pushed through swinging doors, holding them open for Cleo and Rhett.

They entered to a cheer. "She's here!"

Cleo beamed. Attendance was large today, at least two dozen people. Thank goodness she hadn't canceled.

"I have books from your holds lists," Cleo said, "and more in Words on Wheels. I can go retrieve books too." She smiled all around, saving the best for last. "I brought my special display. I'd love to show it off. You'd be the first to see it."

"First!" came a triumphant cry from the back. The residents gathered around. Walkers made rubbery squeaks. Wheelchairs bumped. Some knees crooked and creaked. Eyes had dimmed and ears required a boost, but the library could still offer materials for everyone.

Cleo took in the touches of hominess as her hosts assembled. The remains of afternoon cookies, coffee, and milk lay stacked on a cart. Geraniums bloomed in the picture windows. Best of all, there was a pet, albeit not as cuddly as Rhett Butler. An orange-and-blue parrot perched on a plastic palm tree.

Rhett Butler feigned disinterest in the bird, which had a pirate's vocabulary and a defensive beak. Tail held high, Rhett milled among the residents, soaking up ear scratches and treats.

Cleo set her display case on a coffee table. "I did this up in honor of the antiquarian book fair that's come to town." She described the fair and the various exhibits. The price tags of special items drew shocked gasps and comparisons to first mortgages. The money talk led perfectly to Cleo's main point: bookish collections didn't have to cost a fortune. They didn't even have to include books.

The residents oohed and aahed as Cleo showed off dust covers and bookplates. They had a hoot shuffling through stacks of card-catalog slips and a handful of due-date cards.

When deaccessioning books from the library, Leanna had collected the due-date cards that used to rest in little sleeves glued to back covers. It just didn't seem right to throw them away, Leanna said. They held too much history, of books and patrons. Leanna was sure *something useful* could be done with them.

Cleo was glad they'd found a "something." When planning her route for the week, Cleo had asked Leanna to help her choose cards that might interest bookmobile patrons.

Cleo handed one to a lady in a baby-blue tracksuit. "Now, you don't have to share this," Cleo said with a zipping-her-lips gesture. She had a strict librarian's vow of silence when it came to patrons' reading tastes.

"Oh, my gracious," the woman cried. She held the card up. "Look what Cleo found. August through September 1965, I checked out *The Lusty Lord* three times in a row. Then again for all of December. This brings back memories. I had such a stressful family Christmas that year. I *needed* this book. Scotland, men in kilts, steamy romance . . . If my husband had found out . . ."

Girlish giggling ensued, followed by an explanation. Her husband Elijah had been a preacher. "He wouldn't have approved of this sort of lord," she laughed.

She passed around the card and fell more serious. "That was a bit of a risk, wasn't it? I read that book in secret. If Elijah came in the room, I'd hide it under the covers, the carpet, in the freezer, anywhere. But there was my signature right in the back for anyone to see. I guess I just prayed Elijah wouldn't dare touch such a book. Do patrons still sign a card like this, Cleo?"

Cleo explained the new privacy measures and checkout system. "You'd think you're at the supermarket," Cleo said. "Patrons hand over their cards—like you all have—and the digital number goes right into the computer. It spits out a receipt with the due date."

"Where's the fun in that?" a man asked. Cleo knew him as a retired dentist and lover of biographies. "I liked spying on what everyone else was reading. You could start up book conversations that way."

A small, bald-topped man chuckled. "I used to look at the due-dates cards to see if *I'd* read the book. How are you supposed to remember what you've read if it's all anonymous?"

Cleo had a good memory for books. However, even she occasionally opened to a first page to realize she'd read it before. There were parts of the former system she missed too.

"I liked the stamps," she said. "I'd check the ink pads and change the due dates every morning as part of my routine. I aimed to get a good, firm stamp right on the line. It seems so old-fashioned now. Like card catalogs. Young people now have no idea what a card catalog is, other than for decoration."

"Nothing wrong with old-fashioned!" proclaimed the dentist, to hearty affirmations.

As the group reminisced about favorite books, Rhett went from lap to lap. Every so often, Cleo caught him eyeing the parrot, making sure the bird noticed him ignoring it. While the patrons chatted, Cleo indulged in a cookie.

"This has been so much fun," she said, as the hour slipped by. "I needed to relax. I had an . . . *interesting* . . . morning."

Cleo's mother had two uses of the word *interesting*. The first came straight from the dictionary: arousing curiosity, capturing attention. The second implied utterly awful. In her mother's world, the latter might mean inedible recipes or painfully bad amateur theater. In Cleo's experience, *interesting* included mornings beginning with murder.

"We know," the bald-topped man said. They looked around at one another, prompting someone to go first.

"So, can we bring it up now? Can we ask her?" a lady with bright-blue hair demanded.

Franklin chuckled. "I'd say it's due time. Overdue, in fact. Y'all have been *very* patient."

"We most certainly have," said the preacher's wife. "This book talk has been fabulous, but I'm about to burst. Miss Cleo, we all want to know. Tell us about the murder!"

"And the case!" said another. "We know you're on the case."

*   *   *

Cleo accepted another cookie from Franklin. They were small and made with oatmeal and raisins and provided by a registered nurse at a nursing facility. They were justifiable. Cleo assured herself that even her sugar-banning doctor couldn't complain. Besides, Cleo had had an *interesting* morning.

"I didn't want to drag down your afternoon with ugly news," Cleo said.

"Pshaw," said the preacher's wife. "Tell us everything."

Cleo was mildly shocked. The residents demanded details from cause of death to the extent of "splatter." The parrot joined in with a squawk of "Murder!"

Franklin drifted by and murmured to Cleo, "We watch a lot of *Law and Order* here. We just got HBO too."

"Your cousin Dot, we heard she was involved," said the blue-haired lady. "Every time my daughter takes me into town, we go to the Drop By for cookies and root beer. I hope Dot's not arrested. If she is, she'll have to shut the Drop By. That would be a tragedy. A travesty!"

The others agreed, the parrot screamed for "law and order," and voices rose to be heard.

"I heard it was Cleo's boyfriend," a man in the back proclaimed. "The boyfriend's always who done it on the TV. Sorry, Cleo."

Sympathetic sounds swelled, with Henry's and Dot's names riding the waves of words.

Cleo realized she'd been lulled by the book talk and cookies. Of course the residents would know about the murder. News traveled fast in small towns, and unlike young folks, seniors still used their telephones for talking. Everyone for miles around and beyond would be swapping theories, many of which would be wrong.

Cleo stood. "My cousin and my *gentleman friend* are completely innocent," she declared.

The voices hushed, although skeptical looks remained.

"But I *am* worried that they'll be falsely accused," Cleo admitted, to mutters of agreement. "If I tell you what I know, will you keep your ears and eyes open for me?"

Two dozen faces nodded solemnly. To a rapt audience and one murder-happy bird, Cleo stressed Dot's Good Samaritan innocence and Henry's alibi. She elaborated most on Hunter Fox's questionable scouting activities.

"Not to speak ill of the dead," Cleo said as a polite preamble. "But I heard he was conning local booklovers." Indignant grumbles rumbled around the room. "He may have cheated his fellow bookdealers too."

Cleo debated for a moment. She took her audience's age and wisdom into consideration, as well as their HBO subscription. Then, as delicately as possible, Cleo outlined the likely love triangle of Kitty, Professor Weber, and Hunter Fox.

"Ooooo," crooned the preacher's wife. "That's what happened in *The Lusty Lord*. Except there wasn't a murder, and it doesn't sound like this bookseller lady ended up with the lusty guy, either."

Her statement drew titters, but it made Cleo think. "We shouldn't judge a book by its cover," she murmured, thinking of Kitty and the professor too.

The preacher's wife elaborated. "You mean, that stodgy professor guy could be lusty on the inside? That's very possible. He'd have to be some kind of enamored with that woman, or he wouldn't hang around being a *pre*-fiancé while she flirts up some other guy, don't you think?"

Theories flew, and the parrot learned some unfortunate new words.

Later, Franklin helped Cleo pack up. He lifted the display case, making it seem as light as air. Cleo hefted Rhett Butler, who felt like he'd added a pound of treats. Rhett clamored up to drape his front half over Cleo's shoulder. He purred in her ear with fishy breath.

Back at the bus, Cleo pulled down the windows, releasing built-up heat. Franklin clipped the display case back in place, praising the system and Cleo's visit.

"You and Rhett Butler made everyone's day," he said. "I don't know how you'll top it next week unless you come back with that *Lusty Lord* book—or news that you caught the killer."

"Both will be difficult," Cleo said, playing along but serious too. "The library deaccessioned *The Lusty Lord*. That's why I had that checkout card. And a killer, well . . ."

Cleo let Rhett down on her captain's seat, and said with both earnestness and modesty, "I hope the *police* will catch the killer this time, and quickly too. I'm only trying to help Dot and track down the missing books."

The big nurse turned grave. "About those books," he said. "I don't think it's anything, but you got me thinking. My grandmother—my G-mom—she had a visitor the other day. Called him 'Aquaman.' Said he was chatting her up. G-mom's an awful flirt. But now I wonder . . ."

"Aquaman?" Cleo said.

"Yeah, G-mom mixes up words. At ninety-seven, that's her prerogative. So's the flirting. We guessed it was the pool guy. But when you started describing that 'antiquarian' festival, I got wondering. She said they talked about books. She was a school librarian for years. She has more books than you could stuff inside this bus."

"Did she give him any? Sell any on *commission*?" Cleo couldn't keep the skepticism out of her tone.

"Nah, not G-mom. She wouldn't do that. It breaks my heart—she loves those books, even though her eyes aren't that great anymore. She says she keeps them for the grandkids. You ask me, those books are like her kids."

Franklin wrote down his grandmother's address. Cleo knew Bernice Abernathy from her bookmobile route of home deliveries. Bernice didn't drive anymore because of her eyesight, so Cleo brought the library to her.

"I call G-mom every night before bed," Franklin said. "I'll let her know you'll be coming by." His smile was back. "Like I said, it's probably nothing, but she'll love to talk books in any case. You can bet she'll spread the word too."

As he strolled back to work, Cleo buckled up and revved her engine. Word was already spreading: news that Cleo Watkins was out looking for clues, missing books, and a killer.

Chapter Eleven

"Strawberries and apologies." Henry hustled up Cleo's front-porch steps with a paper sack in one hand and Mr. Chaucer panting at his heels. The sun was setting in dusky peach hues. Cleo had been sitting out on her porch, watching the colors change and listening to a nightingale warming up its vocals.

"You shouldn't have rushed." Cleo patted his cheek and found it dewy warm. His hair tufted out, mad-scientist style.

Henry handed over the bag. He'd called earlier, saying he was in line at a pop-up farm stand selling berries.

"Heavenly," Cleo said, sticking her nose in and inhaling the promise of long, sweet summer months ahead. In honor of the berries, Cleo had made buttermilk biscuits for shortcake. On her own, she might have made a meal of just that. However, she had invited Henry for dinner, not just dessert.

"I'm sorry to make you wait," Henry said, as Mr. Chaucer panted up at Cleo.

Cleo understood how he felt, having made similar apologies all afternoon. After the nursing home, she'd zipped through some home deliveries. She'd heard more talk about a handsome man sniffing around for books. She'd collected names and spoken with two women who'd met Hunter Fox.

One of the women had wisely refused to let him inside. To Cleo's horror, the other woman had given him cash, a down payment for selling her books, which he'd promised would make her ten times her investment. Cleo hadn't had the heart to say so, but she feared the woman's books were worth far less than the down payment. Now that the scout was gone, there would be little chance of retrieving her money.

Cleo folded the strawberry sack closed, keeping her dark thoughts away from the tender berries.

"I was running late all afternoon myself," Cleo assured Henry. "But you shouldn't worry. I'm not the one who cooked dinner. *You* did. We're having your leftover chicken and rice. All I did was slice up cucumbers and dill for a salad and whip up biscuits for dessert. Easy."

Henry remained ruffled, more anxious than simple lateness would account for, Cleo thought.

"I was leaving the fair when Gabby stopped by," he was saying. "She wanted me to look at some papers and books and—"

"Sit," Cleo urged. "Let's sit for a spell and watch the sunset. It's lovely out. Tell me what Gabby found."

Henry didn't need further prompting. He unleashed Mr. Chaucer and sank into a padded wicker porch chair. Mr. Chaucer trotted to the porch swing, where Rhett lay. The cat reached down a paw, pushing off his pug friend's head, sending the swing gently swaying. Mr. Chaucer lopped onto his back and pawed back, mostly missing.

Cleo smiled at the four-legged friends and more worriedly at her gentleman friend. "Tea?" Cleo offered, gesturing to the pitcher sweating on the side table. "It's not the good kind, I'm afraid. It's my afternoon brew."

Henry would understand that meant tea tragically lacking both sweetener and caffeine. Age did have its drawbacks, among them low-sugar diets and owl-worthy insomnia if Cleo sipped so much as a drip of caffeine after noon.

Henry accepted a glass and downed the bitter brew like it was nectar. "Ahhh," he said. "That's better. Thank you, for waiting and for the company."

"My pleasure," Cleo said. "Thank *you* for joining *me*. Now, you were saying . . . Gabby had some books?"

Henry kicked off one loafer and then the other and stretched out socked feet. "Gabby wanted me to look at books collected from Hunter Fox's room at the Myrtles. There's some good news. One was Dot's. It's an unexceptional edition of *To Kill a Mockingbird*, but it has her bookplate and her name penciled in."

"That's wonderful," Cleo said. "It proves what she said. Hunter Fox took her books. But only one was there?" She knew Henry had seen Dot's list of lost books. Hopefully, all the bookdealers had studied the list after Professor Weber distributed it.

"Only one, unfortunately," Henry confirmed. His fingers rapped the wicker armrest.

His tapping was contagious. Cleo's fingers danced too, thinking about Dot. Her cousin had again neglected to return Cleo's calls, and when Cleo had gone by the Drop By, a *Closed* sign dangled from the door.

Cleo mentally recited her vow. She'd give Dot time. But not much more time.

Henry stopped tapping and said, "It's odd. He only had a few books, and nothing worth much. No treasures, like Kitty said he'd been finding around town."

"Perhaps he sold most of the books?" Cleo said. "Buddy said Hunter offered a sale the night before the fair opened. That's when Buddy acquired Dot's bird illustration."

Henry suggested that selling his entire inventory seemed unlikely. "Unless he gave it to someone else to sell . . ."

"Kitty," Cleo said, in darker tones than she'd ever uttered a word associated with cats. "She praised Hunter's book-finding abilities and mentioned having her own personal scout. She said she was sharing the proceeds of that 'imaginary' *Gone With the Wind* too. If she had Hunter's books—valuable and basically stolen—that's a lure for a robber." But if a thief had been after the books, why kill Hunter? Why in the alley behind Henry's shop, with Henry's tool?

Cleo decided a comforting dinner was in order. "Let's go inside and enjoy your home-cooked meal."

*   *   *

Cleo's dearly departed husband Richard hadn't been a man of the kitchen. Richard, bless his heart, couldn't boil water without setting off a smoke alarm. His rare culinary efforts were confined to the barbecue, where he'd incinerate hot dogs, hamburgers, marshmallows, and the stray vegetable.

Henry was a meticulous cook, adventurous in his tastes but rarely deviating from recipes. Cleo likened his cooking style to his book restorations. When replacing a cover or restitching a spine, the best restorers didn't leave their mark or add flair that wasn't in the original.

Henry followed the same principles with recipes: if the great Julia Child or Edna Lewis considered a recipe good enough for their cookbooks, then Henry Lafayette followed it to the letter. He'd made Edna's simple but stunning recipe for chicken and rice last night, a perfect comfort food.

Cleo first served a demanding Rhett Butler a can of "Chicken and Gravy Delight." Henry doled out kibble to Mr. Chaucer.

Unlike Rhett, the pug savored his meals one nibble at a time. Finally, Henry and Cleo took the seats she'd begun to think of as *his* and *hers*.

Hers was closest to the stove and sink. She'd claimed it over five decades ago. His, she'd previously considered the "visitor's" seat because it had the clearest view of the back garden.

Cleo peeked outside. A light glowed in Ollie's cottage, warming her heart. She'd offered the little single-bedroom house to Ollie after he graduated from college, knowing he adored his parents but wouldn't relish a return to his childhood bedroom. Besides, Ollie's dad—Cleo's eldest son, Fred—was forever pressuring Ollie to get a "real job," fast. Ollie wanted to take his time and find a career he felt passionate about. Cleo supported that, having found her calling in library work.

Ollie's passion was for the environment. The young man had recently returned from temporary gigs saving oil-soaked shorebirds in Louisiana and leading educational tours along the Mississippi River. He was on the lookout for similar jobs locally.

Cleo hoped he'd stay close and in her cottage. Her grandson was helpful with gardening and opening stubborn jars. He was also delightful company, which Cleo considered more valuable than any rent, which often Ollie couldn't pay.

"Ollie is organizing a benefit for the sandhill cranes at the nature preserve," Cleo said now, since a good dinner required pleasant topics. "The wetland park out by the river, where the old tobacco farm used to be. They're hoping to build a blind for bird watchers and a boardwalk that won't disturb the nesting sites. Ollie's excited."

"How nice," Henry said and passed Cleo the pepper without her asking. The dish was perfectly seasoned, but she always added a little more pepper.

"It's a dance party at the tobacco barn they restored for events," Cleo continued. "I think Ollie's working up the nerve to invite Gabby."

This got a genuine smile out of Henry.

It was obvious to grandmother and gentleman friend and anyone else with eyes that Ollie was smitten with Deputy Gabby Honeywell. Unfortunately, infatuation turned the usually articulate young man into a blushing, stammering fool in the deputy's presence.

"I hope Ollie manages this time," Henry said. "Do you think she realizes he's trying?"

"Oh, I'm sure she does," Cleo said. "Gabby is a professional detective. I think she might even entertain a date if Ollie worked up the courage to speak a coherent sentence to her."

Rhett joined them. He sat in a chair across the table and stared down whoever raised a fork, his attempt at feline mind control. The food was lovely, but Cleo noticed that the pleasant small talk kept withering. Henry finished his meal without his usual relish. *Don't push him either*, she told herself.

"Seconds?" Cleo asked brightly. Rhett perked up and twirled in his seat, suggesting he'd happily have some chicken.

Henry leaned back and stared out the window. He sighed heavily before turning to look Cleo in the eye.

"Ollie's not the only one scared to talk to Gabby Honeywell. I need to tell her something, but first I need to work up the courage to tell you."

Chapter Twelve

C leo got out the sherry, the good bottle she reserved for holidays, celebrations, or bad news. She guessed she was about
to hear something she wouldn't like.

"Should we go out to the porch?" she asked. She preferred
unpleasant words out in the open air, not bottled up and bumping around her kitchen.

Henry carried the glasses and the bottle. Cleo followed,
thinking they hadn't even had dessert. They'd have shortcake
afterward. Surely anything was better faced together and with
strawberries.

The sky had turned blue-black, dotted with sparkles. They
settled into comfy wicker seats. Rhett jumped on Cleo's lap,
while Mr. Chaucer leaned against Henry's shins. Cleo fortified
herself with some sweet sherry and waited.

Henry took a deep breath and let it out with a gust of words.
"I'm a fool, Cleo. I should have said something right away. I got
flustered. There was my awl, in that evidence bag, and all the
bookdealers watching . . ." He turned stricken eyes to her. "Most
of all, I worry you might doubt me. That's my greatest fear!"

Cleo reached over and squeezed his hand. "Doubt you?
Never! Tell me what's going on." She thought they each might

need a double helping of shortcake, with a mountain of whipped cream, maple syrup, and a cherry on top too.

Her gentleman friend rubbed his eyes, sending his wire-rim glasses askew. He left them sitting sideways and turned to her. "You gave me the finest alibi in town. But . . . I wasn't actually here all night. I went out."

Mr. Chaucer whined. Henry scooped the little dog up to his lap.

"Out?" Cleo thought of Kitty, presumably sleeping away the night, believing Hunter was there beside her. There was no comparison, she told herself. Henry's explanation would be innocent. As he spoke, her pulse returned to normal.

Henry smiled grimly down at his pug. "I should say, *we* went out. Neither of us has an alibi. Chaucy here insisted on a visit to the garden a little after midnight. I'd already been half awake. My mind kept going over all the things I needed to do for the fair."

"Understandable," Cleo said. Some nights her mind made lists on constant repeat. Such nights tended to fall before big events or after difficulties, like a tree crushing her library, or a patron found dead in her library . . . or Henry out at midnight without an alibi?

If she hoped to shut her eyes tonight, she'd need to follow the sherry with chamomile tea and the most sleep-inducing book in the house. One of her library patrons swore by *Anna Karenina* for insomnia. Cleo, unfortunately, liked *Anna*.

She tried to soothe Henry. "That's nothing to worry about. So you and Mr. Chaucer went out to the garden for a spell? That's okay. My alibi still holds." She forced her smile up to beaming bright.

"Well," he said, tugging at his beard. "We didn't stick to the yard."

"Down the lane, then?" Cleo said hopefully. Her section of Magnolia extended two blocks up and two down before intersecting other streets. Anywhere along it was almost in Cleo's front yard.

Henry's head shook side to side. "We walked to the park. The moon was out, and it was quiet. Since we were that far along, I dropped by my shop. You know how you get a worry stuck in your head in the night and you can't shove it out? I'd been lying in bed, thinking I'd left a jar of glue open. Isn't that silly?"

Cleo let him chatter about the glue, expensive and archival, necessary for a restoration he was doing. He'd imagined it hardening up, a slow-motion book-repair emergency in the making. Now there was a bigger problem.

"The glue turned out to be fine," Henry said, looking abashed. "It's me who froze up. When you said I was here all night, I didn't know what to say."

"You were in shock," Cleo said gently. She leaned over and reached for his shoulder, tugging him into a partial hug. Rhett joined in, hopping to Henry's armrest and bumping his head to Mr. Chaucer's.

Henry smiled, for a moment at least. He rubbed Rhett's ears as he said, "After I stayed quiet, I felt worse. I know it looks awful too. I've been terrified, thinking you might suspect me in Hunter's death. Heaven forbid!"

"I'd *never* think that!" Cleo nodded to her cat, purring so hard he was drooling, the silly boy. "Neither would Rhett, clearly." She waggled a mock chastising finger at Henry. "How could *you* even think such a thing?"

Henry's shoulders relaxed. "You're the sleuth. It would be logical to suspect me. Wouldn't Miss Marple or Hercule Poirot say so too?"

"My intuition says no," Cleo said firmly. "Miss Marple would agree with following intuition. So would Poirot. Oh, what was it he said about intuition? *Intuition comes from logical deduction or experience? Feelings?* I can't recall exactly, but I know it was clever. I should look it up and reread the book that passage comes from . . . Now, which book was that?" She knew she was delaying, as Henry had earlier with his talk of glue.

Cleo sighed and said, "I suppose we *have* to tell the police?" A devilish idea brushed by. They *could* keep it to themselves. Everyone already believed her. Even Wanda Boxer had backed up the alibi. But she knew the answer.

"We do," he said. "No, *I* do. I wanted to tell Gabby earlier, but I had to talk to you first. I can't bear to keep lying by omission, and it's wrong to let Dot shoulder all the suspicion."

The wicked voice in Cleo's head noted that that's what honesty brought: trouble doubled—two people she loved, now vying for prime suspect. She tugged some of the blame to herself. "I'm the one who insisted you were here all night. I guess I'm a heavier sleeper than I thought."

Henry eyes had a little twinkle as he said, "You were snoring ever so slightly, my dear."

"Never!" Cleo finished her sherry and was about to propose shortcake. Gabby wasn't home yet, and if it got too late . . . well, surely, confession could wait until morning. Perhaps the police would nab the killer by then and there'd be no need to say anything. Then she noticed Henry had out his rarely used cell phone. "I'm texting her," he said, chewing his lip in concentration.

Cleo didn't have to ask who.

"She says she'll be back soon."

Within moments, a car door slammed. Too soon, Cleo thought, and hunkered down in her seat.

* * *

Confession got a delay. The heavy, scuffing footsteps that followed belonged to Ollie, returning home from a meeting at the nature center. Seeing Cleo and Henry, he bounded up to the porch and settled in to enthuse about the record number of sandhill cranes.

"Wonderful!" Cleo exclaimed, feeling she had to exaggerate her responses lest Ollie realize that his grandmother wasn't fully listening. She was *trying* to pay attention. Cleo adored cranes and Ollie even more. "Marvelous birds," she said, dropping this affirmation rather randomly amid Ollie's words.

"They're awesome," Ollie agreed. He whipped out his phone and played their calls at high volume. Clacks and yodels filled the porch and wafted out into the night. Rhett's ears went flat, and his furry face swiveled with feline predator instinct.

"You'd run away if you saw a bird that big," Cleo told her cat.

Ollie played another soundtrack, this time with video. The birds were fascinating and pleasantly diverting. Henry made polite sounds but looked distant.

"They sound so prehistoric," Ollie said with awe. "It's great there are so many out at the preserve, right in time for the fund raiser. Are you coming, Gran? Henry? There'll be dancing." He added, "We're getting a bunch of bands—punk, country, blue-grass, swing . . . something for everyone. I need to learn how to do the swing. Could you teach me, Gran? Henry?"

Cleo was happy to have a reason to chuckle and share a smile with Henry. "We're not *that* old, Oliver," she said. "Swing hit its heyday in the twenties and thirties."

Ollie grinned back. "Just seeing if you guys were listening." He returned to his phone, instantly engrossed and entertained.

Cleo thought her grandson might be more perceptive than he'd let on.

* * *

They knew all the songs of sandhills by the time Gabby strode up the walkway.

Ollie fumbled to mute his phone. "Hey, Gabby," he said.

"Hey, Ollie," she replied. "Hi, Miss Cleo, Henry." She bent to greet the pets. "You had something you wanted to tell me?"

Ollie blushed furiously. "I was going to tell you about the crane benefit. I'm on the organizing committee. There's a party, a dance out at the restored tobacco barn."

Unfortunately—or maybe fortunately—for Ollie, Mr. Chaucer was distracting Gabby with his puggy cuteness. He lay on his back, snuffling and snorting as she rubbed his belly.

"Oh, right," Gabby said, making funny faces back at the dog. "My friend Sam and I bought tickets already. Sounds fun."

Ollie's shoulders slumped. He brushed back the hair that forever lopped across his eyes. It fell back again.

Cleo gave him her most supportive grandmotherly smile. "Sam?" she said to Gabby. "I forget, have I met him?"

"Her." Gabby grinned at Mr. Chaucer. "Sammy Emerson. She runs the new Pilates studio downtown. The one with the juice bar."

"Awesome!" Ollie blurted. "I mean, awesome that you're supporting the cranes. The new juice bar is great too. I love juice. I guess, well . . . I'll see you there. Later." He managed to leave without tripping over Mr. Chaucer, Gabby, or his own feet.

Cleo watched him go. The motion-detector light in the side garden flicked on, then off, and silence settled back down.

Gabby looked up at Henry, her voice as quiet as the night. "*You* have something to tell me?"

Chapter Thirteen

The next morning, Cleo had strawberry shortcake for breakfast. She topped it with a mountain of whipped cream and dolloped cream on her coffee too. "A midweek treat," she told Rhett, serving up a hefty helping of his favorite fishy food.

"We're on our own," Cleo continued. "We can do what we like." She pitched their indulgences as fun. It worked for Rhett, not so much for Cleo.

Strawberry shortcake hadn't worked its magic last night either when Henry confessed his troubles. Gabby had listened patiently over dessert and decaf.

"It was chaotic at the bookstore," Gabby had said, kindly shouldering some of Henry's weighty guilt. "I should have whisked you all away to the station immediately. And finding a body is always upsetting. You were all in shock. In any case, Henry, it's good of you to come forward to clarify the timeline. That's what an investigation is all about. Putting together the pieces."

Henry's midnight stroll had been as wobbly as a jigsaw piece or a pug's sniffing whims. He and Mr. Chaucer had zigzagged across Fontaine Park, stopping at Chaucy's favorite trees and lingering at the fountain. Since they were so close, Henry had decided to stop at his shop. He hadn't stayed long, he said. He didn't talk to anyone, and as far as he could recall, only a few cars and maybe a white van had passed by.

Gabby muttered that there was "always a white van."

Cleo pictured man and dog in the moonlight and shadows. She shivered, thinking of the killer, who could have been feet away, watching the light in Henry's workshop flick on. While in his workshop, Henry had heard a noise.

"A trash can tipping," he said, rubbing his beard, eyes closed in memory. "My neighbor the psychic, Madame Romanov, has had trouble with raccoons and kids messing with her cans." His eyes popped open. "I *did* look out, but I didn't see anything. The alley was dark. There was a light on at Madame Romanov's. I remember thinking she was up late. You might talk to her."

Gabby already had. The psychic had said she hadn't seen, heard, or felt anything. "The spirits were silent," Gabby reported, eyes rolling.

If only he'd gone outside, Henry kept saying. Maybe he could have run off the killer.

"Or gotten hurt yourself," Cleo had countered. *Or killed.* Even now, sipping her morning coffee, the chill stayed with her. Gabby had seconded Cleo's thoughts. The medical examiner placed time of death around midnight, give or take a few hours to either side. Right when Henry was there.

After the desultory dessert, Henry and Mr. Chaucer left with Gabby to sign a revised statement at the police station. Gabby said the timing offered two perks. One, it was still the same day as the crime. Two, Chief Culpepper wouldn't be in.

"I'll have to tell the chief tomorrow," Gabby said. "He might . . . well . . . want to chat with you both again. Especially Henry."

They'd be lucky if a lecture was all they got, Cleo feared. Henry had given a false statement. Cleo had too, unwittingly.

Henry had squeezed Cleo's hand good-night and said he'd go to his apartment afterward. It would be late, and he was sure he wouldn't sleep. He didn't want to keep Cleo awake.

Long into the night, Cleo wished he'd stayed. They could have been awake together. Her mind spun with troubles but no obvious solutions. She must have fallen asleep briefly, because she dreamed she was in Words on Wheels, chasing after a white van with books and loose pages sailing out the back. When the dream hurtled around a roller coaster, she jerked awake and stayed that way until seeking a solution in Words on Wheels. Around midnight, she went out to her bookmobile, flashlight in hand, and scoured the shelves for the dullest book in the bus.

Finding a boring book turned out to be a challenge. Cleo considered a text on auto repair, but that wouldn't do. Words on Wheels had been wheezing lately, and Cleo would love to be able to diagnose the cause herself. Gardening, tax returns, horse jumping, and sign language for toddlers all seemed slightly too interesting too. Finally, Cleo checked out *Anna Karenina*, hoping her patron who swore by it for insomnia relief was right. A chapter in, Cleo did drift off, only to have eight hundred pages fall on her nose and wake her right back up.

After that, Cleo went downstairs, turned on the TV, and dozed on the sofa, with Rhett on her chest and an infomercial droning in the background. She woke with a stiff neck and the oddest urge to order a two-for-one Eggstatic shell-less hard-boiled egg maker.

"Two for one," she said now to Rhett. She rubbed her eyes. Suddenly two-for-one sounded like a good idea. She'd take out Words on Wheels today and combine work with sleuthing: a two-for-one trip delivering books and hopefully tracking down leads.

*   *   *

Bernice Abernathy, known to her nurse grandson Franklin as G-mom, lived with her daughter on a cul-de-sac resembling a caterpillar, with a twisty spine, round head, and little streets sticking out like stumpy legs. Cleo turned down a leg, parked, and left Rhett snoozing in his crate. The air was cool and gushing through the open windows, and she didn't plan to stay long.

Bernice, ninety-seven years young, answered the door wearing a skirted full-piece bathing suit, wraparound sunglasses, and a shower cap.

"Cleo Watkins, the sleuthing librarian," Bernice said with a big smile. "Come in! I just got back from my aquarium aerobics class."

Aqua aerobics, Cleo interpreted, an exercise she'd never tried and likely never would. Cleo preferred her encounters with water to be poolside, preferably with a book in one hand, sweet tea in the other, and a sunshade overhead.

Bernice removed her shower cap to reveal a cute gray pixie cut. The glasses stayed on.

"I like to start the day off with exercise," Bernice declared, slipping on a robe. "Gets the blood flowing."

Cleo had started the day off with dessert. She vowed to work in some power strolling later.

They settled in on floral-print sofas and made pleasant small talk about one another's libraries, former and present.

"I loved working at the school library," Bernice said. "But now I have more time for *me* and my own reading."

Since Cleo had come in Words on Wheels, she conducted official library business, confirming that Bernice knew about all the new audiobooks, free to download from the library.

"You bet I do," Bernice said. She even listened with fancy headphones on now, she reported, after a young mother at the pool complained.

"Claimed my romances were too steamy for the children." Bernice cackled happily. "She was right! Franklin gave me a pair of headphones." She mimed hand-sized earmuffs and bobbed her head to an imaginary beat. "I look like a DJ at the pool now."

Cleo smiled, enjoying the image of DJ Bernice. Most of all she was happy that the library could provide for all patrons, even those with failing eyesight. Business officially done, Cleo eased into her ulterior motive for visiting. "Franklin told me that a man interested in books dropped by the other day."

"The hot aquaman—anti-quarium, antiquarian, whatever you call him," Bernice said, waving a bothered hand. "Franklin said you were gathering the dirt on him. I'm surprised he didn't come visiting you too. He said he was especially interested in *lady librarians.* He seemed nice enough. Great voice. Not bad to look at either, from what I could tell. It's a pity about him."

"Yes," Cleo said carefully. "You know he's . . . passed on."

"Murdered! Heck yes, I know. That's all we talked about at water class this morning. Now I get a bona fide private detective at my door!"

"Amateur only," Cleo clarified.

The elder woman dismissed the distinction. "When you get to be our ages, Cleo, you know what you're good at and titles don't matter." She clapped thin hands and chuckled. "Go ahead. Interrogate me. I didn't do it! Although I *will* confess: I led that foxy man on. I let him sniff around my bookshelves and beg to see my old atlas collection and my Agatha Christies. Bet you'd like to see those too."

Cleo didn't have to beg. Soon enough, she found herself on aching knees in Bernice's family room/library, a cool interior room lined with bookshelves. She was at the last and lowest shelf, still searching for an elusive Poirot.

"I don't see the *Poirot Investigates*," Cleo said. "Ah, there's *The A.B.C. Murders*. That's the one with Poirot's quote on intuition!"

"*Intuition comes from experience and little signs*," Bernice said. With more limber knees, Bernice got down on the floor beside Cleo. The older lady pushed up her dark glasses and squinted at the shelf. "That's odd. *Poirot Investigates* should be right next to my Miss Marples." She ran a thin finger across a matching set of volumes dressed up in red leather. Gold letters spelled the titles and the name *Christie*.

Cleo ran her finger along too and felt that tingle Kitty had talked about. Cleo didn't need a signature to feel it, or even a real person. Both Agatha Christie and Jane Marple were real to Cleo, and equal idols.

"Check out my geography section while you're down here," Bernice said. "I have a bunch of retired atlases. Can you believe, my school was tossing them out? They're valuable for the maps alone, not that I'd ever chop them up."

Like Dot's poor books. Cleo selected an elderly book, the cover as weathered as ancient bark. "Lovely," Cleo said, except as she flipped, she didn't see many maps.

She put it back gently and selected another. It opened to the middle, and Cleo gasped.

"You okay?"

"Fine," Cleo said, automatically. But the book didn't appear to be. She flipped and confirmed gaps in the page numbers.

Bernice pulled herself up. With less elegance, Cleo did too.

"Well, that's plain strange," Bernice said, still thinking about her missing mystery. "I could have sworn that *Poirot Investigates* was in here. That's the really special one. Not many first prints of it around, I gather. The other book guy said it was worth a bundle. The Fox guy didn't seem interested in it. Come to think of it, that's kinda odd too, isn't it?"

Cleo wanted there to be another explanation. "Would your daughter have put it somewhere safe, knowing how valuable it is?"

"Nah," Bernice said. "We agreed, best place to hide it is among all the books. Besides, I want to unload it soon."

Cleo replayed her words. *The other book guy.* Had other scouts been around? A competitor could hold a grudge . . . and have a motive. She asked her hostess.

"Yep, my books and I are popular." Bernice laughed. "We're leading all sorts of men on. This guy was local. Nice. Polite. Not pushy at all. Young. Well, young to me. Around your age, Cleo. Ooo, I could set you up! What's his name . . . ? Something French, like the Revolutionary War guy. Lafitte? Nope, that was a pirate . . ."

"Lafayette?" Cleo said. "Henry Lafayette? I know him well."

"That's him!" Bernice said, slapping the nearest shelf. "My mind! I mean to call him, see if he's still interested in helping me sell. He left a message last month, saying this aquarium whatever fair would be a good opportunity. I forgot . . ."

Cleo took back her theory that a local rival had a motive for murder. Henry helped folks assess books. When he told Cleo about this work, he spoke of the books, never their owners. Cleo took it as his version of her librarian's vow of secrecy. Now she thought it wasn't just for privacy but for safety too, of the books and their owners.

"You showed Mr. Lafayette your atlases?" Cleo asked, thinking she could ask Henry about the missing maps. There was no need to upset Bernice if nothing was wrong. The books could have been damaged back in their school library days.

Bernice said she had indeed shown him and he'd been downright appreciative. "I'd never sell those," she said. "They're not easily replaced. But the Christie books, I could get nice, inexpensive copies for the grandkids to read, and I can listen on my DJ headphones anytime."

Cleo thought that was a lovely idea, as long as Bernice hadn't sold any books to Hunter Fox. She ventured to ask.

Bernice grinned. "Nope. I told him I'd check with my local book guy. That foxy man was offering a lot less anyhow. I'd venture he was trying to swindle an old lady." She laughed. "Didn't work on me!"

Cleo stopped herself from mentally cursing a dead man.

Bernice chatted on. "I do need to find that book and get it sold. I'm gonna surprise Franklin and help pay off his nursing-school loans." She pushed back her dark glasses again and squinted hard at the shelves, muttering that maybe her daughter had borrowed the book to read again.

With a heavy pit in her stomach, Cleo asked, "Did Hunter Fox *borrow* anything?"

Bernice went still. "*Borrow*? You mean, take? No. Like I said, I told him I needed that second opinion from the Lafayette fellow."

"Was Mr. Fox alone in this room?" Cleo asked gently.

"Only when I went to make coffee and get us some cookies. Oh, and I answered the phone. Some woman I didn't know, trying to say I owed a fine for failing to show up to jury duty. Not me! I attended jury a few months back. Took forever to get her off the line . . . I wasn't gone but a minute or five. Ten at the most."

Bernice suddenly looked her age. With a shaky hand, she gripped her bookshelf. "Are you saying, you think he swiped my book when I wasn't looking?"

Cleo didn't answer directly. An idea had struck her. Quite a terrible idea. "The woman on the phone, can you describe her voice?"

"Like she was whispering, but at talking volume. Like she was out of breath from running."

Kitty, in her Marilyn voice? Keeping Bernice occupied while Hunter swiped valuable books? Cleo forced brightness to her own words. "Let's hope your daughter put that book somewhere safe."

Bernice wasn't fooled. The older woman slapped the shelf. "He took it, didn't he? It's a good thing that man *is* dead, or I could kill him myself."

Chapter Fourteen

The best thing about best friends was how they knew what you needed. Sometimes before you knew yourself. Sometimes a tad too quickly.

"I'm not sure," Cleo said, backtracking on the desire she'd edged around over a four-pancake lunch. After leaving Bernice, she'd driven back to town, planning to pick up a snack at the Drop By. When that plan hit a bump, Cleo sped straight to the Pancake Mill and unloaded her worries.

"I sense your unusual indecision," Mary-Rose said. "That alone tells me you need help. Hold on, let me get undressed and cash out table six."

She hauled an apron over her head—the undressing. In the process, she tipped a postcard display by the cash register.

Cleo caught the tower of cards, her heart jumping with ridiculous alarm. Her decisiveness continued to teeter.

"It's just that I did vow to give Dot time," Cleo said, looking out over the Pancake Mill. The lunch rush was winding down, and the air was heavy with scents of syrup and griddle cakes, browned butter, and hot blueberries. In the back, the massive waterwheel creaked, pushed by the wind.

Cleo rationalized aloud, again. "But that was before a killer came around, wasn't it? It is *odd* that the Drop By was closed still when I went by. Dot could simply be taking the day off. Heaven knows, she deserves it. Maybe she gave her assistants the day off too, or they're ill, or . . ." *Or something is very, very wrong.*

"Uh-huh," Mary-Rose said, punching the cash register buttons with brisk authority. The drawer shot open. She doled out change and handed it to a waiting waitress. "Does that sound right to you, Desiree?"

Waitress Desiree shook her head, her expression suggesting she wouldn't bother wasting words on the obvious.

"Exactly," Mary-Rose said, coming around the counter. "Cleo, your instincts are right. Dot doesn't close the Drop By on a whim. You said it yourself earlier: chagrin isn't about to override her good business sense. We need to talk to her. For her sake and for Henry's too. The intervention is on!"

"*Intervention* sounds a bit . . . startling," Cleo said.

"Good. That's the idea," Mary-Rose declared, smoothing her sundress and hoisting a double-decker pie carrier. "You tried delicate and giving her time, Cleo. If I go with you, I can be the one who asks her straight out. You can be the good cousin."

Mary-Rose stopped to chat with some diners. Pancakes bubbled on tabletop griddles. The do-it-yourself cakes ranged from perfect rounds to abstract blurbs and tiny drops of dripped batter. Mary-Rose often joked that her customers paid to do their own cooking.

Of course, the fun of forming and flipping cakes was part of the attraction. The other draw was the glorious view. Outside, the appropriately named Pancake Spring glistened. Swimmers crisscrossed the deep clear waters, leaving diamond paths across the round, natural pool. The resident trio of peacocks strolled along the banks.

"Okay," Mary-Rose said, rejoining Cleo. "Let's get this intervening going!" She pushed open the door and they stepped out. Mary-Rose set off toward the gravel parking area, tucked from view by a dense screen of palms and ferns.

"I know you're worried, Cleo," Mary-Rose said. "That's why this is good for you too. Your worry might be worse than the reason. For all we know, maybe Dot's selling books and shutting up shop because she's aiming to retire or take a vacation down to Florida."

Cleo shuddered. Those sounded like awful reasons to her. Still, either was preferable to Cleo's worst-case scenario of Dot needing cash for something truly terrible, like a health problem.

"You don't believe that," Cleo said. "I've never heard Dot say she wants to retire."

"No," Mary-Rose admitted. "I don't believe that. But we'll find out. We have to be direct, no dancing around. It's like flipping a pancake: fast, decisive, no hesitation." She glanced over at Cleo. "Oh, don't give me that look, like I'm terrorizing kittens. I'm just warming up. Some verbal stretching."

"I did give her time," Cleo reasoned again. "But now . . ."

"Now you have two loved ones who are prime murder suspects," Mary-Rose said. "You've been more than reserved, Cleo." Mary-Rose grinned. "Ha! The *reserved* librarian! You've been *on hold. Overdue* to intervene." She swung the pie carrier. "It is too bad that Dot had to go and threaten Hunter in public and that Henry had to stroll over to the crime scene without an alibi. Oh, and somehow lose track of a murder weapon." Mary-Rose made a *tsk*ing sound.

Cleo kicked gravel, sending it rolling to the dark shadow of a fern.

"I've been meaning to ask," Cleo said, "The day of Dot's argument at the fair. When Henry and I chased after her, you and Mr. Chaucer stayed back at Henry's stand. Did anyone come by?"

"To steal a murderous awl, you mean?" Mary-Rose said. She tapped her forehead. "I've been thinking of that. I've been hanging around you too much, Cleo. I'm developing a suspicious mind, but I'm afraid I'm going to disappoint you."

"You could never disappoint me," Cleo said, covering preemptive disappointment. "Why?"

"That sweet little pug got all sad, seeing you and Henry run off. Mr. Chaucer and I followed after you. We would have caught up too, except he met a Great Dane he had to greet."

Cleo filled in the blanks. "So you weren't watching the stand." She added quickly, "Not that you should have been."

Mary-Rose sighed. "I wish I had stayed. I did see a bunch of those bookdealers gathered outside the doorway when I looked back that way. Does Henry think that's when the awl went missing?"

Cleo kicked some more gravel. "He's not entirely certain he had that particular awl at the demo. He has entire walls and shelves of tools, you know."

"I'm the same way with whisks," Mary-Rose said supportively. "Can't resist them. Can't keep them straight."

They waited for a car to drive by, waving to the occupants. Puffy clouds floated overhead, and a peacock sang out its wild yodel. Cleo wished they could spend the afternoon reading beside the spring, like the peaceful picture on Mary-Rose's bookplate.

When the car passed, Cleo said. "Henry hosted the bookdealers in his shop the night before the fair opened. The awl could have been swiped then too. Which suggests premeditation."

"Meaning it had nothing to do with Dot or Henry or Catalpa Springs," Mary-Rose summarized. "I never thought I'd hope for premeditated murder." She pointed up the drive. "I assume we're taking your ride?"

Cleo had parked Words on Wheels just off the berm, facing out. "If you don't mind," Cleo said. "You know I love to drive."

"There's nothing I love more than getting driven around in a bus full of books!"

Cleo's ride had a cat lounging on the hood, fluffy belly aimed at the sun. Rhett never strayed far from the bus at the Pancake Mill. Cleo suspected he feared the wandering peacocks. She called his name and clicked her tongue. Rhett slid an eye open, like an alligator considering its options. Cleo knew he'd come running when she rattled his treats and started the engine.

Mary-Rose buckled up. "Last one in," she sang out as Rhett bounded up the steps. He hopped into his crate for his treat. Mary-Rose held the pie carrier in her lap. It was milky opaque, but Cleo sensed there was something besides pie inside.

"So what did you bring?" Cleo asked as she navigated up the gravel drive. Branches hung low overhead, a tunnel of glorious green.

"It's a secret," Mary-Rose said.

Cleo smiled, betting this was a secret she'd like.

*　*　*

Dot lived in a white clapboard cottage with cornflower-blue shutters and a riot of rhododendrons.

"Okay," Mary-Rose said, stomping up to Dot's door. "On the count of three, we start pounding."

"We're not a SWAT team," Cleo protested. "Gentle, remember?" She held Rhett Butler on her shoulder. His claws poked through her cardigan. He could use the *gentle* reminder too.

"Okay, you know best. *For now.*" Mary-Rose scanned the shrubbery with suspicion and added darkly, "I've got your back."

"You have whatever's in that pie carrier," Cleo said. "Be prepared to thrust your secret dessert at her as soon as she opens the door. Rhett and I will be right beside you."

When Cleo knocked, she feared Mary-Rose's storm-the-cottage tactics had rubbed off on her. The knock sounded too loud and reverberated through her fist. Rhett tensed, digging in his claws.

"Good," Mary-Rose whispered.

Not good. "Yoo-hoo, Dot?" Cleo called out in a merry trill. She raised her fist again, planning a light, happy tapping to the beat of *shave and a haircut, two bits.* She knocked out the melody twice, and her mind wandered, wondering about the origin. A more important question was how she'd evict the song from her head.

"I have an earworm," she was saying as the door swung open. Dot stood before them in a ruffled sunflower-print apron. Her cheeks were rosy and her hair smooth.

"Dot!" Cleo and Mary-Rose exclaimed simultaneously.

"We came to—" Cleo stopped short. Did one announce an intervention?

"We came to bring you swoon pies," Mary-Rose said, stepping past Cleo and over Dot's threshold. "Come along, Cleo. Thanks for having us in, Dot," she said, although Dot hadn't managed to utter a word. "I'll take these to the kitchen."

Relief swept Cleo over the threshold too. Dot wasn't in shambles, in her personal upkeep or her home. And Mary-Rose had brought her famous "swoon pies," her version of moon pies, marshmallow-filled chocolate-cookie sandwiches.

"I . . . ah . . ." Dot said.

Cleo let Rhett down and gripped her cousin in a hug. She was so glad to see Dot, she wasn't even bothered by her cousin's obvious fluster.

108

Rhett trotted after Mary-Rose, knowing the route to any kitchen. Dot's graciousness came back with a gush. "Where are my manners? Come in. I'm so sorry. I was going to call you, Cleo! I was! Time slipped away, and now I'm entertaining and—"

"Entertaining?" Cleo's emotions mingled. There was relief that Dot appeared well. But there was also a dash of hurt mixed with vexation. Dot was *entertaining* instead of returning her cousin's worried calls?

Dot's hands flew to her apron ties. She lowered her voice. "It's the president of the Georgia Antiquarian Book Society. I'm so honored! He took time away from the fair to personally bring me some news and a book. One of *my* books! Come say hi." Dot bustled down the hallway, leaving Cleo gaping behind her.

Cleo caught up with Dot just outside the kitchen. Rhett had made himself at home, staring expectantly at the fridge. Mary-Rose stood beside Dot's small kitchen island, introducing herself and her swoon pies to the stony face of Professor Dean Weber. Cleo reached for Dot's elbow.

She drew her cousin back into the hall and whispered, "What is *he* doing here? He could be a *murder* suspect!"

Dot's eyes widened.

Mary-Rose's voice boomed from the kitchen. Cleo recognized the tone as creating a cover. "So," Mary-Rose proclaimed. "I take two big old chocolate-cake cookies and fill them with a whole mess of marshmallow and then dip half in chocolate glaze! Swoon!"

The professor turned toward the doorway. Behind his back, Mary-Rose shot Cleo a shushing gesture.

Cleo decided she didn't care if he'd overheard. The man was a suspect on her list, and here he was, suspiciously in her cousin's kitchen.

Professor Weber eyed Cleo stonily. "Mrs. Watkins," he said. "I've been hearing a lot about you."

He didn't elaborate, so Cleo only smiled. Maybe he'd heard of her lovely bookmobile or how she'd solved several recent murders.

Dot bustled in and began tidying her immaculate kitchen. She whisked a dishcloth over the counter, her nervous tic. Her words were just as brisk. "That nice Buddy Boone found my other bird book—the Audubon—at the professor's book stand this morning. Of course, Professor Weber didn't realize it was *mine*. Buddy only noticed because of my bookplate. I feel like I owe you some payment, Professor. Buddy too. He should have come with you so I could thank him as well. Please tell him I'd love to give him a finder's reward or cookies or—"

"No payment necessary," Professor Weber said. "It's hardly an exceptional copy of *Birds of America*. Once Mr. Boone pointed out the book and your *pencil* signature—which is not a good permanent identifier, by the way, and not a benefit for resale—I felt it my duty as society president to return it to you personally. Provenance and legitimacy are the cornerstones of the antiquarian business, as I've often said. I've distributed your list of missing books to all the dealers. Now that I know even more details about your supposedly missing volumes, we have a better chance of identifying them."

Dot blushed and gushed thanks, then explained to Cleo and Mary-Rose. "The professor asked about any identifying markings, especially for my most valuable book, so if—*when*—it's located, I can get it back." Dot's voice had risen to nervously hopeful. "See? It'll be fine. Just fine."

Fine except for a murder inquiry. And Dot and Henry being suspects. And a more likely suspect dropping by Dot's house. Cleo wondered about the professor's intentions, both in visiting and in inquiring about Dot's book. The polite, southern lady side of Cleo's brain argued for nice and noble. Her sleuthing side countered with just the opposite. Identifying details could help him find Dot's books. They could also help him—or Kitty—hide them.

"How did you acquire that Audubon book?" Cleo asked him. Mary-Rose nodded strenuously, suggesting intervening in the professor's business was going well.

He looked down his nose at her. "Miss Peavey gave it to me as a thoughtful gift, knowing I enjoy natural history. I was unaware it had problematic origins. She was surely unaware too. Mr. Fox is—*was*—responsible for acquiring it."

Encouraged by Mary-Rose's bobbing head, Cleo said, "Did Miss Peavey acquire many other books from Mr. Fox?"

His face didn't move, except a narrowing of his eyes. "Miss Peavey's business with Hunter Fox was none of my business."

And he didn't like that one bit, Cleo guessed. She'd been right in thinking he knew of Kitty's flirtations with the book scout.

"Tea?" Dot said too brightly. "Coffee? Some of these lovely swoon pies?"

"No," the professor said. "I have to return to the fair. I've spent too much time on this unnecessary trouble already."

"Sorry!" Dot said.

Not sorry, Cleo thought.

He left with a stiff "Good day" and a haughty refusal of swoon pies for the road.

"He *is* a chilly one," Mary-Rose said. They watched out Dot's front window as he drove off. "I thought so the other day. Now I know it. No tea? No swoon pies? Not caring that his fiancée was swooning after a hot con man?"

"*Pre*-fiancée," Cleo murmured. "Or he's pretending not to care."

"Pre," Mary-Rose said huffily. "If he gave her that big diamond ring and she took it, I bet he doesn't see much distinction."

Dot had locked up and was leaning with her back against the door. "I'm sorry!" she blurted. "I should have called you both earlier. I was about to, truly, when Professor Weber stopped by. I'm sure he was just being nice, and you all are being *so* kind. Thank you for the swoon pies. They're my favorite, and here I was being so rude! I don't deserve them."

Mary-Rose led the way back to the kitchen. "You're never rude, Dot. We, on the other hand, have an ulterior motive. The swoon pies are to sweeten the blow. Cleo here is going to ask all about books and money, and we're not leaving until she gets answers. This is an intervention."

Chapter Fifteen

They returned to the kitchen. Mary-Rose served sweet tea and swoon pies while Cleo revealed her greatest worry.

"Are you okay?" Cleo asked. Her heart raced as she asked, "It's not your health, is it?"

Dot hung her head. "No. Not *my* health. It's the Drop By."

Cleo was relieved, but only momentarily. The shop was Dot's heart and soul, like the library and bookmobile were for Cleo.

Dot said, "Remember when the air conditioner at the store broke back in March? Fixing it revealed trouble with the vents and the furnace and then more trouble with the plumbing and refrigeration, which popped up some code violations that need fixing—fast—and then the taxes came due and . . ."

Dot paused for a breath, slumping back in her seat. "I got behind on everything, and it all snowballed," she said. "I couldn't think how else to catch up other than to sell some stuff." She cast worried eyes around her kitchen. "I didn't want to take a loan out on the house and end up in trouble here too."

They sat around the rectangular table tucked in Dot's breakfast nook. Dot's father had made the table to fit. Dot had sewn the yellow gingham café curtains for the three walls of windows.

Outside, hummingbirds zipped between a syrup feeder and the rhododendrons.

Cleo reached to grip her cousin's hand. Mary-Rose pushed the platter of swoon pies closer. Even Rhett abandoned his refrigerator watch and trotted over to hop on Dot's lap.

"Thanks, Rhett," Dot said. "Thank you all. I needed to get that off my chest." In what Cleo took as a good step forward, Dot accepted a swoon pie.

"Dot," Cleo said gently. "You could have told us. Everyone would *want* to help. Me, April, all of the family—"

"Me," Mary-Rose chimed in. "You know what our mothers would say: *a trouble shared is a trouble halved.* Or cut in thirds in this case, or tiny crumbs once everyone gets involved." She brushed up cookie crumbs to make her point.

"That's exactly why I couldn't tell you all!" Dot said, so forcefully Rhett threw back his ears. "I don't want to go lending anyone else my problems. April has the kids' college tuitions to worry about and the cost of living in California. You both have your own work and bills. This is *my* problem. I'm the one who had my head in the sand and didn't look up until things got too dire."

Cleo had been raising a swoon pie to her lips. She put it back down. "How dire?"

Dot took a deep breath and exhaled the spiraling troubles. "If I can't fix the code troubles by the end of the month, I'll have to close the Drop By. If I can't open the shop, I can't pay the repair bills or the taxes."

Mary-Rose and Cleo hurried to make sympathetic sounds and platitudes. *It will be okay*, they said.

"No," Dot said, with uncharacteristic brusqueness. "I'm thinking it's a sign. I'm getting to that age. Besides, no one *needs* a downtown grocery anymore."

Cleo mostly managed to cover her horror. She took a large bite of swoon pie so she wouldn't have to talk.

"Close the Drop By?" Mary-Rose said, expressing Cleo's feelings for her. "Dot, that would be a tragedy for the whole town! Is it what *you* want?"

Dot shook her head so vigorously, her hair batted at her eyes. "No, not at all. I love that shop, and I'd hate letting my kitchen and clerk helpers go. They're like family. But I won't take out more loans, from the bank or anyone else."

Cleo put down her cup. Intervening was more wrenching than she'd anticipated. She decided it was time to get it all out. "So you tried to sell your signed copy of *Gone With the Wind*."

Dot raised sad eyes. "Yes. Hunter Fox said I could get nearly *thirty thousand* for it. Can you imagine? He'd take about six thousand and I'd get the rest, he said. It would have solved all my troubles and then some. I enjoy *Gone With the Wind*—you know that, Cleo. Margaret Mitchell's signature is a true treasure. But I don't need a rare or expensive book to love the story just as much. The way I figured, I found that book for a reason. It was going to help me. Hunter seemed like he wanted to help too, but then at the fair he pretended we'd never had a deal at all."

Cleo reached out and gripped her cousin's hand.

Dot sniffled. "I made a fool of myself at the fair. Then I compounded it. I went to the Myrtles that evening and tried to reason with Mr. Fox. I know he was in his room. I heard him and a lady talking and laughing right before I knocked, but then they wouldn't open the door."

Kitty, Cleo thought grimly. Kitty had claimed it was Dot who couldn't be reasoned with. Dot who was "pounding" on Hunter's door. Cleo's look must have betrayed her concern.

115

Dot squeezed her hand back and said, "Yes, I know. It looks like I was crazed for those books, doesn't it? I tried to explain to Gabby when I gave my statement. I didn't want to hide anything, and I knew the police would find out I was there. I'm a fool . . ."

"No, you're wise to tell Gabby everything," Cleo said and told her about Henry's revised statement.

Dot's eyes widened. "So Henry doesn't have an alibi either? Oh, but it's okay. Henry doesn't have a motive." She shot Cleo a wry smile. "Unlike me."

Mary-Rose scoffed. "I kicked Hunter Fox out of the Pancake Mill. You could say I have a motive too."

Cleo recognized that Mary-Rose was being supportive. Still . . . "Please," she said. "I don't need any more loved ones as suspects."

Dot had broken away from Cleo's grip and was twisting her napkin. "I know I should have sold my books through Henry. I didn't want anyone to know my troubles. That's why I've avoided calling you all too. I've been cowardly. I've made everything worse. Now there's no fixing it, and I should own up to that."

Mary-Rose slapped the table decisively. "Anything's fixable, especially plumbing. I know some retired contractors who do volunteer work if we can muster the materials. I'll send them over to the Drop By this afternoon."

Cleo rallied too. She couldn't help with repairs, but she could with books. "I'll keep hunting for your *Gone With the Wind*," she promised. *And the killer who might have it . . .*

* * *

By late afternoon, clanks emanated from the plumbing bowels of Dot's Drop By. Long legs in jeans and loosely tied sneakers stuck out from the cabinetry.

116

"Oops!" Ollie said from inside. His sneakers floundered for grip. What had been an intermittent drip turned into a distinct splashing, and Ollie uttering those panic-inducing words, "Don't panic!"

"Ollie, are you okay?" Cleo wanted to inquire if the plumbing was okay, but that might sound rude, as if she didn't trust Ollie's skills. Which she didn't.

"He's doing a fine job," Dot said, hovering at Cleo's shoulder. Dot raised her voice. "As long as you're careful of yourself, Oliver. Don't get hurt down there. I have cookies waiting when you're done. The store-bought boxed kind, nothing I made here."

Dot was taking health-code regulations seriously. She'd relented to opening the grocery part of the store but not the deli, thus avoiding any fines or infractions. She'd glumly told Cleo that probably no one would come by.

Ollie gave assurances from under the sink.

The door chime dinged, and Dot hurried out to the front. Contrary to Dot's low expectations, the store was filling up fast. Word was spreading, and locals were coming to show their support. Cleo was proud of her town and of Ollie, who'd stepped right up too.

After their intervention at Dot's house, Cleo had dropped Mary-Rose back at the Pancake Mill. She was taking Rhett home—and hoping for a catnap herself—when she noticed Ollie lying in a hammock hung between the catalpa trees. Her grandson was nodding over a book and still in his pajamas. When she'd told him of the difficulties at the Drop By, he'd swung into action, almost falling out of the hammock with enthusiasm to help Dot, whom he and Cleo's other grandkids thought of as their favorite "auntie."

He'd learned all sorts of skills on his recent Gulf Coast gig, he claimed. Soldering, plumbing, carpentry . . . Cleo had thought he'd spent his time photographing sunsets and shampooing oil off shorebirds.

"Ow! It's okay!" he cried out now. "Hey, Gran, can you hand me that whatcha-call-it thingy? The one with the round head that swirls around and makes the clacking noise?"

"A ratchet?" Cleo eyed the tools Ollie had assembled from the garage, her husband's old stash. Dear Richard could fix just about anything. She wished he were here to help Ollie.

"Yeah, that's it. I've got this. Don't worry, Gran."

A half hour later, Ollie emerged, smudged and damp but declaring victory over the drip. Cleo offered the highest of grandmotherly praise.

Ollie turned self-effacing. "Yeah, well, it's not much, is it? There's the whole underground pipe part that needs to be dug out. I wish there was more I could do. If Auntie Dot gets in contractors, I could help them."

Cleo squeezed her grandson's arm and felt a pang of preemptive nostalgia. She hated to think that the Drop By might close. It would mark the end of an era, for her family and her town. She and Ollie made their way to the front of the store.

"Whoa," Ollie said.

"Good gracious," Cleo echoed.

The line of customers stretched all the way to the ice cream freezer. Folks were buying just to buy, Cleo guessed. A lady held an armload of canned corn. Another man was buying out the cake mixes, and a mom and toddler were stocking up on ice cream sandwiches. The tip jar overflowed. Dot stood at the cash register, flustered but glowing.

"Everyone wants to support her," Cleo whispered. She pinched her palm to keep herself from tearing up in public.

"That's it!" Ollie crowed. He bent and kissed Cleo on the cheek. "We can start an online fund raiser! That's something I'm actually pretty good at!"

Cleo followed him outside, where she greeted and thanked friends and neighbors. Basking in the sun and warm words, she thought things might work out after all. All she needed was that book and a suspect for the police to nab.

The warmth lasted until she glanced across the park and saw another crowd, this one outside the Gilded Page. Cleo squinted. Through the pinks and purples flowering in the park, she spotted a lavender gown. The person wearing it turned slowly, arms raised to the sky.

Madame Romanov! Cleo didn't have to be a fortune-teller to guess that this crowd wasn't good news.

* * *

"Close your eyes . . . hold out your palms. Do you feel the cold fingers on your skin? The murdered man's touch? He's with us!" Madame Romanov jangled her bracelets. Slim, her double-wide dachshund, trotted off with jingles on his collar. Madame moaned, and the group of a dozen or so people giggled nervously.

"I feel something!" exclaimed a twenty-something woman in a tiny sundress. "A chill is crawling up my chest!"

Her friend squealed and grabbed her arm. "I feel it too!"

Cleo had crossed the park at brisk stomping pace. Thus she'd arrived glistening, her mother's polite term for sweaty. Matched with the light breeze, a chill was only natural.

"You're feeling the wind," Cleo said.

Grumpy rumbles passed through the crowd. Cleo was ruining the fun. Madame Romanov broke contact with the beyond and pointed to Cleo. The psychic's dark eyes looked wild, like they might see into Cleo or beyond. A fresh shiver crawled up Cleo's neck.

"Look, we have a special guest. Very special," Madame Romanov proclaimed. "This woman is a conduit to the other side. She finds the dead. She's drawn to them. Don't get too close to her, or you too might be taken."

Cleo recognized some locals among Madame Romanov's audience. "It's true," one of them whispered. "She's a librarian who finds dead people!" Another waved and mouthed, "Hi, Cleo."

Cleo guessed the rest were tourists. The clues were easy: Cleo didn't recognize them, for one. Second, they carried book-fair tote bags and had glossy town maps sticking from their pockets. The squealing woman whipped up her cell phone and snapped some photos in Cleo's direction.

"I am *not* a *conduit*," Cleo said huffily. The psychic had her eyes closed again, her pointy chin raised to the sky. Slim had wandered off to mark the corner of Henry's bookshop.

Cleo tried to reason with the audience. "A man has been killed. This is not a parlor game. It is a serious crime, and the police are searching for help and witnesses. Madame Romanov, did *you* witness anything?"

The psychic began another slow-motion dance, circling Cleo. "The dead seek justice. This woman, the seeker of the dead, is on the wrong path. A dangerous path. Spirits, help her find the way."

Cleo frowned. Was the psychic trying to tell her something or simply misleading her audience?

The woman in the sundress and her friend rushed to Cleo's side and snapped a selfie, giggling and then skittering off, like Rhett when he played games of imaginary prey.

"Oh, for goodness' sake!" Cleo exclaimed. Beyond the crowd, she saw Mr. Chaucer snoozing on his pillow in Henry's window. A bearded face peeked out and just as quickly drew back. At least Cleo hadn't gotten herself glistening only to be irritated. Once the coast was clear of spirits and selfies, she'd check in on him.

Madame Romanov chanted on. "The killer is close." She pointed a wavering finger toward the front door of the Gilded Page. A *Closed* sign hung from it. The hours were written out in gold paint across ebony-painted wood panels: *The Gilded Page Antiquarian and Rare Books. Monday through Friday—when open. Weekends and holidays, nights, special occasions, and inclement weather—at whim.*

Henry could add an addendum, Cleo thought. *Closed for murders and psychic disruptions.*

Wary of looking like a death conduit in further photos, Cleo forced a neural, pleasant expression on her face.

"Feel the killer . . . you *know* the killer," Madame Romanov was saying, waving her hands too close to Cleo's face. Chubby Slim ran by and barked. The crowd murmured.

Suddenly, Cleo did feel something, the thrill of an idea.

"You knew him," Cleo said. "On the morning Hunter Fox's body was discovered, you already knew his name, Madame Romanov. How? Did he visit you?"

"His spirit visited me." Madame jangled her bangles. "He came from beyond. He told me his name."

"Did he tell you his killer's name?" Cleo asked, playing along.

Madame Romanov ignored the question. "We're done here. The spirit portal has closed. Come along, people. Let's continue our tour. The ghosts of the Myrtles Bed and Breakfast call to us. I have explored its hallways of many mysteries and hear its ghosts calling to us now. Listen . . ."

Cleo heard birdsong, the honk of a horn, and the tittering of Madame's tour group.

The psychic took off at a speed-walking pace, leaving her guests and Slim to trot after her.

The door to the Gilded Page cracked open. Two worried faces peered out.

Mr. Chaucer woofed and waggled his back end.

"Are they gone?" Henry said.

"Off to chase ghosts at the Myrtles," Cleo said. "I didn't know it was haunted."

Henry leaned out and scanned the street before ushering Cleo inside.

"I didn't know my shop was haunted," he said. "I came back from the fair to walk Chaucy, and she was out in the alley. She called my place the 'Killer's Workshop' and accused Chaucy of being possessed."

Mr. Chaucer sneezed and almost toppled over.

"He just has some springtime allergies," Henry said defensively. His expression brightened. "I'm glad to see you. I had an idea . . . I'd like to invite you out on a date."

Cleo's first thought was that it was odd timing.

Henry grinned. "The bookdealers are getting together at the Myrtles tonight for an after-dinner cocktail hour, all members and their guests invited. You and I could go . . ."

"And listen in and ask questions." Cleo beamed back at her gentleman friend.

"A sleuthing date," he said.

He always knew just what she wanted. "I'd love to!"

Chapter Sixteen

Cleo almost slept through her date. Henry was picking her up at eight PM, downright late for going out for Cleo. To prepare, she'd had an early dinner and then settled on the sofa with Rhett, intending to rest up and read. Reading turned to heavy eyelids and a bobbing head.

Just a little lie-down, she'd told herself, stretching out with Rhett on her chest. *I'll only rest my eyes for a minute.*

Over an hour later, she jerked upright, upsetting her book and her cat. The clock read 7:34. Cleo hustled upstairs. Rhett followed, meowing complaints, thinking it was time for bed and thus his bedtime treats. Sulky, Rhett offered no help as Cleo dug through her closet, wondering aloud what to wear.

Cleo chose a peachy linen dress topped with a deeper-hued cardigan. The night, seeping in through her open window, was still softly warm. Peach would match the season and have the added benefit of camouflaging the orange fur Rhett was enthusiastically rubbing against her hemline.

Cleo fluffed her hair, touched up her mascara, and was wondering whether lipstick was too much when the doorbell rang.

Rhett bounded downstairs. Cleo grabbed shoes and tinted lip gloss and hurried after him.

"Hello," she said, swinging the door open and expecting a kiss on the cheek.

"Hello," Gabby repeated, smiling brightly. "Why, you look lovely, Miss Cleo."

Cleo hid her surprise by patting her hair. "Henry and I are going to a cocktail party," she said, leaving off the sleuthing portion of their date.

"I know," Gabby said, and her smile fell. "About that . . . Henry might be a smidgen late."

Cleo's stomach did flips, even as Gabby hurried on in chipper tones, saying it was nothing to worry about. "He's, ah, just a little busy answering some questions for the chief. All voluntary. I'm sure they're about done by now."

Cleo had been steadying herself on the door. She swung it open wide. Gabby stepped in, only to be halted by a fluffy orange Persian flopping at her feet.

"Deputy Rhett Butler," Gabby said, squatting to his level. "Henry and Mr. Chaucer will be here any minute." She glanced up at Cleo, biting her lower lip.

Cleo read trouble.

Gabby kept her gaze on Rhett. "I didn't get a chance to tell Chief Culpepper about Henry's revised statement until this afternoon. The chief had Henry come into the station to clarify some points, that's all. They were still at it when I left the station. Henry had said you had plans to meet tonight. I thought I should drop by and let you know."

Clarifying didn't sound terrible, yet Gabby was still biting her lip and concentrating too diligently on Rhett.

Cleo waited, sensing Gabby had more to say.

"And . . ." Gabby said, lingering on the word before spilling out more. "The chief charged Henry with giving a false statement. But don't worry. That's usually only a misdemeanor, a fine or community service, or a lawyer could get the whole thing dropped." Gabby ended encouragingly, "It's hardly worse than a speeding ticket."

Cleo ran a hand through her hair, mussing her carefully arranged layers. "Poor Henry! Does he have a lawyer with him?"

"Not unless Mr. Chaucer has a law degree." Gabby avoided Cleo's eye.

"Outrageous!" Cleo declared.

"I am sorry," Gabby said. "I tried to report it like it was no big deal, but it is kind of a big thing. Henry no longer has an alibi. The killing was outside his shop, with his tool. I can see where the chief is coming from, even if as a friend I don't believe Henry hurt anyone."

Cleo reiterated that *anyone* could have grabbed that awl. Henry had no motive. Henry was a good man.

Gabby let her vent. "I know," she said. "If it makes you feel better, Miss Cleo, we're looking into all the booksellers. I spent the entire day doing background checks."

A wicked thought struck Cleo. She'd feel better if Gabby had found someone with a criminal background. "Any good news from your research?" she asked.

"Yes," Gabby said immediately. "Most booksellers are good people, just like you've been saying."

"Oh," Cleo said, disappointed. Then she realized there was still an opening for bad behavior. "Most? Is someone not good?"

Gabby hesitated. She scratched Rhett's ears and asked him, "Should we tell her?" After a moment and some encouraging purrs from Rhett, she turned to Cleo. "Okay," she said. "I'm not revealing anything you couldn't find with some Googling. Our

Miss Kitty has a little shoplifting problem. I should say, book-lifting."

Cleo drew a sharp breath.

"Now don't go jumping to conclusions, Miss Cleo. Shoplifting books isn't a pathway to murder. It seems Kitty 'accidentally' took an expensive book from a store a few years back, and from a library more recently."

"A library!" Cleo stomped her sandal. Her stomp landed softly in the thick entryway carpet but felt justified. "That's terrible. Theft from the library is theft from everyone." She wasn't mollified when Gabby reported that Kitty had paid for her crime: a small fine and community service.

Cleo huffed. "What about Hunter Fox?" She imagined a lengthy record of crooked deeds.

"Clean as a proverbial whistle," Gabby reported, scratching Rhett's chin. "Which could mean he was a very good con man, if you're right about his book-scouting ways. Or his victims were too embarrassed or shy to press charges."

Like Dot, Cleo thought. If not for the murder and having to give a statement, Dot might not have told anyone about her troubles.

Gabby was listing other society members with publicly discoverable misdeeds. A couple of medievalists with speeding tickets. Cleo could empathize with that. She'd been known to have a lead foot.

"Professor Weber had some bad online reviews of his bookselling business," Gabby was saying. "The most surprising thing about him is that he's loaded. Serious family money. Maybe that's what Kitty sees in him? Then there's Henry," Gabby said.

Cleo drew in a breath.

"Spotless," Gabby said.

"Of course he is," Cleo said, turning to reinspect her hair. She'd never doubted her gentleman friend, not for a moment.

"Kind of disappointing," Gabby said. "Except for Henry. I mean, if I'd found an out-of-town stabber, that would be something to dig into."

Cleo checked her watch. Eleven minutes past eight.

"I'm sure he'll be here soon," Gabby said. "How was *your* day?"

Cleo recognized Gabby's kind attempt to distract her. "I have something for you to look into," she said and described her encounter with Madame Romanov. "She told me I was on the wrong path. I wonder if she knows what the right path is? At the scene, did you or anyone else give her Mr. Fox's name?"

Gabby stood, rolling her shoulders and neck as she did. Rhett jumped up to the banister post beside her, demanding more attention. Gabby rubbed his ears. "I'm sure I didn't say anything to Ms. Romanov. Crime scene 101, you don't give up the name of the victim before notifying next of kin." Rhett purred as Gabby considered. "I don't think the chief knew the victim's name at that point. You told me. Then the chief was busy, so I didn't have a chance to tell him right away. The techs and EMTs wouldn't have known, most likely. Why do you ask?"

Cleo explained. "Madame Romanov knew the name Hunter."

Gabby raised an eyebrow. "She wasn't doing that psychic guessing thing? You know, how they pick up on little things you don't realize you've dropped and run with them?"

"Possible. Kitty mentioned *Hunt.* It's not hard to guess the name Hunter from that, I suppose, but thinking back, Madame also mentioned *fox.* 'Fox in the henhouse,' I think she said. It could be a coincidence . . ."

"Or not. I'll look into her some more."

Footsteps fell on the porch, shoes and little pug feet. Mr. Chaucer and Rhett were going to have a pet play date while Henry and Cleo were out.

Gabby pulled the door open and stepped back with it. Mr. Chaucer trotted in, Henry fast at his heels. "So sorry I'm late," Henry said, making a beeline to Cleo. "I was, ah . . . delayed. Speaking with someone. A little trouble. Nothing to worry about."

Cleo hugged him, holding back her desire to pepper him with questions. They'd talk when they were alone and the dear man had a cocktail in his hand.

He kissed her cheek. "Ready for our sleuthing date, my dear?"

At a muffled chuckle, Henry spun around.

Mr. Chaucer waggled his back end at Gabby, stepping out from behind the door.

"Sleuthing date?" Gabby said. "I knew you'd be looking into this, Miss Cleo."

Cleo stiffened her stance, preparing to issue rousing justifications. Every moment the chief spent falsely accusing Henry was a moment of investigation wasted. She'd scour the county for clues. She'd—

Gabby held up a palm. "I'm not stopping you. All I ask is that you kids be careful tonight, okay? And Miss Cleo? Let me know if you find out anything."

* * *

The Myrtles Bed and Breakfast occupied an antebellum Italianate mansion as pretty as a layer cake. Delicate porches and lacy balconies trimmed three stacked stories. Elegant crepe myrtles lined the walkway. By summer, the trees' graceful limbs would bend with frothy confections of pink, lavender, and magenta blooms, with wedding parties vying for bookings and photo shoots. The building, with two wings to either side and a ballroom in the back, was large enough to host extended families, as well as small conventions.

Cleo and Henry entered arm in arm, holding on tighter as they tipped back their heads to admire the eighteen-foot ceilings and glittering chandelier.

They were greeted by Nina Flores, one of the current owners. Usually bubbly, Nina looked twitchy and frazzled.

"They're in the ballroom," she said, with a jerky gesture toward the back.

"Is everything going well?" Henry asked.

Cleo noted a pulse thumping under Nina's eye.

"An innkeeper loves all her guests," Nina said in a monotone. She lowered her voice. "My husband Karl and I appreciate the business, Mr. Lafayette. We truly do! But these old-book people are a handful." She clutched thin arms to her chest and shivered.

Cleo realized it was chilly. No, downright cold. She was glad she'd worn a sweater.

Nina said, "The air conditioning is down as low as it will go. Professor Weber insists it has to be arctic for book preservation. I went out and bought dehumidifiers for his and Ms. Peavey's rooms because they claimed it was 'dangerously humid' in here. I've upgraded *her* to the penthouse suite, but she's still going on about suing us."

"Kitty's upset about the break-in?" Cleo asked, pitching her tone to sympathetic, fishing for information.

Nina's exhale heaved her sideways. "I'm not saying she *wasn't* robbed, but she won't tell the police exactly what's missing, which is strange, isn't it? She did leave her key in a bar for anyone to swipe. She can't blame us for that."

Cleo leaned in and lowered her voice. "Do you think it was one of the other bookdealers who swiped the key?"

Nina Flores scanned the grand foyer, eyes roving from the green velvet drapes to the grand piano. She didn't bother to whisper.

"I do! A whole bunch of them were out together. Who else would know Kitty's room number or care so much about used books? I even have a theory about which one of them could have done it."

Cleo's hopes rose. She held her breath.

"Who?" asked Henry.

"Any of them!" Nina crowed. "They're all crazed. Crazed for books. They even have a term for it. They were *laughing* about it over breakfast. *Bibliomania.*"

She spun and stalked back to guard the front desk.

Henry and Cleo held their chuckles until they were away from Nina's twitchy ears.

"I shouldn't be laughing," Henry said. "But 'any of 'em'? That doesn't narrow the suspect field, does it? Or clear me."

"Or me," Cleo said. "Bibliomania. It's a real condition and we're stricken." She was glad for the laugh. On the way over, Henry had "confessed" about his trip to the police station.

"I did make a misleading statement," he said, ever diplomatic.

"I'm the one who misled first," Cleo said ruefully. She gave the heavy oak doors to the ballroom a solid shove, and she and Henry paused at the threshold, taking in the ornate space. Red wallpaper embossed in stripes covered the walls. Cloud murals soared high on the coffered ceiling, and the marble floor had so many ripples it seemed to move. Nina's husband Karl manned a backlit bar, polishing a glass and warily watching the chatting antiquarians.

"Everyone *seems* well behaved," Cleo said, noting that the bookdealers were dutifully wearing name tags and keeping their voices at a low rumbling level. "I was telling Mary-Rose the other day, book people are *good* people."

Henry sighed. "I'm sorry one might be proving you wrong. The bad apple . . ."

"Or two bad apples." Cleo's gaze landed on Kitty, convicted library-book thief. A half-dozen men, including her pre-fiancé, stood around her. She was laughing theatrically at something one of them said. She threw a hand to his arm, gripping the speaker while batting her eyes at the rest. Professor Weber stood stoically at her side.

"What do those two see in each other?" Cleo mused.

"A love of books?"

Cleo squeezed his hand. A shared love of books was a lovely thing. "Yes," she said, still dubious. Kitty loved "southern delights," but the professor had scoffed at *Gone With the Wind*. "What's his specialty?" she asked.

Henry listed French and German philosophers and nonfiction, particularly natural history. "Opposites attract?" he suggested.

They made their way to the bar, where Karl scowled suspiciously and persisted in polishing the glass.

Cleo wondered about opposites attracting. It was such a common saying, one took it as truth. But was it? In her experience, folks bonded more over their commonalities.

"He's very wealthy," she murmured to Henry.

"She's very . . . vivacious," Henry said.

"Flirty and gorgeous," Cleo translated. Wealth and beauty seemed more than enough attraction for some folks, although not for Cleo.

Karl greeted them with a sharp nod. "Bet you need a drink," he said. Henry ordered a glass of red wine for himself as well as Cleo's request of sparkling water with a slice of lemon. "Heard you got an escort to the police station this afternoon." He raised an eyebrow questioningly.

Henry flinched.

"Henry was helping the police gather information," Cleo said in her most authoritative librarian's tone.

"They'll need help." Karl handed over their glasses. "This is bad business. I'm seeing it right here at the inn. Robbery. Complaints about the breakfast. Fights. Not that *I'm* blaming you, Henry." He added, in the same rote monotone his wife used, "We appreciate you recommending us as Catalpa Springs' premier bed-and-breakfast."

"Fights?" Cleo asked. She rattled her ice cubes, hoping to tame down the bubbles.

Karl pointed with his chin. "That Marilyn Monroe woman, Kitty Peavey, and Professor Weber got bickering over breakfast."

"What happened?" Henry asked.

Karl raised his chin. "An innkeeper never gossips," he said stiffly. He picked up the glass and resumed over-polishing.

Cleo repeated what Gabby had said to her. "It's not gossip if it's true. Like you say, the police need help."

Karl regarded her solemnly. "Are you on the case too?"

Cleo nodded just as seriously.

He leaned across the bar. "The professor, he said something along the lines of, 'I know what you were up to with Hunter Fox.' Well, I think we *all* guessed what she was up to with Mr. Fox, if you get my drift."

Cleo did. "Interesting," she said to be encouraging. She took a sip of her drink. The bubbles fizzed at her nose.

They all looked over at Kitty, who was fluttering a hand at her cleavage. "She tried that Marilyn Monroe act on me," Karl said, scowling. "She sounded all out of breath, saying I could be her 'hero' if I gave her the key to Hunter Fox's room after it was sealed by the police."

"*Very* interesting," Cleo said again, more truthfully this time. What would Kitty want? Perhaps it was as innocent as removing evidence of their relationship. Or evidence of a criminal kind?

Henry said, "I'm guessing you didn't let her in?"

"You guess right!" Karl said. "I had to put a padlock on the door since his key wasn't with his . . . you know."

Body, Cleo thought with a shiver. *Another missing key.* That was interesting too.

Karl polished the glass furiously. "I thought, if some killer thief still has that key, I don't want anyone going near there, Miss Peavey included. That and if I'd given in to her request, it wouldn't just be the police after me. Nina would kill me, assuming I succumbed to flirtation temptations. We'd have another murder on our hands."

He laughed. Cleo drew her cardigan closer.

"Sorry about the air conditioning," Karl said, misinterpreting her shiver. "Seems that penguins and old books need the same temperature."

Cleo smiled. "Did Kitty say why she wanted to get in the room?"

"Books," Karl said, with a disgust Cleo would have paired with palmetto bugs or book butchery. "What else is there with this group? She claimed she'd left some of her 'valuable inventory' in his room."

Cleo glanced at Henry. Her gentleman friend was frowning.

Henry said, "She wanted books from Mr. Fox's room? Cleo, remember how Gabby asked me to look at the books found in his room? There were hardly any. I wonder if he was robbed too?"

"Hey, now," Karl protested. "My wife and I run a secure establishment."

Henry was rubbing his beard, his prelude to an idea taking form. Cleo expected him to inquire about access to keys, rooms, or books. His question surprised her and made her glad he was her sleuthing date.

"The argument at breakfast," Henry said. "When Professor Weber told Kitty he knew what she was up to. What did she say?"

"Ah," Karl said, actually putting down his sparkling glass. "I'm glad you asked. That's the best part. She said, 'I know what *you've* been up to, darling.' Then he said, 'Frankly, my dear, I don't give a—'"

Karl cut himself off abruptly and reached for the glass. Giggles bubbled behind Cleo. Moments later, Kitty Peavey appeared at her side.

"Drinks all around, barkeep," Kitty exclaimed breathlessly, waving her diamond dangerously close to Cleo's nose. "We're celebrating. I said yes! My Dr. Dean and I are now officially engaged!" She lowered her eyelids seductively at Karl. "If you offer us a sweet deal, we'll consider coming back here for our wedding."

Karl shuddered, and Cleo doubted it was from the penguin-appropriate chill.

Cleo glanced over at Professor Weber. He stood stiffly as colleagues raised congratulatory toasts around him. He wasn't joining in. He wasn't professing or boasting or even looking pleased. To Cleo's eye, the newly engaged man looked stunned.

Chapter Seventeen

"I guess that argument between Kitty and her professor wasn't that serious after all," Cleo said.

She and Henry stood by a potted fern as large and flouncy as a peacock. Cleo edged behind a frond, feeling it gave her permission to gawk at the assembled bookdealers. She needn't have bothered to hide. All eyes were on Kitty and her lusty rendition of "Diamonds Are a Girl's Best Friend."

Professor Weber accepted congratulatory handshakes, still looking somewhat dazed. "Maybe the argument *was* serious," Henry said, surprising Cleo. Usually, Henry was the more optimistic and rosy-eyed between them. "What if Kitty feared Professor Weber was going to break up with her? Now she's made a big public announcement about saying yes. He'd look bad if he called off the engagement."

Cleo considered that. "Kitty seems like someone who likes to get her way. But what if it's the opposite? Professor Weber got *his* way, didn't he? His romantic rival is out of the way, and now the engagement he wanted is finally official. Karl could have misinterpreted their argument. It might have simply been a heated discussion about books."

Henry grinned. "Books do arouse passions, as you've often said."

Cleo nodded seriously. She had said it before, in past murder investigations too. "I'll say it again." She told him about Bernice Abernathy, her missing *Poirot Investigates*, and the atlases lacking maps.

Cleo said, "When I hinted that Hunter Fox might have 'borrowed' her valuable Poirot, Bernice said she'd like to kill him herself." Cleo sipped her drink. Much of the fizz had gone out of it. "Of course, that's just a common, awful saying. I certainly don't suspect Bernice. Not that she's not capable—Bernice's knees are more limber than mine and she does aqua aerobics—but she's legally blind these days. She couldn't have driven into town at night, let alone catch a man unaware in the alley. It goes to show, though. Hunter Fox got around town and made enemies over books."

Henry's shoulders slumped. He took a gulp of wine. "I hope Bernice's atlases are intact. They're gorgeous. I spent a lot of time assessing her library. I'd hoped she'd let me sell some of her books. I have a buyer who collects Agatha Christies and would treasure *Poirot Investigates*. Does that make me sound mercenary too? I worry that all of us bookdealers will look bad to you because of this business, Cleo."

"Never," Cleo said firmly. "You'd be helping her book find a worthy new home. Bernice would still have the book—or the money—if she'd gone through you. So would Dot. What still perplexes me is how Hunter found them."

"I certainly didn't give him their names and addresses," Henry said.

Cleo patted his arm. She knew he hadn't. "There's another visit I don't like." She reported on Professor Weber's visit to Dot's home.

Henry had already heard. News had spread around the fair. "Professor Weber made quite a show of going to return that book, calling it his presidential duty. I don't think he was happy about it. The bookdealers were mixed about Buddy's role too. Some praised Buddy's keen eye. Others were saying . . . well . . . that he was nosy and should have minded his own stall."

Cleo sided with praising Buddy.

"Look," she said, nodding toward the doorway. "There's Buddy now. I'd like to thank him—and pick his brain."

"A fellow snoop," Henry said. "Our sleuthing date is back on track."

* * *

Buddy beamed at Cleo's thanks. The collector of Georgia books and ephemera was looking jolly but pinched in an out-of-date blazer a few sizes too small. The royal-blue sleeves ended above his wrists and tightened around his shoulders. Strangely, the matching slacks ballooned too large and long and flopped over his well-worn boots.

He held a cocktail glass filled with bright-blue liquid, festooned in a little paper umbrella and orange slices. He'd raised it in greeting, calling it "something special to celebrate the happy couple."

Cleo glanced at the happy couple. Professor Weber appeared to be professing. Kitty had an arm looped through his and was sipping a massive blue drink similar to Buddy's.

Cleo shifted closer to Henry, who was asking Buddy about his day at the fair. A comforting list of book talk went by: items Buddy had sold, happy customers, nice conversations, intriguing items he meant to look for. Cleo let herself drift into bookish thoughts.

"I went by your cousin's store this afternoon, after the fair closed," Buddy said, snapping Cleo back to attention. "It's a real cute place. I'd have gone in, but it was packed! So many people, I thought it must have been a private party."

Cleo smiled. "That's a good way of putting it. It was a party of sorts, a show of support for Dot and the Drop By."

Buddy frowned. "Because of her troubles, being suspected of murder and all? Boy, this is a real nice and supportive place you've got here."

"No!" Cleo said and then felt bad when Buddy flushed and apologized.

"Sorry," Cleo said. "I mean, no one who knows Dot would ever suspect her of murder." Cleo felt her fingers cross in a fib. If Chief Culpepper could suspect Henry, he could suspect Dot too. She hurried on. "Dot's having a little bit of financial trouble at her store." She wasn't spilling any secret. People all around town knew now, and once Ollie launched his online funding campaign, anyone on the Internet could know too. "People came out to shop in a show of support."

Buddy approved. "I'll be sure to drop by and buy something myself. Miss Dot seems like a fine, upstanding lady. A lady who loves books is the best kind of lady in the world. In my humble opinion."

Cleo caught Henry giving her a mushy look. She blushed and reminded herself that they'd come on business.

"Tell us about finding Dot's book," Cleo said. "She's so happy to have it back. How did you happen to come by it?"

Buddy was attempting to sip his drink. The glass was fishbowl shaped and the floating orange slices and paper umbrella blocked access. Cleo idly wondered what the concoction was. She bet it was sweet and fruity, and she half wanted to try one herself. Once again, she reminded herself of their purpose. A killer could be among them. At the very least, clues could be. She had to stay alert.

Buddy managed a side slurp. A bit of blue dripped on his boot. "I was taking a little break, that's all. Kitty said she'd look out for my books and any buyers who might come by while I was gone. We're stall neighbors, you know, and I'd been watching hers quite a bit. She likes to go get coffee or chat with folks. This was the first time I asked for the return favor. I don't like leaving my stuff, but I wanted to go see what everyone else had. The big dealers, you know?" He twirled the little paper umbrella. "Like yours, Mr. Lafayette. I was heading for your display of gilded and illuminated pages."

Cleo never tired of looking at those either. Henry had a minor specialty in medieval manuscripts, full books but also partial pages and covers. He had some on display in a glass cabinet similar to her bookmobile case.

"Those pages are amazing, aren't they?" Cleo said. "To think of a scribe touching the parchment so long ago. It always gives me a thrill."

Buddy's eyes lit up. "That's the word. A thrill. I like to think of the paper too. Paper's so fragile, right? Yet it's rugged as all get out. Think of the hundreds of years those pages have been around." He flushed. "I'm sounding silly, aren't I?"

"Not at all!" Henry and Cleo said simultaneously.

They all found themselves grinning like giddy kids at book prom. "The fair really is a special event," Henry said. "I do hate to see it marred by tragedy and . . ."

"Bad behavior," Buddy said, filling in the blank. He looked sadly into his cheery drink.

Cleo felt bad for bringing him down. "You helped my cousin immensely," Cleo said. "She'd been really down, feeling tricked and misled. The return of that book helped her remember the goodness in folks."

Buddy flushed and mumbled something that sounded like "Aw, shucks."

Cleo couldn't help but smile. She hadn't heard an *aw shucks* in years.

"It was nothing," Buddy said. "Really, truly, nothing. Like I said, I was just browsing. When I got to Professor Weber's stall, he was busy talking to real customers, so I could take my time perusing without feeling like I was in the way. I saw that there book of birds and gave it a look. I remembered it was on that list the police gave out, the list of Miss Dot's missing books. Then I noticed the bookplate. I collect those, you know. Where'd Miss Dot get that plate done? It's beautiful."

Cleo explained the foreign-exchange student and their personalized bookplates. "I have my own and so does my friend, Mary-Rose. Our library does too. We all have the original plates for making more copies as we need. I could get you some if you like."

"That would be real nice," Buddy said. "I'd pay you—"

Cleo cut in with a refusal. "You've already paid us in kindness." She prompted him on with his story. "When you showed the book to Professor Weber, what did he say?"

Buddy shrugged. "To be honest? He looked kinda mad. It's subtle with that guy, but he got chillier, you know. He tried to brush it off too. When I showed him Miss Dot's signature, he told me it was in pencil and didn't mean anything. But then some local lady came by and confirmed it was Miss Dot's. Said she had been in a book group with Dot and knew it for sure."

Cleo gave silent thanks to diligent local booklovers and Buddy too.

Buddy shrugged. "I said I'd track down Miss Dot and have her come look at it. The prof, he said he'd handle it. He must have felt bad or embarrassed or whatever to take it back in person." He shoved aside an orange slice and sipped his drink. "I wish I could've looked through more of his books," he said. "He closed up his shop after that, threw a cover over everything, and basically told me to skedaddle."

Cleo turned to frown at the professor. A jolt shot up her middle. He stared straight back, at her and her little group.

Trying to cover, Cleo smiled brightly and raised her glass in a celebratory salute. He looked away, and she did too, unnerved by his reaction.

"Buddy," Cleo said. "I have some titles to add to that list of missing books, from other ladies around town. If I gave an expanded list to you, could you keep an eye out?"

"Sure could," Buddy said. "I've got a good memory for books." He began listing everything he'd seen on Professor Weber's stand to prove it. Cleo's hopes sank as the titles droned on. None sounded like the books she sought.

"And then a few about the afterlife and a real old book about medical astrology and another about communicating with the dead and magic and stuff," Buddy said, wrapping up. "That's sure not on Miss Dot's list. Doesn't sound like Professor Dean Weber, for that matter, although I guess they're kinda philosophy."

He and Henry chatted some more about the professor's collection. Other bookdealers joined them, medievalists who gabbed about Old English until Buddy drifted off, making excuses. Cleo didn't mind staying on the sidelines of the conversation. It gave her time to people-watch and mull over a possibility.

As the evening wore down, she and Henry congratulated the mismatched couple and commiserated with the twitchy innkeepers. They were on their way back home, Henry driving at his usual tortoise speed, when Cleo put her thoughts into words.

"Those astrology books that Professor Weber has . . . they sound like something Madame Romanov would like, don't they?"

Henry got her hint immediately. "Something she lost to a con man? Do you think that's how she knew Hunter Fox? I did talk to her about books once. She said she has some that might be valuable in magic circles. It's not my area of expertise, but I told her I'd be happy to do some research. We could ask her."

Cleo had her arm out the window, her hand waving in the warm night air. "She's unlikely to tell us. She'd be a suspect, just like Dot, if Hunter conned her out of valuable books."

Henry parked in front of Cleo's picket fence. They walked arm in arm to the door, where claws and paws scrabbled on the other side. Cleo was tired but reluctant for the evening to end.

"It's late," she said. "I think you should stay. You live next to a possible suspect."

"*I'm* a possible suspect," Henry said. "With a misdemeanor charge."

"All the more reason for me to keep an eye on you," Cleo said, reaching out and patting his soft, bearded chin. "Besides, your shop is haunted and you wouldn't want Mr. Chaucer to become possessed."

Henry smiled and pressed his hand to hers. "I gratefully accept." He followed her in and greeted his waggling pug. "I promise that Chaucy and I will not go walking at midnight ever again."

"At least until the killer's caught," Cleo said, locking the door behind him.

Chapter Eighteen

A ringing interrupted Cleo's dream. An insistent buzz followed closely by another and another fast after that. For a moment, she felt relief. Her dream had morphed into a terror but with no apparent monster, nothing visible or obviously scary. Like the murderer, she thought drowsily, someone ordinary. The buzz continued. Cleo's eyes popped open as Rhett stomped on her stomach and meowed.

On the other side of the bed, Henry mumbled and shifted. A pillow half covered his head. Was it the buzzing he was blocking, or had she been snoring again? Cleo glanced at the bedside clock. Six fifty-five.

On a typical Thursday morning, Cleo would be up by now. However, she and Henry had stayed up late talking. Ollie had dropped by too. He'd seen her kitchen light on and stopped in, excited about his online fund raiser. He'd already raised several thousand dollars in his Donate to the Drop By campaign. He swore that Dot was about to go viral. Cleo found that somehow disturbing. Viral had never seemed like something she'd want.

Downstairs, the buzz turned to noisy knocking.

"Oh, for heaven's sake!" Cleo whispered. She threw on a bathrobe and didn't bother with slippers. Rhett beat her down the stairs. He was sniffing, flat eared, at the door when she reached the foyer.

Cleo ran through possible visitors as she positioned a bifocal lens against the fish-eye peephole. Mary-Rose would wait quietly for a decent hour. So would Dot and other friends. Ollie wouldn't get up this early unless he'd stayed up all night. He'd never rudely buzz and pound.

Blurry beige filled the peephole. The police uniforms were beige. Gabby?

Cleo blinked to refocus. The beige blur continued to block her view. Someone was standing too close. Cleo looked down at Rhett. His ears remained back. He had a bad feeling about the visitor. So did she.

"Who is it?" Cleo called out, keeping the door solidly locked.

"Police!"

Cleo recognized the blustery bellow of Chief Culpepper.

"Open up! I know he's in there!"

Cleo repeated a whispered, "Oh, for heaven's . . ." She didn't bother to smile when she opened the door. She stood firm, fists on her hips, Rhett swishing his tail at her feet.

"Chief," Cleo said crisply. "This is awfully . . ." *Rude* came to mind. "Early and abrupt," she finished, filling the entrance so he couldn't barge in.

Over the years, she'd learned that Chief Culpepper awoke on the petulant side of bed. *Bless Mrs. Culpepper's heart*—but then the chief's wife got to hustle her grumpy husband off to work in the morning. The big man looked particularly grouchy this morning, wearing a pouty expression and suspenders resembling crime-scene tape.

Beyond his broad shoulders, Cleo noticed a welcome face. Gabby shot Cleo an apologetic look and mouthed, "Sorry."

"Good morning, Miss Cleo," Gabby called out, craning over the chief's shoulder. "We're sorry to bother you so early. We're looking for Henry."

"We have some more questions for your no-alibi boyfriend," the chief said. "And this." He waved a paper at Cleo's nose. She fought the impulse to bat it back.

"Henry's sleeping." However, as Cleo said this, a snuffling pug wobbled down the stairs. Mr. Chaucer reached the door, woofed, and then sneezed on the chief's boot. He was followed by shuffling slippers and a yawning Henry.

"Who is it?" Henry said, sounding drowsy. He sharpened up when he saw their guests. "Is something wrong?" he asked. "The shop? Is someone hurt?"

Cleo realized that annoyance had overridden what should have been her rational reaction to police at the door. Thank goodness no one was hurt. Other than Henry's spotless reputation.

"The chief has some questions," she said to Henry.

"And a warrant," Culpepper said. "Deputy, let's get a move on. Show them the court order."

Cleo accepted the paper, only because Gabby was the one extending it, again with that *sorry* look.

"It's a search warrant," Gabby explained, although Cleo had gathered as much. "To search the Gilded Page."

"Let's get back there," Chief Culpepper said. "We will build this case nail by nail, rock solid, and I didn't get up early to stand around waiting." He turned and stomped off down Cleo's steps.

Gabby hung back. She whispered, "He wanted to burst into the bookshop on a 'raid.' I'm really sorry to rat out your location here, Henry, but I didn't want the chief to get more worked up and break down your shop door."

"Deputy!" the chief bellowed from the driveway.

"Hush!" an angry female voice bellowed back. "Quit your yelling before it's seven!"

A humbled "Sorry, ma'am," came from the chief.

Wanda Boxer! Cleo had to smile. Wanda had managed to find a sentiment they shared. Everyone did have something in common.

* * *

"Why did they rouse me out of bed and drag me down here if they don't want me inside?" Henry said, peering inside the Gilded Page. He sounded a tad grumpy. Cleo empathized. She felt on edge too. First her dream, then the unpleasant wake-up call, and now the weather.

Wispy mare's tail clouds raced across the sky, riding a wind that felt like hot breath. Pollen clogged the blustery air. Everything, from the air to Cleo's mind, seemed hazy.

Mr. Chaucer sneezed. Cleo's nose twitched too, and her hair batted at her eyes. She'd be happier inside, but as soon as they'd gotten to Henry's shop, the chief had evicted them.

They weren't the only ones waiting outside. A police suv stood prominently at the curb, siren silent but lights flashing. Passing pedestrians stopped to inquire. A ladies' walking group paused to wonder if Cleo had found another body.

The wind gusted again, and Cleo nudged closer to the shop and Henry, who was staring through the window. He and the nosy pedestrians had a clear view, with all the lights shining inside.

Cleo said, "It'll be okay. Gabby's in there and . . ." Suddenly her shoulder was open to the wind. Henry was going inside. Cleo and Mr. Chaucer hurried after him.

"You can't do that," Henry said. His voice sounded strained, and Cleo guessed he was struggling to keep calm. She saw why.

Chief Culpepper held a book by its covers, splayed open, as he gave it a vigorous, upside-down shake.

"Why not?" the chief asked. "Because you're hiding something?"

"Because you're hurting that book!" Cleo exclaimed. "You'll break its spine." She rummaged in her purse and found her cell phone. When trying to take a photo, Cleo often messed up and pressed video record instead. This time she wanted video. She aimed the lens at the chief.

"Hey," he said. "Shut that off, Miss Cleo."

"I won't," Cleo said firmly. "I'll call a lawyer if I have to." Her daughter-in-law Angela was a lawyer, and a good one too. Unfortunately, Angela was out of town on a family vacation. If Cleo needed legal help, she had no doubt Angela would hurry back. Angela loved her work, and she wasn't a big fan of vacations. Cleo understood both. Whenever someone suggested that Cleo retire or take a cruise or an extended trip down to Florida, she could only think *why?* Why leave when she loved her job, home, family, friends, and cat?

But Angela was far away in North Carolina. Cleo thought of another threat, more immediate and possibly more terrifying too. "My grandson is an expert in viral online causes. He'll share this video to the worldwide web of booklovers, and you'll be in trouble."

Chief Culpepper's small eyes widened. He righted the book and made a show of flipping delicately through its pages, page by page, with the flick of his thick index finger, until the same finger moved toward his lips.

"No! No, no, don't lick your finger!" Henry exclaimed, waving his hands.

Cleo moved in closer with her camera. Her hand was shaking, but she figured that was fine. Horror flicks these days prized shaky camerawork.

"Ah, Chief?" Gabby said. "This warrant only permits us to look for the possible murder weapon. A hammerlike object? I don't think it would fit in a book, but how about I check all the shelves just in case?" She added, "The boring grunt work. You'll understand the workshop better than I will . . ." While the chief's back was still turned, she shot Cleo an exasperated look.

Cleo appreciated her intervention and appeal to the chief's self-importance. He stomped off toward the back, agreeing that of course he'd understand the tools better.

"Thank you," Cleo said softly when they heard him clattering around the workshop.

"I *am* sorry," Gabby whispered back. "I can't argue with the chief's rationale for a search, though. We're missing a murder weapon. We have to look."

Henry was tending to the book Culpepper had left sprawled on top of a shelf. He ran a hand over its cover before carefully easing it back among its book companions. He joined Gabby and Cleo. "But I thought you had the weapon. My awl."

A bang came from the back, followed by an "Ow!" and cursing.

Gabby bit her lower lip. "We're looking for a hammerlike object now. Something blunt, with this size head." She indicated a circle the size of a walnut.

"But Mr. Fox was stabbed . . ." Cleo said.

"Not before he was whacked on the back of the head." Gabby grimaced. "The medical examiner just completed the autopsy. There was a double homicide in Claymore. We had to wait in line."

Cleo's first thought was that awful things happened in Claymore, the sprawling, restless town to their west. She quickly corrected herself. Awful things happened in Catalpa Springs too. She took Henry's hand and squeezed.

"I'm missing a hammer," Henry said quietly.

Cleo felt the same urge she'd had with Dot. To hush the dear man up. He was already in enough trouble. Both he and Dot were too helpful for their own good.

"How do you know?" Gabby asked.

Instead of answering, Henry led the way to his workshop.

The chief's ample backside greeted them. He was bent over, pawing through a box of the dense cardboard used for covers. "Bunches of junk everywhere," he mumbled. "How's anyone supposed to find anything in here?"

Henry pointed to the pegboard wall, where the white paint outlines marked each tool's proper place. He'd tidied recently. Tools filled all the outlines except one: a hammer with a long handle, bulging head, and viciously clawed end.

*　*　*

"I noticed when I was putting up my tools the other night," Henry said. He and Cleo sat on one side of his workbench. Gabby and the chief were on the other. Mr. Chaucer was under the table, snoring. "I kept thinking it would turn up, but it hasn't."

Cleo was grateful that the chief seemed to be losing interest. He'd accepted coffee from Henry and was letting Gabby ask the questions. Gabby always asked good questions.

Gabby led Henry through a timeline of the hammer's last-known whereabouts.

"I'm quite sure I had it before the social I held over here," Henry said. "That was the night before opening day. It's tradition. The hosting shop owner—that's me—invites all the antiquarians to come by. I displayed some of my favorite antique tools on my table here. I didn't put most back on the pegboard afterward. I just stuffed them in my carrying box to take to the demonstration the next day."

"The demonstration that many people attended," Cleo reminded everyone, and especially Chief Culpepper. "At the table that was open to the public and left unattended." Guilt gnawed at her. Henry had left his table unattended because she was chasing after Dot, butting into Dot's troubles.

The chief rubbed his forehead. "I need more coffee." He held out his cup and Cleo and Henry jumped up, vying to refill it.

Caffeine seemed to wake up the chief's interest in other suspects. "So you're again claiming that any of those book types, or anyone, could have strolled by and swiped the hammer, like that awl. Then, or the next day at your demo table?"

"Yes," Cleo answered, since Henry was hanging his head. She guessed he didn't want to pin the blame on his colleagues.

"Was anyone else here for the social?" Gabby asked. "Other than fellow booksellers, I mean?"

"I dropped by briefly," Cleo said.

The chief muttered, "Of course you did."

Henry's eyes drifted to the distance. If he could have seen through walls, he'd have been looking at the alley, the crime scene.

"My neighbor dropped by," Henry said. "She got a package of mine by mistake. She didn't stay, just came through to find me in the workshop."

"Your neighbor Madame Romanov?" Cleo turned to Gabby. "Have you asked her whether she knew Hunter Fox?"

"Mrs. Watkins," the chief snapped. "The police are doing the questioning here."

Cleo did her best to look contrite. She knew Gabby would tell her later anyway.

"This hammer," Gabby said, guiding the conversation back to the reason for their search. "Does the outline on the pegboard give its general shape and length? Could you positively identify it as yours if it turns up?"

Henry could. He opened his workshop laptop and produced a series of photographs from all angles, some with a ruler included.

Rather than expressing gratitude, the chief frowned. "Why all the photos of a hammer?" he demanded.

A flush rose over Henry's beard and spread to the tips of his prominent ears. "For posting to a bookbinders' tool forum." He shot Cleo a bashful look. "It's a chat group. We talk about techniques and, well, tools mostly. I guess I'm a geek online."

Cleo thought it was sweet. She could see how it would be fun to chat with friends all over the world with similar bookish interests.

Gabby scanned through the photos. "It's the right size. Vicious-looking thing . . ." She glanced over the screen and added, "Sorry. I'm sure it's perfectly nice for what it's meant for, but that claw part looks like something off a pterodactyl."

Henry explained. "It's called a backing hammer, also known as a folding tool. The single claw is used to manipulate the spine during the rounding process. To create a hinge on the book board, allowing the cover to open."

He reached for a nearby book and ran his finger down the cusped curve between spine and cover.

Cleo marveled. Here she spent her days around books, and she had never particularly pondered how that common curve was so essential.

The chief cursed under his breath. "I don't want to know what it does to books. I simply need to know if it killed someone. If you own it, Mr. Lafayette, and I find you're hiding it, then that's two murder weapons. Two! That and lying to the police would make you a pretty good suspect, wouldn't it? Of course, if you cared to confess and explain yourself . . ."

Henry blanched. Mr. Chaucer leaned into Henry's shins.

Cleo thrust her fists to her hips. She knew the chief was making valid points. However, he was missing the one fact that outshone them all. Henry was a good person.

She couldn't change the chief's mind by telling him that. Instead, she said, "Henry had absolutely no motive to hurt that man."

"Unlike your cousin," Culpepper countered. He downed his coffee and exhaled with satisfaction.

Cleo worried he'd had too much of a caffeine boost. "Why, that's just as absurd. Dot would never—"

The chief held up his hand. "Let's get all our murder weapons in a row first, shall we? Deputy, search the rest of this workshop and look for that whatcha-call-it hammer. Once we find that, we can hammer in our investigative nails." He looked pleased with his play on words in a way Cleo didn't like.

She didn't like his final words to Henry either.

"I'll be seeing you soon, Mr. Lafayette," he said, making a hammering gesture. "We have a lot to talk about."

Chapter Nineteen

A disapproving clucking met Cleo at her picket gate. Cleo winced. She knew that sound. Wanda Boxer was warming up for a tongue-lashing. Two options came to mind. Cleo could duck and hustle around the side of the house to her back door. Or she could face the inevitable, already in progress.

"I never!" Wanda declared, her voice like a rake across a sidewalk. "First the police haul your boyfriend in for lying. Now they come by raiding your home at dawn. You're bringing down our neighborhood, Cleo. Bringing it down!"

Wanda stood beside a camellia. She looked pleased. The shrub looked tortured.

Cleo strode briskly up her pathway. "Good morning, Wanda," she said, as if her neighbor's rudeness had sailed over on mute. "Lovely day." She was glad now that Henry and Mr. Chaucer had stayed back at the Gilded Page. Henry had given Gabby permission to search his entire shop and his apartment too. He had nothing to hide, he'd said.

Cleo believed him. She felt that Gabby must too. By extending her search to every book and reading nook, Gabby could then surely tell the chief they'd found nothing. They could move on to other suspects, like Kitty and Professor Weber and Catalpa Springs' premier psychic.

"It reflects badly on the neighborhood *and* your library, you shacking up with a potential killer," Wanda bellowed. "Your cousin's still a big-time suspect too, isn't she?" A *tsk-tsk* carried in the blustery breeze, and then Wanda turned disturbingly cheery. "Ah, Mrs. Stolberg, have you heard? Cleo's dating a murder suspect!"

Mrs. Stolberg, a neighbor two houses down, had been strolling up the sidewalk with her wolfhound. Hearing Wanda, the woman veered herself and her dog into the street. Wise move, Cleo thought. Traffic was light in their neighborhood, and better to risk a speeding car than a head-on encounter with Wanda on a spring morning.

So rude, Cleo thought as she hurried to her porch. She bit her tongue. From reading magazines in Words on Wheels, Cleo knew that one should avoid engaging with a bully or the modern equivalent: a troll. *Troll* seemed apt for Wanda, lurking amid her devastated landscape.

Cleo yanked open her door and hurtled into the calm sanctuary of her front porch.

Wanda's words wormed through the screen. "I'm retracting my alibi for your boyfriend too!" Wanda yelled. "You tricked me!"

Cleo fumbled with her keys, urgency making her muddled. For a moment, the nightmare feeling returned, the feeling of a pursuer closing in. But like in the dream, there was nothing obvious, nothing there beyond Wanda and her words.

Ill words could strangle and terrify too, Cleo thought. As soon as the killer was caught, she'd turn her attention to gardening. She'd get Ollie to help her plant a thick evergreen hedge along her border with Wanda. Images of spiky hollies or a dense bamboo grove filled Cleo's head.

Once inside, Cleo exhaled. "Unseemly," she informed Rhett Butler, who bounded to the foyer. "Uncouth," she vented. "There is no excuse for such bad behavior."

Rhett yelled a meow that Cleo chose to take as agreement. Her cat scampered off to the kitchen, where Cleo fed them both treats. Tuna Delight for Rhett. The last of the strawberries and a toasted biscuit for herself.

The belated breakfast brightened Cleo's mood. So did plans for the day ahead. She had a busy bookmobile schedule, including a stop outside the book fair this morning. Around eleven, she'd go by the elementary school for recess, always a fun stop. And after lunch? That's when she hoped to fit in some sleuthing, namely visiting Madame Romanov.

She pondered her approach when it came to the psychic. Should she give a pretext for her visit? Dropping by for a palm reading or a talk with Hunter's spirit? Looking for Henry's misdelivered mail, Madame's reason for visiting his shop the night of the social?

Cleo got up to wash her dishes. She knew two things: dishes left in the sink didn't wash themselves, and she didn't want to go see Madame Romanov on her own.

*   *   *

The wispy clouds had grown brooding cumulus heads by the time Cleo parked near the Depot. She sat in her captain's seat, flipping through a gardening magazine and watching folks hurry by, umbrellas in hand. A few spits of rain dotted her windshield.

Cleo liked rainy days, the best for cozying up with a good book. Unfortunately, such days tended to drive down bookmobile business. She'd had a handful of visitors, most dropping by to chat, presumably about the weather.

"Looks like rain," they'd say, before edging toward the topic of murder and Cleo's theories. She consoled herself by touting the innocence of everyone's top two suspects, Henry and Dot.

She was getting ready for her next stop at the school when a flash of bright color caught her eye. Kitty Peavey strolled from the Depot. She paused under the eaves and then out to the dim daylight, palm up, checking the weather. Cleo expected the "proprietress of Southern Delights" to retreat from the hair-frizzing mist. Instead, Kitty sashayed down the sidewalk and straight for Words on Wheels.

"I've been meaning to visit your cute bus," Kitty said, entering with a cloud of perfume. "Aw, what a sweet kitty cat," she cooed at Rhett, who sat on a shelf, looking grumpily out at the weather.

Rhett immediately flopped and purred, and Kitty gushed more pretty-kitty praise.

Cleo's feelings toward the woman rose. She reminded herself that Kitty was a suspect, for murder and various book crimes. Thus warned, Cleo extended cautious greetings. "His name is Rhett Butler," she admitted when Kitty asked.

Kitty clapped. "How cute! You and your cousin really are true *GWTW* fans!"

"We are," Cleo said, swept by a chilliness that wasn't blown in with the weather. "She has the police looking for her valuable signed copy, the copy Hunter Fox acquired under . . . misleading circumstances." Cleo's manners kept her from outright bad-mouthing the recently deceased.

"Bless him," Kitty said with a pout. "That man was the best scout ever. He could sniff out high-value books like a bloodhound, I tell you. 'Look low, look high,' that was his motto." Seeing Cleo's perplexed expression, she said. "On the shelves, for treasures other buyers miss. I suppose it's the same in the library. Folks focus on eye height."

"It is true," Cleo said. She was guilty of it too, although she did have the dual excuses of bad knees and a height of barely five feet three inches.

Kitty shook her head. "Poor Hunt. He told me he was coming into something *big* too. It's a shame."

"Big?" Cleo asked, her interest piqued. She stood to lean back against the dash and watch Kitty's face. "A rare book?"

"I don't know," Kitty said with a sorrowful sigh. "All he said was, he wasn't going to have to spend so much time digging around dusty old bookshelves and attics and chatting folks up." She looked up, and Cleo saw a true tear in her eye. Kitty recovered quickly, flicking her hand and leaning back down to inspect Cleo's traveling display.

"Why, this is cute too," Kitty said. "What a sweet idea to display these old due-date cards. But why are they special enough to care about?"

"Signatures," Cleo said, stepping to the case. "There's a former governor who grew up in Catalpa Springs." She pointed out a long-ago mayor and a minor-league baseball player. "And the best, the author Shirley Macon James. I'm sure you know, she lived just outside Catalpa Springs for a spell in the 1950s. She wrote her novel—"

"*Into the Waves*," Kitty breathed, clasping her hands. "She wrote that around *here*? Oh my goodness, I'd clean forgotten. You all should be putting that in your tourism ads, instead of that lie about this place being safe. Shirley was such a timid little thing, wasn't she? Bless her heart."

Kitty had leaned so low her breath fogged the glass. She was squinting hard, and Cleo wondered if vanity kept her from wearing eyeglasses.

"You have a *signed* copy of her book too? Oh, my!"

"A second edition," Cleo said, aiming for modesty, but with pride seeping through. The reclusive author had dreaded book signings and passed away young, making autographed copies of any edition a rarity.

"That is a true delight." Kitty tapped the Plexiglas with her right index finger. The nail was shiny red with a perfectly long, square tip. Cleo recalled Kitty fussing with that same nail on the morning of Hunter's death. She must have had it fixed. Cleo wondered how she'd broken it. *In a scuffle?* Goose bumps rose up Cleo's arm. Kitty, by her own admission, had been with Hunter the night of his death. They had a business relationship and possibly a romantic one too. Cleo knew money and passion were both prime motives for murder.

Kitty tapped faster, bringing Cleo's mind back to the bookmobile and blustery day. The taps ended in a decisive thump. Kitty straightened. "I *have* to have this." Her eyes fixed on Cleo. "Let's deal. Tell me your price. We'll work down from there."

"I'm sorry," Cleo said, the apology a polite formality only. "This book is not for sale. It's a *library* book, part of our special collection. We don't even lend it out. I'm thrilled you recognize Miss James. Gothic romance isn't so well known, nor is she. As you know, this was her only book. She passed away far too young." A car-versus-pedestrian accident had taken her life, eerily similar to the tragedy that took young Margaret Mitchell. Sadness struck Cleo. What other books might the world have enjoyed if those women had lived longer?

A cloud passed over Kitty's face too.

"It's tragic," Cleo said, realizing she'd tactlessly mentioned death to a woman who'd just suffered a loss.

"Fifteen hundred," Kitty said.

"What?" Cleo was momentarily taken aback. "Oh, the price? No, I'm serious, Miss Peavey. The book is not for sale. The special collection is—"

"Oh, don't say 'special,'" Kitty said. "Tell me, who around here comes to see this *special* book? Anyone? Who appreciates it?"

Hardly anyone, Cleo thought guiltily. The special collection was housed in the Reference Room at the main library. Patrons visited the room for its wood-paneled splendor and solemn silence. Few, however, ever asked to see the books locked in the glass-fronted shelves.

Kitty continued, waggling a chastising finger at Cleo. "Don't tell me you and your library staff appreciate it, either. I mean, who *really* cares? I, on the other hand, will *love* this book and take proper care of it."

"We take good care of our books," Cleo said. "Patrons regularly visit the special collection." Her cheeks flushed, knowing she was tiptoeing to the precipice of an untruth. When Cleo had checked the request record for Shirley Macon James's signed work, she'd been shocked to see the book hadn't felt the touch of a hand in over three years. Cleo vowed to do more.

"I'm highlighting the book here to build up interest," Cleo said.

Kitty curled her lip. "By driving Miss Shirley around in a derelict bus? It's *warm* in here, in case you haven't noticed. Worse, it's humid. Do you even have air conditioning?"

"Of course," Cleo said, not mentioning that the AC wheezed tepid until Words on Wheels reached highway speeds. Forty-five miles per hour achieved mildly temperate. Fifty and above offered a chance of chilly.

Cleo patted her hair, "This display is only temporary. Back at the library, we have nice, cold, dehumidified conditions." But not as arctic as at the Myrtles Bed and Breakfast. Most library books and library patrons didn't need to be refrigerated.

Kitty hovered close to the case again, running her finger in a circle over the book below. When she stepped back, her hand glided over the latches holding the portable display case on the shelf.

"Can I touch the book?" she asked.

In other circumstances, Cleo would have readily agreed. Kitty, however, was a known book thief.

"Ah . . . not today," Cleo said.

"Oh well," Kitty said, her tone cheery again. "Cute case, nicer book. I'll get my hands on it someday. Soon, I hope." She left with a singsong, "'Bye, for now!"

Air seemed to whoosh out with her and then right back in a misty gust. Cleo closed the door firmly, feeling a sudden need to protect the books from the uncontrolled climate and Kitty Peavey too.

Chapter Twenty

"So . . . we're lying?" Mary-Rose held a shopping bag in one hand and a large purse slung shieldlike across her chest. Dressed in a rosy raincoat and red rubber boots, she looked ready for the weather. And battle.

"No," Cleo said, automatically fibbing. Cleo glanced across the street to Madame Romanov's purple-shingled cottage and said, "We'll give a partial truth. We'll tell Madame Romanov that we're interested in her second sight. That's true. I *am* interested."

Mary-Rose made a scoffing sound. "I'm sure you are, Cleo. You're *interested* in whether she'll slip up and drop a clue."

"Or drop one on purpose," Cleo said. "She might want to tell us something."

Mary-Rose's eyes narrowed. "What if she did it? What if *she's* the killer? What's our plan then?"

Cleo had called Mary-Rose after lunch. Her friend had immediately intuited that Cleo was looking for backup. They stood where they'd met up, at the corner across from Henry's shop, with a fine view of the crime-taped alley and Madame Romanov's cottage. Individual shingles were painted in varying shades of lavender, grape, and eggplant, like scales on a psychedelic lizard. A light glowed behind lace curtains, and a neon sign flashed OPEN: *Welcome. The Seer Sees All.*

"Well . . ." Cleo said, hedging. In the case that Madame was a killer, Cleo's plan was hoping the psychic didn't give her guilt away by attacking them. She mentally acknowledged that it wasn't her best plan ever.

"Oooh," Mary-Rose said. "I know what we can do. We'll ask her to 'see' how the killer did it. That way, she can say without implicating herself. That worked on Ted Bundy, the serial killer. I just saw a documentary. He gave up all sorts of sins, talking in a hypothetical third person. It was creepy beyond creepy."

Mary-Rose rested her canvas shopping bag on her boots. Green-gray curls of kale poked out. She'd been at the farmers' market and then to Dot's, where she'd bought an "excessive" quantity of chocolate bars.

Cleo considered no quantity of chocolate excessive, especially on a cloudy day with talk of serial killers. She was about to propose that they have some chocolate, for fortification and courage, when Mary-Rose hoisted her bag and strode across the street. Mary-Rose was tugging open the psychic's creaky wire gate when a sunny greeting sailed up the sidewalk.

"Hey, ladies." Gabby Honeywell strolled toward them, her ponytail swinging and a large backpack slung over one shoulder.

"Hi, Gabby," Mary-Rose said, frozen halfway through the gate. "Nothing going on here!"

"Exactly what all the innocent people say to cops." Gabby grinned at Cleo, head shaking. "I was just finishing up my fruitless search of the Gilded Page."

She paused while Cleo exclaimed, "Of course it was fruitless!"

Gabby continued. "Imagine my surprise, looking out the upstairs window. My favorite neighbor and my favorite pancake maker, heading for a witness's home, acting *furtive*."

Mary-Rose dropped her shopping bag and set about repinning her loose bun, murmuring about "furtive."

Cleo went straight to confessing. "We're just visiting. I think Madame knows something."

"You think she'll tell you outright?" Gabby said, adjusting her backpack. "Or do you plan to trick it out of her?"

"*Trick* sounds dishonest," Cleo said.

"We're lying," Mary-Rose said, a hairpin between her lips.

Lie sounded worse. "Madame is the one lying," Cleo said. "I'm sure she knew Hunter Fox. She might have been a victim of his book scouting. She has—or had—magic books she considered valuable. People like to talk with me about books. She might reveal something she wouldn't tell you."

"That's the truth," Mary-Rose affirmed, patting her redone bun. "Cleo's like a book whisperer."

Gabby was scowling at the little cottage with its wild purple scales and riotous garden. "It's not a *bad* idea," Gabby conceded. "Madame wouldn't let me inside when I interviewed her. I wondered why. But I don't like the idea of you ladies going in there alone. What if you're right? If she had bad dealings with Hunter Fox, then she's a murder suspect."

"Oh, we have a plan for that too," Mary-Rose said. "We're going to get her talking in the hypothetical, like Ted Bundy."

Gabby rubbed her temple as if pained. "How about this? I'll wait right outside, and if anything—anything at all—doesn't seem right, you leave immediately, okay? If you can't leave, yell. Loudly."

Cleo nodded obligingly. She didn't predict they'd be shouting.

Mary-Rose, however, was looking worryingly eager. "Leave it to me," she said. "I'm an acclaimed amateur screamer." She turned and unlatched the gate.

Gabby raised an eyebrow.

"Community theater," Cleo explained. "Mary-Rose did the *Phantom of the Opera* scream several years running."

"So listen for that," Mary-Rose called back.

*   *   *

"She certainly likes wind chimes," Cleo said.

"It's like an infestation of 'em," Mary-Rose said, frowning.

Cleo understood her friend's reaction. The gusts sent up cacophonies of clanking in every discordant tone. Chimes hung all around the porch, from trees, and even from a bird feeder, where a harried finch flung seed to the ground.

Mary-Rose added to the ringing. She pressed her finger on a doorbell that screeched.

Unearthly *wooooo* sounds surrounded them.

Cleo spun, her eyes scanning all directions, including upward. A bird's nest nestled in the upper right corner of the porch. Behind the tight circle of twigs hovered a black box with a mesh front.

"Speakers," Cleo said, pointing. She turned and identified three more in the other corners. "Surround sound," she added with distaste. Cleo found the technology disorienting and dizzying, even in movies.

Mary-Rose wedged her finger into the buzzer. "Nice," she said as the ghostly howls surrounded them once more. "I'm thinking of getting surround sound for my sun porch."

"You are?" Cleo realized she should sound more supportive. "I mean, how nice."

"Of course, I wouldn't want it making these silly sounds," Mary-Rose said. "I suppose it adds to the fun, though. Listen, Cleo, I had a thought. We should warm Madame up before we start asking about stolen books and murder. What if I say I want to contact my great-gran, the one who inflicted freckles and bony ankles on me?"

"You have lovely ankles," Cleo countered, but she saw another potential trouble. Mary-Rose loved to get caught up in a good story, especially campfire ghost tales. Inconceivably to Cleo, Mary-Rose utterly adored getting scared. "We have to be on guard," Cleo warned. "Don't let her lull you with sound effects and ghost stories. She's a salesperson too, like those appliance salesmen you cautioned me about the other day. She's selling a scam."

"That's half the fun, isn't it?" Mary-Rose said. "I want to see how she does it."

A voice came at them from all directions. "The other world is watching. The beyond sees all . . ."

Mary-Rose grinned back at Cleo. "Don't make the beyond angry, Cleo Jane," she whispered. "Don't you worry, either. I am ready to scream." She inhaled deeply as the door swung open, seemingly on its own.

Mary-Rose stepped boldly in. Cleo followed with more reasonable caution. She peeked behind the door, expecting Madame Romanov to pop out and yell, "Boo!" The reality was scarier. No one was there. They were met only by the thick scent of incense.

An antique globe lamp glowed dimly in a corner. Potted plants clogged the windows, and filmy fabrics with shimmery threads plumed from the ceiling and walls. A round table took center stage, dressed in purple satin, like the floor-to-ceiling curtains behind it.

"Look, a crystal ball!" Mary-Rose exclaimed, pointing to the centerpiece. "Oh, this *will* be good." She called out, "Yoo-hoo, Madame? Beyond? Anyone home? We've come to commune with the spirits."

Cleo's eyes adjusted to the dimness and zeroed in on something that could tell them more than any crystal ball.

"Books!" Cleo started for a wall of shelves, partially covered by filmy fabric. She lifted the cloth and tipped her head to read the spines. The titles revealed Madame's interest in crystals and Russian history, astrology, and dog training. The shelf at eye level was tight with books. Cleo remembered Kitty's words, Hunter Fox's scouting motto: *Look high, look low.* The lower shelves were filled. The upper had a gap of several inches, with books from either side tipping into it. Cleo stood on her tiptoes, but the shelf was above her level.

"Sit! Sit before the crystal seer," a female voice demanded, coming from above and all directions. "Visitor, step away from the books! Move to the crystal ball."

"You heard her," Mary-Rose said. "To the crystal, Cleo."

"It doesn't sound like Madame Romanov," Cleo whispered, following Mary-Rose to the table, where chairs were wedged tight as teeth. They pulled out two and sat with knees bumping.

Mary-Rose whispered, "Play along. Remember? We're all fibbing here."

The curtains behind the table rippled. Cleo heard scuffling and feet and, she was sure, a muffled giggle. What was going on? A wavering, otherworldly voice filled the room, female but youthful.

"To whom do you wish to speak?"

"I'll go," Mary-Rose whispered. "Amelia-Rose Honoree," she said, loudly giving her great-gran's name.

"She knew you were coming," the voice proclaimed. "She says she wants you to . . . ah . . . see her in your every freckle."

"Oh . . ." Mary-Rose said, nudging Cleo. "The family freckles! That almost gives me chills."

"Almost," Cleo muttered.

"Amelia-Rose also says you should stand strong on your feet and legs," the voice said. "You carry her . . . her . . ." Mumbles and mutters filtered out before the voice blurted, "Her visage! You have her visage."

"Yep, that's the truth," Mary-Rose said. "My bony ankles are her very visage, right between my strong feet and legs." She nudged Cleo. "Your turn. Go ahead, ask for your dead guy."

But now Cleo had a different question. She wanted to know who was behind the curtain. *The Wizard of Oz* came to mind, one of her favorite movies and books too. Her grandmother had owned a later edition of the original 1900 novel, replete with gorgeous illustrations. Somewhere in a long line of relatives and visitors, book borrowing and swapping, it had become lost. Cleo made a mental note to look for a copy at the fair.

Cleo cleared her throat. "Madame, will *you* appear to us?"

Mary-Rose whispered, "Good one."

The curtains ruffled and rippled. A crash sounded in the back, followed by a muffled curse. "The spirits are restless," said the voice. The *woooo*s began again. "Feel the spirits approaching."

"I do feel something!" Mary-Rose exclaimed, wiggling in her seat.

Cleo did too, a bump at her ankles, fast and firm . . . and furry? Claws skittled on the wood floor.

"Oh!" Mary-Rose said. "Oh my gracious, the spirit just licked my foot! Begone, beast, or I'll scream."

"No!" Cleo cried, imagining Gabby racing in, gun drawn. She pulled back the satin tablecloth to reveal a chubby dachshund grinning up at them. "Behold, the beast," she said to Mary-Rose.

"Slim!" the voice hissed from behind the curtains. "Slim! Come, Slim."

"Aw, little angel!" Mary-Rose proclaimed, bending to pet the panting pup.

While Mary-Rose gushed on Slim, Cleo slipped out of her seat. Slim was no Toto. She'd have to pull back the curtains herself.

The heavy satin opened with a fine plume of dust, revealing two young women. Teenagers, Cleo guessed. Goths, she suspected, although perhaps there was an updated term for the tortured-hair, blackened-eye look.

"Hey, you're not supposed to see behind the curtain," said one. She had blonde hair reminiscent of Wanda Boxer's shrubbery. Shredded. Pained. Hacked. Her companion wore all black, from her outfit and heavily ringed eyes to what looked like rusty nails protruding from her earlobes.

Cleo gave them her best grandmotherly smile. "Oh, you were very good. You had us fooled. Are you apprentices of Madame Romanov?"

They exchanged a look that Cleo easily read. *Old people are so gullible.* Cleo held her smile, happy to play along. For now.

"Sure," rusty-nail girl said. "Yeah, we're apprentices to the Great Madame Romanov."

Her blonde choppy-haired friend snorted.

"Lovely," Cleo said. "I'm sure Madame Romanov feels fortunate to have such fine apprentices. Where is she, by the way? My friend and I want to get in touch with her, and the spirits too, of course."

"She's somewhere . . . beyond here," the blonde said, jutting out her chin. "Do you want your palms read? Fortunes? Tarot? Reiki? We can do that."

Cleo politely declined. "When you say that Madame Romanov is 'somewhere,' where might that be?"

The teens stared back blankly. They could be skilled actresses, or they might not know. Cleo waited, stretching out the silence, an interrogation technique she'd effectively employed as a mother, a librarian, and a sleuth.

The blonde broke first. "Look, she's somewhere, okay? It's fine we're here. I'm her niece and we're, like, magic apprentices, like you said."

Cleo interpolated key information. Madame didn't know they were here. She might not approve. They didn't know where she was.

"Do you know *why* she left?" Cleo asked.

The blank looks returned until the rusty-nail girl said with teen exasperation, "Because she wanted to. Maybe the spirits told her to go. She sees spirits." She paused and then intoned darkly, "The seer sees all."

"Does she, now?" Mary-Rose popped her head inside the curtain. "Why, look at this, behind-the-scenes sorcery. Isn't this cozy?"

Chubby Slim trotted in, wagged his tail, woofed sharply, and ran back out.

"Slim!" the rusty-nail girl said, clapping her hands at him. He didn't reappear.

The room *was* rather cozy, Cleo thought. Once, it had probably been a dining room. Now curtains blocked the windows and wires and cables stretched between overtaxed outlets and electronic devices. Cleo hazily identified routers and a multiline phone, headsets, and a big-screen computer showing a dozen or so tiny video images. She stepped closer, recognizing the scenes.

"Hey, that's private," rusty-nail girl said, stepping to block Cleo.

Playing up the image of elderly befuddlement, Cleo said, "Look at this, Mary-Rose. Madame can watch a dozen TV channels at once."

"What fun!" Mary-Rose said, clapping her hands and playing along. "We could watch all our shows, Cleo Jane. Oooh, and look, there's a pretty photo of the porch and the crystal ball and Slim, chewing on a chair leg, naughty little angel! She *can* see everything, even the birds out in the garden." Mary-Rose pointed to a square image just off-center. In it, the nervous finch flicked away his seed.

Madame could also hear, Cleo guessed. Headphones were plugged into the machine. If clients chatted on her porch or in the parlor, Madame could listen, gathering clues for her supposed fortune-telling.

Another scene interested Cleo even more. A camera showed the back edge of the carriage garage, a line of trash bins, and fluttering yellow ribbon. The alley. *The crime scene.*

Cleo backed away slowly, trying to cover her thrill. Madame Romanov might have recorded the killing. Gabby could get a warrant, and Henry could be cleared, and—

Worry interrupted Cleo's good thoughts. Why hadn't Madame come forward? Where was she?

"You really don't know where your aunt is?" Cleo asked the niece. "I don't want to alarm you, but there was a crime recently."

"Yeah, like everyone knows that," the niece said.

"Everyone," her friend confirmed. "You, like, shouldn't go back in that alley. It has bad spirits. We can feel them."

Cleo felt frustration, but a growing conviction that the niece had no clue as to her aunt's whereabouts. She touched Mary-Rose's elbow and forced a bright smile at the teens. "We'll come back when Madame is home. Any idea when that will be?"

They nodded their heads in a synchronized negative.

"You sure you don't want a Reiki session?" the friend said. "Palm reading? Future prediction? Past-life regression? We're as good as Madame Romanov."

"I'm sure you are," Cleo said truthfully, digging in her purse for tips. "Thank you for your time. This has been very *entertaining*." *And very useful*. She predicted that Gabby would think so too.

Chapter
Twenty-One

L ater that afternoon, Cleo went to find Henry at the fair. His stall was at the far end of the Depot. The location offered a good view of the other dealers and visitors. However, Cleo guessed it wasn't the best spot for drawing in customers. The two tables closest to him stood empty, and Henry had his nose in a book. Mr. Chaucer lay under the table, flat on his back, his legs twitching in a canine dreamtime romp.

"You're all alone back here," Cleo said, rousing Henry. Mr. Chaucer kept on snoring.

"Not quite." Henry bobbed his head backward. Behind him, at another otherwise empty table, slouched Gabby's colleague, Sergeant Earl Tookey. The young sergeant wore civilian clothes, a rumpled plaid button-down, jeans, and a University of Georgia Bulldogs cap. The hat covered his eyes. His mouth gaped slightly open, and Cleo guessed he was sleeping as soundly as Mr. Chaucer.

"What is Sergeant Tookey doing?" Cleo said, suspecting she already knew the answer.

"He's been my shadow today," Henry confirmed. "Seems I'm under police surveillance." He smiled. "I prefer to think of it as police protection. There is a murderer about."

Cleo huffed before reminding herself that Sergeant Tookey was a nice young man with a keen interest in cookbooks. In his free time, the sergeant competed in barbecue contests and was a local celebrity for his winnings in smoked-meat categories.

"Police time would be better spent looking for the murderer than watching you," Cleo said loudly. Tookey kept snoozing.

Henry looked drowsy too. "The Thursday lull," he said. "It's been a slow day for everyone. The final shoppers will be waiting for the upcoming Friday and weekend bargains." He looked up the row. "It doesn't help my customer flow that those two stands closed up early."

"For the day?"

His rueful look suggested otherwise.

"They went *home* early?" Cleo said.

"They didn't feel safe." Henry's cheeks flushed. "I got the impression they think *I* could be the killer. Word has gotten around about my revised statement, and Sergeant Tookey isn't exactly undercover."

An ache lodged in Cleo's limbs. Poor Henry.

Henry stood, stretched, and gave her a weak smile. "I've assured folks that it's a misunderstanding. I think my close colleagues believe me. I've told them we have fine detectives in Catalpa Springs too." He twinkled at Cleo. "Even finer amateur sleuths."

Cleo blushed.

Henry came around the table to give her a peck on the cheek. "Do you have any good news? Clues? Suspects?"

"I do have something new," Cleo said. "Mary-Rose and I visited your psychic neighbor."

Henry chuckled. "I bet that was fun."

Under the table, Mr. Chaucer awoke with a snuffle. His big eyes blinked several times before he recognized Cleo and his curlicue tail wagged.

"Chaucy will be demanding a walk," Henry said, as Mr. Chaucer yawned, looking more inclined to demand another nap. "I need to stretch my legs too." His books were safely locked in their cabinets. He asked the woman a few stands up to watch over them. She nodded in sleepiness as much as agreement.

They ambled slowly, at drowsy pug pace. "I'm sorry I missed the visit to Madame's cottage," Henry said. "I've only been inside once, another case of misdelivered mail. I went in and a ghostly voice ordered me to sit at that table. You bet I did what I was told. The voice kept on saying to sit, so I kept on sitting. Finally, I realized the words were on repeat. She'd left a recording on."

Cleo could picture the scene and Henry dutifully following orders. "She has an impressive electronic surveillance system hidden behind curtains." Cleo described the "apprentice" teens and video cameras. "Gabby found the camera pointed at the alley—it's as tiny as an eyeball. Gabby's hopeful that they can get a warrant to search the property and collect any recordings."

Henry thumped his forehead. "I should have known she monitors that alley. She basically told me a while back. She was having trouble with raccoons tipping her trash cans. She said she *sees* every move they make. I thought she meant she was using her special powers."

"Oh, they're special powers, just not psychic."

"This is a wonderful development," Henry exclaimed. "The video will show the killer. It'll prove that neither Dot nor I was there."

Cleo had initially felt the same rush of optimism. "Yes," she said.

"What?" Henry asked.

Cleo didn't want to be a pessimist, but something didn't feel right. "Madame Romanov didn't come forward about her video monitoring. Why?"

Henry nodded slowly. "She doesn't want her seeing technique revealed? She's afraid? Of the killer?"

"Or afraid of the police," Cleo speculated, getting a shocked gasp from Henry. Cleo told him about the empty spot on Madame's bookshelf and how Madame had seemed to know Hunter Fox's name. "Or," she ended in a brighter tone, "she simply forgot to say anything, and the video's right where it should be, with the killer's face as clear as a sunny day." She reached out and squeezed Henry's hand.

He squeezed back. "I'll hope for the best."

Cleo would too, but she'd keep sleuthing out the worst.

Their stroll was nearing the end of the row of bookstalls. Buddy's red-and-white-checkered tablecloth was a bright flash of color. At the next stand, Kitty Peavey was waving around her feather duster. She'd been busy chatting when Cleo came in, and Cleo had been glad. She was hoping Kitty would forget about getting her manicured fingers on the library's copy of *Into the Waves*.

Henry stopped to talk with Buddy.

"Slow afternoon," Buddy chuckled. "Makes me want to pack up and go fishing."

Henry agreed. "Me too, and I don't even know how to fish."

Cleo took the opportunity of their small talk to peruse Buddy's offerings. He had some copies of *Gone With the Wind*, she noted, simple reading copies in good condition.

"I can't say this fair's a bust, though," Buddy said, turning his attention to Cleo and his inventory. "I picked up some items I wouldn't mind keeping for myself if it comes to that." He pointed to a book on fishing lures and fly ties.

Cleo looked at it with interest, thinking it might be just the book to cure her insomnia.

"And this . . ." Buddy said, grinning like a kid playing hooky. He reached under his table and drew out a clear plastic folder. "I'm not putting it out, because it's too good for the likes of me. I'm only showing folks who might appreciate it. If no one bites here, I'll put it up in an auction." Buddy's cheeks were red, his voice excited. "I got a by-golly deal, and from Hunter Fox too." He added quickly, "May he rest in peace."

Henry and Cleo leaned in as Buddy waved his thick hand over the folder, palm up like a game-show hostess in overalls. In awed tones, he said, "A letter from James Oglethorpe to some English lord dude. Gander at that date: 1738!"

Henry studied the page, making appreciative murmurs.

Cleo wished her twin grandsons could see this. The boys had recently done a middle-school project on James Oglethorpe, founder of the English colony of Georgia. He'd been a humanitarian beyond his time, with dreams of reforming prisons, aiding the poor, and keeping Georgia free for all. Cleo bent close to Henry, cheek to fluffy beard. She thought of the man, so long ago, sitting at a desk, simply writing a letter. And here she was, within nose length of a page he'd touched.

"My!" Cleo said. "How exciting!"

Buddy grinned. "I know, right? I can hardly believe it. I mean, it cost a mint, by my standards. But it's worth it. I think I can make two thousand back, more than twice what I paid."

"Hunter found this?" Cleo asked. "I wonder where?"

"Old box of junk, sitting around an attic. It's in out-of-the-way towns like this where treasures can still be found, Hunter said, and he was right about that." Buddy glowed with pride.

"Congratulations," Cleo said. Good news was something to celebrate, and she was more than ready to cheer it.

"Ahhh." Henry had picked up the clear folder and was holding it up to the light.

"What?" Buddy's smile froze. "Aw, don't tell me. If it's bad news, I don't want to hear."

Cleo didn't want to hear either.

Henry turned the page, eyeing it from both sides. "Could we examine it?" he asked. "I have gloves at my stand."

"I have gloves!" Kitty Peavey swooped over. "Couldn't help but overhear you mention Hunter. Poor Hunt. Rest assured, Mr. Boone, that man would never sell you something for *less* than it was worth. Always the other way around, with him. So clever." She sniffed dramatically before retrieving a pair of blue gloves as thin as air.

Henry tugged them on, with only one finger poking a hole out. He carefully removed the letter and placed it on the clear sheet.

"What are you looking for?" Buddy asked. "The paper seems right—old and dingy. I figured that was good."

"The paper looks fine. It's the pressure of the signature," Henry said. "A forger—"

Kitty sucked in air. "Hush! Don't say that awful word around here!"

Henry continued on evenly, "Sometimes a signature doesn't match the text. Say, there's a letter from the same general time period with no signature or one that's been removed or cut out.

A forger can use the space to add a famous signature. Signing a single name is easier than forging an entire document, like a letter."

He ran a finger at the bottom of the page and then behind it. "The page doesn't appear to be torn recently. But the indentation of the signature, the impression made by the pen . . . You can see how it's different from that behind the letter text. I wouldn't swear by it, without analysis of authenticated Oglethorpe writings, but I'd say that the letter and signature are by two different people."

"The signer probably isn't Oglethorpe?" Cleo said, disappointed for Buddy's sake and let down too. She'd *wanted* it to be real.

Buddy's shoulders slumped. "Shoot! Good thing I didn't pay what I thought it was worth. Still . . . shucks!"

"I'm sorry," Henry said. "I truly am. I'd have loved to buy this myself. I saw a similar item up for auction last autumn, but it was beyond my means. It's why the handwriting in the letter gave me pause. It seemed different from the document I'd seen. But, again, you should take it to an expert. I know a museum archivist who could help. We've worked together before authenticating—or deauthenticating—pieces."

Kitty gave a disapproving huff and muttered something about "meddling."

Buddy shook his head. "I believe you. Guess I will be keeping this for myself after all."

"Win some, lose some," Kitty said with a shrug. Then she smiled. "I guess Hunt won after all."

"Unless someone tricked him first," Cleo pointed out.

"No," Kitty said scornfully. "You think someone around here happened to have a fine forgery sitting around her attic, just waiting for a gullible book scout to come by?" Kitty countered. She laughed, theatrically clutching at her chest. "Oh, or a master forger is living here in little old Catalpa Springs? Ha! Hunt always knew what he had. He could tell a cheat at a thousand paces."

Because he was one, Cleo thought.

Kitty touched her stiff blonde waves. "Good thing I *know* my Margaret Mitchell signature is authentic. No question there!"

Cleo couldn't help herself from taking the bait. "I thought you said we were only *imagining* that signed *Gone With the Wind*."

Kitty beamed. "That's right, imagining sure builds *excitement*, doesn't it? I'll have buyers eating out of my hand by the end of the fair, lining up to buy it. You keep thinking of our deal too, Miss Cleo! I'll even raise my offer. Two thousand."

She swept off in a wave of flowery perfume, leaving Cleo's nose wrinkling.

"So you're book dealing now too?" Henry asked, his tone joking but baffled. "Two thousand?" He looked down at his pug, whose wrinkly face quivered with concern. "Chaucy, we're getting cut out of all the local business."

"No, you're not," Cleo said, aiming her words at the worried pug. "The book Kitty wants isn't for sale. She thinks she can buy the library's copy of Shirley Macon James's *Into the Waves*."

Henry cocked his head. He, Buddy, and Mr. Chaucer sported nearly identical looks of male confusion.

"It's a southern Gothic romance," Cleo said, to murmurs of "Ah, yes," from Henry, who had an excuse, given that he specialized in texts written several centuries earlier.

"It's not a widely known work," Cleo admitted, "but a classic nonetheless. Miss James lived just outside Catalpa Springs while she was writing it, not far from the Pancake Mill. Mary-Rose's family knew her quite well. Like Margaret Mitchell, she was uncomfortable with fame and passed away far too young."

"Too young, tragic, and one big hit," Buddy said. "Kinda wrong how that brings up the value of a signature." He glanced back at his letter. "If it's real," he said, glumly slipping the paper into the protective sleeve.

Over at her stall, Kitty was back to twirling her feather duster, looking bored.

Cleo noticed that the French translation of *Gone With the Wind* no longer occupied Kitty's display case. A sign had taken its place. She pushed back her bifocals, but the text was angled away.

Buddy noticed and said, "That sign says *Inquire about a true delight. Gone With the Wind*, that's all I've heard about, all day long. Twenty-five thousand, she's asking. Can you imagine that? Here I was planning a deluxe vacation with my three-thousand-dollar letter."

Henry looked as deflated as Buddy, but Buddy cheered up faster. "I'm actually glad you caught the problem, Mr. Lafayette. Someone had to get the 'fair curse.' I'm just glad I didn't pass it on by selling a fake."

Henry shook his head sadly.

Buddy lowered his voice. "Did you hear the rumors about a bigwig antiquarian getting caught passing off a fake after last year's fair? I didn't get a name and I'm not gonna ask. I mind my own business." He patted a stack of books, including several fine and affordable copies of *Gone With the Wind*. "I'm sure there's no problem with these."

Cleo reached for the top copy and flipped through. The book was lovely, and the price seemed almost too reasonable. "I'll buy this one. I'd like to have my own copy to reread in the bookmobile."

Henry chuckled. "One for every room of the house and every vehicle too?"

"One of every edition except those a bookmobile librarian can't afford." She handed over a twenty and insisted that Buddy keep the change.

"The *Gone With the Wind* Kitty has," Cleo said. "You know I fear it's Dot's, but I haven't been able to look at it to confirm. When Kitty describes it to folks, what edition does she say? May or June or . . . ?"

Buddy frowned. "I don't know. Just first edition. First is first, right? She's talking up the price most of all, and I feel real bad, thinking Miss Dot won't be getting that. It's not right. If Kitty ever brings out the actual book, I'll call you right away. Although that might not help . . ."

"How do you mean?" Cleo said, fearing she knew.

"Professor Weber told everyone to look out for Miss Dot's bookplates and the identifying marks on that rare *Gone*, didn't he? But it's like Mr. Lafayette said about this letter: marks can be added. Or removed. I made a point to stroll back over to Professor Weber's stand this morning and look around, all casual like. He had a title on Miss Dot's list. William Bartram's *Travels*—the reproduction, not anything pretending to be from the 1700s." He glanced sadly at his letter. "Anyway, I looked inside, expecting to see Miss Dot's bookplate. Nope."

"Not hers, then," Cleo said.

"Who knows?" Buddy said. "The front page, where she stuck her other plates, was missing."

Henry huffed. "Unacceptable. If any book or seller is questionable, it's bad for all of us."

Buddy nodded gravely. Mr. Chaucer whimpered.

Henry said, "Buddy, I'm going to ask you a favor. Will you let me alert the members to this forgery? Probable forgery, I should say. It won't reflect badly on you, only the man who sold it to you."

"He can't care anymore," Buddy said. "You do what you have to. I won't speak ill of Hunter Fox, though. My mamma always said, you're courting bad luck if you speak ill of the dead."

Cleo looked out over the Depot. Hunter hadn't conned only laypeople like Dot and Bernice. He'd swindled his fellow antiquarians too. If someone had lost more money and professional pride than Buddy had, then Hunter Fox had made his own bad luck . . . and a motive for murder.

Chapter
Twenty-Two

The following afternoon, Cleo sat on her front porch, enjoying the simmering warmth, and the company of her favorite neighbor and cat. Rhett lounged in a patch of sun. A cardinal chirped in the magnolia, and scents of flowers and fresh-cut grass wafted through the screen.

The noisy source of the chopped grass marred the mood. A Weedwacker buzzed frenetically over at Wanda's. The looming cloud of crimes damped the atmosphere even more.

Gabby flexed socked feet, stretched to rest on the porch rail. The chief had ordered Gabby to avoid excessive overtime pay. Cleo had advised the young deputy to kick off her shoes and rest for a spell. It was Friday, after all.

"How was your day?" Cleo asked, after giving Gabby time to sip her iced tea—the proper, sweetened kind. "Any sign of Madame Romanov? Any word on her?"

Gabby groaned, not a good sign. "No sign of her. I don't know whether to be worried or irritated. As for words on her, I've read and heard way too many of those."

Cleo raised a go-on eyebrow.

Gabby obliged. "Her real name's Tina Roman, from Miami. She and her sister and a niece moved up here a few years back to get a fresh start, the sister says."

"A fresh start implies leaving trouble behind," Cleo observed.

"Indeed it does. Trouble of her own making. Down in Florida, Tina worked as a cleaner in a cathedral. Seems she had a bad habit of listening in on confessions and got herself fired. I found that out from a nice, talkative lady in the cathedral's bookstore." Gabby stretched so that her toes were in a spot of sun.

"Book people are helpful," Cleo said, and then qualified. "Usually."

"When they're not conning folks and possibly murdering one another," Gabby agreed amiably. "Tina's former boss, the priest, would only say that Tina had been asked to 'avoid further contact' with his parishioners and had left 'voluntarily to reassess her spiritual interests.'"

Cleo, who'd been drinking unsweetened tea, tasted a fresh bitterness. "No contact? That seems harsh for a priest. Do you think she was eavesdropping for information to use in her fortune-telling?"

Gabby rattled the ice cubes in her sweating glass. Beads ran down in little rivers. The air was steamy, like summer had sneaked in early. "I think she was more direct. Why bother with fortunes if she already had confessions?"

"Blackmail," Cleo said. She didn't like the evil word hovering about her porch and had the urge to get up, open the door, and shoo it out.

"Mind you, I'm only speculating," Gabby said. "So was the bookstore lady, who admitted to reading a lot of mysteries and thrillers."

Cleo issued a favorite philosophy: reading nourishes a healthy brain and imagination. Then she added, "Was there any evidence of blackmail?"

Gabby shrugged and plunked her feet back down to the porch planks. "There might well have been, but no one pressed charges. Tina Roman rented a fancy condo with an ocean view. On a church cleaner's salary? Her sister worked for a vehicle repo service. She had the condo next door. Between them, those ladies had the skills to hustle money."

"Interesting," Cleo said, loading the word with implications.

"Sure is. I'd like to find her." Gabby frowned toward Wanda's yard. "I'd like to go over to Wanda's, too, and disable that Weed-wacker. What a racket! Here she complains about me. Do you know, she called in another complaint this morning, saying my vehicle woke her up at three AM? I was out on an emergency call, an accident!" The young deputy sighed and added, "I hope I didn't wake you up."

Cleo admitted she'd been conked out on the sofa with the TV on. "Infomercials are the only thing that puts me to sleep recently. I've tried boring books—"

Gabby interrupted. "Wait, *you* think there are boring books? Which ones?"

"I'll never tell," Cleo said primly. Actually, she hadn't found any sufficiently boring. She remembered Buddy's fly-fishing book. Maybe she had something similar in the bookmobile, no offense to fly-tying enthusiasts . . .

The sun had moved beyond the porch, prompting Rhett to rise and stretch. Cleo patted her lap. He hopped up and head-bumped her chin.

Cleo said, "Infomercials are the only thing that bores me to sleep. The only trouble is, I wake with a neck crick and strange urges to shop. This morning, I felt I *had* to have a motion-detecting light for my toilet bowl. I stopped myself, but barely."

"No, just no," Gabby said, chuckling. She curled her long legs up under her and breathed in deeply. "Ah, this is nice. I needed this, Miss Cleo. I was getting a little too obsessed by our Madame Romanov, disappearing like she actually has some supernatural ability. We have a trace on her phone, but it's off. Her relatives claim they have no idea where she is. You ask me, if she's not hurt—which I dearly hope she isn't—then she's guilty of something."

Cleo rubbed Rhett's chin and mused aloud. "Blackmailer or killer?" Rhett purred equally loudly for both.

"That is the question," Gabby said.

The Weedwacker at Wanda's faded, suggesting she'd moved on to annoy the neighbor on the far side.

Cleo tried to relish the relative peace, but another question buzzed around her brain. "What about Madame Romanov's video cameras? Did you find any recordings yet?"

Gabby's heavy sigh gave the answer. "The camera system was a great find on your part, Miss Cleo. That and Madame's unknown whereabouts got us a warrant to search her cottage. Unfortunately, her surveillance isn't as high-tech as it looks. It records on DVDs. Crazy, right? Talk about old school."

Cleo *could* talk about old school. She still used her old record player. She kept her grandmother's working Victrola in her sitting room and housed unknown numbers of her sons' eight-tracks and tape cassettes in the attic. DVDs sounded high-tech enough to her.

Gabby was talking about the cloud and cell phones. "Tech guys can usually dig that stuff out even after it's erased," Gabby said. "But with a DVD, all you have to do is pick it up and take it with you or toss it in the landfill and it's gone. There's a gap in her DVD library for the day of the killing. Either she took it or someone else did."

Cleo stuck on a word. "Her library . . . Did you check out that empty spot on her shelves?"

Gabby smiled wide. "I did. You were right. There was dust all around, except for an outline of books. I asked the niece. She said her aunt kept 'special' magic books up there. The niece knew for sure because ever since she was little, she'd wanted to see those books. Her aunt kept them up high, out of reach, claiming they were too 'dangerous' for little girls to read."

Cleo *tsk*ed. "What's dangerous is discouraging reading, especially in little girls."

Gabby crunched an ice cube and added, "Yep. That and messing with a killer."

*   *   *

Later that evening, Cleo sat at her kitchen table with Ollie and Rhett. A gentle breeze wafted in the open windows, carrying a chorus of courting tree frogs.

Henry was out at a Georgia Antiquarian Book Society board meeting. Cleo wondered if Sergeant Tookey had tagged along, surveilling. If so, the sergeant was likely enjoying a good long nap. Henry had said the meetings went on for ages, with tedious readings of procedures and expenditures. He'd wished he could join Cleo for her planned Friday-night-leftovers feast.

Cleo wished so too. She was happy to have another lovely dining companion, though, both for company and for emptying the fridge.

"This is amazing, Gran," Ollie had said, as Cleo hauled out every leftover in the house. He'd already happily finished off the chicken and rice, a slice of ham, cold asparagus, two deviled eggs, and a few token leaves of lettuce, the last straight from Cleo's garden.

The sweet boy had also come bearing pie, an entire black-bottom pecan pie, rich dark chocolate topped in caramelized pecans. The pie was now down to nearly half.

Cleo had taken a sliver and then another for evening-up purposes. It was wrong to leave a pie lopsided. Ollie had consumed two massive slabs, with a double side of butter-pecan ice cream. He'd gotten the pie from Dot, who'd received it amid a flood of supportive treats.

On the phone earlier, Dot had joked with Cleo, "There are so many dishes showing up on my doorstep, it's like I'm hosting my own wake, except it's just the opposite."

Mention of a wake had sent a chill up Cleo's arms, but she knew Dot intended joy. With the help of donations and volunteers, the Drop By would live again.

Ollie put down his fork and rubbed his flat belly in contentment. "Ah . . . that hits the spot."

Cleo noted that he had a spot on his forehead, a smudge of mud. He'd been helping Mary-Rose's contractor friends dig a plumbing line at the Drop By. Cleo smiled at him, warmed by the pie and her kind grandson.

"You've been such a help to Dot," Cleo said, with a twinge of guilt. For all her driving around in search of clues and victims, she hadn't found any of the missing books, let alone the killer. Ollie, on the other hand, had been doing literal heavy lifting, digging through muck and mud and root-clogged clay pipes. His heavy lifting continued online. Cleo inquired about his fund-raising site.

"It's going awesome," he said. "We hit fifteen thousand this afternoon. Fifteen! There should be even more now. It'll snowball, and then, Auntie Dot, viral cause!" He waved his fingers like a magician conjuring.

It did sound like magic to Cleo. "Fifteen thousand . . . ah . . . viewers?"

Ollie issued a happy guffaw. "Dollars, Gran. Plus change."

Cleo's hand flew to her heart. "My gracious, Ollie. Who in Catalpa Springs has that much money?" Her little town had a smidgen less than three thousand residents, counting those in the rural reaches. That number included children and retired folks and those with no Internet and little money to spare.

"It's not just Catalpa Springs," Ollie said, nibbling a bit of the cookie pie crust. "It's everywhere, anywhere. Strangers will give to causes they believe in, even if it's nothing they're ever going to see. Like me, I just gave a few dollars to protect pika in Colorado." He swiped back the loopy locks always falling over his eyes.

"Pika?" Cleo said, deciding she needed another extra sliver of pie to help her digest all this information.

"They're these small montane animals. Picture a high-altitude hamster. They're in trouble from their mountains getting too warm. I'd *like* to see one someday. I want them to stick around. But they're nowhere near here."

Rhett purred loudly.

"No mountain hamsters for you, Rhett Butler," Cleo said. She praised her grandson for his generosity and gave silent thanks to all the donors, friends and strangers alike.

"This is a good reminder for me," Cleo said, getting up to clear the table.

Ollie jumped up to help.

"I get caught up in suspicion in times like these," Cleo continued, head shaking with disappointment in herself. "I've been going around ranking folks on likelihood to commit premeditated murder."

Ollie laughed. "Gran, you wouldn't be a very good sleuth if you thought everyone was innocent. Besides, online benefactors wouldn't give money to faraway critters or endangered downtown shops or strangers' medical bills if everything was going great. We're righting wrongs! Only you're braver. It's a heck of a lot safer to give ten bucks to cute animals or Auntie Dot's store."

As soon as Cleo placed clean plates in the dish drainer, Ollie plucked them out and wiped them dry. Cleo had never seen the need for a dishwasher, except after big holiday meals, when she secretly coveted one. Then, however, she'd miss moments like this, time slowed down with her grandson.

Ollie reached for another plate as Cleo scrubbed silverware. "Can you imagine what Granddad would have said about you chasing after killers?"

"Your granddad was a lovely man," Cleo said. "But, yes, he *might* not have approved." He definitely wouldn't have, just like he wouldn't have approved of her speeding down the roads in a big yellow library on wheels.

He wouldn't have stopped her. Richard wasn't a bully, and she would have put her foot down firmer if he'd tried. He would have grumbled, though, and still expected his dinners on the table, promptly by five fifteen. Cleo glanced at the clock ticking above the sink. It was past seven, way beyond dear Richard's appointed dining hour, to be completed in time for the six o'clock news.

Her landline rang, startling Cleo from a haze of memories.

"I'll finish the dishes," Ollie said. "You get that antique technology on the wall." It was their running joke, Ollie's youngperson marveling at phones on cords.

Cleo answered with a laugh in her voice and was rewarded by joy in return.

"Good evening!" Dot exclaimed.

Dot would be at her landline in her kitchen. They'd be linked by curly phone cords and the lines running across town.

"You'll never believe it," Dot said, her voice high with excitement. "It's my books, Cleo. My books have come home!"

Chapter
Twenty-Three

A dark feeling pressed at Cleo. She couldn't explain it. Nor could the bright lights and happy chatter in Dot's kitchen shake it away. Cleo covered with a smile. Heaven forbid she turn into the family downer. They already had one of those in a second cousin, a man so morose he could bring down a party with cupcakes and kittens.

"This is a wonderful development," Cleo said brightly to reinforce the positive facade. The words sounded too sharp to her ears. *Something's not right.*

"It *is* wonderful." Dot clattered around her kitchen in a ruffled peach apron and a whirl of excitement. Seemingly simultaneously, Dot brewed decaf, got out the nice china cups and saucers, arranged a plate of freshly baked cookies, and wiped and tidied her sparkling counters. Dot kept cookie dough in her freezer, ready in perfect portions she could pop in the oven in the event of guests and good news.

"But not your *Gone With the Wind*? That wasn't in the package of books?" Cleo had to ask. She ran her finger down the small stack of texts, although she'd already checked twice. The books, left in a bulging bubble-padded envelope beside Dot's front steps, now sat atop Dot's kitchen island, carefully arranged on a fresh tea towel beside a potted hyacinth.

Gone was definitely not among them.

Dot's counter cleaning picked up speed. "No. Not *yet*. Not in this package, but it's still very nice of someone to return these books, isn't it?"

"Really nice," Ollie agreed, munching on his second chocolate-chip cookie. "This cookie's the best, Auntie Dot."

He was right, of course. It was nice, and Dot did make the best chocolate-chip cookies. The cookies were as large as tea saucers, soft in the middle and buttery crispy on the edges. Chocolate chunks jutted out like little mountains, dusted with glittering crystals. Salt on cookies still shocked Cleo. As in, how shockingly good it was.

Cleo, having already indulged in black-bottom pecan pie, had broken off a third of her cookie and given the rest to Ollie. The third still lay on her plate. It wasn't only her doctor's sugar-avoidance prescription that kept her from enjoying it. The anonymous return of the books was odd. Unnerving. "So there was no return address or note or *anything* identifying who left the package? You found it by the steps?"

Dot nodded happily.

Cleo asked, "May I see the envelope?"

Among Dot's many fine traits was the patience of a saint. She fished the envelope out of the trash bin tucked under her sink. She even indulged Cleo's request for paper towels to handle the envelope without leaving fingerprints and a fresh ziplock bag to store it in.

"Freezer-safe or regular ziplock?" Dot asked, always accommodating.

Cleo chose freezer, the thicker the better to seal in what she was sure was evidence.

"I'm going to call Gabby," Cleo announced.

"Cool!" Ollie said, his cheeks flushing on cue.

"If you must," Dot said, with uncharacteristic resignation.

* * *

Gabby showed up in the company of Sergeant Earl Tookey. Cleo was glad to see that the young sergeant wasn't pinned to Henry. Perhaps this meant the chief had moved on to other suspects.

Tookey's eyes lit on the platter of cookies. "I worked up an appetite tonight," he said.

Gabby rolled her own eyes. "Snoozing at that book meeting?"

"You have no idea," Tookey countered, yawning as if in Pavlovian response. "That book board could bore a person to death." He glanced guiltily at Cleo. "No offense, Miss Cleo. I'm sure it's thrilling if you're into that kind of thing. Your boyfriend was very well behaved. No criminal activity."

"He always is well behaved," Cleo said crisply, but Tookey was distracted, edging toward the cookie platter.

"Please," Dot urged. "Eat up." She pushed the plate toward him and bustled off to wipe down her faucet. Scents of bleach and chemical lavender mingled with sweet baking aromas. The counters gleamed. Dot's kitchen must be as sterile as an operating room, Cleo thought, frowning. It wasn't necessarily a good thing. Dot cleaned when she was nervous. She must be concerned about the anonymous package too.

Cleo could empathize. She'd been the recipient of an anonymous box of clues once. It had shaken her, the thought of someone sneaking onto her porch, dropping the box, and fleeing. For a while, she hadn't known if the sender was good or bad, which had been even more unnerving.

Tookey was engaged in the serious business of choosing the perfect cookie. His hand hovered over the plate. He finally selected one with a round middle and lots of chocolate chunks.

"Good choice," said Ollie, who'd been watching. "That'll be a softer one." He blushed and added, "Hi, Gabby. Deputy Honeywell. Neighbor. Nice to see you. I mean, not nice, 'cause this is business, but it is nice that Auntie Dot got her books . . ." Wisely, he grabbed another cookie and joined Tookey in munching.

Cleo showed Gabby the package as Dot bustled about, pouring glasses of milk for Ollie and Tookey and spritzing the refrigerator door with cleaner.

"So you have no idea who left this, Miss Dot?" Gabby asked. "You didn't see anyone drive by? Hear anything?"

"No," Dot said, putting down the spray bottle. "Other than it was someone awfully nice."

"Or the killer," Tookey said, his bluntness muffled by a mouthful of cookie.

Dot gasped and clutched her cleaning towel.

Cleo was glad he'd said it. Better Tookey than her. Dot wouldn't fault the sergeant, who was just doing his job and clearly under the influence of cookie bliss.

"Oh," Dot said quietly. "I didn't think of it that way."

Gabby caught Cleo's eye, and Cleo read the deputy's rueful smile. Cleo had thought of it that way, and Gabby knew it.

"Best to be abundantly cautious," Gabby said, as Dot pushed the cookie plate closer to Sergeant Tookey.

He obligingly took another. "Yeah, good idea."

"We'll have to take the books with us as evidence," Gabby said. "I'm sorry, Miss Dot. It'll just be temporary until we can get them checked out. We'll give you a written receipt listing each one."

"Checked out?" Dot said. She reached a hand to the stack. "Oh, but Gabby, they're fine. Just fine. All these books are perfectly intact, unlike my movie edition and my bird book. That's so upsetting, such fine books chopped to bits and sold off in pieces. But I'm choosing to move on. I'm concentrating on the good."

Tookey made agreeable *mmmm* noises.

Gabby shot Cleo a pleading look.

"Dot," Cleo said tenderly but firmly. "These books are evidence that could help stop a killer. The police have to have them checked for fingerprints and other evidence. Right, Deputy Honeywell?"

"Yep," Tookey answered before Gabby could. He licked melted chocolate from a finger and drank down his milk.

Gabby was busily writing out a receipt, her head tipped to read each spine.

Cleo kept on. "Of course, whoever sent these books might be completely innocent."

Gabby ripped off the receipt and handed it to Dot. "That's right. It could be just a nice, anonymous Good Samaritan who didn't want to get officially involved in a murder investigation."

"Completely understandable," Cleo said, although not to her. She was drawn to investigations. It was the puzzle that intrigued her most. And justice.

Dot tugged her apron tie loose and retied it tight. "I'd rather . . ." she said hesitantly. "I don't really want to . . ."

"You don't want to let them go again," Gabby said kindly. "I understand. But like Miss Cleo said, you could be helping us solve a crime, a robbery or maybe even the murder. As you know,

Kitty Peavey reported a robbery on the morning of the murder. Perhaps the robber took some of these books."

And killed Hunter Fox, Cleo mentally filled in.

"You think a thief took the books and then sent them back to me? Why?" Dot asked, her tone high and incredulous.

Put that way, it did sound unlikely, Cleo thought. Why wouldn't the robber simply keep the books? Or not take them to begin with? Cleo considered the titles: A couple of Walt Kelly's *Pogo* comics from the 1960s. A Faulkner in fine condition and a handful of other southern authors: Zora Neale Hurston, Flannery O'Connor, and Eudora Welty. The books looked like the library's copies, common editions suitable for a pleasant read.

"Robin Hood did stuff like that," Tookey offered. His round face glowed. Cleo took it as sugar overload until he brought up books. "My grandparents had a whole huge set of Robin Hood books," Tookey said. "I read and reread 'em all the time as a kid. Come to think of it, they might've influenced me to become a cop."

No one mentioned that Robin was the outlaw. Cleo could see how it made sense. Robin was the hero of the stories, bringing justice.

"*Robin Hood of Great Renown*, that was the title," Tookey said, smiling. "Hey, I wonder if those books are worth anything? They're really old. Like 1900 old. Ancient."

"They're priceless," Dot said firmly. "Tell your family to hold on to them, Sergeant Tookey. Don't let them out of your sight."

* * *

Ollie had driven Cleo over to Dot's in his Jeep. Cleo's personal vehicle, a classic convertible inherited from her father, had been blocked in the driveway by Words on Wheels. Besides, Cleo didn't want to hog the fun of driving, even if Ollie's vehicle had nowhere near the handling of her convertible. The Jeep swayed like a rowboat on a roiling sea.

Cleo already felt unmoored. She discreetly gripped the armrest as Ollie made his way down quiet residential streets. A full moon winked through the treetops, casting long shadows. As they passed Madame Romanov's cottage, Cleo took advantage of being a passenger to stare. The antique globe lamp glowed in the window. More than complete darkness, the lamp suggested no one was home. Henry's shop came into view next. A sliver of light seeped through the back curtains, his workshop.

"Could you drop me off at the Gilded Page, please?" Cleo asked. "I'd like to tell Henry about the returned books."

"Sure thing, Gran." The Jeep swayed to a stop. Ollie leaned over and pecked her on the cheek. "You need a ride back? You can call me whenever if you want. I'll be up late watching the fund-raising page, counting the money rolling in for Auntie Dot. She doesn't need that old *Gone With the Wind*."

Cleo smiled, recalling Ollie in his little-kid years. Getting him to sleep on Christmas Eve was as impossible as stopping a bunny from hopping. Ollie loved the anticipation. He wanted to stay up and watch for Santa and count the presents almost more than he enjoyed unwrapping them.

"I'll be fine walking home," Cleo said, adding thanks to her considerate grandchild. It was only a few blocks, she said. Henry would escort her. She didn't mention that perhaps he'd stay over. She hoped he might. She seemed able to sleep better with him at her side.

Ollie's grin sank to serious. "Okay, but be careful, Gran. You don't really think the killer sent Auntie Dot's books back, do you? Seems kinda soft and sentimental for a killer. Or super-creepy."

Cleo's sweet grandson quickly brightened. "Or maybe it's just a nice burglar like Sergeant Tookey said. A Robin Hood, robbing from the bad bookdealers and giving books to good folks."

"Let's hope," Cleo said in her best grandmotherly tones. A beneficent burglar was better than a murderer, although neither was ideal.

Ollie waited chivalrously in his Jeep, now rocking with music. Cleo rang Henry's doorbell. She read the *Closed* sign and the hours written in gold paint.

After a long minute, the door opened a crack. Henry peeked over a chain lock. His face brightened, and Mr. Chaucer wriggled out to snuffle at Cleo's feet. Cleo greeted Chaucy while Henry closed the door to undo the chain.

When the door opened wide, Cleo waved to Ollie. Her grandson tooted his horn, and the Jeep rattled off.

"Is everything okay?" Henry asked. He wore a leather apron with pockets across the front. The silvery ends of tools jutted from the pockets. Cleo thought of the missing hammer and was relieved when he ushered her inside and relocked the door.

"I have good news," Cleo said. "Yet somehow I can't help but think that it's actually bad."

Chapter
Twenty-Four

For over an hour, Henry and Cleo had sipped mint tea and speculated on the mystery of Dot's returned books. They'd come to no conclusions, other than that Henry insisted on escorting Cleo home. The full moon shimmered above Fontaine Park, where Mr. Chaucer stopped to sniff the namesake fountain. The little pug circled the burbling fountain once, then once again.

Cleo enjoyed the pause in the park. She wasn't often out at this time, just past ten on a Friday. In the darkness the floral perfume seemed sultrier, sounds clearer: laughter from a group of young folks, the soft hoot of an owl, a car with a wheezy motor.

Unable to locate the owl, Cleo watched the car's taillights blink down Main Street. Streetlamps cast warm glows. The businesses were tucked in for the night.

Except one.

Past Dot's Drop By, the yarn shop, a bank, the shoe store, and a lunchtime café, a neon light flashed.

"The bar . . ." Cleo said as Mr. Chaucer moved on to a lamppost.

Henry smiled. "You want a nightcap? I have a good bottle of bourbon back at my place. It's closer and probably nicer than . . . what's that bar called?"

"Skeet's," Cleo said. Then she remembered that Skeeter O'Malley, the owner, had recently upped his image. "Skeet's Gastropub and Beverage Lounge," she said, drawing a chuckle from Henry.

Cleo didn't frequent the bar, but Skeet's rebranding had been the talk of the town, mainly because all he'd done was raise his prices and rename his offerings. Locals in the know could request the "secret menu," where the original prices of Skeet's many fried delicacies lived on. Skeet was known for fried dill pickles, double-fried catfish, and conch fritters so absent of any seafood that Skeet was said to have relabeled them vegan.

"Skeet's is the closest bar to the bed-and-breakfast," Cleo said. "It's the *only* bar in easy walking distance, really."

"Ah." Henry grinned. "I see where you're going. Yes, it's also where Kitty Peavey left her room key the night before she was robbed and Hunter Fox was killed. I heard all about that from the bookdealer rumor mill." He held out an elbow. "Shall we?"

Cleo took his arm. "We'll just pop in and ask around," Cleo said. Then she reconsidered. "Oh, but it is late. You're probably tired."

"I'm wide awake and honored to accompany you on another sleuthing date. Do you think Mr. Chaucer can come too? I could leave him home, but a guard dog might be useful.

Cleo smiled down at the wobbly pug. "Skeet doesn't mind flaunting the law a little, and he has a barroom bulldog, I hear."

When they entered the bar, Cleo's first impression was cozy, like she imagined English pubs must be. Her second was a dash of betrayal. For as long as she could remember, a bar had occupied this building. For just as long, her relatives had dubbed it a veritable den of iniquity, a no-go zone for folks who kept decent hours and stayed in after dinner.

Cleo looked around admiringly. The ceiling sported decorative tin tiles, the bar gleamed, and Johnny Cash crooned from the jukebox, singing about watching his heart. Patrons filled the booths, tables, and barstools with a gentle din of chatting and laughter. The resident bulldog lay by the jukebox, stubby tail wagging but otherwise unmoved.

"Look," Henry said, nodding toward the end of the bar. "There's Kitty." Henry also noted Buddy Boone and a collector who specialized in fishing and boat-themed books. His gaze lingered on another group of bookdealers, two men and a woman who collected and restored medieval manuscripts. One was helping restore a stunning copy of *The Canterbury Tales* for a museum, Henry said.

Cleo detected longing in Henry's tone. The dear man had worked hard to arrange the fair, yet with all the troubles, he'd hardly gotten to enjoy any bookish fun.

Cleo squeezed his arm. "Why don't you go and talk with them? Sometimes the best information comes from not looking for it."

"I see what you're doing," Henry said, smile lines fanning his eyes. "Nope. Sorry. I'm here to help."

Cleo would shove him toward fun if she had to. She patted his arm firmly and said, "Go on. Honestly, it *is* a help. This way, it looks like we're here for you. You're my cover, and we're dividing our expertise."

He relented. "Okay, but I'll buy you a drink first. If you have any trouble, Chaucy and I will be right across the room. Who's the target of your sleuthing expertise? Kitty? Buddy?"

"Skeeter," Cleo said, and enjoyed his surprise. "Bartenders are like librarians, I imagine. They likely see a lot and overhear even more, and I expect they're very good at reading people."

* * *

"Code of silence," Skeet said. He was in his forties, with an anchor tattoo on one wrist and a bulldog's grinning face inked on the other. He wore leather suspenders and a fedora that Cleo guessed came with his new gastropub image.

She smiled at him over a frothy stein of root beer. "I understand. As a librarian, I have the same policy." She tucked back her hair, took a sip of her fizzy, sweet drink, and tried again. "But a murder investigation takes precedence, even for priests." *And librarians too.*

Skeet declared he was no priest. He turned to pour a beer, and Cleo feared she'd taken the wrong tack. She'd asked Skeet if he'd seen Hunter Fox the night before his death. Asking about a recently murdered man might have been too forward, not to mention impolite. What would her mother have to say about her manners? She sipped some more and smiled, imagining Mama's reaction to her daughter, sitting in a bar way past bedtime.

Skeet slid the beer down the bar and wiped up the streak of froth. He sidled back to Cleo. "I've heard about you. You drive the bookmobile? I like those flames on your bus. That's a real nice airbrushing job you have."

Cleo glowed. She loved those flames.

"I've heard you . . . look into things," Skeet said, his ruddy face pinched in a frown.

"Like any good librarian," Cleo said. "I like things orderly and cataloged. Plus, I'm helping my cousin and my gentleman friend, who've been under undue suspicion." She glanced over at Henry, who was chatting happily with the medievalists.

Skeet's frown softened. "The chief of police came in here the other day, asking questions, throwing all sorts of *undue suspicion* on my business practices and my Margaret. Said she was a health-code violation." Seeing Cleo's head lob in a query, he clarified.

"Margaret's my bulldog. She doesn't bother anyone and gets a bubble bath every Sunday."

"She's lovely," Cleo said, reaffirmed in her theory that even the most opposite of folks could bond over beloved pets. They could bond over shared insults too. "The chief calls me a nosy amateur," she said.

Skeet flashed a gap-toothed grin. "Yeah, an amateur who's solved his cases, I hear." He kept cleaning the counter, seemingly thinking.

Cleo considered how much she should reveal. People confessed to bartenders, didn't they? "It's my gentleman friend," she said, nodding toward Henry. "He's being wrongly accused. I need to identify another suspect. For his sake. For the town's too. We can't allow a killer to go free."

Skeet put down his cleaning rag and looked Cleo in the eye. "Your gentleman friend's the antiquarian book guy? I heard about him being hauled in for questioning. Saw Sergeant Tookey following him around town too. People are saying it looks bad for him, all kinds of evidence piling up."

Cleo held her breath.

Skeet leaned over the bar. "But if he's the wrong guy, all that attention's wrong. Worse than wrong. A man's got nothing if he doesn't have his reputation."

Cleo nodded vigorously.

"I'll tell you what I know," Skeet said, leaning across the bar. "'Cause I'm worried about someone too."

He'd seen Hunter Fox the evening before Hunter died, Skeet told Cleo. "Those book people were in here, partying." Skeet jerked his head hard to the right. At the end of the bar, Kitty Peavey was twinkling at two men with name tags dangling down their polo shirts.

"He was with her," Skeet said. "Blondie there. She had a bunch of book dudes buying her drinks." He frowned. "Better when someone else buys her drink. She sure doesn't tip like a movie star." He grinned. "Or a librarian."

Cleo had tipped Skeet double the price for the two root beers Henry ordered. It wasn't a bribe. She was supporting a local business . . . and a fellow observer's keen eye. Skeet was saying that Hunter Fox and Kitty left together.

"She forgot her keys?" Cleo said.

Skeet shrugged. "That's what she *says*. Came in here yelling at me later the next day, like every problem she had was my fault. I told her, I clean up after I close up. I didn't find any keys." He paused to take an order and retrieve a plate from the kitchen. When he returned, he had a bowl of fried pickles. He dipped one in ranch dressing and gestured for Cleo to join him.

A sudden wariness swept over Cleo. She swiveled to scan the room.

When she turned back, Skeet was eyeing her. "Who are you looking for? Cop or criminal?"

"My doctor," Cleo said. "She shows up whenever I'm out and about to be naughty with my diet. I've already had pie tonight and part of a cookie. Now root beer and pickles? I feel like a kid at the county fair."

He laughed. "These here are all-natural, locally grown cucumbers, pickled by a resident hippie type. They're practically a health food." He jabbed a thick finger at the gastro menu to prove it.

"Thank you," Cleo said, to cover both the justification and the treat. Her mouth was watering already. Cleo adored dill pickles in all forms, and she never argued with fried.

"So," Cleo said, "Did you overhear anything that Kitty and the deceased man were talking about?"

For a moment, a cone-of-silence look flashed across Skeet's face. Then he shrugged. "Books," he said. "That's all this crowd talks about."

At Cleo's prompting, Skeet recalled Kitty and Hunter bragging about a "big" book they'd acquired. "Big, as in worth a bundle," the bartender clarified. "I'll tell you, ma'am, I've heard criminals with more manners than those two. They were making fun of some old . . ." He paused and reworded. "I mean, some 'seasoned' lady they'd gotten one of the books from."

Cleo helped herself to another pickle, giving it a healthy dunk in ranch dressing. "That may have been my cousin Dot who owns the Drop By. She lost a valuable book to Hunter Fox. She was tricked."

"That's not right." Skeet sent another dark look down the bar. Kitty was oblivious. With each fresh bubble of laughter, she leaned into her companions.

"So this is who I'm worried about," Skeet said. "I didn't tell the cops 'cause it wasn't directly about the dead guy. One of my regular customers, she got in a fight with Blondie there. I'm talking a shoving, slapping, yelling match outside the ladies' room."

"Oh my," Cleo said, encouragingly. She was encouraged too. A lead!

"I told 'em to take it outside," Skeet said. "Since then, my regular hasn't come back, which is unlike her. If you find her, tell her I have her back this time. Her name's Tina. You might know her as . . ."

"Madame Romanov," Cleo said.

"You do get around detecting, don't you?" Skeet said.

* * *

Buddy had joined Henry and the medievalists, who were deep in conversation.

Henry pulled out a seat for Cleo. "We're talking about hidden fore edges," he said. "Fascinating, absolutely fascinating."

When Henry got drawn back into the book talk, Buddy explained, "It's these secret pictures painted on the page edges of a book. Cool, huh? Like when you look at the book closed, it's nothing but plain gold gilt. But then if you fan them, like a card deck, a picture appears." He shook his head. "Amazing things, books."

"Marvelous," Cleo agreed. She sat back and sipped the remains of her drink, half listening as the antiquarians geeked out. The other half of her mind turned over Kitty and Madame Romanov. A fight the night before Hunter died. A fight about a book. A swindled book of magic?

"A secret, hidden in plain sight," one of the medievalists was saying of fore edges.

Like the killer, Cleo thought.

"How's your cousin?" Buddy asked, interrupting Cleo's muses.

"Happy," Cleo said, which she hoped was true. "Some of her books were returned tonight."

"That's wonderful! Someone brought 'em back to her store or what?"

"They were left anonymously at her home." Cleo opened her purse and retrieved the list she'd made of the titles. "When you found Dot's bird book at Professor Weber's stand the other day, did you happen to notice any of these?"

Buddy scratched behind his ear. "They're familiar titles, aren't they? They're popular. Popular's not Professor Weber's thing."

He made a good point. "Most are by southern authors," Cleo said, thinking aloud. "Southern delights?"

"Miss Peavey? Yeah, could be. But would she give 'em back anonymously? She makes a show of things." Buddy named some other society members who liked southern classics. He pointed to a title. "Now, *I'd* love to have that one."

It was one of the comics on the list, Pogo the possum and his pals in the Okefenokee Swamp. Cleo's kids had adored Pogo, and Ollie did too. Like Ollie, Pogo cared about the environment, including swamps and all the creatures who lived there. Buddy chatted on about reading *Pogo* as a kid, and Cleo thought how books had different value to different people.

Buddy eventually yawned and announced it was past his bedtime. "I'll sleep better knowing Miss Dot got her books back."

His yawn was contagious. Cleo hoped she'd sleep well too. Henry and the others stood, and Mr. Chaucer wobbled to his feet.

They all made their way out, waving to Skeet as they left. After good-nights and promises to chat more about books and restorations, the medievalists and Buddy headed for the Myrtles. Henry, Mr. Chaucer, and Cleo turned toward her home. Cleo glanced back into the bar as they passed. Kitty was laughing and raising a drink. Skeet was polishing the bar, and Margaret the bulldog likely still snoozed by the jukebox.

If Mr. Chaucer hadn't had spring allergies, Cleo might not have seen what she did. The pug erupted in a string of sneezes.

"Bless you!" Cleo said, her gaze swinging from the window to Mr. Chaucer, who wobbled but managed to stay upright. Her eyes caught on a dusty white van wedged in the pull-in parking.

She inhaled sharply. "Look!" she said, and then immediately corrected. "No, don't look."

But Henry already had. "Oh, it's Professor Weber," he said. "I wonder if he's looking for Kitty?"

The engine was off. The professor had been leaning on the steering wheel, his gaze locked on the view through the window. On Kitty, Cleo was sure. She clutched her cardigan closer.

"We should say hello," Henry said, jolly from his book chat. He turned toward the van.

He was stepping off the curb when the engine roared to a start and the van jolted into reverse. Professor Weber didn't look back, not to check the street for oncoming traffic or to see if Henry Lafayette—stumbling onto the sidewalk and scooping up his pug—was okay.

Henry sputtered. "What was that about?" He recovered his good-natured equanimity. "Maybe he didn't see us."

The professor had seen them, Cleo was sure. He'd seen his fiancée too.

"He was watching Kitty," Cleo said softly.

"Watching . . ." Henry repeated. "Looking out for her?"

A prickle crept up Cleo's neck. She suddenly felt they were being watched. She turned and Henry did too. Kitty Peavey had stepped close to the glass. She stared out at them, her face as rigid and chilly as her fiancé's.

Chapter
Twenty-Five

Cleo lay in bed in the warm bliss of deep Saturday-morning sleep. The quilt was perfectly cozy, the pillow just right, her limbs so relaxed they felt like lead. She hadn't had such a good rest in days, even weeks.

Bang! Bang, bang!

The disturbance melted into Cleo's dream, a joyful if surreal fantasy in which she was cooking with her Granny Bess and her mother. They were all the same age, a sprightly forty-something, and making biscuits on Granny B's old enamel table.

Bang!

Biscuit cutters sliced the dough. *Bang, bang!* A sheet pan fell to the floor, and the prickly sensation of a nightmare crept along Cleo's skin. Granny B was gone. So was her mother. Cleo stood alone at the table.

Meow! A furry forehead bumped Cleo's nose. The tickle of whiskers followed, and a whiff of tuna.

"Rhett," Cleo mumbled. "Too early." Cleo yearned to return to the happy dream, but it had fizzled away. With a sigh, Cleo forced her eyelids up. In the darkness, she blearily made out Henry, tugging a flannel robe over flannel pajamas. A brief flash of contentment returned. She wasn't alone.

Mr. Chaucer woofed. Henry made soft *shhhhh* sounds.

"I'm awake," Cleo declared with the blustery force of the drowsy. "I'll get it."

Henry had already slipped out. Footsteps of man and pug rattled down the stairs. Cleo groaned at the clock. Who was pounding on her door before six? Chief Culpepper, after Henry again? Irritation sparked. She kicked covers from her feet and wriggled out from under Rhett, who hopped off the bed and bounded down the hall, meowing for breakfast.

Cleo was at the top of the stairs when she heard Henry giving a more pleasant greeting than she would have managed.

The pleasantries were not reciprocated. Sharp words barged up to Cleo's ears. "I'm calling the police! You've brought crime to our doorsteps. Again!"

Wanda! Rhett Butler turned tail and trotted back to the bedroom. Cleo wished she could too. Instead, she trudged downstairs.

"Wanda," Cleo said with a sigh. "It's early, and . . ."

"And that bus of yours has attracted the criminal element like I've been saying all along! I told you, Cleo Watkins. You're attracting juvenile delinquents and social-media strangers and disreputables and—"

Now Cleo felt too awake. *My bus? Words on Wheels?* "Wanda, what's happened to the bookmobile?"

"It's gotten itself broken into. Weren't you listening?"

Cleo gasped. She pushed past Wanda and trotted across her porch and down her walkway, oblivious to the damp chill biting at her bare feet.

At the gate, Cleo gaped. Henry stopped behind her, issuing soothing sounds.

"I told you so," Wanda said, sounding pleased.

Mr. Chaucer caught up and woofed nervously.

The door to Words on Wheels swung partially open, crooked on its hinges. Cleo tiptoed over the gravel drive. When she reached her bookmobile, she tenderly touched its side, as she might comfort a wounded being. Then she reached for the door, needing to get inside and check.

A warm hand touched hers. "Wait," said Henry. "This is a crime scene. Let's call Gabby."

"I've already done that," Wanda said. "For once, those police are taking me seriously. Figures, since you're involved, Cleo."

Gabby's screen door slammed a moment later. The deputy herself jogged up a few seconds after. They all met on the front sidewalk between Cleo's and Gabby's homes. Gabby wasn't in uniform, but she was more dressed than Cleo, in faded jeans and a baggy sweatshirt. Her hair was piled up in a messy bun.

Gabby eyed Wanda with a healthy measure of suspicion. "If this is another call about my porch door slamming or my car . . ."

"Why do I even bother to report crimes anymore?" Wanda declared in aggrieved tones. "All I get is complaints. Never any thanks. Ingrates."

Cleo noted that Wanda was fully dressed for yard battle—rubbery boots and old floppy pants, the mud-stained windbreaker, garden gloves poking out her front pocket. All that was missing were her weapons of floral destruction.

"Thank you, Wanda," Cleo said sincerely. Emotion shook her next words. "It's Words on Wheels, Gabby. Someone broke in. The door is broken and wide open. I could see my display case on the floor."

"Oh, don't get all weepy. It's just an old bus," Wanda grumbled. "If you didn't make it so flashy, maybe criminals wouldn't be attracted to it."

"Words on Wheels?" Gabby sounded properly outraged. She started down Cleo's driveway.

Cleo padded after her, trying to keep to the grassy edge. "We didn't touch anything yet," Cleo said. "Henry wisely pointed out that we shouldn't leave prints."

Wanda followed along. "Yeah, you two know criminal procedure, that's for sure. Too bad neither of you heard anything. That little dog was no help either."

Mr. Chaucer gazed nervously up at them, his wrinkles deepening and his eyes wide.

"Good boy," Gabby said to him. To the humans, she said, "Miss Cleo, you need shoes, and I need gloves and my evidence kit. Let's go get those and meet back here. Wanda, we shouldn't keep you. How about I come over later and get your statement? You were right to call this in. Thank you."

Wanda snorted. "Try and shove me off, will you? Well, I'll stay right here if I want, *thank you* very much. I don't want more crime erupting when you all turn your backs again."

Cleo knew she must be shaken because she felt Wanda made a good point.

Rhett waited on the porch steps, frowny-faced from the dewy damp and lack of attention to his breakfast. Cleo fed him and then went upstairs to change. Henry did the same, doling out kibbles for his worried pug.

Cleo's emotions hovered between those of the pets: worried and vexed. Mostly, she was upset with herself. "I was negligent in my librarian responsibilities," she said when she and Henry met back up in the foyer. "I left my collectibles display in Words on Wheels. I should have brought it in. I got lazy and considered it safe."

He made soothing sounds and added a supportive hug. "The break-in might not be related to the display. It could be like Wanda's always said. Kids, pranksters, common vandals. Besides, didn't you say that most of the items in the display weren't worth that much? That was your point, right? That collecting doesn't have to cost a fortune."

His hair was mussed and poking over his ears in all directions. Cleo reached out and smoothed it, ending with an affectionate touch to his cheek and his fluffy beard. She knew the dear man was trying to make her feel better.

She felt awful. "Except for the one valuable book," she said. "The book Kitty coveted."

Henry didn't try to offer false cheer. He squeezed her arm and said, "We don't know yet."

Cleo knew.

*   *   *

Chief Culpepper pulled up with lights flashing. He ignored Wanda's complaints about the book-related crime wave and blustered at Gabby, who had snapped on gloves and was prying the bus's door open. Cleo steadied herself on her picket fence. Her lovely display case lay on the floor. From where she stood, she could see some book covers and due-date cards scattered inside the case.

"A book will be missing," Cleo predicted. "Possibly a signed due-date card too."

"A book and a due-date card?" the chief said with undisguised exasperation. "I got out of bed early on a Saturday for this?"

"Burglary is a major crime," Wanda snapped. "A small step away from home invasion and cold-blooded murder and outright mayhem."

"This was a valuable book," Cleo said, united in indignation with Wanda. "Part of our library's special collection."

The chief shook his head. "What's so *special* about it?"

Cleo explained. "This book had a signature by Shirley Macon James. We also had her signature on the due-date card too. It was quite . . . well, special."

She looked around. Henry was nodding supportively.

Wanda scoffed, any camaraderie gone. "Are you talking about *Into the Waves?* Romance tripe. Better that it's not in the library, I say. *Children* go to libraries, Cleo. They shouldn't be reading junk."

"It's a romance?" the chief asked with a frown. "My wife reads those." He didn't sound happy about it. Cleo thought again that Mrs. Culpepper was a woman of great patience and tolerance.

And then there was Wanda . . . Wanda rallied every year for Banned Books Week, on the side of banning.

"It was a robbery," Cleo said, enunciating firmly. "A crime against the library and thus everyone in Catalpa County." She held her chin high and dared the chief and Wanda to dismiss that.

Wanda turned her attention to Cleo's hedge, grumbling that it needed a good clipping. The chief stomped over to the bus and offered Gabby advice on hurrying up.

The display case lay a few yards away, protected from the ground by a plastic sheet. Gabby was still inside Words on Wheels. She'd already dusted the door and told Cleo that it could have been too easily wrenched open with a few common tools and a little muscle.

Overhead, a golden sunrise was burning off the dew, but long, thin clouds wisped at the horizon and a restless breeze kicked around the pollen. Both Wanda and Mr. Chaucer were sneezing.

Chief Culpepper turned back to them, tugging his suspenders. "So," he said. "If that book is so *special*, why'd you leave it in the bus?"

"Bookmobile," Cleo specified, but her face went hot with chagrin. "I did mean to take the display case inside for the night," she admitted. "But then I went out—over to my cousin Dot's. As you know, she received some of her *stolen* books back."

"*Allegedly* stolen," the chief muttered. "*Allegedly* returned anonymously. No one saw anyone drop off that package. Who's to say your cousin didn't steal those books back herself and then pretend to get them back?"

I'm to say. But Cleo knew disagreeing with the chief would only make him dig in harder. She forged on with her own confession. "Mr. Lafayette and I went out last night. We got in late, and I'm sorry to say, I forgot." She was sorry. Very sorry.

"You went out? Where?" the chief asked.

Cleo realized she'd been a little too honest. "Oh, out to speak with some folks," she said, with the mumbled reluctance of a truant schoolkid caught out.

"And those folks were *where?*" the chief persisted.

"The, ah . . . gastropub," Cleo said.

"Skeet's?" Wanda crowed. "Skeet's *bar?* Cleo Watkins! First you're giving false overnight alibis for your *boy*friend, and now you're hanging around bars until all hours. It's no wonder you forgot about your bus and books!"

"We were there because of books," Cleo protested.

The chief was shaking his head as if disappointed.

Wanda suddenly had somewhere to be. She hustled away, cackling. Cleo knew where she was going: off to her phone to spread gossip.

Gabby stepped out of the bookmobile, tugging off her gloves. "Words on Wheels is too popular, Miss Cleo. You'll have prints from half the town and then some inside. Do you have any theories to get us started?"

Cleo didn't hesitate. "Kitty Peavey. She wanted that book. She tried to buy it, and when I said no, she said she'd 'get her hands on it.'" Cleo searched her memory. "'Soon,' she said." Cleo kicked at some gravel. She could kick herself too. She'd been warned, and she hadn't paid proper heed.

"Miss Peavey?" Chief Culpepper outright laughed. "A pretty gal like her, breaking into an old school bus in the middle of the night? I can hardly see that. Why, she's recently suffered a break-in herself." He pushed out his chest and suspenders. "I'll go speak with her personally, make sure she's doing okay."

After he'd left, Gabby said, "Off the record? I *can* see Miss Peavey doing this. It really wouldn't take much burglary skill to get in this bus. More than that, she's determined. A determined woman will get her way."

Chapter
Twenty-Six

Wanda was back in her garden, whistling with unsettling merriment, when Cleo sneaked out a few hours later. Cleo eased her screen door closed and tiptoed down the walkway. She was alone and on foot. Earlier, Henry had given her a ride back from the repair shop, where Cleo's favorite mechanics had promised to commence emergency surgery on Words on Wheels.

It would be an easy and quick operation, the mechanics had assured Cleo. They'd throw in a general checkup for free. Her bus would be better than ever.

Except it wouldn't, not for Cleo. The mechanics could fix the door and make it more secure. They might even get the air conditioner to puff above tepid. But books were the vital organs, and *Into the Waves* would still be missing.

Cleo was sure Kitty Peavey had the book. Unfortunately, Chief Culpepper was just as sure Kitty was innocent.

Kitty had an alibi, the chief reported. He'd called Cleo to tell her and to warn her against "maligning" visitors. The lovely Miss Peavey, according to the chief, had spent the night in the arms of her fiancé.

"Lucky man," the chief had added wistfully. "A lucky man."

Vexed by his report and tone, Cleo pointed out that alibis from loved ones could be suspect. As soon as the words were out, she regretted them. *Words spoken in haste*, her mother would have warned. *Regretted at leisure.*

"*You'd* know all about that," the chief retorted. "Are *you* sure Mr. Lafayette was with you all night? I should remind you, he's a top-tier person of interest in a murder investigation."

As if Cleo had forgotten!

Henry would be at the fair by now. Rhett was staying at home, sunning on the front porch. Cleo's destination was unsuitable for cats. She was heading for the Drop By, where she hoped to find a glorious mess of exposed plumbing and electrical wires.

The sky shifted between sunny heat and cloudy bluster. Cleo resolved to focus on the partly sunny in the forecast and the situation. She practiced as she strolled past Gabby's cottage, where wildflower seeds were sprouting faster and thicker than weeds. They'd be gorgeous soon. Gabby had spent a whole weekend digging out the beds, her first attempt at gardening.

Cleo admired a freshly painted fence and stopped to greet a friendly calico cat. When she reached downtown, she soaked in the flower-filled park and the lovely library. She beamed when she looked down the street and spotted a crowd outside the Drop By.

How nice, Cleo thought, now in the rhythm of positive thinking. Cleo stubbed her toe on a bump in the sidewalk at the same moment her optimism tripped.

A crowd? It was nearly ten. Dot should have opened by now. Cleo stopped behind the throng of people.

"What's going on?" she asked the nearest person she recognized, Jamal Kennedy. The young man had graduated from high school with Ollie and now boasted a degree in botany and a job raising otherworldly orchids. Cleo saw him periodically when he stopped by Words on Wheels to check out science fiction and graphic novels as thick as the classics.

"It's wild, Mrs. Watkins." Jamal looked down at her from his height somewhere above six feet. "Everyone's saying an innocent dude's getting railroaded for a murder he didn't commit."

"I've been saying that too," Cleo said, tucking her hair behind her ears.

He nodded solemnly. "Then that settles it, and you're in the right place."

Cleo was where she'd intended to be. What she didn't understand was why everyone else was here.

"Is it a rally on the innocent man's behalf?" she asked. In that case, she was definitely in the right place.

"Nah." Jamal bent lower. "This is—*they say*—where the real killer's hiding out. Everyone's gathering in a quest for justice."

Cleo willfully resisted the logical but terrible implication. "The *real* killer? Here?"

"The lady who owns this place. Who'd think it? She makes the best cookies."

* * *

"Get inside, Gran, quick." Ollie ushered Cleo in, shielding her from the crowd and a particularly pushy young man with a sculpted beard, a handlebar mustache, and a microphone. Ollie locked the door and practically pushed Cleo down the nearest aisle.

Ollie moaned. "This is my fault."

He barreled on, speaking fast over Cleo's murmurs of "No, no."

"It is!" he said, leaning back against a shelf tidily stacked with canisters of oatmeal and golden bags of grits. "*I* started that fund raiser. *I* got Auntie Dot online exposure That's where it started. Online! People—strangers—got interested in Auntie Dot and her missing book and the murder, and well . . ."

He rubbed both hands over his face. "A chat group got going last night, just to talk about the murder of that book scout, which seems good, right? I mean, you want to turn up new information and theories. But then everyone turned on Auntie Dot. They're saying she stalked that guy Hunter and killed him and he had it coming, which maybe he did, but . . ."

"It's okay, Oliver." Cleo reached out a soothing hand.

Her grandson shook his shaggy-haired head. "It's not. The fund-raising site shut down our page and sent back all the donations. That's not even the worst of it. There's a true-crime podcaster in town! The guy outside with the beard and the mic."

Cleo hadn't listened to podcasts, although she thought she might like them. As a child, she'd enjoyed radio serials. Her whole family had, gathering in the sitting room or on the back porch to listen. From Ollie's expression, she knew she wouldn't enjoy this one.

"Just listen," he said, taking out his phone. "It's the first episode, and it's . . . it's . . ." At a loss for words, he turned up the volume instead.

Ominous music filled the breakfast aisle, the kind that might introduce a true-crime drama on TV. A voice followed, a man's, deep and foreboding. "Catalpa Springs, a tiny town few have heard of, let alone dared visit, calls itself the 'safest little town in the South.' A lure? A lie? Safe? Not these days. What follows is a tale ripped from the pages of dime-store noir. A desperate woman scorned, a bookdealer—"

"Cleo, is that you?" Dot's voice trilled down the aisles.

Ollie scrambled to press mute while Cleo greeted Dot with a hug, finding herself at an unusual loss for words.

"I suppose you've heard," Dot said when they released each other. She tugged at her apron ties, knotted tight at her front. "I've gone viral. Like the flu."

"Auntie Dot, I'm sorry!" Ollie shook his head as if still in stunned disbelief. "It was going so well too. We'd raised a ton of money."

A knock at the front door interrupted him, a happy tapping to a shave-and-a-haircut beat. Ollie ducked down. He gestured for Cleo and Dot to do the same.

"It'll be that podcaster," Ollie whispered. "Don't talk to him. I admit, I listened to his last season. He's good. He went after a nun who'd been acquitted of murder. Who knows if she was innocent, but he made everyone think she'd done it."

Dot tidied some cereal boxes and murmured that she was sure it would all blow over. "Don't you worry, Oliver. All the dirt comes out with the wash, as our mothers used to say, right, Cleo?" Dot shifted some bottles of cane syrup down to the baking section. "We've had a run on syrup," she said. "I wonder what folks are making? Pies? Popcorn balls? Glazed ham?"

Cleo would normally have enjoyed syrup speculations. Now she worried that Dot was in shock . . . or denial.

The seven-beat knock came again, louder this time. Cleo felt her pocket buzz. She had her phone close for surgery updates on Words on Wheels. Now it seemed frivolous to worry about a wounded door.

I'll just check, Cleo reasoned. It would be rude to ignore the repairmen if they needed her permission to proceed with some treatment.

Gabby's name popped up in a text, prefaced by a smiley face. *It's the police, open up. Please? We'll come around back.*

"It's Gabby," Cleo said. "She's coming around the back."

Ollie brightened and loped off, ducking around the back by the freezers. Cleo and Dot followed. To Cleo's dismay, Gabby wasn't alone.

"Amateurs," Chief Culpepper declared, stomping inside with so much bluster Cleo could have sworn she saw a cloud of disapproval following him. "If I've told you once, I've told you a million times, Miss Cleo, amateurs such as yourself and that podcasting pest from Atlanta only muddy up the investigative waters. I do *not* appreciate having my investigation questioned or having to address wild theories. Innocent members of the public can get hurt. Like Miss Peavey."

Cleo firmed her spine. "Like my cousin."

Standing in Dot's shop, with Dot wide-eyed in front of him, the chief had the grace to apologize. "I *am* sorry, Miss Dot, but that podcaster and the chat group did make some good connections. You *did* threaten the man and go to his room the night he died. Now I learn you were banging on his door like that mob out there?"

Dot's cheeks flared red. "No. Not banging. Tapping. I only wanted to talk, to reason with him."

"Uh-huh," the chief said skeptically. He turned to Gabby. "And Deputy, why wasn't I made aware of the desperate financial situation here at the Drop By?"

Gabby gazed back with serene calm. "I did mention so in my reports, sir."

"That's my fault too," Dot said. "I didn't want anyone to know."

Cleo took her by the arm and translated. "What my cousin means is, she didn't want to advertise her finances. No one likes doing that."

"Then I went and advertised them all over," Ollie said with a groan. "I was trying to help. Auntie Dot would have closed the store rather than bother anyone."

Culpepper stretched his suspenders. He looked out toward the light of the street. The crowd was drifting away. The podcaster trotted after passersby, thrusting his microphone at them. Most scooted away.

More banging came from the kitchen area.

"What's going on back there?" the chief asked.

When Dot explained the contractors, his small eyes narrowed. "How are you paying for that?"

"They're volunteering," Ollie said. "Some guys Mary-Rose Garland knows who do good deeds."

The chief peeked in the back room and left soon after, muttering that it was all a big, muddy mess and getting worse. Cleo couldn't argue with that.

Gabby stayed behind, saying she needed to go over Dot's statement with her. She drew out her cell phone. "I'm not mentioning this to the chief until I confirm it. A techie friend is helping me trace where the bad rumors about you got rolling, Miss Dot."

"Mean rumors turn into avalanches on the Internet," Ollie said grimly.

"True, but avalanches start somewhere. Look at this." Gabby held out her phone. "One person started talking about the murder and insisting Henry was innocent."

"A wise person," Cleo said.

Gabby scrolled down her screen. "Then that same person gets going about Miss Dot's connection and motives. Really whipping up incriminating evidence. Look, here's the detail about Miss Dot going to Hunter's room at the bed-and-breakfast the night before he was killed and—"

Cleo took back her wise-person comment. The online commentator sounded as bad as Wanda Boxer, but with a worldwide reach.

224

Ollie's height let him crane over Gabby's shoulder to read the phone screen. "User name, TinaTheSeer."

Cleo and Dot crowded close.

"Madame Romanov!" Cleo adjusted her bifocals to inspect the thumbnail-sized photo. It wasn't the psychic herself but just as recognizable: a chunky dachshund wearing a purple cape. Slim.

"Why would she do this?" Cleo asked, and then immediately answered herself. "She's guilty, Gabby. This is proof in itself. She's shifting the blame."

"But why go after Auntie Dot?" Ollie said.

Dot said in a small voice, "If it's Madame Romanov, she doesn't like me. I caught her shoplifting a while back."

Gabby frowned. "You did? I didn't hear about that."

A frenzy of banging came from the back room. Dot waited until the noise subsided and said, "I'd never call the police about a little shoplifting. I figured she *needed* what she was taking. I offered her a free lunch, but she accused me of being condescending. She said she'd only been practicing her 'art,' her sleight-of-hand moves. I did apologize. I hadn't intended to offend her."

Gabby made a note of the shoplifting. At Dot's insistence, she also dutifully recorded that Dot hadn't meant any harm. "I'll put it all in a report. If this is Madame Romanov making these posts, it's good information. We can deduce a lot from them."

"She's manipulative," Cleo said.

"That," Gabby agreed. "And she's alive."

Cleo felt momentary guilt. In her vexation, she'd forgotten that Madame Romanov's safety had been in question.

Gabby pointed to her phone again. "She's close by too, or in contact with someone locally. See here? TinaTheSeer knows intimate details about your plumbing line repair, Miss Dot." Gabby grinned. "Either that or she is psychic."

Cleo and Ollie scoffed as one.

Gabby slipped her phone back in her pocket. "Speaking of plumbing, if you're still digging that line, I can come by and help later. I'm not allowed to do any more overtime today." She grinned. "I need to keep up my garden-digging muscles."

Ollie perked up. "That would be awesome. I'll bring something to eat. It'll be like . . . like a picnic!" They made plans and talked about times and foods and parted with cheerful *see yous*.

Cleo and Dot waited until the street looked clear of podcasters and then slipped out. Cleo walked Dot home, determined to keep up a positive conversation. By the time they reached Dot's house, Cleo felt they'd complimented every spring flower and singing bird in Georgia. Then she hit on a positive that made her genuinely smile. "There is some good to come out of this. Ollie . . ."

Dot smiled back. "He's done it, hasn't he? Ollie almost sort of made a date with Gabby."

Chapter
Twenty-Seven

M ore good news came when Cleo was sitting at Dot's kitchen table, enjoying tea and caramel cookies. Dot had made the cookies earlier, planning to give them out as an afternoon snack to volunteers and well-wishers at the Drop By.

"Sorry," Cleo said as her phone buzzed. When she saw who was calling, she crossed her fingers for good luck.

"The repair shop," she said, and Dot crossed her fingers too.

"Well," drawled one of the look-alike brothers who ran the repair shop. "I've got some bad news, Miss Cleo." The chuckle that followed verged on a giggle. He was outright laughing when he said, "You won't have the air conditioner as an excuse to speed down the highway anymore. You'll be shivering at five miles per hour."

Cleo let out the breath she'd been holding. "You're a genius!"

"I'll drive you over to the repair shop," Dot said when Cleo ended the call. "How about we take some cookies to the men too? I made dozens, way too many. Oh, and I could take some by the book fair to thank Professor Weber for bringing by my book and Buddy for finding it. And Henry, of course, and anyone else who'd like some."

Cleo opened her mouth to issue a warning. Dot was too nice, too sunny and trusting . . .

Before she could say a bad word, Dot said. "I'll be careful, Cleo. I won't talk to podcasters or psychics. I know I was too trusting before, but just look at all these cookies. Besides, it never hurts to be nice."

* * *

"Take her for a spin," the mechanics had urged. "Crank up the air. Give the door a workout."

The door opened with the silkiness of warm cream. The brothers had installed an inner brace, hopefully making it harder to break into. The door was better than ever, as they'd promised. The engine hummed and sipped on fresh oil.

As nice as spinning would be, Cleo decided to save it for later. She followed Dot back to town at Dot's sedate speed. When Dot pulled over at the Depot, Cleo waved and gave the horn a mighty honk. She kept going, out Elberta Street, named for the railroad-ready peach that gave Georgia its Peach State nickname.

Cleo continued to drive slowly, following the abandoned tracks and thinking about other changes. Peaches had fallen from their pedestal. Several years back, blueberries had grabbed the state title for the biggest fruit crop.

At least that was a change Cleo could easily adapt to. The year the blueberry news broke, she and Mary-Rose had come up with a recipe for peach-blueberry cobbler that was downright divine.

Cleo's thoughts turned to the Pancake Mill, where blueberry pancakes would be sizzling on the griddles. Her stomach rumbled. Her fingers tapped the steering wheel, listing all the reasons why she should spin out to the Mill. She should test her bus. She'd had a most unsettling morning. Besides, she'd had only coffee and cookies for breakfast. Cookies didn't count as breakfast.

Cleo pressed the gas and turned on the air conditioner. The arctic blast blew her hair back.

"Good gracious," Cleo murmured. She turned off the air, opened her window, and let the warm, muggy scents of a passing wetland sweep in. She could make a stop on the way, a bookmobile stop to absolutely justify a second breakfast. She had some books for the residents of Golden Acres Nursing Home tucked in the shelf behind her seat. Thank goodness those hadn't been touched or taken.

Nurse Franklin greeted her in the lobby, where the air was thick with the scent of peonies. The towering nurse held a vase of the frilly flowers in his hand, pink and complementing his hot-pink scrubs.

"Where's your furry sidekick?" Franklin asked, leaving the vase on the reception desk and taking a heavy tote bag of books from Cleo's hand.

Cleo explained that Rhett had stayed home. "I had a little trouble with my bookmobile this morning," she said. "It shook up my plans for the day." It had shaken her up too.

"The break-in. We heard." Franklin clicked his tongue in disapproval and added, "Just so you know, no one's taking any stock in the rude rumor that you failed to notice because you'd been out carousing in a bar with your bad-boy criminal boyfriend."

"Wanda Boxer!" Cleo exclaimed.

Franklin gave a deep, rolling chuckle. "Yep. That would be our source. Our receptionist is on her gossip hotline." He winked down to Cleo. "Most of us think your bookseller boyfriend is innocent, and everyone says you should kick up your heels all you can."

Cleo thanked him.

"My pleasure," Franklin said. "I like delivering good news. Here's more. The bibliophiles are gathered in the sun-room." He offered to escort her there. "It's uncanny, actually, you showing up. Everyone was just talking about you. Were your ears buzzing?"

Cleo groaned. "Because of Henry and the bar? He's innocent! It's a *gastropub*." She silently gave thanks that Wanda hadn't heard of the podcast yet, although that wouldn't last long.

A lady slowly rolling up the hall in a wheelchair flagged Franklin down and asked to be taken to the "event." He swooped her along. After pleasantries and introductions, he turned back to Cleo.

"Nah, the bibliophiles don't have time to dwell on gossip, not when they have books." He bent to wheelchair height. "Right, Mrs. Slater?"

She gave a sprightly if slightly off-color affirmation.

"That's right. Heck yeah," Franklin agreed, winking at Cleo.

Cleo held the door for Franklin and his passionate friend. She stepped after them into a room filled with giggling ladies, a handful of pink-cheeked men, and the pirate-tongued parrot. The women filled a collection of soft chairs, sofas, and wheelchairs arranged in a loose circle.

The parrot perched atop his plastic palm, clucking what sounded like "Hot, hot, hot." The men were grouped around a card table, with cards and potato chip bags scattered about.

When they noticed Cleo, the preacher's wife led the cheer of greeting. "You'll never guess what we got our hands on," she said, clasping her own hands in excitement. "*The Lusty Lord*! The very book from the library! Can you believe my daughter bought it from the library book sale a few years back? We're having read-aloud story time, right, girls? Gentlemen?"

"We're only here to play cards," a man protested, too gruffly.

His compatriots blushed and ducked behind their cards as the ladies had a good laugh. "Liars," a female voice cried out, echoed by the bird.

"They're here for the good parts," the preacher's wife said. "I had forgotten just how *lusty* this lord is!" She stuck in a bookmark and waved off Cleo's apology for interrupting. "We all need some iced tea and a cooldown," she said, handing the book to Cleo.

Laughter and the clink of ice cubes filled the room. Cups of iced tea and lemonade were passed around.

Cleo opened to the front cover and smiled. It was the library copy, all right. There was the lovely bookplate showing the likeness of the Catalpa Springs Public Library. Another stamp hovered over it, in blue ink and blocky capital letters. *Withdrawn.*

A day decades ago flashed to Cleo's mind as if it had happened moments before. Her work mentor, the head librarian who'd hired her, had gathered the library staff together to discuss the stamp. At the time, they'd been stamping *Discarded* in red ink. Cleo's mentor thought that sounded too rude and awful. Cleo agreed. After much debate, they settled on *Withdrawn*. The word was easy to fit on a stamp, but it didn't capture the difficulty of removing any book.

Recently, Cleo and her protégé, Leanna, had revisited the library's deaccessioning process and the stamp. They'd volleyed around other possibilities for the wording. *Retired* took first place for Leanna. Cleo, however, had issues with the word. "Heavens," she'd sputtered to Leanna, "it isn't like the books are moving down to Florida." She'd probably overreacted. *Retirement* was a trigger word for her.

After that, she and Leanna had wavered between too silly and tragic. *On permanent holiday, with gratitude for years of service. Gone but not forgotten. Passed on to other pastures. A good book looking for a forever home.*

In the end, they'd stuck with plain *Withdrawn*. Cleo now wondered if they should try again. Perhaps *Retired* was preferable.

The preacher's wife broke her thoughts, raising her glass in a toast.

"To all the library books we've loved before," she said, to a rousing chorus of "Hear, hear" and a parrot yelling, "Lusty liar, lusty liar!"

Cleo wondered if that could fit on a stamp—the toast, not the parrot's outburst. She'd ask Leanna. When the toasting died down, Cleo got down to business, passing out books residents had requested. She'd leave others at the front desk for residents who weren't attending the reading.

After everyone had inspected their new items, Cleo said, "You all know, I've been wrapped up in some trouble lately."

"We know you wouldn't date a killer, Cleo," a voice called out.

"Not knowingly," another qualified.

"Nothing wrong with kicking up your heels at a club, either," still another said. Others agreed, and a call went up for Franklin to take them clubbing.

Cleo felt her brow furrow, but she thanked them for their support. "I need all the help I can get," she said, hoping to shift the conversation away from Henry and clubbing. "Remember how I asked you about victims of the book scout?"

"The con artist," came a mumble.

"Had it coming!" declared one of the men.

The preacher's wife issued a loud "Rest in peace!"

"We've been keeping our ears out," Franklin said, when the din settled. "You know about my G-mom. Good thing she doesn't drive, or she'd likely be a suspect too." *Tsk*ing tongues and sympathy rose when he told them about Bernice's missing Poirot.

More names flew around the room, relatives and friends of the residents. Cleo already knew about most of them.

"This is all very helpful," Cleo said. "But here's what's puzzling me most. How did Hunter Fox know whom to visit? He's not from here. What's the connection among all these good booklovers?"

Silence fell for long moments before one of the card-playing men thumped the table. "A mole! The scout had an insider, a local. Yeah, and the spy killed the scout and ran off with all those valuable books!"

The group eyed one another with some suspicion, as if the murderous local might be among them.

"What about a book group?" the preacher's wife suggested, with excessive brightness. Names of local book clubs circulated. The Who-Done-Its, Dante's Devotees, Babes and Books. A few names on the list of Hunter's victims intersected. None overlapped entirely.

Another resident, a lady with proper pearls, raised her hand. "I have it! He sensed 'em! He's a psychic, like the lady the police are looking for. That's it! He and that psychic woman Madame Bovary—"

"Romanov," someone corrected.

"Like I said," the speculator continued. "What if she fed him the info and then knocked him off and ran off with all the books?"

The cardplayer grumbled that she was stealing his theory.

Cleo liked the idea of Madame's guilt. However, she had no belief in Madame's psychic powers.

Chatter bounced around the room. Mrs. Slater, the woman who'd come in with Cleo and Franklin, coughed pointedly. In a raspy, birdlike voice, she said, "I know what I'd do if I wanted to find out something. I'd go to the library."

All eyes turned to Cleo.

That's exactly what Cleo would do. Her stomach clenched. It was an equally good and horrible idea. To think the library—*her library*—might be involved. Cleo quickly talked herself out of the possibility. "Hunter Fox did visit the library. My wise colleague, Leanna, turned him away. We have a strict privacy policy."

"What about all the free talks and programs at the library?" Mrs. Slater persisted. "Remember when we all went to see that local author, the true-crime lady? She scared me silly! We had our photos in the paper afterward. We all looked blurry, probably because we were shaking like leaves in a tornado, we were so terrified." She laughed happily at the memory.

"That nice man at the bookstore did a workshop before Christmas too," another lady said. "Oh, but wait . . . is that your *friend*, Cleo? The man with the bookstore and the murder weapon and no alibi and . . ." The woman fell silent.

Cleo was speechless too. She half heard words fly around the room.

Shhh . . . she's trying to remember.

She can't remember which boyfriend? Does she have so many, she can't keep 'em straight? Like Lady Lucy and the lord!

"The newspaper," Cleo said aloud.

"There's that," the preacher's wife said kindly.

"The newspaper printed a photo of one of Henry's workshops." Cleo remembered that Henry had objected to the headline, deeming it tacky. "*Local Booklovers Eager to Cash In on Their*

234

Shelves," Cleo murmured. It was something like that. Cleo had attended an earlier workshop, so she hadn't gone to the one featured in the newspaper. Dot had, though. So had another lady on the list . . .

"Yeah," Franklin said, squinting out the window as if he might catch sight of the memory. "I drove my G-mom to that. She clipped out the photo. First time she'd ever been in the newspaper."

Other names filled in. Cleo would check at the library to be sure, but she feared they'd found the connection. Henry! The poor man would feel awful.

"The mole," the cardplayer said.

"The bad-boy boyfriend," someone else whispered.

"Well!" the preacher's wife exclaimed loudly. "Let's get back to that lusty lord, shall we? Remember, when last we knew, it was a gusty day for a kilt . . ."

Chapter
Twenty-Eight

They were being watched. Cleo felt the gaze pressing on her back. Goose bumps crawled up her neck.

"They're getting closer," Cleo whispered. She could swear she heard footsteps. Beside her on the gently swaying glider bench, Mary-Rose seemed unconcerned, gazing out at the sparkling spring waters and the rippling reflection of the Pancake Mill.

"Ignore them," Mary-Rose said. Against her own advice, she twisted. "Shoo! Go on, you've had your pancakes."

Low chuckles and feathers ruffled in response.

Cleo glanced back. The Pancake Mill's trio of "guard peacocks" stopped, like children playing a game of freeze. If birds could look offended, they did. They gradually unfroze. The male fanned his tail and stomped. The females waggled their fancy fascinator-hat feathers.

Cleo had to chuckle. "Their expressions! I swear, we've offended them."

Mary-Rose turned back. "Don't let them see you laughing. They get petulant when their feelings are hurt."

"Shooing doesn't count as rude?" Cleo said, relieved to see the birds strutting off down the bank.

"They're spoiled rotten," Mary-Rose said affectionately. "They think they deserve unlimited pancakes anytime I'm out here walking."

Rhett demanded tuna treats every time he trotted into Words on Wheels. A little spoiled rotten wasn't a bad thing.

The bench settled back to a gentle sway. Cleo had come straight from Golden Acres, disturbed by the events of the morning. Mary-Rose had offered up her listening ear, butterscotch pie, and a stroll around Pancake Spring.

"I can see how it *could* look bad for Henry," Mary-Rose said, returning to the topic they'd been discussing before the guard-trio appeared.

Cleo stared at the rippling waters. It *did* look bad. She'd called Leanna at the library when she arrived at the Pancake Mill. In a few clicks of her keyboard, Leanna had found the newspaper photo, a dozen smiling participants and Henry, and all their names handily listed in the caption.

"The chief might even say this is Henry's missing motive," Mary-Rose continued. "Say Henry was angry or jealous that Hunter Fox swooped in and got to those local booklovers and their valuable books first."

"Mary-Rose!" Cleo sputtered. Down around the curve of the spring, the peacocks cackled in response.

Her best friend held up a placating palm. "Now, Cleo, I'm only playing devil's advocate. Or Chief Culpepper's advocate. Besides, if we weren't talking about Henry, this is what *you'd* be saying as our town supersleuth."

Some sleuth. All Cleo had managed to do was get Henry into deeper trouble. Just like Ollie's good deed with the fund raiser had backfired for Dot. She said so to Mary-Rose, aware of the whine in her tone.

"It's always darkest before the dawn," Mary-Rose said, as sagely as if she'd just come up with the saying herself.

Cleo kicked her feet. She was aware she was wallowing. Sometimes one needed a good wallow with a friend. And with pie too. Cleo was about to suggest that they continue their walk and thus justify a second slice.

"So what are we going to do about it?" Mary-Rose said briskly. "It's not like you to sit about, Cleo. Let's sum up. What do you know for sure?"

"That Henry and Dot are innocent," Cleo said.

"Yes, okay," Mary-Rose said patiently. "What do you know for sure about the crimes?"

Cleo considered. "I'm certain Kitty Peavey took my library book. I'm sure she has Dot's book too. Or that she did have it before her room was burglarized. I wish I could get in there and look around."

"So what's stopping you?" Mary-Rose said. A sun hat shaded her eyes but not their sparkle.

What indeed? Cleo had already asked, nicely, and Kitty had denied having the book. The chief had probably asked nicely about Cleo's missing library book too, which Kitty had also denied. Dot was wrong, Cleo thought. Sometimes it did hurt to be too nice. Not that Cleo would ever tell her sweet cousin that.

"You're right," Cleo said. "What are we waiting for?" She hopped off the bench on an upswing.

Mary-Rose stood too, smoothing her sundress, printed in bright abstract florals. "I'm glad you said we, Cleo. Otherwise, I was going to intervene again."

* * *

"She's on the move," Henry whispered.

From her bench in the park, Cleo pictured Henry a few blocks away, deep in the Depot, the cell phone pressed to his fluffy beard. He was a good spy.

Henry had called to report that the fair was closing up for the day. Kitty and the rest would likely be on their way back to the Myrtles for afternoon aperitifs and snacks.

"Cat's on the prowl?" Mary-Rose said when Cleo ended the call.

Cleo was glad to have Mary-Rose with her, lifting the mood with spy talk. Mary-Rose checked her watch, announced that it was "zero five hundred," and settled in to wait for ten minutes precisely before heading to the bed-and-breakfast.

When they arrived, they found Nina Flores slumped in a seat behind the reception desk.

"Is Kitty Peavey in?" Cleo asked.

"We have an appointment," Mary-Rose added firmly.

Cleo decided that wasn't a lie. She was overdue to speak with Miss Peavey.

"Upstairs," Nina said, making Kitty's presence sound as welcome as a termite infestation. Dark circles underlined Nina's eyes, and she wore a puffy winter jacket. Frigid air blew from the air-conditioning vents.

"How have you been doing?" Cleo asked.

Nina shivered. "As well as can be expected. At least we haven't had *another* robbery at the inn. These bookdealers, they attract trouble! I'm counting the minutes until they all check out. I'm praying their final soiree tomorrow night won't end up in some kind of crime too."

Mary-Rose smiled. "Cleo's looking forward to the soiree. She and her gentleman friend have been taking ballroom dance lessons for the occasion."

Cleo flushed. "We haven't had time to practice," she said. What with murder and thefts and unfounded accusations hogging her dance card. "I tend to step on toes," Cleo said.

"It won't matter," Nina said darkly. "They'll be tipsy. Miss Peavey's ordered extra liquor. She's the self-appointed organizer. She nixed the flowers I ordered, saying they had too much pollen. She nixed the band too, since they didn't know any Marilyn Monroe–era music. It'll have to be a DJ, I told her." She pointed in the vague direction of up. "She's in the penthouse. Room three A. Take either stairway and you'll get there."

"Party planning," Mary-Rose groaned as she and Cleo made their way up a grand marble staircase. "I feel for Nina. I adore a soiree, but can't stand all the decisions. In fact, that's why I stuck to two menu items at the Mill. Hard choices: take 'em or leave 'em." Mary-Rose stopped on the second floor. "Which way?"

Cleo laughed. "I hardly see how pancakes and/or pie is a hard choice." She looked around. She'd never been to the "penthouse" third floor. The stairs on the main, second floor ended in two dim hallways stretching out to either side. "Nina said either way. There must be back stairways at both ends?"

Mary-Rose grumbled about the low light of the candle-mimicking sconces and potted-plant forest as they followed a dogleg hallway to the left. Each door was bordered by sizable potted palms. Cleo touched one, confirming it was silk. A backlit *Exit* and staircase sign looked out of place in the antique decor. The stairs led up to the third floor and back down to the first. By the top, Cleo was more out of breath than she cared to admit.

They stepped out to a hallway done up in dizzying floral wallpaper and a chaotically swirly carpet. In her flowery dress, Mary-Rose was almost camouflaged.

"Here," Cleo whispered. A clump of potted palms marked Suite 3A. Cleo aimed her fist to knock but froze when voices filtered out. She leaned an ear toward Kitty's door. Mary-Rose joined her.

"Professor Weber," Cleo whispered, as a male voice spoke on the other side.

"I love you," he was saying. "You know that's why I try to protect you from doing something . . . foolish. No, dangerous."

Mary-Rose raised an eyebrow.

"Foolish?" Kitty's voice was so sharp it seemed to slice through the door. "Is that what you think of me and my collecting?"

"It's what I think of *collecting* that could land you in jail." His voice rumbled too close to Cleo's ear.

Cleo reared back, picturing him so close they might be touching.

"You need to stop such *extreme* collecting," he continued. "We're engaged now. This could get embarrassing for me. For us."

"Oh?" Kitty's voice rose in indignation. "Shouldn't *I* be embarrassed about *your* naughty behavior? What if word of your little trouble gets around? Mmm? Wouldn't that be embarrassing for you? For both of us?"

A slap hit the door.

Cleo's heart jerked. She tugged at Mary-Rose and mouthed, "Let's go."

Mary-Rose dug in her sandals and held up a finger. "It's just getting good," she whispered and put her ear back to the door.

Cleo was about to do the same when the door flung open. Professor Weber stepped out, face hardened, a muddy flush high on his cheeks.

241

"Oh," Cleo said, stuttering the first thing that came to mind, which also happened to be the truth. "Professor Weber, you startled us. We came to see Kitty. Is she in?"

"What do you want?" he asked.

"We're just stopping by for a visit." Cleo turned her tone to bright with a touch of befuddled that younger folks—even those a decade or two younger—never failed to fall for. "Did we get the wrong room? Oh, dear . . ."

"She's in there," he said, and without another word, strode down the hall and down the stairs.

Kitty appeared in the door, her golden curls as stiff and perfect as her posture. "Ladies," she said breathlessly. "Have you come to apologize for calling me a robber? Bless your hearts! I forgive you." She made to shut the door in their faces.

Mary-Rose slapped a palm on the wood. "What a pretty room," she said, pushing the door farther open.

Cleo smiled and added cutting sweetness. "Apologize? Why, no. We came by to make a deal. Shall we come in?"

Kitty's face hardened, but then her eyes glittered, and Cleo guessed she'd said the magic word. *Deal.*

* * *

The penthouse was more of an attic, with dormered ceilings slanting to within a few feet of the floor. Although wide, the room felt crushed and close. The chaotic decor of the hallway continued, with added conflicting touches of floral armchairs and throw pillows. However, it was Kitty's additions that made Cleo's head spin.

A mountain range of clothes rose from the king-sized bed. Where did Kitty sleep? Perhaps she had stayed with her fiancé last night, Cleo thought. Shoes littered the floor, and a brigade of massive suitcases crowded the walls. Then there were the books.

"My, you do have a lot of books," Mary-Rose said, a diplomatic understatement. While Kitty's clothes seemed confined to the bed, books were stacked on every other smooth surface including the floor.

Cleo stared, scanning one stack and then another. Locating the books she sought would be like finding the proverbial needle in a haystack. Or a book hidden in a library.

"Looking for something?" Kitty asked.

Cleo kept scanning. Her eyes caught on familiar covers, on classics and books she'd seen at Kitty's stand at the fair. She didn't see *Into the Waves* or *Gone With the Wind*.

"Looking to deal, you said?" Kitty asked, tapping a high-heeled foot impatiently.

Cleo and Mary-Rose had planned their tactics earlier. They'd fib, for the greater good. "I want my library book returned," Cleo said. "In return, I won't tell the police how I *witnessed* you breaking into my bookmobile." Cleo forced her fingers to remain still in her lap. Lying—even for the good of wronged books—wasn't her strong suit.

Kitty sauntered to the squat windows looking out over treetops and on toward the Depot.

She was still gazing out when she said, "I think you're bluffing. A lying librarian." She turned, flashing a bright smile that stopped at cold eyes. "I like that. I'm going to have to disappoint you, though. I don't have *your* book. I got my own copy, and it's not for sale either. I'm sure you understand that."

Kitty strode to the far side of the room. She shoved apart the line of suitcases, revealing a partially open safe.

"Isn't this a delight?" Kitty said, holding up a book. "To think of Shirley Macon James touching this page with her tragic fingers." She clasped the book to her chest before holding it out to Cleo.

Cleo took it, her fingers trembling. Instantly, she knew, like she'd know her own child or cat. "This is the library's copy," she said.

Mary-Rose jumped up and began snapping photos with her cell phone. Like a fashion photographer, she dipped and angled and zoomed. They'd had this planned too.

"Is it?" Kitty said, in a high, incredulous tone. "How can you tell? I don't see any *evidence*, do you? In fact, all I see are a bunch of little differences."

Cleo turned to the inner front where the library's bookplate would reside. The paper was smooth and unmarked, an aged white. No bookplate. Cleo flipped a page. There was the signature, Shirley Macon James. It looked the same, except for an underline flourish, something Cleo couldn't see the shy, reserved Miss James ever doing. The line was in ink, almost the same color as the signature. Almost, but not quite and not right. Heart thumping, Cleo turned back to the front, as if the bookplate might appear.

"Lovely, isn't it?" Kitty cooed. Before Cleo could answer, Kitty swiped the book from her hands. She clasped it to her heart again before sashaying over to the safe. She put the book in and drew out another.

Cleo felt herself being tugged, as if by an invisible thread, toward the book in Kitty's grasp. *Gone With the Wind*, open to Margaret Mitchell's signature. It had to be Dot's book. Mary-Rose hovered at her shoulder, clicking photos.

"That's right, it's not imaginary anymore," Kitty said, posing with the signature page. "This is the real deal. As much as I adore it, I've come around to parting with it. It reminds me too much of Hunter. What do you say to twenty *thousand*? That's a deal, a steal for a 'first first' edition! It's in fine condition. Not like your cousin's, with some ugly crayon scribble on the back cover." She held open the back. It was clean. No purple crayon mark by Dot's niece.

"No," Kitty said. "I can't let it go for so little. Let's say twenty-three thousand."

Cleo's insides twisted. It was like Buddy had warned. Identifying marks could be removed. If that's what had happened, how could she prove the book was Dot's?

"You're an awful person," Mary-Rose declared. She tugged Cleo's elbow. "Come on, Cleo. We've seen enough to get the police searching this place."

Cleo knew Mary-Rose was bluffing. They didn't have anything.

Kitty waggled her fingers in a taunting wave. "You two are *fun*! Go ahead and try. Chief Culpepper won't bother me." Her voice was wispy high. "I have an alibi. I'm a victim." Her voice hardened. "In any case, your cousin wasn't robbed. She gave her books away." Kitty opened the door wide. When they staggered into the hall, she slammed it behind them.

"Well, that was successful," Mary-Rose said, refastening her hair into its loose bun. "Mostly."

"Successful?" Cleo had held the book in her hands and let it get yanked away.

"We've confirmed she has the books," Mary-Rose said. "Now she's your prime suspect for sure. Or is it Professor Weber and his 'naughty behavior'?" Mary-Rose cringed dramatically. "I don't think I want or need to know about that!"

Cleo roused herself from thoughts of the book and recalled the couple's argument. "I do," she said. "I want to know what Professor Weber did that could embarrass him."

Mary-Rose murmured, "Dying from embarrassment."

"Or killing to avoid it," Cleo said.

Chapter
Twenty-Nine

"I promised a friend I wouldn't say anything," Henry said. "It could cause . . ." He shifted in his armchair, looking uncomfortable. "Embarrassment." He recrossed his legs, clad in light-beige slacks and pale-blue argyle socks. On his lap, Mr. Chaucer snuffled and sneezed before returning to sleep.

Cleo sipped sherry, sweet as candy. She and Henry were in his cozy, book-filled apartment above the Gilded Page. Before them, tall windows looked out over Fontaine Park, where the treetops ruffled as if swept by waves.

Embarrassment was exactly what Cleo wanted to hear about. She held her tongue, giving Henry time to consider. Breaking a promise to a friend would be a conundrum. She would have qualms too. However, she hoped Henry would come to the logical conclusion that murder was far worse. So was being wrongfully accused of murder.

After their visit to the bed-and-breakfast, Mary-Rose had headed home for a dinner date with her husband. Cleo had come straight to Henry's shop. When she arrived, the lights were off and the *Closed* sign dangled from the door. She hadn't worried. She knew he'd be in, and it hadn't taken keen detecting to reach that conclusion.

First and foremost, Henry had said he'd be at his shop, and Henry Lafayette was a man of his word. Second, there was Sergeant Tookey. Cleo had spotted the sergeant sitting on a bench at the center of Fontaine Park. He was crunching his way through a party-sized bag of Zapp's kettle chips, his head swinging like a metronome. Methodically, he took a chip and looked toward the Gilded Page. He took another and shifted his gaze to Dot's Drop By. Back and forth, chip by chip.

"You're busy," Cleo had stated, pausing by the bench where he and several hopeful, hungry sparrows sat.

Tookey politely offered her a chip, which she shared with the birds. "Double overtime," he said, managing to sound both happy and burdened.

"Double surveillance?" Cleo was unable to keep the bitterness from her tone.

He thrust the bag of chips at her again. She peeked inside, saw it was nearly empty, and declined with thanks. Tookey was working, after all.

"Yep," Tookey confirmed, tipping the last chips into his hand before emptying the shards at his boots. Birds flew in from all directions. "Chief's orders. But don't you worry. I'm doing some off-the-books surveilling too." He pointed to his right eye and then aimed his finger in an arc, encompassing the whole of downtown. "I have my eye on all these suspicious book types. I'm on the lookout for that psychic lady too."

Cleo praised him and was rewarded with words she'd wanted to hear.

"I don't like the idea that the killer's someone local," Tookey said. "Especially anyone nice like Henry or Dot." He turned toward the Drop By and said wistfully, "I'd miss those cookies . . ."

Now, looking out over the park, Cleo squinted through her bifocals, trying to see if Tookey was still out there. She didn't see him and hoped he'd left, following a better suspect. Besides, the weather was turning. Rain spit at the window. The treetops waved, and a deep, distant rumble made Mr. Chaucer whimper.

Henry sighed heavily. "Embarrassment isn't usually deadly," he said slowly.

"It could be," Cleo said. "I imagine folks have killed to save face. People who think their reputation is everything."

She'd already told him what she and Mary-Rose had heard, eavesdropping on Kitty and her professor. Now she thought back to the fair when Henry had tentatively assessed Buddy's big find—the Oglethorpe letter—as a fake.

"That day," Cleo said, recalling the situation out loud, "Kitty seemed more upset with your diagnosis than Buddy did. She said something about 'meddling'?"

"I feel bad for Buddy," Henry said. "He walked over here with me at lunchtime when I came home to feed Chaucy. He wanted tips on how to pick out fakes in the future. It's nice of him not to blame me for delivering the bad news." He added darkly, "Like some people."

Cleo raised her eyebrows. Henry had turned from the window to look at her. She saw the conflict in his eye, but also a twinkle. "Revealing a secret to a librarian is like confessing to a priest, right?"

Cleo smiled over her sherry. "Librarian's code of silence," she said, miming lip-zipping. "Although you know that only holds for patrons' reading preferences. I'll have to tell Gabby if it's information that can help the police."

"I wouldn't expect anything else," Henry said. "Librarians deal in information." He poured himself a touch more sherry and said, "I did 'meddle,' but only at the request of the wronged party."

Cleo listened intently as Henry described how a friend—a respected collector he'd known for decades—had asked him to authenticate a text he'd purchased.

"A gorgeous book of philosophical essays," Henry said. He spoke admiringly of luminous illustrations before getting to the grittier details. "At first glance it was lovely. When I studied it further, it became clear that it was a copy. A very good copy, with some hand-scribed flourishes and imperfections that made it even more realistic. It wasn't worth more than any modern reproduction. My friend didn't want to make a fuss. All he wanted was his money back from the seller."

"Professor Weber?" Cleo guessed, so Henry wouldn't have to be the first to say the name.

He nodded. "It was awkward. More than awkward. Professor Weber became belligerent. He accused my friend and me of planting the forgery. From there . . . well . . . you know how conspiracy theories can spin up into even more extreme ideas?"

"I know that very well," Cleo said, thinking of Dot and the online conspiracy avalanche.

"Professor Weber got it in his head that my friend and I were trying to blackmail him because he's wealthy, that we were 'shaking him down' and 'holding his reputation hostage.'" Henry raised air quotes around the absurd words. "I remember exactly what he said because he got sent legal documents. I think he wrote them himself—threats to cease and desist, threats to sue. I'm not sure how legal they were."

"How very strange," Cleo said. "He seems so stoic and . . ." She frowned.

"Professorial?" Henry supplied. "Logical? I used to think that too. I suppose I assumed, based on his job and him being president of the antiquarians."

"And appearance," Cleo said. "We judge books by their covers, don't we? Even when we know better." She asked about the ending of the story, which she'd shelve under *Horror*. Thankfully, it didn't have a horrific ending.

"My friend had saved photos of the book from Professor Weber's original online sales listing," Henry said. "Thank goodness! There was a tiny identifying mark, proving the book came from his shop. We were finally able to convince him that he'd been wronged by whoever sold him the book. He was still angry, but he refunded my friend."

Rain splashed at the window in gusts. Mr. Chaucer hopped off Henry's lap and took cover under his chair. Cleo thought of Rhett, who spent storms under her bed. She'd give him an extra treat when she got home.

"Who sold Professor Weber the book?" Cleo asked.

"He didn't say, and I didn't want anything more to do with it." Henry set down his glass. Thunder rumbled, rattling the windowpanes. "He ordered my friend and me to keep quiet about the incident. That's why I feel I can tell you. I'd have been more sympathetic if he'd simply apologized and asked nicely. Instead, he said he'd make sure our reputations were the ones ruined if we told anyone."

Lightning flashed outside. "Rude!" Cleo said.

Henry got up and looked out the window. Cleo resisted the urge to pull him back. The storm was close and dangerous.

Henry said, "I still remember his words. 'I'll *kill* your reputations.' My friend and I laughed it off as the delusions of a small but self-important man."

Chills crept up Cleo's arm, and not only because of the electric fizz in the air. *I'll kill* . . . Hunter Fox had embarrassed Professor Weber by romancing his fiancée. Kitty had flirted back. Cleo hoped Sergeant Tookey really was watching the booksellers. She didn't trust Kitty or approve of her book-swiping ways, but Cleo didn't want to see her or anyone else get hurt.

Chapter Thirty

"The final hours," Cleo said to Dot the following afternoon. "The last day of the fair." They sat inside Words on Wheels, Cleo in her captain's seat, Dot on the front bench seat. Cleo had parked the bus near the Depot. She liked taking the bookmobile out on Sundays, prime days for patrons to stock up on reading. She also wanted to keep an eye on the antiquarians while she still could.

"I don't know if I'm relieved or sad to see the fair go," Cleo said, gazing toward the Depot, where a customer backed out the doors, balancing an armload of books.

Dot didn't share such indecision. "Good riddance to this fair and the trouble it's caused!" When Cleo glanced back, Dot flushed. "Oh, please don't tell Henry I said that. I'm sure it was a very nice fair except for the . . . well . . ."

Murder, book thievery, rogue podcasters, and missing so-called psychics. Cleo's stomach tightened. The fair might leave, but she feared the trouble would stay put, especially if Dot and Henry were the only suspects left in town.

"You made lovely finds," Dot said, changing the subject to something sunnier.

Cleo swung her legs over the side of her seat so she was facing Dot. Two tote bags filled with treasures sat beside her cousin:

new old books that Cleo had bought earlier at the fair. Cleo had rationalized that it was her last chance to look for both missing books and book deals. She'd failed to find the former, but she had snagged some wonderful books.

From Buddy, she'd bought a sheet from a *Pogo* cartoon, which she planned to give Ollie for his birthday. She'd also found a copy of *The Wizard of Oz* featuring the gorgeous color illustrations of the 1899 version but reproduced in 2017. It had cost less than filling up her gas tank and was thus suitable for grandkids to read and enjoy.

The real first edition would have set her back tens of thousands. Signed could be as much as a hundred thousand, the dealer had told her. Cleo had thumped her heart.

Dot was flipping through *The Wizard of Oz*. "What a lovely book," Dot said, sounding as far away as Dorothy.

"A bargain," Cleo said, reassuring herself that she hadn't overspent. Book sales were dangerous territory for her wallet, as Mary-Rose had warned when the fair started.

Dot closed the book gently. "A bargain and still a glorious book. It almost makes me wish I'd never found the precious *Gone With the Wind* at that estate sale. Do you think that's what sparked this awful trouble, Cleo? *My* book?"

Cleo's first instinct was to comfort Dot, to tell her no, of course not. "I don't know," she said truthfully. "But even if it did, it's not your fault or the book's."

Dot stood and peered out the windows. "That podcaster came by my house again," she said. "I didn't talk to him or open the door. He set up his microphone on my front step, though, and I could hear everything he said." Dot smiled weakly. "*I* almost started to believe I'm a stalker and a killer. He's very convincing."

"Don't listen to him," Cleo said, with the conviction and guilt of someone who had. With Ollie's help, she'd tuned in last night. Between dramatic pauses and ominous music, the podcaster had raised leading questions. *Just who is Dot Moore? How desperate was she to save her store? Desperate enough to kill? To frame an innocent man, her own cousin's significant other?*

Cleo had always thought "significant other" was a strange, unromantic term, like something mathematical. She liked the podcaster's absurd questions even less.

"He'll tire of pestering you when nothing comes of it," Cleo said, gripping the steering wheel. "I bet hardly anyone around Catalpa Springs listens to his silly podcast."

"I hope you're right," Dot said, hugging Cleo before stepping down. "Have fun at the soiree tonight. Don't step on any toes." Dot grinned up at Cleo.

"Not unless I have to," Cleo joked back.

Dot waved to Cleo and then issued another cheery wave across the street. Cleo frowned. Sergeant Tookey leaned on a lamppost at the crosswalk, sipping from a cup the size of a bucket. When Dot waved, he ducked behind the slender pole, his belly and drink still clearly visible.

Cleo continued to watch as Dot hustled up Main Street toward the Drop By, head dipped. The sergeant waited until she was a block away and then ambled in the same direction.

The last day, Cleo thought again, gripping her steering wheel tighter. She didn't have much time left to find the missing books, clear her loved ones' good names, and nab a killer too.

* * *

At 7:02 PM, Henry tapped on Cleo's door, giving her only two minutes to worry that he'd been delayed for questioning again.

254

Henry looked dapper in a tailored pinstripe suit of light gray, and Cleo was pleased that, by chance, her robin's-egg-blue dress complemented his silk paisley pocket square. Mr. Chaucer wore a matching paisley bandanna. The pug and Persian were having a pets' night in and romped off to tussle in the living room before Cleo and Henry had a chance to pat them good-bye.

Henry drove them to the Myrtles, which was done up in swaths of twinkling lights. Strolling arm in arm up the crepe myrtle–lined walkway, Cleo could almost convince herself they were on their way to a normal, pleasant evening.

Nina Flores broke the spell. "One. More. Blessed. Day!" the innkeeper exclaimed when Henry and Cleo stepped inside. Nina was bundled in a puffy parka. The air conditioning blasted at arctic. Bloodshot flared around her pupils, and she pressed a finger to her temple, rubbing in circles. "After these book people depart tomorrow, Karl and I will have three blissful days off before we host a nice bunch of frat boys on a pledge week. Three whole days!"

"Fraternity pledging?" Cleo said, unable to keep skepticism from sneaking into her tone. "You don't worry the boys might be a bit rowdy?"

"As long as there's no theft, murder, fighting, and the police skulking around, I'll be delighted." Nina jerked her head toward the back. "You know the way. Follow the Marilyn Monroe music."

The ballroom was festooned in more twinkling lights. Karl once again stood behind the bar, polishing a glass. "Bye Bye Baby" played softly in the backdrop. Cleo gripped Henry's arm, urgency meeting uncertainty.

He patted her hand, understanding. "So, who do you want to interrogate first?"

255

Cleo scanned the room. Buddy was chatting with the man who collected fishing books. Henry's friends the medievalists were in deep conversation over by the potted fern. The biggest crowd was at the bar, orbiting in the bright glow of Kitty. Professor Weber stood off to the side, watching his fiancée intently.

"Kitty already looks tipsy," Cleo said. "Maybe it will make her talkative."

They were a few steps into the room when Kitty pointed toward Cleo and Henry. All eyes turned.

"Oh, lookee here," she said, her voice shrill despite a slight slur. "It's my librarian nemesis and her liar boyfriend."

Henry groaned. "Too talkative," he murmured to Cleo.

Kitty pointed at Henry. "He lied about his alibi. Did you all know that? He had no alibi the night our beloved colleague Hunter was killed. Slain!"

Eyes shifted awkwardly from Kitty to her fiancé and on to Henry.

Professor Weber moved close to Kitty and looped a protective arm around her slender waist. She clung to him and sobbed dramatically.

"You're bothering my fiancée," Professor Weber said, turning his stony stare on Cleo and Henry. "You're trying to make her look bad, and I won't allow that."

"I only want to help," Cleo said. She addressed the general crowd of antiquarians. "You all want justice for your colleague Hunter Fox, don't you?"

Murmurs of agreement were drowned out by Kitty. "Justice? The police already have two prime suspects. This man—our host!—owned the murder weapon. *He* had a motive too. Hunter was scooping him on book scouting. Then this woman's cousin *stalked* Hunter. She threatened him and then *supposedly* found his poor deceased body! You can learn all about her motives online. It's everywhere. There's a podcast and a discussion group dedicated to her guilt."

Professor Weber glared around the room as if daring any members to question Kitty's assertions. Finally Cleo thought she understood the connection between the unlikely pair. He enjoyed shielding his beautiful damsel in distress. She enjoyed his protective prestige. Cleo gripped Henry's elbow. She sensed a presence at her other side.

"Drink, ma'am?" The voice was familiar, startlingly so.

"Ollie?" Cleo frowned in confusion. Her grandson was dressed like a waiter, black slacks, white shirt, and black vest. She hadn't known he owned slacks, let alone a vest.

He grinned and bent to whisper past her ear. "I'm undercover, helping Gabby. She's in the next room. The chief is watching the door. Sergeant Tookey's here too. See that palm tree?" He nodded toward a potted palm, sprouting a protruding belly.

Cleo couldn't help smiling. "I'm glad you're all here," she said, taking the proffered flute of bubbly. Henry took one too.

Kitty was raising her glass. "Let's toast our fallen colleague."

Glasses clinked. A cheer rose, but grumbles rumbled below it. Hunter Fox hadn't been beloved by all. Across the room, Buddy raised his glass but frowned. Another dealer rolled her eyes, while others stared at their feet. Professor Weber refused a glass and kept his hands in his pockets.

Kitty downed her entire drink. She swayed slightly, and her drawl blurred around the edges. "In honor of the best scout this society has ever known, I'm offering a *special* deal on a true eye-opening delight. That's right, I have what *you've* been looking for." She giggled and spun, her *you* seeming to address everyone in the room personally. When she wobbled to a stop, she added,

"Inquire privately, and I may let you check out the goods before we make a deal." She swayed toward the bar. A crowd closed in around her.

Music boomed in a zippy beat, not a dance Cleo had studied. She wasn't sure her knees would agree to it. In silent agreement, she and Henry moved toward the nearest wall.

"I didn't know that book people would be such dancers," Cleo said, having to yell into Henry's ear.

He smiled. "The soiree is usually a happy affair, a celebration."

Cleo watched the dancers, many of whom weren't doing anything close to steps in rhythm. Maybe she *could* manage this dance. She was about to ask Henry if he wanted to try when she glanced back at the bar and realized Kitty was gone.

Cleo caught a flash of red exiting the ballroom. She grabbed Henry. "Kitty! She's leaving." They followed, staying back but close enough to see her head up the stairs. Cleo's heartbeat sped up. Was she going to get Dot's book? To sell it?

Ollie and Gabby were nowhere in sight as they climbed the stairs. At the second floor, Cleo hesitated. "Kitty has to come back down. Let's wait here and—"

Henry raised an eyebrow. "And reason with her? I've been thinking. Our only hope might be a threat."

When Cleo's eyes widened, he explained. "A warning threat. We could say that we'll broadcast to all the bookdealers and all the online forums that the book is stolen. No ethical dealer or collector would buy it then. It would be sullied."

Cleo liked the idea. "We'll give her one more chance to do the right thing." Cleo looked down the dim hallways. "There are two sets of stairs to the third floor. I believe they extend down to the ground floor too. We should probably split up and listen in case Kitty doesn't come back this way."

Henry squeezed her hand before disappearing down the dim hall to the right. Cleo wandered slowly down her side, wishing she could lower the music thumping from the ballroom. She stopped at the end of the hall, her eye caught on a bookshelf. A handwritten sign urged guests to help themselves: take a book, leave a book. Cleo loved seeing what people carried along on trips and left behind.

She was reading the back cover of an intriguing British mystery when a crash came from the other end of the hall. She froze. "Henry?"

A grunt followed. It was followed fast by a jangling, a rustling, another grunt, and the bumps and thuds of a struggle.

Cleo swiveled and rushed back, but not before a scream echoed down the hallway and down the steps. All the way down. *Thump, thump, thump*, ending in a groan.

Henry stood at the top of the stairs, disheveled and clutching his arm. Cleo ran to him, her attention focused on making sure he was okay. He raised his other hand, pointing to the grand marble steps. Cleo followed the point, down the stairs to a puddle of red. Kitty lay crumpled in her red dress with an awful red blossoming on her head.

Before Cleo and Henry could react, another scream echoed up. The bookdealers streamed from the ballroom, Professor Weber among them. He finally let out emotion, bellowing his fiancée's name as he knelt beside her. Gabby and the chief pushed through the crowd. Ollie followed, still balancing a tray of bubbly drinks.

"Everyone back!" Gabby took charge, feeling for a pulse and calling for an ambulance. The chief and everyone else stared up at Cleo and Henry. Silence fell, cold and heavy with accusation.

"I was pushed in the hallway," Henry said shakily. "I fell. Then I heard Kitty yell, and—"

"Uh-huh," Chief Culpepper said. "What are you going to tell us next? That Miss Cleo there is your alibi again? That you have no motive? I don't think so. Henry Lafayette, you're under arrest."

Chapter
Thirty-One

"I'm sorry," Cleo said, meeting Mr. Chaucer's worried gaze. The pug trotted out to the front porch and squashed his nose to the screen door. When Henry didn't appear, Chaucy looked back at Cleo and whimpered.

Cleo had intended to go inside and make herbal tea for Gabby and herself. Weariness and worry overtook her, and she sank into the nearest porch seat.

Gabby stood midway between Cleo and Mr. Chaucer. It was nearly midnight, and the young deputy looked as exhausted as Cleo and unsure of whom to comfort first and how. She'd given Cleo and Ollie a ride home from the station, where they'd provided witness statements. At Cleo's urging, Ollie had gone on to his cottage, to bed. Cleo had assured her grandson she'd be doing the same. However, she knew she wouldn't sleep.

Henry had gotten a ride to the station too, in the back of Chief Culpepper's truck. Henry wouldn't be coming home tonight. She'd spoken to him briefly before she left. He'd tried to put up a chipper front, even when making two requests that wrenched Cleo's heart. "The two most important things in the world to me," he'd said.

Cleo replayed them again, gazing out into her dark garden.

You have to believe me, Cleo. I didn't hurt Kitty or Hunter. You believe me?

Cleo believed him.

You'll take care of Mr. Chaucer?

Of course she would. However, she couldn't explain to the little dog why his beloved human hadn't come home.

Her eyes prickled, and she swiped at them. Mr. Chaucer sensed her mood. He looked back with worried wrinkles. "It's okay, Chaucy," she said, pitching her voice to singsong high for the lie. It wasn't okay. Henry was in jail.

Rhett Butler sashayed out the open front door, tail held high. He jumped on Cleo's lap and purred into her chest. Her cat always knew when she needed comfort.

"Henry has a good lawyer," Gabby said, going to pat Mr. Chaucer. The pug waggled his tail but kept his nose to the screen. "He's only charged with assault for now."

"Only," Cleo breathed. The chief had made the lesser charge sound like a threat. One more nail in his rock-solid case.

"He has the best criminal lawyer around," Gabby continued, speaking the words to Mr. Chaucer's worried pug face. To Cleo, she said, "Tex Payne. You should hear the DA curse when Tex gets involved in a case. That man's gotten so many criminals off, you wouldn't—" Gabby bit her lip and stopped talking.

Cleo buried her nose in Rhett's fur. Tex Payne was a swaggering Texan who owned the building next to Henry's shop. He oozed confidence and bravado, wore flashy bolo ties and Stetsons, and appeared at the library whenever John Grisham published a new legal thriller. He was competent, Cleo was sure, but he was a *criminal* lawyer.

"Henry's innocent," Cleo said in a small voice. The night songs from the garden grated at her nerves. The crickets were off-key. The tree frogs incessantly repeated their tunes.

Gabby plunked down on the porch planks. She leaned her back against the doorframe and gently tugged Mr. Chaucer to her lap. "I called the hospital before we left the station. Kitty's still out of it. Unconscious. The doctors say that's good. They want it that way for now. The swelling on her brain should go down. When she wakes up, hopefully she'll be fine and able to tell us what happened."

Hopefully. Cleo couldn't rely on hope. She couldn't sit about feeling sorry for herself and Henry either. She straightened her spine and her mind, replaying the events before Kitty's tumble. She'd given her statement to Chief Culpepper under throbbing fluorescent lights and his blustery prodding. Here on her porch, she might remember more. Cleo was grateful her favorite neighbor was here to listen and seemed in no hurry to leave.

"Right before Kitty tumbled, I was looking at a bookshelf," Cleo said.

"Of course you were. Those are like stinky cheese in a mousetrap to a librarian." Gabby's grin lifted Cleo's spirits.

"Henry was down the other hall. It was dim. Quite dark, really." Cleo frowned, willing her senses to remember everything, anything.

"And Henry said someone pushed him?" Gabby prompted. "He fell into one of those fake potted plants, and by the time he got back up, he heard Kitty falling? Did you hear anything?"

Cleo replayed the first crash. Almost simultaneously, she'd heard a grunt and a rustling. Henry, falling into the plant? A thump? A door? And footsteps, not so much the sound on the thick carpet but a vibration under her feet. She couldn't say how many feet. Then the awful thumps and Kitty screaming, all the way down.

Rhett rubbed his chin to Cleo's. His fur smelled of fresh green grass. His breath had the ever-so-slight whiff of salmon.

"A smell," Cleo said, remembering. "Thank you, Rhett. When I ran to find Henry at the top of the stairs, there was a scent. Something I've smelled before." Cleo shut her eyes for a moment. Then a memory jolted her upright so abruptly that Rhett dug his claws into her thighs. "Incense! Madame Romanov uses it at her home. It clings to her like she's bathed in it. What if it was her? We suspected she's still nearby. Henry said he heard a jingling sound too, like keys. What if it was her bangles?"

Cleo recognized the mix of excitement and pleading in her voice.

Mr. Chaucer stood precariously on Gabby's outstretched legs, his back end waggling. Gabby held his sides so he wouldn't topple. "I'm still trying to find Madame," Gabby said. "I won't stop." She gently lifted Mr. Chaucer from her lap and eased herself upright in one elegant move. The little pug resumed his watch of the door.

"I promise, Miss Cleo," Gabby said. "I'll look into everything. You try to get some sleep. Kitty could be awake in the morning and clear up everything."

Gabby hugged Cleo good-night and patted each pet, instructing them to take care of Miss Cleo.

When she heard Gabby's cruiser rumble down their sleeping street, Cleo ushered the pets in and double-locked the door. They had to be careful. A killer was still on the loose.

* * *

Cleo stumbled bleary-eyed into her kitchen the next morning, feeling the worst case of Monday blues she'd ever had. She turned the coffeemaker on, forgetting to add the coffee. She checked her answering machine, although she couldn't have missed any calls during the night. She'd woken at what seemed like five-minute intervals, overcome with the need to check her cell phone and the landline resting quietly on her nightstand. Both awake and sleeping, she'd dreamed that Henry would call with good news. He'd tell her he was free, exonerated.

Cleo stared dismally at the coffee-free hot water dripping into the carafe. She knew where he was. Still in jail. Last night Gabby had warned that Henry might have to wait a day, maybe two, possibly even more, for a bond hearing. The courthouse was short-staffed and overbooked.

Unless I can exonerate him sooner, Cleo thought.

While Rhett gobbled his breakfast, Cleo let Mr. Chaucer out for a romp in the yard. The little pug ran straight to the gate and pressed his snout to the pickets, searching for his best friend. Cleo had to lure him back in with dog biscuits, a necessary treat when she realized she was out of his kibble.

"We'll go to your place later," she told Mr. Chaucer when he looked up anxiously. A walk would be good for both of them. Good for thinking, and better than sitting around waiting for a phone to ring.

After her own breakfast and placating Rhett with a second helping of Tuna Delight, Cleo clipped on Mr. Chaucer's lead. Together they strolled down the lane and across the park. Cleo saw a few folks she recognized. They averted their eyes when they saw her.

"They just don't want to bother us," she told Mr. Chaucer, but a worry rubbed at her. *Or they think Henry is guilty and don't know what to say to me.*

Cleo let herself and Mr. Chaucer into the Gilded Page, using her key. The pug trotted each aisle, searching for Henry. Cleo flipped on a light and then another. The bookstore felt empty and deserted, although it had spent only a night alone.

In the back workshop, Cleo doled out kibble. While Chaucy ate, she stared at the pegboard wall with its tidy outlines of tools. Her gaze stalled at the outline of a clawed hammer. The second murder weapon? Henry could simply have misplaced the tool. His toolboxes were still stuffed. What if he and the police had missed it in their search?

More out of the need to do something than thinking she'd find anything, Cleo hefted the handled wooden carrier to the workbench and began lifting out each tool. As she did, she tried to imagine their uses. Poking. Slicing. Pounding. Striking. Dark purposes came to mind. Cleo yearned to dispel them. These tools fixed needy books. They were good.

"When Henry comes back, I'll have him give me a demo," she told Mr. Chaucer, who dropped a kibble and woofed.

"I know, it'll be fun," Cleo said. But she'd misinterpreted. Mr. Chaucer growled and ran to the front of the shop, hackles raised.

A chill ran up Cleo's spine. She picked up the first tool at hand—a wooden mallet—and trotted after her guard pug.

"Get! Get away. Ugly creature."

The male voice and mean words made Cleo gasp. She recognized the haughty huffiness before she saw the speaker.

"Professor Weber!" Cleo declared, rounding an aisle. She gripped the mallet tightly but kept her hand lowered. He stood at the first row of shelves, inspecting a book.

"Get this mutt away from me," he ordered, as if Cleo and Mr. Chaucer had barged into his private domain. Mr. Chaucer stood stiff-legged, his wrinkly snout pointed at the professor's shins. The professor flicked his shoe.

"Chaucy," Cleo called, clicking her tongue and repeating his name with artificial cheerfulness. She didn't want the brave pug to get hurt. Mr. Chaucer backed up but remained in his tippy version of an attack stance.

"The shop is closed," Cleo said to their unwanted guest. "You'll have to leave."

Professor Weber ignored her and strode to Henry's wall of history and philosophy offerings. The covers were leather in hues of burgundy and rich brown. He reached for a tome on the top shelf, which Cleo would have needed the ladder on rollers to reach. Cleo loved the look of the ladder. She'd always wanted one for the library and for her personal library too.

"You have to leave," Cleo repeated.

"My fiancée and I were set to leave town today," Professor Weber said. "Now she has to stay in the hospital, and the police rudely asked all the antiquarians to stay on too, as if we have nothing but time."

"How is Kitty?" Cleo asked, her earlier irritation slipping away. The professor had to be worried about his loved one, as she was for hers.

"Awake," he said, and Cleo's hopes soared until he added, "But confused. She doesn't remember what happened, but I do."

"You do?" Cleo frowned. She recalled him running in just ahead of the rest of the soiree crowd, yelling Kitty's name.

"Clearly," he said. "It was Henry Lafayette. Do you not see yet what sort of man Mr. Lafayette is? Do you know, he once tried to blackmail and malign my reputation? He said he was *helping a friend*. I suppose he'll say that now, that he was helping you and your obsession regarding that tawdry *Gone With the Wind*."

"No," Cleo said. "He did none of those things."

"So *you* say. The police don't agree. I'll do my best to see that he's kept in jail." The professor began pulling out books and cracking them open. He flipped pages and shoved them back in.

Cleo inhaled sharply. "He didn't malign or blackmail you," she said, working to keep her voice steady and calm. "He never told anyone—"

Professor Weber swung around, his face lurid. "Ah, but he told *you*, didn't he? I knew he'd break his promise. See? He's that sort of man. Untrustworthy."

Mr. Chaucer woofed and growled.

Cleo wanted the professor gone too. He was taking books from the upper shelf, flipping through them, and shoving them back with little care for their safety and placement.

"You have to leave," she said again. "If you don't, I'll have to call the police."

He didn't respond. His nose was stuck in a book. He turned a page and held it close, frowning. He flipped some more and then reached for another book on the upper shelf. His hand froze in the gap. He raised himself to the tiptoes of his leather loafers and then pulled the ladder over. He needed to climb only a rung to be eye level with the top shelf. When he turned back, his expression chilled Cleo.

Professor Weber was smiling.

Cleo lurched forward and grabbed up Mr. Chaucer, cradling him close to her chest.

"Go ahead and call the police," Professor Weber said, stepping down and pulling a cell phone from his pocket. "We'll see which one of us gets through first."

Chapter
Thirty-Two

C hief Culpepper held up an evidence bag, swinging it back and forth with clear satisfaction. "Well, well, well, looks like I have nail number four in my lock-tight, rock-solid murder case," he said. With his other hand, he raised a stubby index finger, its nail chewed to the quick. "One, owning the murdering awl. Two, lying to police. Three, shoving a nice lady down the stairs." He swung the bag faster. "Four, attempting to hide this hammer, which appears to have traces of blood."

Cleo couldn't take her eyes off the horrible hammer. Her head moved back and forth with the evidence bag as if hypnotized. In her arms, Mr. Chaucer was doing the same thing, only his head swung with a slight delay. She cuddled the little pug closer, unsure which one of them was trembling.

The chief thrust the bag at Gabby, who took it with a look of reluctance and a shake of her head.

"This is all wrong," Cleo said, forcing her eyes to the chief's. "Professor Weber could have planted that. He entered the shop without permission when I was feeding Mr. Chaucer. He—"

"See what I mean?" Professor Weber said smoothly. He stood a few yards away, giving his "witness" statement to Sergeant

Tookey. "This woman is desperate to pin the blame on someone else."

"It's true, Chief, we don't know—" Gabby started to say, but Professor Weber interrupted.

"Chief Culpepper, let me add a fifth nail to your solid case," he said. "Two of the books hiding that hammer are forgeries, although Mr. Lafayette has them highlighted on his website as restored historic gems. They'd sell for a lot of money. If they were real . . ."

Cleo's stomach did double flips. "No," she said softly.

"You'll see I'm right," Professor Weber said. "Hunter Fox must have discovered what was going on here. We've had trouble with forgeries showing up after our annual fairs. Now I know why. One of our own members was passing them off. Mr. Fox must have realized. He was clever when it came to books, I'll give him that."

Tookey kept writing in his notebook, studiously avoiding Cleo's eye. The professor continued on, elaborating on the "tells" of a fraud.

Only the chief looked impressed. "You're a fraud expert, then? I want every book in this place checked. Would you be able to stick around and lend us your expertise?"

Professor Weber sighed heavily as if burdened by greatness. "My pleasure," he said solemnly.

"He can't—" Cleo stammered. "He shouldn't. It isn't right."

"Tookey," the chief bellowed. "Take this place apart. Book by book." The chief yanked a handful of aged tomes from their shelves.

Cleo gasped. She wanted to throw herself in front of the shelves.

"Perhaps I should take Miss Cleo's statement somewhere private," Gabby said, touching Cleo's arm gently.

"Get on that, Deputy," the chief said. He yanked out another thick handful of books, looking pleased. His smugness faltered when he addressed Cleo. "I am sorry, Miss Cleo. I know you're close to Mr. Lafayette. This has to be a shock. Heck, must knock you off your feet, but you know, it's hard to know people's true natures. Lafayette hasn't lived here but what? Four years? Five? What do we know about him? Next to nothing, really."

Cleo knew Henry. He was a good, honest man. Her throat had closed up.

The chief brightened. "The good news is that your cousin's in the clear. Right? That's great for you. I hated to think it, but it was looking bad for her for a while."

Gabby cut in gently, "How about we go to the station, Miss Cleo? Then I can run you home."

Cleo numbly agreed. She couldn't bear to see Henry's store upended. Still carrying Mr. Chaucer, she followed Gabby. At the end of the aisle, Gabby stopped so abruptly Cleo and Mr. Chaucer bumped into her.

"Go around back," Gabby said. "I'll bring the car around." She slipped out the door quickly, but not before Cleo caught a glimpse of the crowd outside, a mini-mob of antiquarians, friends, neighbors, and a bearded man wielding a mic.

Chapter
Thirty-Three

I n Catalpa Springs, the depth of personal trouble could be measured in food. Namely, the kind and quantity of consolation treats appearing at one's door. By the time Cleo returned home from the station, Henry had been charged with murder and her porch resembled the buffet table at a funeral.

Two semi-frozen casseroles, a pie carrier full of cookies, a coconut layer cake, and a ham in a cooler waited at Cleo's front door. Cleo surveyed her porch in dismay. What were folks thinking? The worst, clearly.

"How're you going to eat all that food now that you're by yourself?" Wanda's voice rasped over Cleo's raw nerves. Mr. Chaucer growled.

"Go inside, quickly, quickly," she whispered, scooting the little dog in. She pushed the cooler in after him, with the casseroles and cake on top. Cookies defensively in hand, she turned to face her neighbor. Wanda wielded clippers and a more wicked tongue.

"There's been a misunderstanding," Cleo said, struggling to keep her voice steady.

"Misunderstood by who?" Wanda demanded. Grass clippings coated her boots. A flower petal withered on her sleeve.

Wanda went on, raising the clippers for emphasis. "Who misunderstood, Cleo? The police? The president of those old book nerds? *You?*"

The last word stabbed at Cleo's heart. No, she hadn't misunderstood. Issuing her mother's favorite polite brush-off, Cleo said coldly, "I shouldn't keep you."

To Cleo's relief and shock, Wanda swung around and headed back down the walkway. It was rarely so easy to get rid of her. But Cleo hadn't. She soon realized that Wanda was only gathering reinforcement.

"Yoo-hoo, over here!" Wanda called, trotting to Cleo's gate with a beckoning wave of her clippers. "You're just in time. Hurry! She's on her porch, with a haul of sympathy food."

Cleo glimpsed a mic and a sculpted beard.

"I'm here at the home of the killer's significant other," the podcaster said breathlessly, jogging up Cleo's walkway. "Her neighbor tells me there have been warning signs for months now."

"Years!" Wanda crowed.

"Oh!" Cleo huffed. Gripping her cookies, she stumbled inside, slamming the door behind her. She stood looking down at the small mountain of food, an anxious pug, and a frowny-faced Persian.

"What are we going to do?" she whispered to the pets as questions and knocks beat at the door. Two pairs of round eyes stared back, with just as many answers as she had.

* * *

By late afternoon, Cleo had received a strawberry sheet cake, two plates of cookies, another ham, several salads, and a bottle of bourbon. She'd stashed the extra ham in her freezer and the bottle in her china cabinet and now sat at her table, grimly picking at a plate of salad selections.

Mary-Rose and Dot had come by to "keep Cleo company" and help her eat up the food. They'd barely made a dent in the culinary department. Mary-Rose helpfully helped herself to an oatmeal sandwich cookie. Dot, in a somber, heavy-duty canvas apron, whirled around Cleo's kitchen, sanitizing the counter tops to surgical-room levels. Henry was still with the police.

Cleo stared out to her backyard. Rhett Butler sat in a patch of grass, furry face turned to the fading sun. Ollie ran wide, loping circles around the patch, attempting to engage Mr. Chaucer in a game of catch. The little pug would trundle a few wobbly steps and then plunk back down, always facing the house and the street beyond.

"Mr. Chaucer's waiting for Henry," Cleo said. "He knows something's wrong."

Mary-Rose clicked her tongue. "Tragic little guy!"

Dot wondered again if Mr. Chaucer needed another biscuit and if Cleo needed a snack.

They'd all be food-logged if the sympathy gifting and comfort eating kept up. Cleo appreciated the treats. However, the underlying sentiment irked her. She had strong suspicions that her friends and family weren't offering up indignation that an innocent man was being wrongly accused. Just the opposite. They clearly felt that Henry could be guilty of terrible crimes and that Cleo, in believing in him, was a fool in love. She could tell by the pitying looks and shaking heads and the patronizing *there, there*s.

Then there were the more blatant statements, like "One never knows with the dating scene these days." Cleo doubted many of her friends knew anything at all about the dating scene these days, but they should know that Henry Lafayette was a good and honest man!

Cleo shoved at a chunk of broccoli with her fork and voiced her vexations. "I don't know why everyone's rushing over to console me. Henry's innocent! Can't everyone see that? They should all be out looking for clues, not whipping up sympathy casseroles."

Cleo bit her lip, fighting a pang of guilt. *She* should be scouring the county for clues. For once, she didn't know where to start.

Mary-Rose and Dot shared a look.

"What?" Cleo said, frowning at her cousin and best friend. *Not them too! Could they actually doubt Henry?*

"Professor Weber doesn't like Henry," Cleo said, giving the broccoli a vicious stab. "The man is paranoid. A few years back, he tried to blame Henry and Henry's friend when *he* was the one who'd been tricked by a forgery."

"Yes," Mary-Rose said soothingly.

"The professor could have pushed Kitty," Cleo continued on, feeling belligerent. She didn't want her friend and cousin to soothe and comfort. She wanted them filled with indignation on Henry's behalf. "Kitty was flirty at the soiree. Jealousy is a prime motive."

"That hammer—" Dot said.

"Easily planted," Cleo declared, jabbing her fork at an evasive cherry tomato. "The killer could have slipped into the Gilded Page during business hours or a workshop. Professor Weber could have planted it right before he supposedly found it. He was in the shop for who knows how long before Mr. Chaucer heard him and alerted me. Henry would never . . ." Cleo paused to inhale and caught sight of her friend and cousin.

They had identical pitying looks. Dot reached over and patted Cleo's hand.

Cleo pushed back her seat.

"Motives," she said, standing to let Rhett in. The cat happily took over her seat at the table.

Cleo paced around the table, ticking off means, motives, and opportunity, as the chief had earlier. "Professor Weber had motives. Jealousy. Hunter Fox was his romantic rival. Perhaps Hunter even sold him a forged book? Embarrassment. He was angry and desperate to save face on professional and personal fronts."

"Those are fine motives," Mary-Rose said supportively. "He could have gone to Kitty's room the night of the killing, realized she was out, and guessed where."

Picking up her pace, Cleo said, "Yes, she was selling Hunter's books on consignment. More jealousy. He could have taken those books from her room and then killed Hunter."

Dot shivered but agreed it was a fine idea. "Professor Weber did have my bird book, but then he returned it."

"Only after Buddy discovered it," Cleo pointed out. She wanted Professor Weber to be guilty. Anyone but Henry.

"That gives me chills," Mary-Rose declared. "To think, Dot, he showed up in your kitchen."

Dot frowned.

Mary-Rose continued on. "It's a nice theory, but how can you prove it, Cleo? And what about Kitty? She was your prime suspect before she got shoved down those stairs. Could she be faking her injuries?"

"No, she couldn't have been faking that fall," Cleo said with grim certainty. She'd heard those awful cries.

Mary-Rose persisted. "Is Kitty still claiming she has no memory of what happened? Sounds awfully *convenient* to me."

"The doctors said memory loss was possible with a head injury," Cleo said. "Or she doesn't want to admit who pushed her. Like her fiancé?"

Mary-Rose clicked her tongue. "The romantic partner is sadly often the culprit."

Dot coughed and looked away.

They grew quiet. After a few minutes, Mary-Rose announced that she should be off on errands. Out on the porch, she hugged Cleo tightly and said, "Follow the books, Cleo. That's what you always do, and you always get the answer." She released Cleo and offered to drop Dot off at her shop or home.

Dot politely declined. "I need to walk off all this food," she said, although she'd eaten little. After Mary-Rose left, Dot lingered on the porch, petting Rhett, who'd followed them out. She looked like she had something she wanted to say.

"I should go," Dot said finally, although she still hesitated. She was halfway out the screen door when she turned back and gripped Cleo by both hands. Cleo was shocked to see tears floating in Dot's eyes.

"Oh, Dot," Cleo said. "I am sorry! I've been awfully insensitive, thinking only of Henry and my worries. How selfish! There's still a chance at finding your book, and I know you don't want us to, but the family can help pay those bills for the Drop By. It will all work out."

Dot's head shake sped up.

She's so stubborn, Cleo thought. She vowed to call Dot's niece. If anyone could talk Dot into accepting a family loan, it was April.

"I'm not worried about that anymore," Dot said, gripping Cleo's hands tighter. "I'm worried about *you*. I'm only confessing this because I love you, Cleo."

Cleo's heart jumped at the word *confessing*.

Dot barreled on. "I was sweet-talked by that awful man Hunter Fox. He flattered me and my books. I regressed to a silly teenager, charmed by his attentions. I invited him to my house, to look at my books. I was a fool!" The tears had disappeared. Her eyes were sharp.

Cleo held tight to her cousin's hands. "Dot, what are you saying?"

In the beat of silence that followed, Cleo's suspicious mind whirled. *A confession. Foolish teenage emotion? What is Dot confessing to? Murder? No! But he tricked her, toyed with her heart . . . stole her books and her hope and pride and . . .*

"I'm saying," Dot said slowly, "we're never too old to get fooled in love or blindsided by our emotions. How well do you *really, truly* know Henry, Cleo? He hasn't lived here all that long. We don't know his people or his business or life before coming here, only what he's told us."

Cleo yanked her hands back and gaped at her cousin. Thankfully, her mother's warning of words in haste whooshed back to her. Cleo counted to ten and then ten again. She scooped up Rhett and let him purr calmingly in her ear. Hurt, more than anger, made her cheeks burn.

"I appreciate your concern, Dot," Cleo said, glad she could keep her voice mostly steady. "But you're wrong. Henry is innocent and a good man."

Dot nodded. She didn't apologize. "I hope so. Please don't hold it against yourself—or me—if I'm right, Cleo."

"She's wrong," Cleo whispered to Rhett, as Dot hustled down the walkway. "She has to be."

Chapter
Thirty-Four

I n the darkest hours of night, just before dawn, a storm rolled
up from the south. Branches scraped at the clapboards of
Cleo's home. The big magnolia groaned. Lightning strobed
through the curtains, sending Rhett scrambling under the bed.
Mr. Chaucer nestled in closer to Cleo's side.

Cleo had been awake long before the storm. Now she gave
up, flipping on the light. Mr. Chaucer blinked.

"Sorry," Cleo whispered, although she didn't need to keep
her voice low. She and the pets were alone. Poor Henry was more
alone.

Cleo glanced at her bedside clock. It stared back in big red
numbers: 5:38. Cleo shut her eyes, wishing she could go back to
sleep, but all she could think of was Henry, locked up. She
wanted to see him and tell him she believed in him. Most desperately, she wanted to clear him.

But how?

Images of knives and ripped books and Kitty lying at the
bottom of the stairs swirled in Cleo's mind. When the alley
popped into her mental scene, Cleo fumbled to turn on her bedside lamp. Clearly, there would be no more sleep. Cleo got up
and put on both her robe and a bright tone for the pets.

"Let's go get breakfast," she said. "Doggy biscuit? Kitty treats?"

Mr. Chaucer woofed and trotted off down the hall. Cleo suspected she'd find his nose to the door again. She called to Rhett in singsong tones of "Pretty boy, pretty Rhett. Let's have breakfast." After a few more calls and a lull in the thunder, her cat slithered out from under the bed and raced downstairs, fur mussed and tail puffed.

Cleo put on her robe and slippers and grabbed the top book on her stack of new purchases. *The Wizard of Oz.* Perfect. She needed a distraction from her thoughts and the storm.

Mr. Chaucer bravely dashed out to the backyard, returning to shake off the rain with such force he nearly tipped over. Cleo doled out breakfast for the pets and put on a large pot of coffee for herself. Out back, the palms lashed the flashing sky. No lights shined at Ollie's.

"Youth, when we could sleep through anything," Cleo said. She helped herself to an oatmeal cookie, part of the consolation bounty. Oats made it breakfast appropriate, she rationalized, and it would be delightful with coffee. While the pot burbled, she opened her new book.

"Follow the books," Cleo murmured, thinking of Mary-Rose's parting advice. Rhett hopped to the seat beside her and scowled. Cleo had to agree. The book paths all led to Henry. Henry's workshops, which had inadvertently led Hunter Fox to local booklovers. Henry's tools. Henry's shop and the forgeries on his shelves.

"Supposed forgeries," Cleo said to Rhett. "Supposedly found, by the professor." She practically hissed the last word.

Thunder boomed. Rhett bolted from his seat, and pug claws scampered under the table. Cleo flipped through *The Wizard of*

Oz, her nerves so ragged she could only admire the illustrations. She paused at a favorite. Toto pulling back the curtain, dashing Dorothy's hopes that Oz could help her. Oz the great and powerful was a sham, a fraud. Dorothy would have to save herself.

The chief—and Dot, of all people—had implied that Henry might not be who she thought he was. But Cleo knew Henry. She *did*! She was as sure of this as she was of her love for Rhett and books. But someone else could be the charlatan . . .

Cleo mentally sorted through the antiquarians she'd met. Henry's friends the medievalists *seemed* like true booklovers, with their geeky talk of gilded pages. Buddy collected what he loved. He'd been tricked by a forgery too. Hunter Fox had sold Buddy the forged letter. Had Hunter known it was a fake?

"Surely," Cleo murmured. Kitty had boasted that Hunter never sold anything for less than it was worth. Even Professor Weber had admitted Hunter was clever with books.

Cleo turned her thoughts to the professor. She suspected he was just who she thought he was: an intense, insecure man terrified of looking foolish. A man who wanted Kitty all to himself.

Then there was Kitty, who wore her Marilyn Monroe personality like armor. To protect against what? Cleo helped herself to another cookie. She'd read somewhere that oatmeal promoted brain health.

She took a bite and answered her own question. Kitty was an admitted book thief. Her beautiful cover might distract the other bookdealers, but they'd keep their distance if they realized how far she'd go to get a book she wanted. *Like breaking into a bookmobile!*

Cleo finished her cookie, thinking of another known deceiver, Madame Romanov, hiding behind her curtain, spying on her clients. Had she seen one of the bookdealers on her surveillance video? Someone she knew?

Cleo cycled through the names again, automatically connecting them with the books they favored. *Follow the books. Someone is not who they seem . . .*

The storm crackled. Cleo's hair prickled, not from the electricity in the air but an unlikely idea, an odd incongruity. She closed her book and thought hard. She paced her kitchen for what seemed like miles. The idea wouldn't budge. She waited as long as she could for the first light to break and the storm to wring itself out. Then she dressed, threw on rubber boots and a raincoat, and grabbed an umbrella with a pointy tip. She kissed her cat on his frowny noggin and patted Mr. Chaucer's worried wrinkles.

"You two stay here," she said. "There are too many puddles out." *And too much danger.*

* * *

The Myrtles was quiet except for the soft clink of dishes and pans. Scents of coffee and cinnamon buns filled the foyer. Nina and Karl would be busy fixing breakfast, which was fine with Cleo. She'd called ahead to get a room number, muffling her voice when Nina answered and pretending to be a relative of the guest in question. She felt bad for the deception, but she didn't want Nina worrying about more trouble. The innkeepers had let the antiquarians stay an extra night for free, considering the "unfortunate accident" at the soiree and their assistance in the investigation.

But now that Henry was charged with the murder and Kitty's assault, most of them would be heading home. Cleo didn't have time to wait. If she was wrong, she'd apologize. No harm done. Cleo hurried up the stairs, her wet rubber boots squeaking on the marble tiles.

At the spot where Kitty had come to rest, Cleo paused. What if she was right? *No harm done* wouldn't apply then. All sorts of harm had already been done, and more could come to her. She had to take the risk for Henry's sake. Cleo glanced quickly over her shoulder and hoisted her purse. Then she took a deep breath, gripped her umbrella, and hurried up the steps.

The room she sought was at the end of the hallway where Henry had been waiting for Kitty the night of the soiree. Cleo tiptoed across the carpet, holding her breath and listening before tentatively knocking. Her gentle tap brought no response. Urgency compelled her to knock harder. Nina might have been wrong that the occupant was still inside. The guest might have left overnight.

The noise of her pounding bounced down the hall. She imagined all the doors opening and the bookdealers staring out, whipping off masks, revealing faces and desires she hadn't detected.

She raised her fist once more, but before it reached the wood, the door inched open.

Buddy Boone's ruddy face peeked out. "Oh," he said, sounding surprised. "Cleo. I thought you might be the cleaning lady, come to kick me out early. I think we book collectors might be overstaying our welcome." He opened the door a fraction farther and gestured toward his attire, a bulky bathrobe of fluffy fabric, embroidered with pink crepe myrtle flowers. "I'm glad I get to say good-bye to you, but I'm afraid I'm not fully dressed yet. Can I meet ya downstairs in a jiff?"

He started to close the door before Cleo could answer.

She was ready for such a move. She wedged her shoulder in the doorjamb, her purse along with it, and a shoe and her umbrella over the threshold. The purse contained her cell phone and a tiny canister of pepper spray, but it was the umbrella that made her feel like an armed Mary Poppins.

"I won't keep you," Cleo said, issuing silent apologies to manners.

"Ah . . ." Buddy stammered. "Okay. I guess." He stepped aside, then peeked out to the hallway before closing the door firmly behind Cleo.

"What a lovely room," Cleo said brightly. It was small but had pretty antique furnishings from the four-poster bed to a dresser sporting an attached oval mirror and stacks of books.

"I suppose you have all sorts of books to pack up," Cleo chatted on, stepping toward the dresser. "Did you sell a lot?"

"Enough," Buddy said, scratching his head and frowning at her.

If she was wrong, Cleo knew she must seem like a madwoman, bursting into a man's hotel room before breakfast, before he was even dressed.

"Is there something I can help you with?" He moved around Cleo, blocking her path to the dresser. He looked different in the fluffy bathrobe, she thought, and not just because she'd only seen him in denim and folksy bandannas. There was something . . .

Cleo didn't feel right staring at a man in his robe, arms modestly folded over his middle. She swung her eyes around the room, scanning for more books. Several rested on the nightstand. Cardboard boxes stood in a leaning stack, presumably packed up with his inventory.

"I hope you can help me," Cleo said. "I have a question about *Gone With the Wind*."

Buddy's frown deepened. "Okay," he said, drawing out the word to suggest his confusion. "You still looking for your cousin's book, is that it? It's a real shame that, but maybe when Kitty gets her wits back, she'll be able to help. Shame about her, too, and Mr. Lafayette's . . . ah . . . troubles. Shame all around."

Cleo forced herself not to get distracted by talk of Henry's troubles. "You said you've sold some *Gone With the Wind* copies?" Cleo asked mildly.

"Sure. Is that what you want? A replacement for Miss Dot? I'm kinda packed up, but I could mail her something later. If that's all . . ." He gestured toward the door, and suddenly Cleo realized what had been bugging her.

His belly. Or rather, the lack of it. The man who'd filled out his coveralls was suddenly slender. She covered a surprised gasp with a cough and moved back toward the door.

"How kind," Cleo said. "I'm looking for the edition Dot had. A first first. You know, the 1945 version?" She'd just given the wrong date by over a decade. She watched his face and read vexation.

"Sure, sure. I can look for that. No problem. Now, I'm sorry, but I have to get going before that cleaning lady comes by." He chuckled and waved again toward the door.

Cleo debated. He'd given nothing away but ignorance of a book that, as a supposed Georgia-themed collector, he should know. Was that enough to accuse him of murder? She wished she could see behind him. He hadn't moved from his spot, blocking her view of the books.

"Wonderful," she lied, and hefted her purse higher on her wrist. She imagined tossing it at him, making him catch it. Or she could do the next best thing.

"Oh dear," Cleo said, letting her purse drop to the floor. "Oh, my knees." She nudged the fallen purse with her foot, tipping out its contents: lipstick, sunscreen, a slender paperback for unexpected reading opportunities, pens, cat treats, a comb, a compact, and a shopping list. Fortunately, the pepper spray stayed wedged in a pocket.

Buddy knelt down and began gathering it all up.

"Thank you! Let me just get out of your way," Cleo said. "So kind!" She dodged around him and planted herself in front of the stack of books. Her heart sank when she read the titles. *Fish of the Chattahoochee. Oak Trees of Georgia. A Gentleman's Guide to Groupers.*

Buddy had managed to stuff everything back in her purse. He looked up at her with a sharpness that quickly melted back to geniality. "I don't think you'll be interested in those books," he said with a chuckle.

Cleo was about to reach for the proffered purse. At his words, she froze. Ever since childhood, there had been two phrases that made Cleo Watkins instantly rebel. One began with any version of *young ladies shouldn't*. The other was any assumption that Cleo Watkins wouldn't be interested in a certain type of book.

Young Cleo might have fallen for *Gone With the Wind*, but she'd loved Tolkien and Tolstoy too, even more after adults insisted she wouldn't. *You won't like this* was a challenge. Coming from a man who'd seemed set on guarding those books, it was also suspicious.

Cleo reached for the top volume, *A Gentleman's Guide to Groupers*. To her horror, the contents slipped out and she was left holding only a cover.

"I'm so sorry!" Cleo gaped down, imagining she'd see torn pages. Instead, another book lay at her feet. The burgundy cover was cracked with age. Gold gilt glittered on the edges.

She looked from the book to Buddy. Slender Buddy, whose face was no longer affable.

Simultaneously, they reached to grab the fallen book. He was faster, but when he gripped it in front of him, Cleo could read the title. It was the same as one of the forged histories Professor Weber had discovered at Henry's shop.

"Sorry about the book," Cleo stammered again. "I mean, books. I should be going. I'll get out of your way." Her heart pounded hard, almost drumming out his next words.

Buddy Boone stood between Cleo and the exit. He tightened the robe sash around his slender waist. "I don't think you can now," he said.

* * *

"I'm only here to help Henry." Cleo gripped her umbrella, her last line of defense now that Buddy had tossed her purse aside.

"You're a good woman," he said, stepping closer.

Cleo moved back until her knees bumped into the hard shoulder of the radiator.

"So is your cousin," he continued. "Dot's a fine woman with a true love of books. I respect that. I *understand* that. That's all I understand in this world. Love of books. I'm a simple man at heart."

Everyone has something in common, Cleo thought, trying to calm herself. "I understand that sentiment," she said. "So does Henry. He's devastated that the other antiquarians think he's a book forger." He was surely even more devastated to be seen as a killer, but Cleo didn't want to bring that up.

Buddy shrugged. "Unfortunate that Weber discovered those forgeries at the Gilded Page. Mr. Lafayette would surely have detected them before selling them on to anyone else. He's a skilled authenticator. *De*authenticator, I should say. He questioned my lovely Oglethorpe letter after one look. I should have offered that letter to Professor Weber instead. I bet he would have snapped it right up. I got reckless . . . The *events* of this fair unsettled me."

Events? Like a murder he committed? Cleo tried to look suitably sympathetic. "It was a lovely letter. I was truly inspired seeing it."

He brightened. "Yes. You were happy, weren't you? Others could have been as well. My letter could have been in a museum.

It could have brought me a tidy sum too, to enhance my collecting."

Carefully, tenderly, he placed Henry's gilded book on the bed, caressing the cover before turning back to Cleo. "Like I tried to tell you before, I have to be going. As much as I've adored your town, it's brought me nothing but difficulties. That irritating scout and absurd psychic and you, Mrs. Watkins. I'm sorry you had to be so clever and persistent. What are we going to do about *you*?" He moved closer.

Cleo told the truth, mostly. "I won't say anything. Please, just leave something, some evidence clearing Henry, and I'll wait until you've left town to alert the police."

Cleo inched toward the window and glanced down. They were on the second floor. There was a recycling bin below, jutting with cans and bottles.

"Evidence pointing to Buddy Boone?" he said. "Would that work for you?"

Cleo froze, fearful of stepping into a trap. Perhaps he meant it. "Yes?" Cleo said tentatively. "You aren't really Buddy, are you?" Her voice had a thin tininess to it, even to her ears. "Is that why you had to kill Mr. Fox? Did he recognize you?"

The man who wasn't Buddy seemed to consider the question. When he spoke again, his folksy drawl had been replaced by unaccented steeliness. "Fox recognized a thief. It takes a thief to know one, to see the sleight of hand. It's like a magic trick. Once you know how the illusion is done, you see every move."

Cleo wasn't sure what he meant, but she tried to keep him talking. He was unmasked now. Maybe he'd want to brag. "Hunter Fox saw you stealing?"

His eyes shifted toward the book on the bed.

"Swapping," Cleo said quickly. "Collecting?"

"No harm would have been done," he said. "Fox thought he could blackmail simple Buddy Boone. The psychic made the same mistake."

"Madame Romanov," Cleo said. "Is she okay?"

He smiled easily. "For now. Until she tries to make another swap. She thinks I'm a good-old-boy collector of Georgia memorabilia and cheap books. Everyone does. Except you."

Chills crawled over Cleo's arms. She grasped for ways to appeal to his good side. He must have one, she thought desperately. He liked books. "You found Dot's book at Professor Weber's stand. That was nice of you. Did you send back her other books too?"

"I did," he said, smiling. "I had the opportunity to . . . retrieve . . . some books from Kitty's room, items Mr. Fox had given her. I'll admit, I probably got greedy, taking all those books, but the man had insulted me. I felt it only right that he paid me back. Retroactively."

After Hunter Fox was dead, Cleo interpreted. Buddy had broken into Kitty's room and taken the books Hunter had "scouted" from Dot and other victims.

"Dot was kind to me, so I repaid the favor," he said.

"Dot does love books," Cleo said. "She was thrilled to get them back. Henry loves books too. He's a good man. He never laughed at Buddy Boone."

The fake Buddy Boone gave an elegant roll of his shoulders. "I know. He has an excellent shop. That's why I came to this fair, to collect from it. No one was supposed to get hurt or even realize what happened until I was someone else and somewhere else."

In three quick steps, he moved to a jacket hanging on a door hook. He reached into a pocket. When his hand reappeared, metal flashed, thin and sharp.

"You came here alone, Mrs. Watkins. How brave of you. Noble. Foolish." He pointed the metal at Cleo. "The awl," he said. "A bookmaker's friend. A useful tool. I am sorry, Mrs. Watkins, but how can I continue my collecting if I am always looking over my shoulder, waiting for you to appear?"

He moved closer, and Cleo knew words would no longer work. She grasped her umbrella and thumped the spike down three times, loud against the floorboards.

For a moment, nothing happened. Cleo's thudding heart seemed to clog her throat. She feared she really was alone. Long seconds passed before the door burst open and with it Gabby Honeywell, gun drawn and yelling for Buddy to drop his weapon.

The fake Buddy swiveled, lunging at Gabby, who dodged left and managed to grab his arm. The awl fell to the floor. He howled as she twisted his arm behind his back.

"You are . . . under . . . arrest," Gabby said, through the effort of hauling back his other hand.

He yanked it away and looked ready to strike Gabby. Cleo didn't have time to think. With both hands, she gripped the umbrella and pulled it back to shoulder height. Decades ago Cleo had played South Georgia softball. She'd always felt she had a mighty swing still residing in her. Just like riding a bike, Cleo thought, as she whipped the umbrella forward, hitting his wrist with home-run strength.

He yelped and grabbed his arm, giving Gabby the upper hand. The deputy had wrestled him to the ground when Sergeant Tookey lumbered in.

"Dang," Tookey said, frowning right back. "I almost missed it. You said I should watch the back, by the kitchen."

Tookey recited the Miranda warning. Gabby slumped to the bed and Cleo sank down beside her.

"You had me scared, Miss Cleo," Gabby said, regaining her composure. "Let's not do that again, okay?"

"I hope we won't have to," Cleo said, patting back her hair. Her face felt flushed. Her elbow ached and her heartbeat was still thumping on high. But she'd gotten him. *They'd* gotten him. She couldn't hold back a giddy smile, and when she glanced at Gabby, she saw her favorite neighbor was grinning too.

Cleo managed to look properly serious as footsteps raced down the hall. One by one, the bookdealers crowded at the doorway, vying for a view.

Chapter Thirty-Five

Cleo and Henry embraced in the police station lobby. Together they pushed open the station doors and stepped outside. The clouds had parted and the air was softly steamy.

Henry breathed in deeply and closed his eyes. When he opened them again, they were glistening.

"Let's go to my place," she said, taking his hand. He knew his shop had been searched, but she didn't want him to face the mess right away. Besides, Mr. Chaucer was waiting. "Someone is very anxious to see you," Cleo said.

They walked slowly, dodging puddles and soaking up the sunshine. Cleo talked and Henry listened in stunned silence.

Her picket fence was in view when he finally said, "Buddy? But . . . he seemed so nice. He was so helpful, finding Dot's book."

"*Seemed* nice," Cleo said. She reconsidered. "Maybe he *is* nice, in some ways. He took a liking to Dot. But he's also a killer, a thief, and a forger. And he's not Buddy Boone."

They approached Cleo's gate. A metallic snapping sound came from the next yard. Too late, Cleo raised a finger, urging silence.

"Cleo, is that you?" Wanda Boxer appeared at their fence line, clippers gleaming with a green tinge. Plant blood, Cleo thought, and realized she was giddy and shocked and shaken all at once. Thank goodness her kitchen, their four-legged friends, and all those treats were only a few steps away.

Wanda aimed the clippers at Cleo and then slowly over to Henry. Cleo wished, for once, that Wanda's gossip line was faster. Then she'd know. She'd know Henry was innocent, vindicated. Cleo didn't want to be the one to explain it to her. Wanda, she felt, would only spout negatives, and Cleo didn't want her glossy happiness marred.

"Morning, Wanda," Cleo called out. "Turning out to be a lovely day, isn't it? Quite a storm last night . . ." She hurried up the walkway, Henry close behind her.

"Don't you run off, Cleo Watkins," Wanda ordered.

"Go inside," Cleo whispered to Henry. "I'll fend her off."

He didn't budge. "You've done way too much fending for my sake today."

"You," Wanda said, re-aiming the blades in Henry's direction. "You are a lucky man."

Cleo gaped. "You heard? Already?"

"I'm on spring break," Wanda said, in a tone others might use to announce sick leave. "What else do I have to do?" She scowled at them over a butchered camellia. "Really, Cleo, the things you've been up to lately. Fighting criminals, frequenting bars, staying out until all hours . . . Keep it down over there, is all I have to say. I don't want to hear any big party celebrations tonight. And you . . ."

She narrowed her eyes at Henry. "You better appreciate a woman who goes cavorting around, putting herself in danger to clear your name."

"I do," he said warmly and embraced Cleo in a bear hug. The kiss that followed had Wanda huffing. The sounds of frenzied snipping and pruning followed them into the house, where Mr. Chaucer spun in wobbly circles of joy. Henry scooped him up and let himself be smothered in sloppy pug kisses. Rhett bounded up, meowed sharply, and led the way to the kitchen.

Cleo ushered Henry into his seat at the table.

He sat, looking slightly dazed. "Wanda's right. You put yourself in danger. You could have been hurt, and that would have been the worst thing in the world for me."

"Worse than prison on a murder charge?" Cleo tried to joke. "Worse than getting kicked out of the Georgia Antiquarian Book Society?"

His face was serious. "Far worse."

Cleo pictured the flash of the awl in fake-Buddy's hand and Hunter stricken down in the alley.

"Gabby was with me," Cleo said, doling out treats for the pets. "I told Gabby what I suspected but couldn't prove. She came with me and waited down the hallway. Sergeant Tookey always believed in you too. He was staking out the downstairs, in the vicinity of cinnamon rolls."

Cleo put on coffee—decaf for her jumpy nerves—and dragged out goodies: cookies, cake, and pie. "And salads," she said. "I have a bunch of salads too. The unhealthy kind, mostly, with bacon and cheese."

Henry looked puzzled. "You've been cooking?"

"Folks dropped by," Cleo said obliquely. She was glad when he took a cookie and didn't question why folks had dropped by with a buffet.

He smiled. "I think we deserve something sweet. You especially. How did you come to suspect him, of all people? When I was in that cell, I kept trying to guess who was responsible. I decided it must be Professor Weber."

Cleo told him about Buddy's mistake regarding the first edition of *Gone With the Wind*.

"I didn't know about 'first firsts,'" Henry said. "I probably could have guessed the approximate first publishing date, but not exactly."

"But you're not a specialized collector of Georgia books," Cleo said. "Buddy claimed to be a fan of *Gone With the Wind* too, and he had several copies at his shop, different editions. Now I wish I'd looked more carefully at each and the pricing. Maybe I would have guessed earlier."

"His act was so convincing," Henry said. "He looked the part, sounded the part . . ."

Cleo tried to explain how that had tipped her off too. "He was almost too perfect, if that makes sense. Too much in character, and yet that character wasn't quite right. I started making a list of who would be the most surprising guilty party. Not Kitty, Professor Weber, or Madame Romanov. Not even the medievalists, although I did wonder about them when the forged history books turned up in your shop."

The coffee burbled. Cleo poured them big mugs. "I also considered who had the opportunity to swipe your tools and plant evidence and forgeries in your shop. Buddy was keen on your shop and came to town early to visit it. When I thought about it, he seemed keener than his supposed collecting interests warranted."

Henry rubbed his chin thoughtfully. "He followed after us, that first day of the fair when Dot argued with Hunter Fox. He would have gone right past my demonstration table with all my tools."

Cleo had thought about that too. Buddy had been carrying a bag. He could easily have slipped in the awl and hammer. Perhaps an extra awl too, the one he'd brandished at her.

Henry shuddered. "He came by the shop several times. I left him alone sometimes, to browse while I got things from my workshop and walked Chaucy. I thought he was simply interested in books."

"He was," Cleo said. She suggested they take plates out to the back porch for some fresh air. The day felt scrubbed by the storm, fresh and sweet. They sat quietly, the pets at their feet, for an hour or so, long enough that Ollie's curtains twitched open.

Cleo tried to let her mind wander down pleasant paths, to summer gardening plans and her bookmobile route, all the places she'd go with Words on Wheels' new door and ice-cold air conditioning.

But a dark thought kept popping up. She knew she needed to tell Henry, even if it might upset him most.

Cleo took a deep breath and said, "I think Buddy—whoever he is—planned long in advance to swipe your books and replace them with the fakes. It sounded like he came here specifically to target you."

Henry sat back in his seat. "So I *did* bring this on us. How awful. If I hadn't pushed so hard for the fair to come to Catalpa Springs, none of this would have happened." He sighed. "The Georgia antiquarian bookdealers might not forgive me."

The phone rang inside. Cleo considered letting it go, but her phone manners were ingrained from an era before robocalls. She still held the hope that every call would be a real human she wanted to speak with.

Cleo answered and listened, twirling the cord around her finger as she did. Her smile grew wider with every word on the other end.

"I think they'll forgive you," she said, seeing Henry peering anxiously inside. "No, I *know* they do." Cleo reached for Rhett's harness and the keys to Words on Wheels. They all needed to see this, and they'd arrive in bookmobile style.

* * *

As they passed by the library, Cleo beeped in happy honks. Leanna and a handful of patrons ran out and waved from the front porch. Cleo issued another burst of the horn as they circled the park and rounded the corner. The Gilded Page came into view, and Cleo saw that good graces were on their side, in more ways than one.

A parking space long enough for a bus stood empty in front of Henry's shop. Best of all was the crowd. Not an angry or accusatory mob, but a mix of happy locals, a beaming Dot, and contrite antiquarian bookdealers. Professor Weber stepped out from among them, waiting on the curb.

Cleo swung Words on Wheels into the spot and threw out the stop signs. "Ready?" she said. Rhett hopped out of his peach crate and was first down the steps. Henry and Mr. Chaucer hung back.

"Professor Weber?" he said warily. "What do you think he wants? To search my shop again? To accuse me of fraud and forgery and pushing his fiancée?"

"I'd say he's here for the same reason as the rest," Cleo said. "To apologize."

Professor Weber blocked their way down the bus steps. He held out a hand. "Mr. Lafayette," he said stiffly. "Open up, and we'll get your shelves back in order. Can't have your books lying around in stacks. It's bad for their spines."

"Go on," Cleo urged. Looking dazed, Henry walked to open up the shop, his pug trotting at his side. To Cleo's relief, Henry's look turned to joy as friends and neighbors kept halting his progress, wanting to shake his hand and pat him on the back. Cleo scooped up Rhett and followed, blushing from the cheer raised in her honor.

Eventually, after handshakes and hugs, the locals moved their impromptu party to the park, where the bakery and Dot brought out treats. The antiquarians got to work inside, tidying Henry's books and workshop, praising his work, and—best of all—apologizing.

"I never took the rumors of the 'fair curse' seriously," Professor Weber said brusquely to Henry and Cleo. "I considered it made up, a hypochondria at best, an excuse for bad behavior at worst. There are always a few bad deals. Now I wonder . . ."

"You wonder about your own collection," Cleo said bluntly. "You were tricked by a forgery. You even sold that forgery before you realized." She put her hands on her hips, elbows out, almost hoping he'd deny it. She'd taken on a killer this morning. She could stand up to an insecure bully.

His expression hardened. Cleo drew a deep breath, prepared to let it out with truth and indignation.

"I suppose I owe Mr. Lafayette an apology for that," he said grudgingly. "I plan to do a thorough examination of my inventory and any sales since the fair two years ago, when I hosted."

Cleo used her breath for another righteous truth. "That's wise," she said. "You'll also return any stolen books that you and Miss Peavey still have in your possession."

When the professor chuffed in misplaced indignation, Henry said, "The Georgia Antiquarian Book Society takes ethics seriously, as you've said."

"I never . . ." the professor blustered. "Those are unfounded accusations. You shouldn't insult Kitty when she's fragile and recovering in the hospital."

"Who's insulting whom?" Gabby Honeywell strode up, grinning at Cleo. She had a backpack slung over one shoulder, her hair bobbing in a high ponytail. "Leave some suspects for me to interrogate, Miss Cleo."

Professor Weber scowled. "This woman is *insulting* me and my fiancée."

"Oh, I'd say rightfully so," Gabby said. "I have some questions for you too, Professor. Our 'guest' down at the police station won't say much about himself, but he's happy to spill about the rest of you. Like your fiancée. Miss Kitty can't help her kleptomania. I get that. It's a disease. Hunter Fox helped satisfy her book urges. Did you? Did you help her rob Miss Cleo's bookmobile?"

The man's face darkened. "Kitty was under immense strain after Hunter Fox's death. We all were. When she's under pressure, she . . . she acts out and engages in risky behavior. Like you say, it's a mental health condition. She'll go back to treatment. I'll watch over her. I'll take care of her."

Cleo frowned. "Did you watch when she robbed my bookmobile?"

He scowled. "No. I had been watching her that night, worried she might be overly stressed and anxious after Fox's death. You and Mr. Lafayette drew her attention to me. She gets upset if she thinks I'm smothering her with my concern. In a way, it's your own fault that bookmobile was robbed. If you'd left me alone, I could have dissuaded her. I've gotten her through past *episodes*, and I'll help her through this." He paused and then said, with a hitch in his voice, "I love her."

Love. More than ever, Cleo understood clinging to love through precarious times. She touched Henry's hand and said, "The Catalpa Springs Public Library may be able to forgo pressing charges if Miss Peavey returns *Into the Waves*. Although she did mar it in her attempt to disguise her actions."

Gabby scowled, proving she was very good at playing bad cop. "I don't know. She stole from a public institution, from all of us! Wouldn't you say that library principles are at stake, Miss Cleo?"

"I would," Cleo said.

The professor's stony face seemed grayer.

"Then there's this," Gabby said. She hitched her backpack down and unzipped it, drawing out a clear plastic evidence bag holding a book.

Cleo recognized the contents immediately. "Dot's book!" Behind it was a mailing envelope with express-delivery markings and Dot's address on it.

Gabby nodded. "We found this in our suspect's room at the Myrtles. It suggests he pushed Ms. Peavey down the stairs. It appears that he intended to mail it to Miss Dot. He really does seem to like her. It will have to stay in evidence for a bit, but Cleo, you can let Dot know the book will be coming back to her."

Gabby looked Professor Weber in the eye when she said, "Because we all *know* it belongs to Dot Moore. If Miss Peavey tries to say otherwise, I'll have to call in a respected book restoration expert." She paused and nodded to Henry before continuing. "I'm sure such an expert will easily detect how Kitty tried to hide identifying marks by slicing out the identifying crayon marking in the back. Receiving stolen goods is a crime, as I'm sure you're aware," Gabby said, using the professor's own pedantic tone.

She pulled out another list with Cleo's own handwriting, the list of missing and stolen books. "Most of these books were found in the suspect's room, in the boxes he was packing up to take with him. A few are still missing. Professor Weber, you had one previously, a book of birds. I'll warn you, anyone possessing these could be charged with possession of stolen property."

Cleo realized the shop had gone quiet. The antiquarian book-dealers stood at shelves, miming interest in books, but no pages turned. Cleo knew they were listening intently.

Professor Weber knew too. "Hunter Fox gave that bird book to Kitty. She stored it in her safe and later gave it to me, knowing I'm a collector of natural history. I'll recheck my inventory, as I said. We all will." Murmurs of agreement filtered across the shelves.

"Yes, you will," Gabby said. "We'll check Miss Peavey's inventory too. In fact, let's go do that right now, shall we?"

Under the gaze of his colleagues, the professor ducked his head and meekly followed Gabby out the door.

Chapter
Thirty-Six

Late the following week, Cleo put on her freshly polished dancing shoes.

Henry Lafayette adjusted a bow tie. "Too formal?" he asked. "Too polka dot?"

"Just right," Cleo said. "Polka dots are perfect for a party."

Furry faces followed them to the door.

"You two guard the house," Cleo said. Rhett galloped off down the hallway, meowing dares for the pug to follow him. Mr. Chaucer shot a worried look at Henry before woofing and wobbling after Rhett.

Cleo and Henry arrived to find the party already buzzing. Dot's Drop By was lit up with string lights and a joyful crowd. Cleo was among the happiest of all to see the door sign turned to *Open* and the code inspector's "passed" paperwork pinned to the specials board. Dot was looking resplendent in a fresh gingham apron with waves of ruffles.

Dot enveloped Cleo in a hug. "I couldn't have done this without you and Ollie and everyone!"

Dot was misty-eyed, and so was Cleo.

"No weeping at parties," Mary-Rose said, swooping in for hugs and wiping a happy tear from her eye too.

Ollie and Gabby joined them. Cleo noted that Ollie seemed to have gotten over his stammers. "We have two parties in one night," he said, bending to kiss Cleo on the cheek.

"We're off to Ollie's crane fund raiser after this," Gabby said. "Are you coming, Miss Cleo? Henry?"

Cleo and Henry shared a smile and an understanding. They'd gladly donated to Ollie's cause. However, that dance party started at ten, when Cleo and Henry preferred to be tucked into bed reading. "I think I've had enough late nights for a while," she said. "Unless we stop off at the gastropub for a nightcap."

Gabby chuckled. "You deserve a rest. Did you get all those missing books back to folks?"

"I returned the last one today." Cleo had been busy, adding stolen-book returns to her bookmobile route. She'd completed the satisfying task that afternoon. On the way back to town, she'd stopped by Golden Acres. The residents had wanted all the news and had given her the "honor" of reading the final, blush-inducing chapter of *The Lusty Lord*.

Bernice Abernathy had been there visiting her grandson and friends and had praised Cleo for tracking down her swiped Poirot. She was going to sell it, but through an honest dealer this time, Henry Lafayette. Bernice intended to give her grateful grandson the gift of paid-off nursing-school loans. Her missing map pages had been found among the stolen items. Henry was going to rebind her treasured atlases at no cost. They'd be better than ever, he promised.

Mary-Rose clicked her tongue as Cleo ticked off all the people who'd been affected. "Awful and unnecessary. That con man Hunter Fox hurt a lot of people and books." She frowned. "So did the killer. Did you ever find out his real name, Gabby?"

"Johnathon Prince," Gabby said. "We think that's his real name, at least. He went by a lot of aliases, not only the Buddy Boone persona. He'd put them on as it suited him, like the clothes and accent and even a fake pregnancy belly pillow, which gave me the creeps. He liked being unrecognizable, in person and online. I think it made him feel invisible and powerful. He could take what he wanted. 'Collecting,' he called it."

Henry shifted in his polished loafers. "The society members are like family. We all know each other. Maybe we should have noticed who we *didn't* know as well. But like you said, so much interaction happens online now, where it's hard to know who's real. I looked back and realized 'Buddy Boone' had been on some of the book restoration forums I chat on. That's probably where he learned of my books and decided he wanted to steal them."

Cleo shivered, and Dot fluttered off to serve up more free ice cream. She'd gotten big tubs, sugar cones, and sprinkles, all of which she was giving away for free.

Gabby leaned toward Cleo and whispered, "This is tacky of me to ask, but is Miss Dot going to sell that book? The pricey one?"

Cleo nodded. She'd expected to feel sadder about the sale of Dot's *Gone With the Wind*. So had Dot. "Dot loves that book, of course, but she realized it's the memories she treasures most, us reading *Gone* when we were young and the thrill of discovering that precious signed copy in the estate-sale box. The online fund raiser was set to be restarted and the podcaster had broadcast Dot's innocence, but Dot asked everyone to donate to their favorite charities instead. She feels like the book should be the one to help her, that she found it for a reason and that it came back for one too. It will go to a good home. Henry is going to make sure of that."

Henry nodded. "I have a buyer who will treasure it," he said. He squeezed Cleo's hand. "You'll appreciate that the buyer promises not to lock it up in a cold safe. She's going to loan it to her library for their special collection so that more people can enjoy it."

Cleo loved that idea, and so did Dot. Cleo's own special collection was intact again too. The signed copy of *Into the Waves* was in a glass cabinet—locked but prominently displayed in the main library. Leanna had even made arrow signs, like a treasure hunt, pointing the way to it.

Gabby rocked back on her heels. "Buddy—Johnathon Prince—kept going on about how that's all he cared about. Books. Caring for them. Wanting them. Collecting almost seemed like an addiction. He *had* to have them."

"Bibliomania," Cleo said under her breath.

"It's not uncommon," Henry said, and then qualified. "What I mean is, there's a draw—a tug—to books. Thank goodness murder and stealing aren't usually involved. I don't think he came here intending to kill, do you, Gabby?"

Gabby shook her head. "No. Definitely not. He only planned to rob you, Henry, and leave you with a passable forgery, which he considered generous and polite. Hunter Fox had the unfortunate good fortune of spotting the swap. Then Hunter made the fatal mistake of getting greedy."

"I was right at the shop and didn't see," Henry said. He explained to the rest. "I gather it was the night I hosted the social? Everyone was at the shop, milling around, looking at books." Henry flushed. "I was too busy chatting and showing off."

"No," Cleo soothed. "You were only highlighting your wonderful books."

"Buddy prepared the forgeries beforehand," Gabby said. "Meticulous copies he based on library books and online resources. You didn't use those books every day, right Henry? Buddy was counting on that. If and when you did notice the trouble, he'd be long gone."

Henry shook his head. "I *might* have noticed, eventually. The two forgeries were very well done, but not perfect. It's not like I open and check every book regularly. The covers looked fine."

Cleo said, "I have books I don't look at for years. I'll admit, I have some—several, more than several—I haven't gotten around to reading. I find it comforting just knowing they're there, on my shelves."

The rest of them nodded. They understood.

Henry groaned. "I may have helped him rob me, posting my restorations and photos of my inventory online." He smiled. "But then, the great libraries are going digital now, and I think it's the most wonderful thing. We can see into marvelous ancient texts without leaving home."

Cleo focused on the positive too. "We can't deprive all the good booklovers because of a few bad actors," she said. "If only someone honest had spotted Buddy swiping those books, it might have turned out much differently."

"Blackmail," Mary-Rose intoned.

Gabby said, "Yep. Hunter Fox thought he was blackmailing some memento-collecting good old boy. But Hunter didn't just want money from Buddy. He thought they could be partners of sorts. Buddy would do the stealing and forgeries, and Hunter would pass the items off to bookdealers. Hunter told Kitty he was onto something big. She thought he meant a big book, but he pictured an easy life with easy money."

"Hunter paid with his life," Cleo said. "Madame Romanov is lucky she didn't meet the same fate. She must have realized just in time."

"That psychic premonition," Mary-Rose laughed.

"Right, or her video cameras," Cleo said, rolling her eyes. "I hear she's back in town. Back from 'vacation'?"

Gabby confirmed this. "Yep, Madame aka Tina gave a statement. At first, she claimed she contacted Buddy Boone out of the goodness of her heart, wanting him to repent." Gabby paused for skeptical snorts from her audience.

"I know," Gabby said. "We didn't buy that. We finally threatened her with arrest for withholding evidence, and she confessed that she'd asked for payment in exchange for her video recording. He was supposed to leave it in the alley, at the crime scene. Instead, she saw him—or someone who looked creepily *not* like him, thinner and dressed differently—breaking into her house. She got out and ran, leaving her dog behind."

"Terrible behavior, deserting her pet," Henry said. "That woman is not to be trusted."

Gabby agreed. "I don't think she'll be in the psychic business much longer. Word of how she derived her powers is spreading. She has agreed to help our court case, in exchange for us looking the other way about running off with evidence. She has the video of the murder, and she can help with the assault on Kitty too."

"The jangles," Henry murmured.

"The incense," Cleo added.

"She was there," Gabby confirmed. "Or, rather, hiding nearby when it happened. She and Nina Flores know each other from Madame's ghost tours. Nina was letting her bunk in a utility room on the second floor—right along that hall where you were waiting for Kitty the night she was shoved, Henry. There was a cot in there and a tape recorder with a remote control that made ghostly sounds. Nina said having a ghost added 'value.'" Gabby shook her head dubiously.

Cleo agreed. "I can't see who goes to a relaxing bed-and-breakfast to be scared by noises."

"Right?" Gabby said. "Madame admitted she was watching Buddy the night of the soiree, hiding in that little back staircase that leads downstairs. When he made for that very staircase, aiming to follow Kitty, she panicked and bolted. That's when she ran into you, Henry. Literally."

"I thought Buddy was accounted for in the ballroom," Cleo said, shaking her head.

Gabby had too. "No one missed him from the party. He was the kind of guy who faded into the background, which suited him perfectly. He sneaked upstairs, grabbed that book from Kitty, and shoved her. He never meant for you to get hurt, Henry."

"But why?" Mary-Rose asked. "Why risk revealing himself to steal from Kitty? Was he doing it for Dot?"

In a way, it seemed noble, Cleo thought. Like Robin Hood. She was feeling conflicted until she noticed Gabby shaking her head.

"Dot's book was a bonus. The whole reason he stuck around Catalpa Springs was the video evidence. Madame Romanov had been in contact with him. She left an anonymous note under his door, saying she'd 'send him a sign' and they could 'make a deal.' She even tried to convince him she was an ally by starting up that online chat group casting suspicion on Dot. She said she understood why he killed Hunter. Hunter swindled her out of her magic books and deserved 'what he had coming.'"

Mary-Rose shivered.

"I had to return those magic books to Madame's niece," Cleo said. "Madame refused to see me." The niece had been delighted to get her hands on the "dangerous" books, and Cleo had been delighted to give them to her.

Gabby shook her head. "She was scared to talk to you, but toying around with a killer? Foolish and greedy. That greed indirectly led to Kitty's assault. Remember at the soiree, when Kitty hinted that she had something 'special,' 'just what you're looking for,' and going on about making a deal?"

"I thought she meant Dot's book," Cleo said. "Although she was ambiguous."

"It was open to interpretation," Gabby agreed. "Buddy took it as a 'sign' from his blackmailer that Kitty had the video. He must have been getting desperate. Kitty was carrying Dot's book in a clutch. He yanked it away before he pushed her. When he realized it was just the book, he decided he'd return it to Dot. A small penance. He's been going on and on about what a great guy that makes him, how it redeems him. He said he always left 'masterful duplicates' to replace the books he 'collected' too, so the victims shouldn't complain."

Cleo gazed up the aisle to where Dot was joyfully handing out ice cream cones. She could understand anyone taking a liking to Dot. However . . . "That hardly redeems murder," Cleo said. "And what about the other books? The books Hunter swindled and Buddy stole? He had those packed up to take with him, didn't he? That's not great-guy behavior."

Gabby shrugged. "He considered those as payback for the mess Hunter put him in. He didn't know their owners. They didn't bring him the world's best cookies like Dot did."

Gabby grinned as one of those cookies suddenly hovered over her shoulder, snagged from a passing platter by Ollie. The two twenty-somethings drifted off into the festivities to enjoy cookies and each other's company.

Later, Cleo and Henry strolled through the park. A bluegrass band had set up by the fountain. Kids ran around, giddy with the night, lights, and ice cream.

Cleo felt their excitement surge through her.

"We never got to implement our dance moves," Henry said, smiling at her. He held out a hand.

"I don't know bluegrass steps," Cleo said, eyeing the bouncy dancers warily.

"I think we've reached the age where we can do whatever we like," Henry replied. He held her close, and they danced cheek to cheek to their own rhythm.

"What if I asked you never to go chasing after killers again?" Henry said, as their slow waltz took them by the fountain.

Cleo leaned back and took in his smiling face. "You wouldn't do that, would you?"

"No," he said, grinning. "I'd never want to squelch your natural talents and passions. But can I ask one thing? Next time, will you wait for me to come along with you?"

Cleo didn't hesitate. "I will," she said.

She thought of the whirlwind week, starting with Mary-Rose warning of heartbreak at the book fair.

Henry raised her hand. Laughing, Cleo spun in her shiny shoes, feeling like a kid again, like she was flying above the earth. She came to a dizzy stop in Henry's arms, but her joy kept twirling up to the treetops and beyond. She'd been right, so happily affirmed: books would never break her heart, and neither would Henry Lafayette.

Recipe

Mary-Rose's Famous Swoon Pies

Cookies

2 cups unbleached all-purpose flour
1/2 cup unsweetened cocoa powder
1 teaspoon baking soda
1/2 teaspoon table salt
1/2 cup (8 tablespoons) unsalted butter, softened to room
  temperature
1 cup sugar
1 large egg
1 cup buttermilk, room temperature
1/2 teaspoon vanilla extract

Marshmallow Filling

6 tablespoons unsalted butter, softened to room temperature
7 ounces marshmallow creme or fluff
1 cup powdered sugar
1 teaspoon vanilla extract
Pinch of salt
1 tablespoon milk (more or less as necessary to make the filling
  a thick but spreadable consistency)

To make the cookies:

Preheat oven to 350°F. Line a cookie sheet (12 x 17 inches, or use
two smaller cookie sheets) with parchment paper.

311

In a medium bowl, whisk together the dry ingredients: flour, cocoa powder, baking soda, and salt.

In a large bowl, using a hand or stand mixer at medium speed, beat butter and sugar until pale and fluffy. Add egg. Beat until well combined. Add vanilla.

Reduce mixer speed to low and mix in about a third of the milk, followed by a third of the dry ingredients. Continue, alternating between dry and wet ingredients, until well combined.

Divide the batter approximately in half. You will bake the cookies in two batches. Scoop out batter using a rounded tablespoon or ice cream scoop to make 12 mounds. The cookies will spread, so space them as far apart as possible on the pan. A dozen will just fit on a 12 x 17 inch pan. If you have smaller pans, use two pans or bake in batches.

Bake for 15 to 17 minutes. The cookies are done when they spring back if gently pressed.

Remove cookies and cool on a rack. Repeat with the remaining batter. Let the cookies cool completely.

To make the filling:

Place all ingredients except the milk in a large bowl and beat until fluffy. If the filling seems too stiff to spread, add a little milk (a tablespoon or less should do).

To assemble the cookies:

Flip over half the cookies. Spread the marshmallow filling on the flat side. Sandwich with remaining cookies, pressing down slightly so that the filling spreads to the edge.

Enjoy!

Acknowledgments

I owe more than I can ever express to my family for their love and support. Thank you to the inspiring writers of Sisters in Crime and to generous readers of early drafts, especially Cynthia for your kind encouragement and critiques. To Eric most of all, thank you for our time together and for listening to way too much talk of murder.

Many thanks to my wonderful agent, Christina Hogrebe, for inspiring this series and finding it a perfect home at Crooked Lane Books. To my fabulous editor, Jenny Chen, thank you for all your support and insights and for making Cleo a better sleuth. Thanks to Jesse Reisch for the gorgeous cover illustration, Jennifer Canzone for the lovely book design, Ashley Di Dio for publicity and marketing prowess, and Rachel Keith for meticulous copyediting.

Most of all, heartfelt thanks to library lovers and readers for joining Cleo on her bookmobile adventures.